Rain on the Wind

WALTER
MACKEN
Rain on the Wind

BRANDON

Published in 1994 by
Brandon Book Publishers Ltd.
Dingle, Co. Kerry, Ireland.

Copyright © The Estate of Walter Macken 1994

British Library Cataloguing in Publication Data is
available for this book.

ISBN 0 86322 185 8

Cover illustration: Steven Hope
Typesetting: Brandon
Printed by The Guernsey Press, Channel Islands

Chapter One

A BIG GREY gander it was.

Its neck was sticking out to the farthest extent, just clearing the grass, and a most terrifying hissing was coming out of its open beak. The boy looked at it solemnly, with a tin mug raised in a small pudgy fist. Behind him his brother was pulling at his shoulder and calling, "Come away, Mico, I say! Come away, will y', and lave 'm alone!"

Looking at them there, if you didn't know that all the fishing people put their boys in short red petticoats up to the age of nearly seven, you would have taken them for two little girls. Both of them had short curly hair, fair in colour, and they wore jerseys over the swinging red petticoats. Their feet were planted firmly on the short grass, very green grass that was littered with the droppings of the geese.

High over them the sun was shining brightly – shining on the calm waters of the Bay to one side of them and on the green grass under them, and glinting blindingly off the rows of whitewashed thatched cottages with here and there the brown nets slung on the pegs driven into the walls. It was a grand scene that would have been very peaceful indeed if it wasn't for the gander.

The gander didn't like Mico, and behind the gander his

flock of pure white geese were backing him up, in a narrow phalanx, their necks swinging above the grass and they hissing.

"Come on, Mico," said the taller of the two boys, pulling at the stubborn shoulder of his brother and hopping on the grass with his bare feet. "That oul gander bit Padneen O Meara yesterday."

"Go on," said Mico, firing the tin mug accurately and hitting the gander with it right on the back of the neck. Even the taller boy stopped pulling at Mico's shoulder then, and looked in amazement at the gander. The long neck went lower, slid along the grass, turned, and the body of the gander followed his neck, slid to the grass, over on his back and he lay there, paralysed, with his webbed feet sticking up ridiculously into the air.

"Now y' done it," said the tall boy. "Y' murdered 'm. Now me mother'll be after you in earnest!"

"Dead duck," said Mico, pointing with a small fat finger. "Dead duck." And he laughed, a small gurgling laugh coming from his five-year-old chest.

"If we're caught we'll be kilt," said his brother, looking around nervously. The look reassured him. He saw the long line of white houses looking over the grass at the sea away in the distance across the waste of the Swamp in front of them. Behind those the lines of other houses ran, built up on the Fair Hill. Some of the thatches you could see, and in the higher-up ones you could see the blue of the sky reflected in the narrow windows. But the gangling half-doors were deserted. They stood alone on the great green in the hot-sun silence. They were all alone except for the spasmodically kicking gander and the silenced geese. Silenced for a very short time.

Almost as if they were swinging into a practised military movement the geese came to arms. They all hissed first and then, except for four who circled the stunned gander, they made for the two boys, evil in their eyes and the dreadful hissing in their beaks. Determined!

"Go way!" said Mico, raising a hand at them. They came on. "Go way!" he said, raising a bare foot at them, but they came on. The taller boy stopped pulling at Mico. He backed away.

"Oh, bejay, they'll ate 's," he said as he backed.

Mico stood his ground. He kicked out with a foot again and the nearest goose pecked at it viciously. Mico pulled it back, without a cry, even though it hurt him, and he backed back too. "Go way!" he said hopefully again, but the geese had noticed the first crack in him and they came on more determined than ever, more loudly than ever, and they spread out their wings as well, so that they seemed to have doubled in size and numbers, and they made in a body for Mico. Mico turned and ran. His thick little legs twinkled over the grass and the geese followed after, their hissing changed now to a triumphant cackling. The grass verge ceased and Mico ran down on to the road. He turned there at bay, but the geese came on after him in a veritable fluttering of cackling victory, so Mico crossed the road and came to the edge of the quay, his eyes searching for his brother. All he could see of him were the two terrified eyes peeping over the edge. He was standing on the stone steps leading down to the water, and Mico joined him there as quickly as he could. The geese came on as the two boys looked at them. Then they looked down at the water lapping below. The tide was on the turn. The sea had flung back the river from the estuary and was licking at the bottom steps. Mico went to pass his brother then, but the brother had thought of it at the same time. He turned to go and pushed past him, and the next thing he knew there was the small body of his brother heading for the water. He saw the sea grasp him and the red petticoat hold him up for a time and then he saw him sink, and the boy didn't wait for any more. He opened his mouth and a scream came out of it, sufficiently high to startle the geese above, then he turned and raced up the steps, his terror of the geese forgotten, so that his coming sent them flying in all directions in undignified haste.

He reached the grass border then and with his legs flashing and his arms out he ran towards one of the houses in the centre of the long line of houses and he was screaming, "Mammie, Mammie! Mico fell into the sea! Oh Mammie, Mammie, Mico fell into the sea!"

Mico came to the surface again.

He thought the water was very nice if he could manage at all to stand up in it, but it was very unsubstantial. From where he was now he could see the water heaving where the river met the rising sea between Nimmo's Pier and the Docks. He saw the houses on the other side of the river fronting the Long Walk, and they white with their wash and gaily decorated by the many blankets, sheets, and towels hung from the upper windows to dry, and he could see the hulks of what were once big sailing ships rotting in the sun on the far side of the river and whitened by the gulls who used them lavishly as conveniences. The water was green and very soft where he was now, and under him was the glitter of the sun on rusty tin cans and chamber-pots and bent bicycle wheels and the offal of the village, because here the people dumped their unwantables.

Mico started to sink again, and he thought how unpleasant it would be to be tasting this nasty water.

Devil a down did his head go, though, because the man leaned out of the pucaun boat beside him and stretched a long pole with a hook on the end of it and he curled it under the body of Mico and held him on the top of the water. The hook curled under Mico's fork, and his little hand went around the smooth timber and he looked up along the pole to the gnarled nut-brown hands that held it, up the blue-jerseyed sleeves, and let his eyes rest then on the calm blue eyes that were looking at him with a laugh in them.

"Hold tight, Mico," said the old man. Behind the blue eyes that were deep sunken and sheltered by the peak of the broad brim of the black Connemara hat, Mico recognized his grandfather, and as always when the old man was near,

Mico felt that everything was going to be very smooth from now on.

"Gran," said he then in the middle of a laugh, "I hot the gander."

"Begod," said Gran, "yer the devil's own, Mico. Yer mother'll kill yeh."

Thought of his mother sobered even Mico.

Hum, thought Gran to himself. "Hold tight now, Mico, and I'll haul you aboard." Mico's small hands were tightened whitely on the pole. His fair curls were flattened to his head and made the awfulness of the birth mark that covered one side of his face almost completely seem very obvious. It was a terrible mark. It stretched from his forehead, took in half of his left eye, spread over the whole side of his face, and then lengthened like a flat dark purple finger into the jersey at his neck. It always made Gran feel sad looking at the mark. God's finger, they called it, when they didn't call it anything worse.

He pulled him slowly towards the bulging side of the black boat, the fresh tar on it glittering green from the reflection of the sunlit water. The water lapped gently against it, and the tall mast on it with the tarred ropes swayed as he bent down and caught the child by the slack of the petticoat and lifted him into the air.

He held him up there for a time at the length of an arm, looking up at him laughing and the water dripping down from him.

"Put me down, Gran, put me down!" said Mico, so he hauled him in and put him standing beside him in the belly of the boat, his feet and clothes dripping water on the smooth limestone blocks laid in a pattern as ballast. "Here," he said then, "off with the oul wet clothes, Mico," and he hauled off the jersey with a practised sweep and after that pulled the petticoat with the white cotton top over his head too, and left Mico standing up there, a sturdy little man of a boy with the baby creases still faintly visible above his knees and the fading pot belly. His legs were tanned to above the knee, and his arms and neck and the rest of him was as white as the inside of an eggshell. "Hop around there now," Gran said then, "until I get something to dry you with."

He mounted up to the bow of the boat and stretched himself full and leaned down into the hatch there and hauled out some sort of a rag. "It's not too clean, Mico, oul son," he said looking at it, "but what matter?" and he came up to the child and went on his hunkers in front of him and started to rub him down with the cloth. There were only a few spots of tar on it so it didn't destroy him. Mico giggled and clasped his arms across his chest. "Yer ticklin' me," he said. "Devil a tickle," said the old man. "Turn around now, till we do the back." And he turned him around and applied the cloth to him. "Up there with yeh now and dry out in the sun. If we had a clothes-line aboard we could hang yeh out on it like a pair of drawers." He lifted him up on top of the hatch and took the wet discarded clothes in his strong hands and squeezed them dry over the side.

"Were you a baby, one time, Gran?" Mico asked then.

"Of course I was," said Gran indignantly.

"The same as me?" asked Mico.

"The spittin' image a yeh," said Gran.

"Why haven't I whiskers too so, Gran, like you?" asked Mico.

"Ah," said Gran shaking his head sagely, "He oney gives them to oul fishermen like me."

"If I'm a fisherman, will I have one a them?" Mico asked.

"You will, nothing surer," said Gran.

"Then I'm goin' to be a fisherman," said Mico emphatically and stretched a small hand to the fishing-frame beside him and impaled a finger on a sharp hook. He let a yell out of him.

"Holy God, Mico," said Gran, "you're the devil's spawn for gettin' into trouble," moving up to him resignedly.

"I only wanted to see if it was sharp," said Mico.

"Don't move it now, you devil," said Gran, "or you'll drive it into your finger and we'll never get it out." He lifted the frame carefully and unloosed a few rounds of the brown line and then caught up the finger and looked at it. The barb hadn't gone through. "Be easy now, will you?" he said, "and I'll get it out and don't pull away from me."

"Will oul Biddy Bee murder me, Gran, for hittin' her oul gander?" Mico asked.

And then the storm broke over them.

There was the cackling of frightened geese above their heads and the sound of running feet and women's voices raised, and the sound of Mico's brother's voice raised a little hysterically, a little theatrically, and other young voices joining in too, and shortly Mico and Gran looked up to see a forest of faces looking down at them from elongated bodies. It's a strange thing, Gran thought, how big people look when you see them from below and how strange their faces are. He picked out the face of his son's wife easily enough. Her hair was brown and it was pulled back in a bun from her narrow face. A narrow face over a square jaw. That's an odd thing now, he thought. Her nose was aquiline, and she was tall and carried herself very well. Her eyebrows were square and as yet there was no grey hair in her head, and the drab blouse she wore tucked into the heavy red petticoat with the apron over that made from a canvas sack couldn't hide a well-built body. Time enough for the grey hair, Gran thought.

"It's there you are!" she said then. She has a hard voice, Gran thought; she has lost the soft Connemara burr that was in it.

"He's all right," said Gran. "I saw him fallin' in. I pulled him out."

"You could have shouted," she said; "you could have shouted and let us know he was safe, and I runnin' out with my heart in the palm of me hand expectin' to find him floatin' in the sea. What about Tommy here? What about the fright he got? His heart is flutterin'. D'ye see how pale he is?" gathering her sniffling son close to her apron with a hand that was bleached with soap-suds.

"So well he might be," said Gran, "when 'twas he pushed the little fella in."

"I did not, Mammie, I did not," said Tommy in a screech. "I did not push him in. He hot the gander and the gooses chased 's and we went down the steps together and Mico slipped on the green yoke and slod in."

"That's right now," said a young gentlemen with a snotty nose, beside them. "Mesel and Twacky saw the gooses after them. Jay, it was great gas to see the oul gooses after them!"

"Come on up our that, you now," said Mico's mother to him ominously, "and I'll teach you something."

"What about me gander?" asked a cracked voice coming up behind them. She pushed her way forward, a stick, a crooked one, supporting her bent body. It was noticeable that the other kids gathered made way for her politely, for wasn't she a witch? She had a curved nose and a red kerchief over her hair tied in a knot under her chin. "What about me gander?" she reiterated. "The oney support oo a poor widow woman, and he lying up there now on the broad of his back stretched out like a corpse for all the world to see, and what'll me poor geese do without their husband if he dies and how am I to live without me geese, and where am I to get another gander? Ah, the devil created you, you little bee yeh, and if I get at yeh it's the back of me stick I'll lay across yer backside, mother or no mother!"

"Come on up our that now, Mico," said Mico's mother.

Mico stood there looking up at them, his hands behind his back. His hair was drying and was standing up around his head. He had a low forehead and his eyebrows already were dark and thick over his eyes. Brown his eyes were, but the nervousness he felt had them pulled down so that the melting effect of them was lost. The birthmark was livid against the white of his skin.

"I oney hit the gander because he wanted to bite 's," said Mico.

"Hey, Biddy Bee, Biddy Bee!" roared one of the kids. "Look at the oul gander! He's up on his pins again."

This brought all the heads away from the direction of the boat as they looked back towards the green sward.

"To the praise of God he is," said Biddy, raising a hand and a stick in the air. "Me gander has the use a the legs again. Not that I'm forgettin' you," she turned back at Mico, "you young murderer yeh, but what good could be in yeh and where yeh kem out of, a Connemara get and a father that's oney a Claddaghman for three generations?"

"Now shut your filthy tongue," said Mico's mother aggressively.

"Not an inch of it," said Biddy in a screech, "and keep away from me and me belongin's, Ma-am, d'yeh hear, or it's the curse a the widow's weeds I'll put on you and yours, and if I see that brat of a bee of yours comin' within an acre of me geese again, I'll gut him as sure as there's a God in Heaven!" and with the last word off she went.

The face of Mico's mother was very red with suppressed anger, so she leaned out and gave the snotty-nosed boy a hearty clout on the ear.

"Be off with ye, ye ferrets!" she said. "A person can't put a foot outside a door but yeer all out spyin' around to see what ye can see and report what ye can hear. Be off with ye, the lot of ye now, before I lose me temper!" and they backed off precipitately, the injured one roaring like an impaled bullock and running towards his house, his red petticoat flying and the most appalling screeches coming out of him.

"Come on up here from that at once, Mico." She bent back to him again.

"He'll be up after you, Delia," said Gran quietly. "I'll bring him up meself in a minute. He's all right, I tell you. I dried him off and the sun'll do him fine and I'll be up with him."

He looked quietly into the angry harassed face glaring down. His own eyes were firm as they could be on occasion.

"Well, it won't save him," she said going. "I'll teach him

- 13 -

to be bringing disgrace on 's and frightening the life out of his brother."

She was gone then; they were all gone, and peace reigned over the waterside.

"Will she bate me, Gran?" Mico asked in the middle of the peace.

"Well, now, Mico," said Gran, "mebbe we'd be able to circumlocate her. We'll give her a little time to be coolin' off." And he winked a bright blue eye at the child. Mico grinned back at him. 'Tis a great pity about the mark, Gran was thinking. If it wasn't for that he'd be good-lookin' too. The brown eyes were nice and his cheeks were square and his mother's jaw looked better on him than it did on her. The nose was a bit squat. It was like his father's big nose, Gran thought, before someone sat on it. But flat like that, he thought, it suits the big face he has. He'll be big too, he thought, like his father. It's a good job, he has the quiet eyes, he thought then, because it's wanting quietness he'll be, once the time comes that he takes to looking in the mirror.

Aren't the ways of God very strange now! he mused, as he coiled the inch-thick tarred rope at the stern of the boat. The things He does to people. Why did He have to be taking a purple paintbrush to the face of a child?

Mico felt the boards hot under his bum, and wiggled, almost ecstatically. It was grand to be in his pelt like that and feel the sun on him. It was blinding on the rising tide too, and the boat was rocking gently. It seemed a grand boat to the eyes of Mico. He knew the front look of it from seeing it coming home from the fishing. It was like part of the house down at the quays. A great sturdy bow on it, swelling out into two black breasts in front and then curving bigly to the flat tail. Like the Vikings' boats long ago, Gran told him. Like that, they med them, only longer. And all the men of the Claddagh down here were Vikings too. All the way they had come to this place thousands of years ago from the cold black seas of the North. They were here before that stinkin' oul town was even thought of. He'd say that, thumbing at the town of Galway disdainfully, where it lay across the river. We were first here, Gran would say. The Claddagh was the very first town in the whole of Ireland, and 'twas we built it, until them upstarts came from God knows where and set up in the opposition across the river, and then started to look down on us, the things, as if man for man we weren't better than fifteen of them any day in the week.

Gran was still a fine man even if he was over fifty.

He wasn't big. He was made fine. His back was as straight as the tall black mast that rose on the boat and he filled his blue jersey well and there was still a lot of flesh left on his legs to swell the rough black cloth of them. His hands were what gave away his age. They were very strong but the tendons stood out on them. His beard made him look older than he was because it was iron grey and clipped by himself with scissors so that he looked like the advertisement on the packet of cigarettes, the Players ones. An older edition, that was all. His face was nearly black, it was so brown and weather-worn, and the corners of his eyes were made up of a million wrinkles from having to close them against the glare of the sea. He was a quiet man and a kind man, and a better man there wasn't in the whole of the Claddagh if you were in serious trouble and wanted to be talked out of it. He had all the quiet philosophy of his forty seagoing years in his eyes.

Mico's father, Micil, took after him.

Micil Mór is a big slob, they said. Micil Mór is a great big eejit. But they said it softly, and indeed they said it straight up to his face. He was so big that you had to say it up to him. He was the biggest man in the province of Connacht, so he was. He was the height of a door and a half-door and he was the width of a full door. That'll give you some idea of the size of him. And he had a laugh to go with that. Of a summer evening when all the fishing boats would be coming home, black silhouettes with the sun going to bed behind them in the Bay, one of those calm sound-travelling evenings, the people waiting out here on the quays would know the boats were coming in when they would hear Big Micil laughing out beyond the Lighthouse.

"Will me father be comin' home soon, Gran?" Mico wanted to know. "When will me father be comin' home?"

"Begod, he'll better be soon or it'll be too late to be goin' after the fish at all," said Gran, rising and peering over the quay wall towards the bridge crossing into the town where the pub was.

"Lookit, Gran," said Mico, pointing out towards the estuary, "lookit the gooses with the long necks."

"Thim is swans, Mico," said Gran.

There were two of them with three ugly grey cygnets scrabbling after them, making a poor show of imitating their dignified progress.

"They're like the boat, aren't they, Gran?" Mico said.

"That's true, Mico," said Gran; "they're like the boat. Thim is white swans and the boat is an old black swan."

Mico laughed.

"The boat isn't a swan, Gran," he said.

"That's all you know, you poor ignorant eejit," said Gran, leaning against the gun'le with a black corncob pipe in his gob and his hard fingers busy with a knife clipping a square of plug tobacco. "Long ago," he said, "when we had princes in Ireland, rale princes instead a the merchant wans that'd steal the milk out a yer tea, when we had the real ones, every time they'd die they'd put them in a boat, just like this now, shaped like a swan, and they'd send them out to sea and they'd set fire to them, and d'yeh know what'd happen then, Mico?"

"What, Gran?" Mico asked breathlessly.

"The whole thing'd go up in flames and sink into the sea, and out a the water right up into the sky ther'd rise up a white swan. That's true. Every one a them swans out there is a prince that's dead. That's why yeh must never do nothin' to a swan, Mico. You must never hit a swan on the back a the neck with a tin can, like you would an oul gander."

"Bejay, Gran," said Mico, "I'd never do that to a swan. A prince, is it?"

"A prince indeed," said Gran, "and the wans that lay the eggs is princesses. A more useful occupation, I must say, than what some a the lassies do be at now. You know when the swans go flying, Mico?"

"Yeh," said Mico; "kind a whing, whing, they go, like – like when yeh tie a string to a can and swing it in the air."

"That's the very thing," said Gran. "Well, that's the very sound our boat does make when it's out there in the sea with the sail set and she close-hauled. Ah, sails as sweet as a swan, she does, Mico, and you hear the whing, whing, like you said, in the ropes."

He was looking up the mast, the concealed part of his neck a white contrast to the rest of his face.

"Jay, Gran," said Mico, "I'd love that, so I would. When can I go, Gran? When can I be goin' out with ye?"

"Soon, Mico; when the body does be bigger and the sleep doesn't be comin' over yer eyes in the early evenin'. Yeh'll never feel now so you won't."

"Jay, I wish I was big now, Gran," said Mico, fervently. "I wish I was as big as a house, so I do."

"Up with yeh now, up the steps," said Gran, giving him a smart smack on the bare bottom. "I'll bring up the clothes with me."

Mico swung out of the boat agilely and ran up the smooth worn steps that led to the top of the quay. Up above there was green grass on the rectangle of quay that pointed a finger into the river. All along here there were three quays like it pushing out, forming a shelter for the fishing boats, whose masts were rising higher and higher over the quays as the sea disdainfully raised the level of the river. There was activity now about the quays too. Men gathering up the brown nets that were placed out on the grass to dry, and the black figures of men coming from the white cottages with boxes on their shoulders and boxes under their arms, and the boats were gradually swallowing the piles of ropes and nets and lobster-pots, and from some of them trails of blue smoke were rising where the coals were being lighted in the iron trays below the hatches.

Mico stood there nakedly on the quay watching the swans or raising his head to follow the flight of the big gulls that swung lazily over the estuary, screaming and swinging and diving. Then Gran made his slow way to him and he slipped a hand into the horny hand of the other and they made their way across the road and up on to the green grass, and they set their steps towards the centre of the row of white houses, and the sight of the geese placidly grazing away in the distance with the grey gander raising his head to look about him, set Mico's mind back a half an hour or so, and his heart started to thump.

Maybe she wouldn't bate me this time, he thought, and even if she does maybe it won't be too bad.

The grass bent under his feet and tickled his bare toes. They were near the door of the house when they heard the voice calling from behind.

They stood and turned. They saw the big figure of Micil rounding the houses from the road and come lumbering across the grass. "Hi! Hi!" he was shouting. Mico left his grandfather and ran towards him. When Micil saw the small naked figure closing on him he halted and looked and then threw back his head and hit his knees with his big hands and laughed, and Mico laughed too, running towards him, and spread his arms, and Micil Mór bent down then and scooped him into his chest and paused and flung him high in the air, and Mico had to scream at the suddenness of it and then laughed again as the rough cloth of the arms caught and cuddled him.

"And what happened, me great fella?" asked Micil, holding the wriggling nakedness out from him and examining it. "Didn't I come runnin' when I heard you were drownded lavin' me lovely half pint a porter undrunk on the counter, and it's alive you are all the time."

"I fell in," said Mico, "and Gran hauled me out and me mother was mad, and Biddy Bee sez she'll put a curse on me on account of I hit her gander with a mug."

"My God," said Micil, putting him up on his shoulder and walking towards the old man, "can I not let yeh out a me sight for a minute that you aren't up to your neck in trouble?"

"It wasn't me fault this time," said Mico, wriggling himself to the tickle of the harsh blue cloth of his father's coat. "It was the oul gander." He put one fat arm around his father's head. The head was massive and covered in a peaked cap. Below that his face was very brown and was decorated by a close-cropped black moustache. Mico could have fitted his brother beside him on the shoulder that bore him, and there was room on the other shoulder for two more boys or a full-grown man. Me father is the biggest man in the world, Mico could say to the other kids in the bouts of boasting that went on.

"What happened at all, Father?" Micil asked Gran when he came up to him. He always called him "father". He was very respectful to Gran. That was the way he was brought up, to respect his parents and their parents. It was a tradition in those times that was dying hard with the grown-up people. Always like that it was in the old times, as we all know, before fellows starting writing books and making films for all to see where the love of a father was derided, and it was a wonder somebody didn't start a campaign to have all the ould wans drowned when they reached the age of fifty.

But Micil liked his father very much. Sometimes he wouldn't agree with him on various matters, over his marriage for example, of which Gran hadn't approved. Or about the fishing sometimes. But he never contradicted him or denied him. He just did what he wanted to quietly in a subdued manner and left it at that.

"'Twas a good job," said Gran, "that the news a your son's

near drownin' brought you outa the pub below or we'd have to go fishin' be the light oo a candle. What ailed you to be so long? D'yeh see already every boat in the place is ready to pull away from the quay and here we are without the bit in our mouth or a tip-tap done when we should be hoistin' the sail now and be on our way."

"Ach," said Micil, shoving a finger into the son's ribs, making him bend and twist and gurgle, "haven't we a fine boat and two good men in it and can't we show anyone in the Claddagh our stern if we want teh? He wasn't hurt, was he?"

"Devil a hurt," said Gran. "'Twas him did all the hurtin'. Delia was mad at him. Swore she'd bate him. So we delayed a little with our coming."

"Frightened she was, that's what," said Micil. "I nearly died mesel. Young Twacky that came runnin' in. Hi, he sez, Micil, Mico is in the sea by the bite of a goose and Biddy Bee is batin' 'm, and Mico's mother gev Padneen a clout in the snout. All in wan piece. Begod, I left the pub on the hop then, I can tell you. But sure there isn't a stiver wrong with him. Eh, Mico?" Lifting him down from his shoulder and slapping him on the back.

They stood in front of the house then.

Even though it was in a middle of a row of all the same kind of houses it was different. The thatch seemed to be a little more yellow and the whitewash a little more white and there was a blue glint on the small panes of the narrow windows. Behind the windows there were geranium pots with the flowers in bloom, pink ones striped with red. He went in the half-door and Mico followed in his shadow.

"God bless the woman of the house," said Micil Mór cheerfully as he entered. He had to bend low to come in and when he stood up the roof seemed to be very near his head. It was a roof of blackness. From the smoke of the turf burning in the open fireplace. Cheerfully, dimmed by the great glare of the sun outside, the fire burned. Delia was bending over a pot at the hearth, and she stood up as they came in and wiped back a wisp of her hair that had fallen over her face.

"Did you hear what Mico did?" she asked. "Did you hear the like of that? Isn't it worse and worse he gets?"

"It was an accident," said Micil Mór. "How could he help falling into the sea? Aren't they always falling into the sea?"

"He could help hitting the gander with a mug," said Delia querulously. "He could help that. Disgracin' us and havin' the whole of the Claddagh listenin' to Biddy readin' us."

"Now, now, Delia," said Micil, stripping the navy-blue reefer jacket from his jersey-covered chest. "Don't be takin' it like that. Be thankful God didn't have him drowned on us."

"It might be better for him, and for us too if he was," said Delia in a tight voice.

There was a silence in the house then. Micil looked at her, his coat in his hand, and his eyes were troubled and he was frowning. Mico stood in the open doorway, his hands behind his back and his eyebrows pulled down. Gran stood behind him, his hand resting on the half-door. Even Tommy who was eating a slice of bread and jam in the corner near the fire stopped chewing as he sensed the silence.

There was much behind it.

There was, Delia thought, much and much, but good God, what makes me like that? She would have taken the words back if she could. They were just the meaningless jumble of her irritation. She could never forget bearing Mico. Was that, she wonder, what was wrong with me about him? His birth was a red searing flash of pain in her every time she looked at him. He had been too big and too troublesome and too slow. He had not come from her for forty-eight hours after she got the pains. Forty-eight hours! The sweat running down her in rivulets. Her lips bitten through; her grasping, sweating hands pulling at the strop tied to the end of the bed. And when she saw him with the mark of God on him, she wondered what devil had been mocking her, or what her secret sins might be that God should have cursed her.

Her first-born was tall and straight and his nose was thin and his hands were narrow and sensitive and his forehead was broad and high, and he was quick too. He could do things years and years before Mico's reflexes seemed to work. Where he would be tall and graceful she saw the squat body of her second son. Powerful and squat, but what beauty is there in squatness and what beauty in a face marked like that?

"We will have the tay now," said Micil quietly and hung his coat on the dresser.

She turned away to the fire, her hand going to the canvas apron and bringing up a fold of it to blow her nose.

"Come over here, Mico," she said, "until I put some clothes on you. What made you bring him home like that, Father? What'll the people say?"

"I don't give a goddam what they say," said Gran. "What has he to show but what the rest of them have?" He sat at the table near the door. It was a white scrubbed table under the window. The chairs around it were wooden ones, their seats scrubbed as white as the top of the table and powerfully built. Gran threw his hat on the window beside the flowerpot and reached for a potato with a fork, speared it and began to peel it. There was about a stone of potatoes in the centre of the table, bursting flourily through their skins, the steam rising from them.

Micil Mór sighed and went to the top of the table on the other side of the window.

"Come on, Tommy, amac," he said. "Sit over to your tay." He reached for a potato with his fork and as he peeled it, he regarded his first son. He's a fine lad, he was thinking. His shoulders were broad. Why am I thinking things like this, he was wondering. I love my son Tommy, and I love my son Mico, but I love my son Mico more because God marked him. But isn't that natural that you should? He had a dim idea of what Delia had gone through having Mico, but for some time he had been uncomfortably aware that Mico was distasteful to her. Holy Mother of God, he thought, what put that thought into my head? Isn't it fanciful I'm getting on this June day under the hot sun? She was frightened because he fell into the sea, and when women are frightened they are not like us. They take it out on the things they love. Ah, he thought then, I'm too stupid to be thinking things out. Let them lie.

"Your mother should have bet your bottom, Mico," he said, turning to where she was pulling a dry petticoat over his head. "D'yeh hear! You mustn't go fallin' into the sea. You must stay out of trouble, Mico. D'yeh hear me now!"

"Yes, Father," said Mico with his eyes wide.

"That's right," said Micil Mór as gruffly as possible.

And then, so peculiar is human nature, Delia rubbed her hand on the head of Mico and ruffled it, and said, "Sure it wasn't his fault? How could he help it? Go over now and have your tea, alannah," and she bent to the big plate in front of the fire that was covered with the lid of a tin can and she lifted the lid and laid the steaming plate of boiled pollack in front of them. So Mico was startled again and so was Micil and they looked at her and ate their potatoes, and she came and sat in the middle of her two sons and bent her head and blessed herself and then served the steaming fish on their plates.

"All the same," she said, "he'll have to be off to school the very tomorrow. We'll have to let the Master have the handling of him now."

"Isn't he a bit young for school?" Micil asked, his mouth full.

"He'll have to be handled," she said determinedly.

"School," said Gran disgustedly. "School indeed."

"Well, I've med up me mind," she said, "and he'll just have to be off, that's all. I'll put a pair of trousers on him in the morning and he can be off with his brother."

Trousers, Mico thought. Well, that's something. For some time now he had been hoping for a pair of trousers. Because the red petticoat was going out of fashion, even among the young. There were some people even in the Claddagh now, who weren't putting their boys into the red petticoat at all, but slamming them straight into the trousers after the napkins just like the snobs in the city. Trousers is good, Mico thought, but school is very bad indeed. The boys of Claddagh were very healthy in the main, despite the poverty of their housing and the precarious methods by which their parents lived on the whim of the sea, and healthy boys as everybody knows are the devil's spawn. In all the Claddagh there was only one man capable of bringing them to heel with a look or a word or a wave of his walking-stick. That was the Master. Even little Mico had been brought up on the tales of him. And the knowledge that some day he would be in his power had caused even he to stand quietly and watch his passing, the small man in the short jutting beard and the hairy trousers, as they called the bright Connemara tweeds which he wore. Bejay, that's terrible, thought Mico, thinking of being in the same room as him.

"Ah, well," said Micil, "I suppose he has to go to school some day. Times passes too, doesn't it? Very fleet it is. I remember the first day I went to school then. Pa was there too in them days. A young man he was then and had no whiskers. I never thought then the day would be dawning that I'd see me second son going off to school. Yeh better be good in school now, Mico, do yeh hear? Don't be gettin' into trouble in school. No man can save you there."

"I will," said Mico.

"Ah, the poor little fella!" said Gran. "What do they want schools for? In my day all yeh had to do was learn the counting and a few words to be able to write your name in a book. What more does a fisherman want? Doesn't God Almighty himself teach him his lessons out on the open sea? They have a University up there. A big College. And do ye know somethin'? There isn't a man up in that College that I couldn't blind with the knowledge of the things I learned from God. There!"

Micil Mór laughed.

"Mebbe, mebbe, Father," he said; "but times is changin'. Mebbe Mico won't want to be a fisherman. Mebbe he'll want to be a professor in the College instead."

"I'd like to be a fisherman," said Mico in a small made-up voice.

Micil looked at him in surprise. His eyes became soft as he peeled himself another potato.

"Ah, we'll see, Mico, we'll see," he said, but he was pleased and he winked at Gran.

"No man," said Gran, "has a greater love a the sea than Mico. Isn't he racin' into it every chance he gets almost?"

"There's time enough for him to think about it," said Delia. "Eat up your tea, Tommy." That finished the conversation, and they got down to a steady eating. Both the older men knew that Delia was in dread of the sea. She had lost a brother in it already, out in Connemara. And when she would be sitting by the fire breast-feeding her first son, six years ago, Micil and Gran had a picture of her sitting there, looking at the child, holding a breast into its avid mouth, and she saying to them, half joking and half serious (her face wasn't as stern then as it was now), "Never near the sea will me darlin' go," she would say, over and over again.

They ate swiftly and purposefully until Gran pushed back his chair and reached for his cap.

"If you have any intention of catching a single herrin' today, Mister Micil Mór," he said then, "you better be puttin' a stir in you. There'll be no more left in the sea than you'd fit into a tin can."

"All right, Father," said Micil. "'Twill be an ease to get away from all the strife an' stress of this blessed day."

They were shortly making their way to the quay.

Under their belts they had the potatoes and the fish and mugs of hot tea with the chunks of pancake that were hot and beautifully doughy and stuck to the stomach. It was made on the triangle placed over the hot turf coals from the fire and baked in the iron pan, and over the pan was placed the lid of a three-legged pot with more hot coals on top of that, so that it came out with a crust the colour of honey and butter melted on it as soon as it touched it. Micil strode ahead with a half-ton of equipment draped over and around him, and his voice was loud and his laugh too as he answered and addressed the many people who spoke to him, for the whole village came alive now as the evening drew in.

Behind him Gran came with a heavy box on his shoulder and his hand up balancing it, and Mico was in his other hand.

He saw that Mico was in a serious mood.

"Gran," he said at last, "will I be likin' school now?"

"Well, you might and you mightn't," said Gran, "but it'll be worse if you go there and think it's goin' to be better than it is. Here's what'll happen to yeh, Mico. You'll spend the next ten years of your life shut up into a small room with a whole lot of other fellas, and there'll be a fella with a big stick tryin' to bate knowledge into you that won't earn you a penny piece when you know it be heart. You know what you'll do now, Mico?"

"What Gran?" he asked as they crossed the road to the quay.

"When you go tomorrow, say to yourself, It's into jail with you now, Mico boy, but I'll put up with it, because when me sentence is over look what I have in front of me."

"What's that?"

"The sky, Mico, and you under it and a boat under you and the mast creaking on it and a live fish jumping at the end of your line, and you a free man. That's what you'll be, a free man. Think of that, Mico. Work hard in your jail so that you'll get it over to hell and get out under the sky. Isn't that the best way to look at it then?"

"I don't want to go to jail, Gran," said Mico.

"We all have to go to jail some time, Mico," Gran answered gravely, "and if we get it over when we are young, mebbe we'll never have to have it when we're old."

The jutting quays were a hive of activity. Already some of the boats were away and were swinging widely into the current of the river. The sun was heading for the Aran Islands and somebody had touched a pink brush to the clouds on the horizon. The bulk of the town on the other side of the river was alive with the winking diamonds of the dying sun on the window-panes, and the cold grey stone of the buildings was mellowed and more beautiful. Even the towering bulk of the artificial manure factory looked blackly beautiful in the rays of the setting sun. The seagulls' feathers seemed to be magically touched with the exotic plumage of the tropics, and the darting terns were white blurs diving into the smooth waters.

There were shouts and counter-shouts and hoarse laughing and apparent confusion on the quays. Only apparent, because the men who were going to sea had been going to sea before the town across was hardly thought of even, nearly thousands of years ago. The plied gear was stacked and stowed and the thick ropes were plucked from the bollards.

Mico stayed up and watched his Gran descending the steps. He saw him go into the narrow hatch with the perishable food, and emerge and go to the stern of the boat where the nets and ropes were neatly coiled, and he sat there then comfortably and pulled his old pipe from his pocket and put it in his mouth. And calmly and unhurriedly Mico's father was untying the heavy rope around the brown sail and freeing it and hooking on the light triangular foresail, and then he got up on the hatch and spat on his hands, winking up at Mico, and he took the rope in his hands and hauled and the heavy sail climbed up the mast creaking musically and protestingly against his strength. High up the mast it climbed, high above the quay, and then the wind took it and bellied it and it flapped a bit and then went taut, and Micil Mór secured it and came diving up the steps and whipped the rope from the bollard and held the leaping boat in one hand as if he had a stallion at the end of it, and he whipped another hand around Mico and rubbed his moustache on his face.

"Goodbye now, Mico," he said. "We'll see you tomorra."

"I wish I was goin' with ye," said Mico.

"Some day, some day," said Micil Mór, and then he was down the steps and flung the rope first and then himself aboard, and the wind being in the right direction it caught at the sail and pulled the boat away from the quay into the middle of the stream, and Gran leaned his body on the tiller and took the pull of the boat on himself, and after leaping for a little it set stolidly and sailed towards the mouth of the river. He paused then to wave a hand at the small figure on the quay, before he brought his practised eye back to the seemingly casual steering of the boat. They cleared the mouth of the river and he headed the boat for the south side of the Lighthouse. He would see the fleet of fishing boats spread out before him, making chunky progress up the Bay, and Micil turned and they caught each other's eyes and smiled, and Micil sat on the hatch and proceeded to light his pipe with a sigh.

It was good, said that sigh, to get away from the land and the women and even the children, because out here you were cut away from it all. You were a part of a thing that had no time to spend on thoughts of women or children, or why your wife mightn't like one son of yours, and why her face had become so stern and why a man had to walk a little more warily with her, even though there were times when she returned to the brown girl he had known with the flashing teeth and carefree eyes and nothing else in her but a great surge of love that met his own just like the river met the sea.

Gran was thinking much the same. How good now it was to be out in the green water again, that was the colour of the skin of a young apple, and the smell of water that had travelled from far out in the Atlantic, and how it didn't seem so long ago at all that he was going out in this self-same boat and behind him on the quay he was leaving a sturdy little boy. Yes, this big man sitting out from him now, and what a laugh he'd get if Gran were to say, "I remember the time I was comin' out in the boat just like this and you were the size of Mico back there on the quay and you sayin' to me, 'I wish I could go with yeh,' and you havin' a red petticoat on you like him."

"It should be a fine night for the fishing," said Micil Mór, his head over his shoulder.

"Aye," said Gran, raising his head and lifting his face to the breeze. "Aye indeed, but ther's rain on the wind."

Chapter Two

"**M**ICK," SAID PA, bouncing the round wooden pointer on his head so that it resounded hollowly, "you're a thick."

"Yes, sir," said Mico, lifting a hard hand to rub his skull.

He was sitting in a long desk with six others up near the top of the class. It was a narrow room with a high ceiling and lighted by two long windows at their backs and two more at the sides. It smelled of the green distemper that covered the walls and of chalk and of incarcerated boys. There were about thirty in the class. But because he was at the top of the class didn't mean that Mico was there in anything more than a metaphorical sense. Pa knew what he was doing. If he thought boys might be inclined to be backward or troublesome, they always came to the top of the class where they could come under the lash of his tongue and eye and whatever else was handy. Mico had been up in the front desk since the day he came to school seven years ago, so according to Pa's chart that will give you an idea of what he had grown like.

"I cannot understand you, Mico," said Pa. "How is it possible for God to create in the one family two boys so dissimilar as yourself and your brother Thomas? He made you

- 30 -

broad, Mico, and he made you tall, but he left out the brains. Do you think that's what happened?"

"It could be, sir," said Mico equably.

Pa looked at him with his lips pursed. The brown eyes were looking back into his own steadily. Not cheekily or insolently (or he would have a buzz in the ear by now) but just an honest look from a pair of honest eyes. Pa sighed. He was a small man. Standing now in front of this seated boy he was barely an inch or two over the other's head.

"What height are you, Mico?" he asked.

"I don't know, sir," said Mico, sighing and spreading his hands. They were very broad hands, and clean too. The fingers were blunt and very powerful, sweating now as he twisted a stub of a pencil in them. His hair had lost its curls and was falling over one eye and was a kind of black-brown in colour. Very thick hair, very tough hair. Pa leaned a delicate hand forward and grabbed a bunch of it.

"Did you endeavour to learn the poem, Mico?" he asked.

"Oh, as true as God I did, sir," said Mico. "Ask me brother."

The class sniggered at this honest answer and were chilled immediately from the glare of a steely eye. All you could ever see of Pa's eyes were the glints in them, because his eyebrows were very thick and he combed them too so that they were like windshields nearly over his eyes. "Did you try hard at the poem, Mico?" he asked, letting the hair go and tapping the knees that came out under the desk with the pointer.

"I tried me level best," said Mico.

"Is that so, Thomas?" asked Pa, raising his eyes towards the back of the class. He caught Tommy's gaze on him. Tommy rose to his feet. He was tall. But he was slenderly built. His hair had remained fair and curly. He is a handsome lad, Pa was thinking as he looked at him. The nose was thin and the cheekbones were high and the eyebrows narrow and curving away from the edge of his eyes. The forehead was broad and the hair was brushed back from it.

"Oh, he tried all right, sir," said Thomas. "But you know Mico."

"No," said Pa, a little nettled by his reply, because he was secretly fond of Mico. "Tell me about him." He walked down a little, one hand on his hip and the other swinging the pointer. Mico heaved a sigh and felt less sweaty as Pa went away from him.

Tommy, seeing cleverly enough that he may have put a foot wrong, was quick to switch on a smile. His teeth were very regular, they were even and white and went around his jaws in grand arcs.

"It's just that he finds it hard to memorize, sir," said Tommy.

"I see," said Pa and then turned back again almost in the middle of Mico's sigh. "Say it again, Mico," he said, "as far as you can, till we hear."

Oh God, groaned Mico to himself, rising to his feet, having to squeeze his big body up, because the desks weren't made for his size at all. He stood there then, the bad side of his face to Pa. The trouble about it was that it was growing with his face. Looking at him from the side you saw a red-purple boy. Small bumps were developing on it too with the years. It wasn't pretty. Pa didn't like it. It disturbed him to see things that were contrary to an ordered nature, so he generally approached Mico from the good side of him. Looking at him that side, the hair falling over the tanned face; the thick black eyebrows over the low forehead; the broad nose creeping into his face over the level lips, and the big chin sweeping into his chest, he was quite handsome in a very masculine way, like you'd say a good boat is handsome.

"Happy the man," intoned Mico with his brow furrowed, "whose wish and care a few paternal acres bound content to breath his native air in his own ground whose herds with milk whose fields with bread whose flocks supply him with attire whose ... whose... That's where I always get stuck, sir," said Mico desperately.

"Said without meaning or punctuation, it's all right to

that. Now, Mico, why can't you learn the rest?"

"I don't know, sir," said Mico.

"Whose trees," said Pa, "in summer yield him shade, in winter, fire. Do you like trees, Mico?"

"Hah?" asked Mico with his mouth open.

"Do you like trees, I asked. You're not deaf as well as dumb, I hope." (Dutiful sniggers from the class at the pun.) "Silence!" thundered Pa.

"Well," said Mico, "trees are nice, I suppose."

"You suppose," said Pa. "Isn't it a strange thing, Mico, that you know a poem called *The Wreck of the Hesperus* and another one called *Rosabelle*? They are the only two poems you could learn in the course of seven years and keep in your head. Isn't that odd, Mico?"

"Well, them are easy, sir," said Mico; "they're about the sea."

"About the sea," said Pa. "Mico, have you no ambition in you at all? Don't you want to be a scholarship boy like your brother? When next year he's going off to be taught in a secondary school, the gate of knowledge wide open to him, where will you be going?"

"Sir," said Mico, "I will be going to sea with me father and grandfather."

"But, Mico," Pa asked, "have you no ambition in you to rise higher in life than a fisherman?"

"Sure ther's no higher, sir," said Mico.

He means it too, thought Pa in wonder, thinking with a shudder of boxes of dead fish lying shoulder to shoulder and head to tail and their scales littering the quays and looking at his own hands and thinking of them bloody with the guts of fish.

Mico liked Pa. He knew that was almost heresy here, where generations had been brought up in fear and trembling and all their adult lives were to be boasting about what Pa did to them, and his cutting *bons mots*, and his biting sarcasm and the trembling rages that took possession of him.

Tommy held a different view.

Tommy was a very clever boy. Everyone in the Claddagh knew that now. If they didn't they weren't long without knowing it, with Tommy's mother going around telling them. "Our Tommy was at the head of the class. Did ye know our Tommy has won a scholarship to the secondary school? Forty pounds a year. Imagine that? He'll end up a professor so he will."

He was a very quick boy. From the first day he went to school he knew all the answers. He was very advanced now. So with his budding knowledge he looked at Pa, and what did he see? He saw a poseur. Oh, clever enough, I grant you, but a small man with limited knowledge all the same, else why would he have remained in a small school in the small town in the poorest part of the West of Ireland?

Pa would have liked many times to take Tommy and beat him into insensibility in the hopes that it would take him down to the level of the other human beings. But he couldn't do it. He was honest and had to admit that Tommy was a very clever boy. You told him a thing and that was that for evermore. He was always right, and his attitude was always impeccable even if the cute mind of Pa could see a little sneer under his smile. Holy God, thought Pa in the vernacular, that the little bastard should be patronizing me! Me! And to be helpless about it. So that now when Tommy was going out of his hands with a first place in the whole County as a scholarship boy, Pa felt in a strange way that Tommy was his first big failure. Odd, that.

Pa sighed.

"All right, Mico," he said, "sit down," and he punched him lightly on the large shoulder. He always advised the boys against becoming fishermen. Not that it did much good. In most cases it was necessity that drove them to follow their fathers, but he could see that in Mico's case it wasn't that. He knew what it meant to be a fisherman. The grinding poverty, the year-after-year hard labour that even criminals wouldn't have to put in. He tried to lift them out of it when he could, which wasn't often.

"All right, all right," he said, "and now we'll hear Master Twacky deliver us the poem in his best Galway accent, and if you dare to say 'oo' instead of 'of', Twacky," he went on ferociously, "I'll hammer the delights of hell out of you."

Twacky stood up and licked his lips and commenced, "Happy the man ..."

The morning droned away with threats and alarums and occasional beatings.

It was near the end of the day when a small face appeared at the window of the school. Its owner had managed to climb up from outside assisted by a few minor comrades. He pressed a hot and sweaty face close to the glass and roared.

"Hey, fellas, fellas, the mackerel is in! The mackerel is in."

He had one startled look at the outraged Pa before he vanished again, but he might as well have thrown a bomb into the classroom. It was only Pa's eye that kept them from breaking into speech, but even his eye was unable to take the gleam from their eyes or to take the bursting tenseness from their bodies. Because it wasn't every year or every month that the mackerel came in. Generally they only came into the Bay and cruised around there and fell to the nets and long-lines of the fishermen, but this was something else. The shoals were in. This was the tocsin sounding, and here was Pa speaking away laconically as if nothing at all out of the ordinary had happened to them.

"For tonight," he was saying, "you will do the following sums. Is everybody ready? Pencils topped? Jotters clean? A new page?" Oh, Jay, Mico was groaning, will he not go on with it, will he not go on to hell with it! In another month, thanks be to the blessed God, I will be finished with it for ever. Sums and Irish and English and Catechism. And finally he had to say it – "Class Dismissed."

For a big boy, Micil's son, Mico, could run very fast and he ran fast now. He was first out of the door on account of his bulk, and he was first to run up towards the boats on account of his speed. His feet were bare like all the rest of them and they were burned brown by the sun and they were broad feet so they carried him fast. He ran along by the church and chased across the road, ran on and he didn't pause or halt until he stood above his own father's boat. He jumped down into it from the quay without going down the steps, and he landed like a bird on the hatch to the terrible amazement of Gran who was doing something in the back.

"What in the name a God," he asked then, "is chasin' yeh?"

"The mackerel is in, Gran," said Mico, barely breathless.

Gran gave his eyes to heaven.

"Holy God," he asked, "Did yeh ever see the like of me brave Mico to be breakin' his neck runnin' to me with a bit a news that I could ha' told him a fortnight ago?"

"Give 's a line or two, Gran, will yeh?" Mico pleaded. "On me oath I won't do nothin' to them. I'll bring them back to yeh."

"And where do yeh intend to go?" Gran asked.

"Down the docks," said Mico. "'Tis better down there. The fry gets trapped and they come in after them. Ah, hurry up, Gran, will yeh! All the fellas'll be there before me."

"Look," said Gran. "Will you learn to be patient, Mico? You won't get one any quicker for bustin' yer thorax runnin' like a bull after them disgraceful fish for which I have no use unless they're gutted and fried while they're still wrigglin' in yer hand. Take it easy, boy, will yeh, and you'll get there all the quicker."

Mico took a big breath and relaxed, even sat down. Then he smiled.

"All right, Gran," he said. "I'm patient now." And looked it too, even though every bit of him was throbbing.

"Fine," said Gran, leaning into the locker and pulling out a line wound on a wooden frame with a heavy lead weight on it above the hooks. "You won't want this thing down there. 'Tis too heavy. In fact all you want for the mackerel when they are in heat like that is a spool of thread and a bent horse-nail." He started to untie the weight from the line. Slowly. Carefully. Mico felt like leaning forward and pulling it out of his hand, but he controlled himself, just biting his knuckles with his white teeth. Small teeth they were for such a big face, and they sloped back a little from the gums. Just like a pike, Gran told him, that's the way a pike's teeth are shaped so that once he bites you he can't let go. "How did ye get on at school today?" Gran asked then, his fingers methodically busy.

"Oh, bad," said Mico. "I'm a terrible eejit, Gran, I must be as thick as a boot. Why did God give all the brains to me brother, Gran? He could have spared one or two for me. If it was only to keep Pa out of me hair."

"You're better off, Mico," said Gran, "to be slow at school. You won't forget whatever you learn the hard way, and you'll know so little when you leave that there'll be plenty of room in your skull to learn all the important things."

"I hope you're right, Gran," said Mico.

"Amn't I always right?" asked Gran. "Here now, this'll do yeh fine" – handing him the frame.

"How about one for me too?" asked the voice of Tommy above smiling down at Gran. Gran looked up at him slowly.

"Don't tell me," he said, "that you're going to spoil your nice hands at fishing for mackerel?"

"Ah," said Tommy, "it's good fun. I don't mind. All the fellows are going."

"Ah, go on, Gran," said Mico, "give him one. I'll see that nothing happens to it."

"For a fella with all the brains," said Gran, "he can mix up a line and make a greater haimes of it than anyone I know."

"Dear God," said Tommy, "the damn thing only costs a few pence."

Gran got a bit red in the face.

"Here, Tommy," said Mico, firing his own one up to him. "You take this one. Gran'll give me another. Go on. You go and I'll be after yeh."

"All right," said Tommy, going and then coming back and

firing his bundle of books tied with a strap into the boat. "Would you mind leaving this up in the house when you're going up, Gran? Tell Mother I may be late home to tea." Then he was gone.

"Late home to tea!" said Gran. "Would you mind leaving this up in the house!"

"Ah, he doesn't mean it," said Mico soothingly. "He does be thinking of other things. Honest, Gran. He does. You know yourself. Come on, have a heart now and give us the other line or the shoals might be gone."

"I don't know why I let him upset me," said Gran. "Isn't he oney a child like yerself when I come to think of it? Why does it matter that he can get under me like that and nothing else in the world can get under me?"

"It's the hot weather," said Mico. He knew it wasn't the hot weather. It was just that Gran could never get on with Tommy. He never did. Since he was young he had always been interfering with the bringing up of him. Micil's Delia was inclined to spoil him. Wasn't that natural? Here was a boy who since he was born was as well shaped as any sinner could ask for. He was a model child. His nose was stuck in books from the day he had learned to spell, and was never out of them, and that was a very strange thing to see in a small house given over to the hard facts of fishing living, where men were always too tired to do anything more than tumble into bed and sleep and eat and figure painfully the proceeds of a fishing trip.

The whole of the Claddagh knew that Delia's son, Tommy, was a young genius, and they also knew that Micil's son, Mico, was a great dunce, and they liked him very much, but a blind cod could see that he hadn't a brain in his head, so he'll end up like the rest of 's, the poor divil, taking a pucaun out to sea and getting dirty and wet and tired and starving when times were bad and nearly starving when times were good, for then there would be a glut and the dirty exploiters of fishermen would pay dirt for fish, and where were you with all your labour and all your honesty, so more power to Delia's Tommy that has the brains so that he can make something of himself, become somebody, make a bit of money for his unfortunate people, so that they wouldn't have to depend on the wilful sea for a living, even when they were old and worn out.

So the dislike Gran felt for Tommy was a thing he couldn't put his finger on, just that he made him uneasy. Was it because he saw here another Claddagh man who was going to escape from the sea? Was it that? Or was it because he was so fond of Mico, and saw that Mico played a poor fourth violin in his own house, with his mother.

"Here," said Gran, practically throwing the other line, freed from the lead, to Mico, "get the hell out of my sight. The whole world is a mess a stinkin' thievery and connivin' and trickery and I wish to hell I was out in the bottom of the ocean with the fish goin' in and out through the sockets of me dead eyes."

"Thanks, Gran," said Mico, leaping up the steps and running. "I'll keep them safe for you," and he ran down the road and turned right to the wooden bridge on top of the lock gate that served to hold back the waters of the Claddagh Basin from the river and the sea. He was leaping across this, pausing to look down on the waters of the lock below, where a few drowned dogs, bloated from their long immersion, waved to and fro, the shape of them barely distinguishable now, and then he heard Twacky shouting behind him.

"Mico, Mico," shouted Twacky, running up to him, "let's go with yeh, will yeh, Mico. Let's with yeh."

Mico smiled as he looked down at the other. Twacky was his own age but only about half his size. The whole place was worried about Twacky, because he didn't seem to be growing at all. His father and mother were worried about him. He had eight sisters and brothers and they were all right, but the youngest of them was nearly taller than he. People were always stopping his harassed mother (Why wouldn't she be? If you had eight one after another you'd

- 39 -

be harassed too) saying, "What's wrong with Twacky? You'd fit the poor fella into a match-box. What are yeh givin' him to ate?" "What am I givin' him to ate?" she'd ask the angels. "Outa house and home he has me et. We have to nail down the plates to stop him aten them. Everything under the face of the earth I've given 'm from boiled cod to lights and liver, crubeens and stirabout for his breakfast, tripe and onions and the fattest oo American belly bacon. God almighty, fed like one a the horses that pulls the coal-carts he is, and looks like that. A tape worm he has, I tell yeh. The *craos deamhan*, the worm of hunger, he has in him, I tell yeh." And the inquirer would go away shaking the head and the mother would go away shaking hers, and Twacky kept on eating like a horse and never growing so that you'd notice it.

So he was small and he wore blue trousers that were supposed to be short ones but came below his knee, making him look even smaller, and his hair was cut into the bone by his father and a little fringe left in front so that he looked like a convict from the back, and like a cockatoo with his bunch of hair from the front. He had a small thin face and the biggest eyes anyone ever saw. Blue they were and had long dark lashes over them. He was very earnest and nervous and always hopped from one foot to another and had a habit of catching his clothes in front with his elbows and rubbing his chest with them as if millions of fleas were excruciating him, but he was as clean as a sandstone. His chin was pointed.

As if, Mico thought, you could resist the appeal in Twacky's eyes!

"Of course you can, Twacky," he said. "Could you not get down yourself?"

"I could," said Twacky, "but I was too late lookin' for a line. All the others were in front a me. The oul fella roared the head offa me. Jay, Mico, we better hurry or ther' won't be one left to us. Jay, did yeh hear Pa at me today, Mico?" (All this as they crossed the bridge and stepped down and headed at a trot for the opening where the green sward they were on beside the river, debouched on to the big bridge that carried the traffic over this rushing torrent that neatly bisected the town.) "Did yeh hear 'm at me? All about that oul pome. Jay, that's a terrible oul pome, isn't it, Mico?"

"It's a stinker of a pome," Mico agreed.

"Jay, he'd be a quare man, Mico, wouldn't he, that'd want to be like your man in the pome, with them things, trees and such, not even wanted to be buried proper, just like an ould horse shot down in the Swamp and thrown into a hole. What kind of a fella'd be writin' tripe like that, Mico?" he asked breathlessly.

"I don't know, Twacky," said Mico. "I bet he never died like that. I bet a fella like that died on a feather mattress with all the people in the world hangin' over his head."

They stopped for a moment as was ritual, to poke their heads through the steel stanchions of the bridge, so that they looked down at the granite supports below them, pointed and shaped like the prow of a boat, so that when you half closed your eyes and saw the water you would think it was the bridge was moving and not the river. Then they pulled away and ran on. They turned down and ran on the concrete rectangle of the fish market and they slithered under the Spanish Arch and ran by the houses flanking the Long Walk and they came to the first opening in the docks and ran faster. Mico saw that the old boat in this small dock was already filling up with the fishers, so they came to it panting and he jumped over the side of it, negotiated the slant in the deck of the rotting timber with great dexterity, and then elbowed his way beside a chap with a fishing-rod and looked down into the water which seemed to be alive with the millions of fleeing fry.

"Hold me legs, Twacky," he called. Twacky came forward and pulled Mico's big bare feet between his arms and his sides and held tight while Mico bent down so that he could reach the rising tide. He waited until a great swirl of the fry came near him and then curled his big palm under them and swooshed them out of the water. Water rose and fry rose and Mico rose laughing and gathering one or two of them, wriggling, from the deck, expertly hooked them, still wriggling, on to the mackerel hooks, lowered the line into the water, almost immediately felt the tug of a ravenous fish at his line, and letting a great "Whoo!" out of him hauled the line in hand over hand and banged the rigid body of the mackerel, striped like a green tiger, on the rotting boards of the deck.

Chapter Three

IT WAS A very old boat. This cut-in from the docks was about ten yards wide and the old boat filled it from side to side. It was so old that when the tide came in it didn't shift it at all. That was because it was so rotten below that the water had seeped in and deposited mud and shingle, and the carcass of the decaying boat was as well anchored as if it was held down by the anchor of a great liner. Hard to imagine that it was once a proud, sturdy sailing ship, but it was there to see if you looked, the stump of the great mast, splintered and rotting so that you could chip it away with your nails. A ship that had sailed into every bay in the country, and could follow the cod into the cold northern seas, here she was now as an ancient platform for hundreds of boys swarming all over her, spoiling her deck with their feet and shoes and bait, and thrashing swiftly dying fish.

It was a sight to see the fry.

They swept in from the bay, literally millions of them, tiny things, with fear and panic in every muscle of their small bodies, beautifully shaped bodies for things so small. They came in droves and sometimes in long green lines, and from below them you would see the rigid bodies of the mackerel, coming up at them. The flurry that came on them then! The swift ordered turns and twists of them in the water, miraculously following the leader like wild geese, and the updiving fish would leave great holes in their ranks and they would close again, and you would see the place like a river of silver as they turned their bodies to flee. And one or two, bitten but not engulfed, would wearily come to the surface and float there, limply, until they sank and you saw the green shape swallowing as they fell.

The place was a volume of sound. On the boat itself and on the two sides of the docks were boys standing and kneeling and sitting with their feet dangling, and boys lying full length. And from their hands went all sorts of lines into the water. Brown lines and white lines and thread lines and blow-lines and even clothes lines.

Fish flew out of the water in every direction. Feverish activity for at least half an hour and then the fry flew from their enclosure and sought the open sea, and there was a lull.

Mico wiped sweat off his face with his hand, leaving thick scales all over him, and relaxed. His line was dangling in the water, and all around his feet there was an array of the fallen enemy.

He took time off to look around him then.

There was a forest of boys and a terrible smell of fish, which Mico didn't mind at all. It was part of his life to be in the middle of the smell of fish. There was a boy beside him who wore a white shirt and grey short trousers with a blue and white belt holding them up. He wasn't using a line, he was using a very nice split-cane trout rod. I bet that's his father's, Mico thought, and wondered with a grin if his father knew that his son and heir was ruining his equipment fishing with it in sea water. The line was attached to what Mico thought was an expensive reel and the line was an oiled silk one he saw with a whistle, and he thought of saying to the boy, Good God, you have that line ruined with sea water; it'll never be any good for trout again, but then he shrugged and thought, Sure it's none of my business.

Twacky was on the other side of him, and at the end of the quay up high he could see Tommy with his line. He was sitting on the quay and his line was in the water between his legs, and he was looking towards the Bay. Mico looked out there too, across the Nimmo's Pier and realized what a grand day it was. It was hot, but there was no haze on the sea. The sky was blue and looking over at the Clare hills it was hard to see them. They were just a deeper blue than the sky. That's how he made them out at all. The Lighthouse looked as white as the feather of a wheeling gull.

And then the fry came back with the mackerel chasing them.

Twacky was the first this time to get a bite.

"Jaysus, lads," Twacky screamed, "I got a whale."

Mico laughed, and sobered a little as he thought that despite all his promises to Gran he had cut a bit off the line for Twacky. Ah, well, he thought, sure I'll splice it back again so skilfully that he'll never know. You will like hell, he answered, not to fool Gran!

He got a pull at his own line then and forgot it and hauled in the twitching fish. A fairly big one. He beat it on the deck until it was stilled and then bent down and got his sharp penknife and cut a slice from the mackerel near the tail. The whole body of the fish wriggled in silent tortured ecstasy. He baited his hook with the triangular piece of fish flesh.

The other boy's fish hit him square in the face, fell from the hook on which it had been only lightly caught and if it had any intelligence it sailed for China after the fright. The freed hook swung and Mico remained perfectly still, having a great respect for freed hooks, but the boy with the white shirt was not very skilful, he swung the end of the rod and Mico felt the point of the hook digging into the side of his jaw.

"Don't move the rod now," he said in a loud quiet voice that stilled the hands of the boy.

"Oh, God," he said, "is it stuck in you?"

"I'm afraid it is," said Mico. "Now listen," he went on,

keeping his head quiet, "don't move a muscle, will you? Keep your hands where they are. I don't know if the barb went in. If it did we're kittled." He leaned out then and caught the line hanging over his head, took a firm grip on it and pulled it so the reel screamed. "Lower your rod now," said Mico, "and go around and have a look at it." It was stuck in his right jaw. He could feel warm blood trickling down the side of his neck already. That'll clean it anyhow, he thought. Then as the boy passed him cautiously Mico took a grip on the rod. "Better give me that," he said and took a firm grip on it and then walked backwards so that they could get away from the throng at the rails, who were too busy pulling fish, anyhow, to realize anything untoward had happened.

The boy went to the right side of Mico's face and peered up at the hook. Mico saw he had red hair and the pale complexion that went with it. He was nearly as tall as Mico but he wasn't too thin. He was filled out well enough. His eyebrows were dark red and were thin. His eyes, widely opened with apprehension, were green. A thin face he had and his white teeth were misshapen, almost every second one criss-crossing the other. The corners of his mouth, closed tightly now, would take an upward quirk at the corners if they were held naturally.

"It seems to be well in," he said after the scrutiny, looking at Mico anxiously.

"We'll see," said Mico, and cautiously raised his hand towards the hook. He felt the top of it where it was tied to the gut and then he ran his fingers down its slender length to where it was caught. For big fingers, the other boy thought idly that they were tender of touch. At the rounded part of the hook Mico tightened his fingers and closed them in, feeling for the barb. The tip of his finger found a little of it.

"I don't think it's in very far," he said, and then gave it a straight pull. He winced as it took some of his flesh. There was a blob of blood and flesh on the end of it. He was amused to see a bead of sweat on the long upper lip of the boy.

"It's all right," he said. "It's out."

"Phew," said the boy in a long sigh. "I was afraid it was properly stuck in the bone of your jaw. Here" – searching his pockets – "here's a hanky. It's not very clean, I'm afraid," he said, "but I think it's clean dirt that's on it."

"It's all right," said Mico. "I have one of me own. Here's your rod and for God's sake look what you're doin' with it. You needn't bait the hook either, that's the best lure in the world on it now." He laughed and went to the side and stretched down and dipped his handkerchief until the sea caught it and soaked it, and then he drew back again and pressed the wetness of it to the jaw. He took it away then and saw where the blood had mixed with the salt.

"Here, let me do it for you," said the other, and took it from him and dabbed it with his fingers until the blood had ceased to well. "You'd want some iodine."

"They get iodine from the sea," said Mico, "and what's on the handkerchief but the sea and that's iodine."

"That's true," said the red-headed one. "I'm sorry though. I was very clumsy. I never did this before."

"Whose is the rod and tackle?" Mico asked.

"It belongs to me old fellow," said the other.

"Does he know you have it?" Mico asked.

"Devil a know," said the other. "I just got home from school and pinched it and ran down."

"Don't you know," said Mico, "that sea water is very bad for tackle like that? 'Tis ruined, so it is. Your oul fella'll be mad and small blame to him."

"Ah, but wait'll he sees all the fish I have," said the other.

"If he's a trout man," said Mico sagely, "he won't like his best tackle being ruined to kill mackerel."

The other boy laughed.

"Ah," he said, "I'll talk him out of it. He's a very nice man."

"Who are you?" asked Mico bluntly.

"Peter Cusack's me name," said the red boy. "And who are you?"

"Mico," said he, thinking that the boy was all right. He smiled.

"You better catch some more mackerel so," he said, "if you want to impress your father."

"That's right," said Peter. "Sure I'll see you afterwards."

They went back to the fishing then side by side, and sometimes Mico dodged the swing of Peter's rod with exaggerated care, and they laughed more and warmed towards each other, the boy in the jersey and the boy in the white shirt, the boy in the bare feet and the boy with the white socks and brown shoes.

And the tide departed and with it the fry and after them the voracious mackerel. The old boat stood up free of the water, the underneath part that you could see now slimy with green weed. Mico never liked the look of the old boat at all when the sea left it. It seemed to be stripped of all dignity and all purpose, and was just a wreck that smelled badly when the sun got at the under parts.

"What way do you live?" Mico asked Peter, as he arranged his heavy catch of fish into a hank.

"Oh, up the west," said Peter.

"We'll be with you so," said Mico. "Come on, fellas!" And he hoisted the fish over his shoulder so that they rested on his back. Tommy was going to protest, to say, "What will Mother say when she sees your jersey all fish scales?" but he knew Mico would just shrug his shoulders in genuine amazement at such a question, so he turned to Peter and walked ahead with him.

"Where do you go to school?" he asked.

"Ah, I'm finished with one now," said Peter. "I'm going to the secondary after the hols."

"I'm goin' too," said Tommy. "I got a school."

"Did you?" the other asked, stopping a little. "So did I!"

They discovered they were going to go to the same school.

"Do you hear that, Mico?" Peter asked, turning back. "Your brother and meself will be going to the same school. Will you be going too?"

"No," said Mico, "I'll be going fishing with my father." Peter's expression showed that he thought this was a peculiar thing, because in the circles in which he moved, scholarship or not, you went on from the national to the secondary school. He left it and talked to Tommy about the school.

"Is he a sissy, Mico?" Twacky was asking Mico in a whisper.

"What d'y' mean?" asked Mico.

"Look at the socks on 'm like an oul girl," said Twacky, pointing, "an' a white shirt an' a belt with colours. And shoes too on 'm in the middle of summer."

Mico laughed. He wasn't sure whether it was at the earnest look of puzzlement in Twacky's blue eyes or the size of his small figure bowed down with the huge hank of fish. "He's different to us," he said then. "He can afford shoes in summer. His father probably has money."

"But, jay, Mico," said Twacky, "even if my oul fella had money I wouldn't wear shoes in the summer. They'd cut the feet offa me."

"You'd get used to it, Twacky," said Mico, "and anyhow he seems to be a very nice fella."

"I suppose he is," said Twacky doubtfully, squeezing the dust of the road up through his toes.

They were walking back by the river up the Long Walk. The river was shallow now, having won its ephemeral battle with the vanishing tide, and it rushed with a kind of sibilant triumphant song over the rocky bed. Some of the stones appeared over the water. The sun was low over the Bay out beyond, and shone kindly on the white Claddagh houses on the other side of the river, and the slender masts of the seemingly rope-entangled pucauns of the fishermen rose against the pink sky. Ah, yes, said Mico, 'tis a great life, and then he was brought up short by the crowd of boys at the Spanish Arch.

There were about twenty of them and they stood and blocked the Arch in a line, a determined line. Mico had noticed some of them down at the docks. He knew all of them nearly by sight, as you would if you lived in a town for a while. But never their names. They were townies too. He could see that well. You always knew. They weren't dressed like Mico and his brother or Twacky. Short torn coats and trousers with the backsides out of them, or trousers where the backsides had been patched and the patches and the backsides were out of them. The dirt of towns on their exposed parts. Hair cropped close or badly in need of cropping. Their faces pale, because they lived in long streets where the houses were tall and shut off the sun.

They stopped Peter and Tommy first.

"Here," said one of them, pushing a hand in Peter's chest, "where d'ye think yeer goin'."

He was a tall boy, nearly as tall as Mico and well built. He had outgrown his suit, and his broadening shoulders had burst the shoulder of his coat so that his skin was seen underneath. He had a bullet head and his nose turned up and his eyes were small.

Peter looked down at the hand.

"Remove that dirty paw, you scoundrel," he said in his best accent. The boy was so surprised that he did so, and then recovering placed the hand back on the shoulder and pushed, and Peter sat abruptly on the ground, the sticky flesh of his hanked fish lapping up the dust.

"Who d'y' think yer talking to?" he asked. Peter looked funny on the ground peering up in amazement.

"That's the way to treat them, Bartley," said one of the minions. "We'll get them Claddy fellas."

Mico felt like laughing at Peter, he looked so funny, and then he became a little annoyed when he saw that one of the pieces of Peter's rod had broken with his fall, the slender top. His mouth tightened and he moved and put a hand under his arm and raised him to his feet.

"What's the joke?" he asked Bartley.

"Who do ye think ye are?" Bartley asked. "Did ye get permission to come over to this side a the river? Ye stick to yeer own place and we stick to our place, and since ye didn't stick to yeer place, we declare that yeer fish are all forfeit, and ye can hand all of them over now and we'll let ye go in peace, and if ye don't hand them over ye'll go in pieces, so take yeer choice now and have yeer pick."

"Mico," asked Peter, "what's this?"

There was no time for Mico to tell Peter what gang warfare was. It was all a little complicated. There was the Claddagh side of the river and there was this side of the river which was ruled by the High Street Gang or the Middle Street Gang, Mico wasn't sure which, and when one went into the other's territory one walked warily. It was all a thrilling part of Mico's younger days, but he thought he had grown out of it. It seemed not.

"Now listen," he said, "yeer about ten to one so I suppose we can't fight ye, so we'll settle with this, that we'll give ye two hanks of the four hanks of fish we have and let us be on our way." I'm getting awful sensitive in my old age, he was thinking, to be avoiding a fight like this, but he thought that Tommy was never much good in a fight and Twacky was too small to be allowed in a fight and he didn't like the thought of Peter's nice white shirt being rolled in the dust. So, thinking of Gran, he compromised.

"You shut your big mouth, Turkey-face," said Bartley. His minions giggled at this sally. Tommy, who had edged back from the bunch at the Arch, glanced at his brother Mico and saw the signs: the paling of the good side of his face and the twitching of his muscle. Oh God, Tommy thought, don't let him fight. I don't want to get hurt. It isn't that I'm a coward or anything, but always when things like this happen I get sweat on my stomach, thinking of the pain of a knuckle on the bridge of your nose or the blinding flash of a fist in your eye – and he turned now to see if he could slide off back the way they had come, but he noticed fearfully that the ring had silently closed around them. Don't let

Mico lose his temper now, he prayed, or I'll be hurt.

Mico was counting ten under his breath. That was Gran. Now Mico, Mico, it's only fools that lose their temper. A fisherman never loses his temper. He has so many things to lose his temper over that he'd be wasted away with disease before he was thirty if he lost it every time he ought to. Take a deep breath and count up to ten and leave the tempers to the lazy perverted, spineless son 'f bitches that live in cities.

He had just reached a count of eight when little Twacky came forward with his face red and the hank of fish swinging in his small hand, and before anybody could stop him he drew out with the hank and he hit Bartley across the face with it, saying, "Yeh dirty Townie scab, yeh! I'll kill yeh, so I will! I'll kill yeh!" And there he was straddling his fallen fish-covered foe and punching him vigorously in the face with a frenzied fish. Twacky was very fond of Mico.

Of course there was nothing for it then but to fight.

Mico used the hank of fish as a weapon, swinging rings all around him until the twine broke and the fish flew in all directions. Then he had to use his fists. But it was hard enough at that, when his big body was swarming with red-faced cursing boys, clinging to him like bluebottles on the eye of a cow.

Peter used the fish too, and Mico was surprised and amazed and joyfully glad to see that Peter was good. His crooked teeth were clenched and when the fish were expended he used his left hand and his poor father's fishing rod; used it as a sword now and a flail again.

Tommy put his hands over the back of his head and kicked out with his feet, and sometimes used his elbow to poke it in an eye, but fists seemed to come at him from everywhere and he experienced all the things he had feared, the blow on the bridge of the nose and the blow of the fist in the eye, so that he held his nose now and his eye again and he couldn't stop from crying out, "Lave me alone, will ye! Lave me alone, will ye!" and as is the habit with boys when they have beaten you into cowardice, they thumped him on the back and kicked him in the breeches and then with yells they jumped to join the milling crowd around the other three.

Twacky was fighting like three men. He was so small you'd have to get near the ground to get a good blow in on him. He was a fearful defender and on some of them he would leap up and clasp his arms around their necks and burrow into them until they fell, when he would deal a puck in the nose and then rise to burrow into another tormentor.

They couldn't come near Mico. He was very big and very strong, and every time he hit there was an opponent suddenly crying for his mammie, dancing around holding part of himself and roaring.

But an unequal struggle it was and could have only one end, ignominious defeat or a throwing into the shallow river, so God sent deliverance to them in a strange way.

A little man was his instrument — a little man like the flail of God who laid about him on convenient bottoms with a blackthorn stick. A little hairy man named Pa, with his beard bristling and the stick rising and falling and he shouting like Jove, "You scamps! You rogues! You flea-bitten city dwellers! Be off with you! Hold back, boy!" He dealt it out with the stick and his practised hand dealt clumps on ears that resounded over the water like a smack of a board on a stone flag. The bewildered boys, holding on to sore bums or smitten ears, backed away from him, resentful of this sudden and unfair ending, and they got off a respectable distance and they prepared to curse him with all their precocious knowledge when he faced them with a new fear.

"I know you," he told them, "I know you all. You, Bartley Mullen, you snotty nose, and you, Pigeon O Flaherty, and you, Wee-wee Johnson. I know all of you and I will now go straight to your fathers and see that they discipline you."

Since they had all been about to threaten their parents on him, this cut the ground from under their feet, but there was worse to come.

"I know you go to the Brothers," he said, referring to that school presided over by the order of teaching monks, "and tomorrow I will go down personally and see that you are all flogged by the Reverend Brother" (naming a man that had put the fear of God into anybody unfortunate enough ever to be in his class). "Over the desks with ye, ye barbarians, until we see will ye descend any more like bandit locusts on the decent peace-abiding citizens that walk the roads. Off with ye now, before I give ye more!"

And they faded away, sheepishly, daunted and thinking many terrible things about the little man, but definitely worrying about the morrow, and Pa turned to regard his decent peace-abiding citizens who were pulling themselves together and licking their wounds.

"I have spent my whole life," he lectured them, "explaining to you that fighting is no way to freedom. There are other ways. The ways of cunning and honesty. Twacky, you are a very fierce young man. You'll have to get a better control on your temper or you'll kill somebody some day."

That made Mico laugh, the sight of little Twacky looking up at Pa, as frightened as a fry, with one of his eyes raw red from approaching blue-blackness. The idea of little Twacky killing somebody!

"And stop whining, sir," said Pa, going over to Tommy, who was picking up some scattered fish and tears still in his eyes. "Face your misfortunes like a man. Surely you have enough brains not to be overcome by inferior intellects. A disgraceful performance. Thomas, dry your eyes and don't be a mollycoddle. Who's this?" he asked then, pointing a stick at Peter who was gathering the broken pieces of his father's fishing rod.

"He's Peter Cusack, sir," said Mico. "He was with 's."

"Cusack? Cusack," said Pa, a hand on his beard. "Oh, aye. You live up near myself, don't you, boy?"

"I do, sir," said Peter. "I know you well to see."

"H'm," said Pa. "You fought well, boy. Now how often must I tell you, Mico, that you are to avoid getting into positions like this? It's disgraceful, this brawling. Leave this brawling and fisticuffs to lesser men, do you hear?"

"We couldn't help it, sir, this time," said Mico. "They were intent on batin' 's. I'll get a few more of the lads tomorrow and I'll teach them manners. If only we had a few more we'd ha' bet them."

"Silence," thundered Pa. "Enough is enough, do you hear? If I hear any more of this talk I'll deal with you myself, personally. Do you hear?"

"Yes, sir," said Mico.

"Good," said Pa. "Well, come now, gather yourselves up, boys, and be off. Your parents will be wondering. And wash yourselves off before you go home. Get rid of the gore and grime and thank you for these" (bending down and retrieving two mackerel and trying vainly to dust them off with his fingertips), "they will be pleasant for the tea, and don't forget to be at school bright and early and no excuses for not having exercises done. Be off now, be off, and God bless ye," and off he went down the Long Walk with his jaunty step and his hairy suit, looking funny enough but very dignified with the two battered fish dangling from his hand.

Mico looked at Peter and saw the twinkle mixed with bewilderment in his eyes. Then they both laughed and when Twacky asked plaintively what ther' was to laugh about, that he wished he could see something to laugh at, they laughed all the more doubled up, and the sight of sullen Tommy sobered Mico, so they gathered up the fish and the bits and pieces and followed Tommy, who had walked ahead of them, silent, with his back stiff.

"Jay, lads," said Twacky then, hopping, "it was a great fight, wasn't it? Did ye see me hittin' that bee Bartley in the kisser, Mico, did yeh see me?"

"I did, Twacky," said Mico. "What did you want to do that for?"

"Jay, he maddened me," said Twacky with his lips tightened. "He med me fur rise. If I was big enough I'd ha' murdered 'm."

"You did enough damage for the size of you," said Mico, laughing.

"Do you always have pleasant interludes like that?" Peter wanted to know, dabbing at a sore eye with a gentle dirty hand.

"Not often," said Mico.

"There's never anything nice like that where I live," said Peter.

Mico laughed.

"There'll be war in your house tonight," he said, "when your father sees the rod."

"Oh, God," said Peter, looking sadly at the remains of what was once a beautiful delicate trout rod, "he'll have canaries."

At the big bridge they went down the stone steps and they washed their cuts and bruises in the river, and after that they washed the dust off the limp fish and then they crossed the bridge and they paused a little where their ways parted.

"Goodbye," said Peter. "Maybe I could see ye again sometime."

"Maybe you could," said Mico. "You know where we live now. Down there" (waving a hand at the Claddagh). "Ask anyone for Micil's Mico and they'll show you our house."

"I'll do that," said Peter. "Maybe ye'd come and see me too."

"We might at that," said Mico.

"Me father has a twenty-two rifle," said Peter eagerly. "Maybe ye'd come with me if I pinched that and we could shoot duck or seals or something?"

"Maybe," said Mico, "if the same thing doesn't happen to it as happened to the rod."

"Goodbye so," said Peter, moving away slowly.

"Goodbye," said Mico, turning down towards the black lock gates.

What a day! Peter was thinking. Imagine having fun like that every day! He turned once or twice before he reached the rows of shops and houses to scan the big figure of Mico and little Twacky hopping along beside him. I'll see him again all right, he thought. I'm sure to. Then he went home to face his father with a light heart and a broken rod.

"He's a nice fella, isn't he, Mico, for a fella with white socks?" Twacky inquired.

"He is indeed, Twacky," said Mico, "and he fought like a hero too."

"He went at them well, for a fella with a clean neck," said Twacky judiciously, "and to look at him you'd think he was a mammy's pet."

Mammy! That reminded Mico. He looked ahead and saw the tall thin figure of his brother increasing his speed as he neared their houses. He'll tell all now, he thought, and of course the blame'll fall on me. Ah, well, he thought, I'm big enough now to take the blame, and they crossed the bridge towards the village, the small and the tall, with spoils on their shoulders and aches in their eyes.

Chapter Four

IF YOU WALK up the town by the main street and turn right where a patch of green grass and some shrubs and flowers are imprisoned by a big square of iron railings, and go down here and up towards the railway station, but bypass the station and walk right ahead to a narrow path that crosses a small railway bridge that used to carry people in an erratic train to the heart of Connemara, you will be able to make your way towards the Barracks on the hill by way of a military footpath that runs beside the railway line.

If you wish you may cross the railway line and walk over to the sea. But it is soggy land and evil-smelling when the tide is out. But once you pass the Barracks, and pause to look at the slit trenches and connecting trenches and barbed-wire entanglements that soldiers build to play with, you will come to different country.

It is fairly wild, but the land is solid under your feet and on your left there are thick woods bisected by the rusty railway lines. But near the sea it is wild and lonely, with occasional beaches of silver sand and strong brown rocks, and you could be alone here all day except for the gulls and odd strange birds that have come from the woods to take a look at the sea. Then if you travel farther and round a headland that covers off the Bay of Oranmore you will come on a strange place. Out in the middle you will see a green island. If the tide is full, you will wonder how on earth the few animals that graze it ever got out there, but if you wait until the tide falls you will see that a long, long man-made causeway leads out to it. Quite a solid enough road when the sea departs until the bad bad weather when the storms tear at it and it has to be reinforced again by cursing men. Walk out along it and you will come to the island. You will be surprised at the green of the grass. It is not the coarse marsh-green that usually sits near the sea, but good honest wholesome grass fit for pedigreed cattle to eat, and many flowers grow on it all the year round, and you will wonder at the size of it if you walk around it. It rises towards the centre, and perhaps that drains it and keeps the grass good and green, and whatever phosphates are in the breezes of the eternal ocean.

Right in the centre of the hill, there is a single thorn tree. In May it is thickly clustered with blossoms and they say that the blossoms on this single tree last longer than blossoms on the thorn tree anywhere else in the world. The trunk of the tree is thick and twisted like the gnarled muscles of an old and mighty man. There are some twelve stones set around the ground in a ring, and the grass is very short and thick at the butt of the tree, and it's most pleasant to sit there in the shade it provides and let the sea winds blow on your face. It is always pleasantly scented. One strange thing about it is that the cattle or sheep who graze the island never come near this tree. Cattle love trees. Some cattle even eat trees, but most cattle love a thorn tree, because its points are sharp and they love to lean their thick hides against it and scratch away the millions of different sorts of flies that afflict their poor hairs in all the seasons. So it is a strange thing that the cows don't come near this tree. Why wouldn't they even come and eat the luscious and obviously tasty grasses that grow under it? They don't and that's a fact.

So what?

So it's a fairy tree. It's all right to shrug your shoulders when you are told all this and say you gave up believing in the fairies when you were six months old, but if you can find any other explanation to fit the peculiarities of this tree, then you are welcome to it. You'll get nobody around here to believe you. If you like to go up the road a piece and talk to a few gentlemen they'll soon leave you in no doubt about it. They'll even trot out the oldest inhabitant, who saw things on that island that no mortal man could ever believe. So there you are.

All round the island, you come abruptly from green grass to rocky shore. No half measures. Green grass, rocks, and then great depths of water even when the tide is out. It's as if some mysterious force below the ocean bed stuck a big finger up through the ground below and kept this island hovering on the tip of it. The wild duck come here occasionally and if any man about the place had the courage to come over to the island in the winter in the late evening he'd get a shot at the wild geese. Nobody ever comes.

So here on a certain evening in early August came to the island across the long causeway, four boys.

Mico led the way across the causeway, his eyes darting here and there measuring it all up, and raising his head to smell at the breeze, a thing he had been taught to do by Gran. ("Use your nose, boy. That's what God gev it to you for. Feel the change of the wind in it. See if there are any fish coming to you from it.") Behind him walked Peter and he was holding the gun. Not very carefully. He was jumping about a bit from one side of the causeway to the other. And behind Peter came Tommy and after him, wagging a small tail, came Twacky.

Getting the gun had been a bit of business. It wasn't that Peter's father wouldn't give it exactly, because from what Mico could see Peter's father would give him the North Star on a plate once Peter had talked him into it. He was a nice man. Mico liked him. A bluff sort of a man with a white moustache and a tanned face that he got from being out so often in the fresh air after every known sort of game, trout and salmon and pike in the summer, and going into bog-holes up to his watermark, as he said himself, after the wild geese and the duck in the winter. There wasn't four inches of the whole County Galway that he didn't know like the lines on his own hand.

The mystery of it all was, Mico was thinking, that Peter should be the most spoiled son in the world, but he wasn't. Because he was very intelligent and felt that his parents were very young and he had to look after them or God knows what they'd do, and apart from the physical crimes he committed he'd chop off his right hand before he'd hurt them spiritually.

"How in the name a God, Peter," he asked, turning back to him now, "did you persuade him to give you the gun?"

"Ah, it was easy enough," said Peter. "Actually I was trying to get the shotgun, but he nearly blew up. He's had it since he was a child and he'd sooner part with me, I think, than that gun. Then I had to be a bit cautious because I didn't want mother to know at all that I was after a gun, so after a bit of play-acting I let him offer me the twenty-two as a compensation."

"God," said Mico, "I hope nothing happens to that."

"Devil a fear," said Peter, "amn't I a born gunman?"

"But will we really be able to kill anythin' with a small yoke like that?" Twacky wanted to know.

"You could kill an elephant with that," said Peter, "if you got him in the right place."

"Whist," said Mico, spreading his arms and stopping them where the causeway ran on to the island. "Do ye see what I see?"

"What is it?" Peter asked.

"Look," said Mico, pointing his finger and lowering his voice. "What's that under the fairy tree?"

"It's a fairy," said Peter in the same muted voice.

"On me oath it is," said Mico, looking at the white un-moving thing.

"Jay, fellas," said Twacky coming up behind them and holding on. "Don't be talkin' like that. Ye have the shivers runnin' up me back."

He looked closer.

"Gwan," he said then, in a loud clear voice. "It's only an oul girl."

They could see her silhouetted up there, her head bent over a book, and the sun going down behind her seemed to make the white dress she wore look misty. She raised her head and looked towards the causeway. They could see the sun on one half of her face. If she was perturbed by their coming she showed no signs of it. She kept looking at them steadily and they stood there looking up at her wordlessly, and when Mico moved up the hill towards her over the short grass as if impelled, they followed him. He stopped on the edge of the shade of the tree and looked at her. She had black hair and it was close-cropped, making her look like a boy, but her chin was rounded and her lips were red. The sleeves of her dress were short and showed her arms burned by the sun, and there were small brown moles on them. A gold wristlet watch she had. Her eyes were brown and very steady and regarded them steadily, her left hand holding the book in her lap which she had made by pulling up her knees almost under her chin. The other hand, with its long thin fingers, was pulling at the grass. Mico, who was not without imagination, thought how disturbing it must be to be faced by four boys if you were alone on an island that was pushed into the Atlantic Ocean. Boys like themselves. Poorly dressed enough, in bare feet, and he, the biggest of them, must look sinister with his face, and Twacky, small and all as he was, looked villainous with his bob and his scowl. He always scowled at girls. They made him feel very uncomfortable. Not a bit of fear did she show. Maybe, he thought then, there is somebody with her and they are the other side of the hill.

"Hello," he said, smiling.

"Hello," she answered gravely.

Then they were all silent, Twacky moving uncomfortably. What do I say now, Mico wondered, or what on earth made me come up here at all?

"Is that a book you're reading?" Peter asked then, coming forward a bit.

"It is," she said.

"Where's your mother?" he asked then.

"At home, as far as I know," said the girl.

"Well, now," said Peter, "isn't it a great wonder that she'd let you out readin' books on a lonely place like this?"

"Do you own the island?" she asked.

"No," said Peter.

"Then wouldn't it be a good idea," she said, "to mind your own business?"

Peter's good humour melted. His face went a bit red. Red-haired people go red easily anyhow, Mico was thinking, and you always know when they are in a rat.

"Well, for God's sake," said Peter, "I was only trying to be nice."

"What are you doing with a gun?" she asked then.

"Do you own the island?" he asked.

"I might do," she said.

"Well, you know what to do with it," said Peter rudely. "Come on out of this, fellas." He went to go on, and then turned back again. "What's the name of the book?" he asked belligerently, his head shoved forward.

Surprisingly, she answered him.

"It's a book by Mr James Stephens," she said, underlining it as if to say, a stupid person like you I'm sure could never have heard of him.

"Who's goin' to translate it for you?" Peter wanted to know then.

"I think you're a very rude boy," she said, her eyes flashing.

Peter, now that he had knocked a spark out of her, turned to go. "We'll go now, lads," he said, making determinedly for the shore below.

"I hope you're not going to shoot birds," she said in a loud voice. It stopped Peter. "Nobody ever shoots birds here. They're not afraid of guns and it would be a mortal sin to shoot birds."

"Is that so?" Peter asked very politely, his red eyebrows high on his forehead. "That's very interesting. Well if you hang around here along enough you'll be seeing a bagful of mortal sins committed." And he turned and this time really went towards the shore.

"Don't mind him," said Tommy to the girl.

"Is he a Galway boy?" she asked.

"He is," said Tommy.

"Strange," she said, as if she had been in Shop Street and had seen an Eskimo buying sausages.

"Do you like James Stephens?" Tommy wanted to know.

"I adore him," she answered simply, with all the fervour of what Mico thought must be her fifteen years.

"I like him too," said Tommy, "if it wasn't for the fairies."

That surprised Mico, and then didn't surprise him when he saw Tommy screwing his eyes eternally over books. Mico had never heard of Stephens unless he was the fellow that made the blue-black ink that came in the big glass bottle that Pa kept on his table.

"Ah, you don't understand," she said a little patronizingly, waving a hand, but a little surprised that this obvious Claddagh boy (you could always spot the Claddagh boys for some reason) should know what she was talking about when her design had been to crush them and make them depart away from this lovely island of hers, where with all the fevers and depressions of her growing years, she often came to "be away from it all", to be silent and read about never-never lands and be alone except for the birds and the deep blue sea that was never blue in this bay but green, green, green, like the grass and like the fumbling emotions of the youthful years.

"Are ye comin' or aren't ye comin'?" Peter was roaring from the bleak shore below, his hand cupping his mouth.

"All right, Peter," Tommy shouted, "we're coming." Tommy could switch his mind in the most amazing manner. One second it was this girl with the close-cropped hair and a fringe straight across her forehead, regular features and a determined chin, her and James Stephens, and the next it was the mechanics of a twenty-two rifle. He saw all the action of it as he went towards Peter, the pulling back of the oiled bolt and feeling the slim length of the cartridge in the fingers; inserting it into the breech; sighting along the barrel; seeing the tip of the foresight; and then the crack.

The girl looked up and saw Mico looking down at her, smiling.

"Peter is very nice," said Mico, not quite knowing why. "It's just that he had a bit of trouble getting the gun from his father and it was such a great gas getting it up here. He had to put it under his shirt and down the leg of his trousers in case he'd be seen. He's always awful polite."

She warmed then. The rigidity went out of her body and the haughty tone from her voice.

"Don't let him kill a bird," she said earnestly.

"To tell you the truth," said Mico, "I don't think he'd be able to kill one if it was sitting in front of him. He's a poor hand at a gun. I've seen him. And we have only ten bullets."

"That's good," she said.

"What's your name?" he asked, surprised at himself again. "I'm sorry," he said then. "I shouldn't be so nosy. It's just seeing you up here under a tree on an island by yourself and not afraid when four scoundrelly-lookin' boys come up to you. Why do you come here?"

She got to her knees then and let the book fall to her lap.

"Oh, it doesn't matter," she said. "My name's Josephine Mulcairns. Why I come here? To be alone."

"You picked a bad day today," said Mico.

"Yes," she said. "Do you believe in fairies?"

"Not now," said Mico, "but I maybe would at night."

"Ah, janey, are yeh comin', Mico?" Twacky was asking disgustedly from a few paces away. Twacky showed on his

- 65 -

face what he thought of girls and it didn't look so good. "Ah, Mico," he went on, "them fellas'll have all the bullets gone and we won't get a crack outa the oul gun if you don't come." At that moment there was a sharp crack like a man flicking a whip, as if to emphasize his point. "Listen, Mico! Come on, will yeh?"

"All right, Twacky," said Mico. "Goodbye now," he said then to the girl, "and I'm sorry we upset the loneliness on you."

She smiled. Her teeth were small and as even as her fringe.

"That's all right," she said. "I don't mind you. But that red-haired boy is a nuisance."

They went and joined the others then, running, and for the next hour they completely forgot the determined girl on the hill with James Stephens. There were a few wild duck around the island and they expended bullets on them. There were folds in the island where they could lie and crawl around, and getting from one side to the other cautiously they would have a quick shot at a canny mallard or the small alert teal. It was fruitless work but it was good fun. The only lives in jeopardy were the human ones surrounding the man with the gun, and in no time at all they had used eight bullets, two apiece, and then Peter used the ninth on a black cormorant – nearly choking himself gobbling a captured fish – and it was when they got to the east side of the island that they saw the three seals far out on the flat black rock.

It was Mico saw them first and he pressed the others to the grass behind him.

"Quiet, will ye," he said, "for the love of God! Get down and then ye can peep."

They remained very still, their hearts beating fast, and then they raised their heads. The seals must have just arrived or they would have been frightened away by the cracking of the gun. Way out behind the Aran Islands the sun was sinking into a bed of dark clouds that were rising menacingly from the west. The water was very smooth, just heaving on the rising tide, and there was a great clarity in the air. It was one of those evenings when sound travels far. They could hear the individual buzzing of the midges that plagued them and the clocking of the grasshoppers hidden in the grass. The Clare Hills were very clear. (That's rain, said Mico to himself.) You could see the stones piled on the raw hills, heaped up piles of unbeautiful stones, as if the angels had disdainfully thrown bags of unwanted granite from heaven.

And there were the seals, as sleek as the smooth stones on the sea shore rolled to a beautiful roundness by God's grindstone. Two of them were on the rock stretching out their necks and body in a line, and out a little was another seal. It would go out from the rock and put its playful head under the water and dive until you could see its behind before it slipped under. Down it would go and then incredibly quickly it would come out of the water like a salmon in startled flight from the same seal's grandfather, and it would land wet and triumphant on the rock with the other two. Then one of the seals would rise to its front flippers, honk unmusically, like an early motor-car horn, and their mouths would meet and they would appear to be biting at one another, and then the one in possession would edge forward pressing his chest against the other and pressing him back, back, until he would tumble and fall splashing into the water with none of his habitual grace. It was grand to watch. Why did they keep it up? They kept it up for ages. One of the seals just lay stretched and let the other repel the boarder. Mico wondered if the lazy one was the male or the female; if the two women were arguing for possession of the male or if it was the other way about.

It was like looking at a play. Twacky would clap his hands and laugh loud whenever the seal was pushed off the rock back into the water, so that Mico would have to keep a large hand over his mouth to stifle him.

Peter broke it up at last. He edged the gun forward.

"I'll take a shot at them," he said, his eyes shining, all the murderous instincts of his game-killing father aroused in him. Mico was going to protest. What a terrible thing he thought, if he was to kill one of those chaps! They looked almost human in their playfulness. It was getting duskish anyhow, he thought, and Peter couldn't kill them. All he can do is frighten them away. The ones on the rock had dried a little and although they still gleamed you coud see the sort of brown-grey colour of them appearing.

"All right," said Mico, "bang away."

"If you dare to fire a shot at those seals," said an angry voice behind them, "I'll report you to the authorities."

The four of them raised their heads, startled.

"My God," said Peter then, as he recognized her. "It's you again!"

He stretched his left hand under the gun, rested the barrel on the hillock in front of his face and took a pull on the trigger.

"Don't let him shoot," she appealed then to Mico, and then stood up and yelled, "Shoo! shoo!" so that it carried over the water and the seals raised startled heads and then with incredible speed slithered from the rock into the sea, and the crack of the gun came at the same moment. They saw the splash it made about ten yards to the left of the rock.

"If I had known," said the girl bitingly, "that you were such an awful shot I wouldn't have bothered," and then she turned on her heel and walked away.

"Sweet God!" said Peter, fuming.

"Here, Peter," said Mico, holding his arm, "don't let her upset you."

Tommy had been thinking.

"It's getting dark, you know," he said. "When does the tide cover the causeway?"

That aroused them. They looked at one another for a moment and then as if they were all pulled by the same string they rose to their feet and ran and ran and ran until they topped the hill, and they didn't pause to look but ran down the other side of the hill and only stopped when they came to the causeway and saw the tide sweeping over it in a torrent.

Then they noticed the girl.

She was standing facing them.

"It's all your fault," she said to Peter. "You and your silly shooting. I would have gone long ago if it wasn't my duty to stay here and see that you shot nothing. And then I was entranced looking at the seals and I forgot. And now what are we going to do?"

"It's not too high," said Peter, "we can walk."

"Not in that, Peter," said Mico. "Look at the sweep of it. It'd take down an elephant nearly."

"Then we'll swim it," said Peter.

"Don't be sillier than you look," said the girl. "It's nearly half a mile and with the tide running you'd end up in America."

"It's my opinion," said Peter to the darkening sky, "that the Chinese were the only sensible nation when they drowned all the girls."

"Maybe we could swim it," said Mico, looking closely at it.

"Aw, jay, Mico," said Twacky plaintively, "I can't swim."

"I forgot that," said Mico.

"And I can't swim, either," said Tommy, "but you'd never think of that."

"We'll have to put up with it, that's all," said Mico. "It's about ten now. We should be able to cross in three hours."

"Holy God," said Twacky, "it'll be one a clock in the mornin' then, and me oul fella'll murdher me!"

"What else can we do?" Mico asked.

"Nothing," said the girl. "You're perfectly right. We'll just have to stay. I don't know what my parents will think."

"They'll think, thank God, maybe she's dead at last," said Peter.

Her lips tightened and she turned away from them and

went up the hill. It was getting quite dark now. There was a quarter moon, rising gigantically on the far side of the causeway, but Mico's eye saw that it would soon be swallowed up by the dark clouds that had insinuated themselves all around the horizon. That's not showers either, he thought, that's good honest, heavy, unrelenting rain.

"I think," he said, "that we ought to go up and light a fire under the tree. It's the only shelter we have, and it's going to rain. Look, would ye go around by the shore and pick up whatever driftwood ye can find? We'll want it all. There's not a bush or fern on the island apart from that tree. Go on, Peter, you and Tommy go around that way, and Twacky and myself will go the other way, and we'll meet on the far side."

The two boys shrugged and walked off. Mico thought that the search wouldn't be very diligent. They always found things to talk about that took their minds off material things like working. He went around by the shore. The calmness of the night was broken now by the gentle lash of the sea on the shore. Like a tiger lashing its tail before it leaped. Twacky kept very close to Mico as they travelled with their eyes close to the ground. Twacky liked the big bulk of Mico in the blackness. Twacky wasn't keen on the dark, to tell the truth. It was a vague fear he had, made up of disturbances of the mind brought on by the tales Twacky's old grandmother used to entertain them with before she died. She was an old, old woman and she seemed to have grown into the hob-seat by the side of the open fireplace, her red petticoat spread and her head covered by a check kerchief, and she had an old dudeen of a pipe that she smoked surreptitiously when she thought the childer weren't looking, and it was gas to see it disappear under the red petticoat if anyone called at the half-door or if one of the kids got up early to answer a call of nature at the primitive privies that the village boasted. She'd be telling ye yarns away there that'd raise the hair on the scalp of the dog nearly, about supernatural things that took possession of the night with the fall of darkness, so that when you were out with an urgent pee, you'd start thinking about what she had told you and you would get a tingle in your spine and your hair it'd gup straight on your head like grass on a green, and back you'd race into the brightly lit kitchen and half of the thing with you that you meant to leave outside, so that you'd be in bed again and you'd be thinking and you couldn't go to sleep because you'd know you'd have to be off again in a minute and you'd have to beat or bribe one of your brothers to accompany you.

"Jay, Mico, it's very dark, isn't it?" he asked in a hushed voice to match the hush of the night.

"It is, Twacky," said Mico, "and I can't see a damned thing more, and 'tis little enough we have here. And that girl up there too, all alone. Will you go on up with her, Twacky, and I'll go around and meet the others?"

"Aw, Mico," said Twacky, "is it to gup and stay with an oul girl?"

"Well, she won't eat you," said Mico.

"Ah, but jay," said Twacky, rubbing himself with his elbows, "they do make me ashamed."

"What of?" asked Mico in wonderment.

"Ah, I dunno," said Twacky. "Just ashamed. I do be sweatin' and I can't get out a word."

Mico laughed.

"All right, Twacky," he said, "you go around and meet them and I'll gup to her."

"But Mico," said Twacky.

"What now?" Mico asked.

Twacky paused. After all, he was thinking, you couldn't tell Mico that you were kind of uneasy in the dark. He looked into the blackness that clothed the island now. You could just see the white outline where the sea was breaking on the shore. Imagine goin' into the middle a that be yourself. He swallowed. "All right, Mico," he said, "I'll do that."

"Good man, Twacky," said Mico, "I'll gup and try and get a start on a fire." He walked away towards the peculiarly silhouetted tree on the top of the hill. Twacky remained until he could hardly hear his feet swishing on the grass and then he said to himself, Sure ther's nothin' at all to be afraid a. Look at all them watchmen fellas that does be up all the whole night and not a sinner within sight of them and nothing ever happens to them, and he set off around the island at a good trot, and he was very relieved to hear the two voices in front of him, and he slowed his walk and approached them as if it was the most natural thing in the world to saunter at this time.

Mico picked the girl out by her white dress. He closed on her and dropped the bundle of driftwood on the grass.

"I hope you weren't lonely," he said.

"A little," she said honestly, relief in her voice. "I thought you all might have gone and left me."

"Ah, now," said Mico, "we wouldn't do that."

"That red-headed boy is capable of anything," she said.

"You'll have to make a little sacrifice now," said Mico.

"What?" she questioned, her voice going up.

"You'll have to give 's a page or two of James Stephens'," he said "to get a start on the fire. I have no paper. There's some old grass here under the tree and I can get a few twigs from the tree here." He rose to his full height and laying a hand on one of the branches of the thorn tree, pulled it towards him.

"No, no," she said urgently, "please don't touch the tree."

"Why not?" Mico asked.

"Well, it's a special tree," she said.

"Is it the fairies again?" asked Mico, resignation in his voice.

"Well, all the people around here say it's not lucky to touch it," she said.

"Sure they wouldn't mind us taking a few twigs," said Mico.

"No, don't touch it," she said. "There's a blank page or two in the book and I'll give you those," and she bent to tear them out. He could almost see her slender fingers feeling for them. He came to his knees again and held out his hand. Her fingers brushed against his and he took the crumpled pages.

When the others came near, the fire was going. Mico had a knack with such things. He always had a match or two in his crowded pockets, in the midst of the fish-hooks and the twine and the halfpenny and the other odds and ends.

Their contribution to the fire fund was pitifully small.

"It was too damn dark," said Peter airily. "You'd want to have the couple of million eyes of the flies to see anything in this light."

"I'm glad ye didn't hurt yeer eyes tryin'," said Mico. "What would the world do if it was deprived of yeer eyes? This'll only last for ten minutes, all we have here."

"Well, friend," said Peter, putting his hand in his pocket and pulling out his father's fishing knife. (It could do everything except talk, this knife; it could gut a fish or hit him on the head or gaff him in an emergency or it could also open lemonade bottles, or more important, it could pull the cork on a bottle of Guinness, a necessary adjunct to all fishing expeditions.) "There's a tree here, and here's a knife," and he reached up and caught a branch of the tree and leaned his weight on it.

"No, no," said the girl, getting to her feet and reaching for him. "Don't do it! You don't know what'll happen."

"What do you mean?" Peter asked, and then the branch broke from the trunk with a sort of sobbing scream.

"Now you've done it!" said the girl.

"Done what?" Peter wanted to know.

"Terrible things," said the girl. "You have destroyed yourself."

"Listen," Peter asked them, "is this one out of her mind?"

"You'll see," she said. Her eyes were wide in the firelight. She kept looking at him as if she expected him to be smitten by a bolt from heaven (or hell depending whether her fairies were good or bad).

"Oh, I get it now," said Peter, putting his foot on the

branch. "The fairies are with us again."

"Jay," said Twacky in a small voice, "maybe you shouldn't have done it."

"Piddle," said Peter, breaking up the branch masterfully. "We have to have a fire. The tree is here and St Patrick drove all the fairies out of Ireland with the snakes."

He threw it on the fire and it burned most beautifully, flaring up, the flame licking greedily at the slender twigs and the thorns and the reddening haws.

"You see," said Mico, gently to the girl, "nothing happened."

"I'll tell you what's wrong with her," said Peter, sitting on a stone; "too much Celtic twilight. She'll be drowned in clouds of Celtic twilight before she's seventeen. What age are you now?" he asked abruptly.

"Mind your own business," she said.

"What do we do now, to pass the time?" Tommy wanted to know. "Tell ghost stories?"

"Ah, jay no," said Twacky, pulling in close to Mico. "I had enough a them from oul Momo."

"Why don't you read us a bit of the book?" said Tommy. "That'll pass the time nice enough. It'll save us thinkin' of what's in store for 's when we get home."

"I will maybe if he keeps quiet," she said.

"I'll guarantee that he does," said Mico, holding a very big fist into the light from the fire. "I'll put him to sleep with this if he as much as opens his gob."

Peter laughed. "All right," he said, "I'll be quiet, on me oath I will."

She read for them from the book. It was called *In the Land of Youth* and she hadn't gone very far when her hearers became very quiet, and in the end even the voice of the girl faltered and came to a stop so that there was silence between them except from the insinuating wind that was gradually heaving the ocean, and the breaking of the waves becoming louder and more frequent on the air, and over them all hung her words about a man hanged on a gibbet at the top of a hill and the finding of a great door opening in the hillside, and the young man going into the land of the strange people who came, silent shapes, to plunder the outer world from their own never-never land buried in the earth. They were all shaken. She couldn't have chosen a more unfortunate subject for such a time and place. Even Mico's phlegmatic soul was shaken a little. Your man accepted it all as if it was true, and here with the fire and the flickering shadows it seemed as real as if it was happening in front of your eyes. It was Tommy that broke the silence.

"Personally," he said, "I'm not keen on the Celtic twilight. You know what I think it was. All these birds, Yeats and the rest of them, writing about fairies and bog cotton and Fionn Mac Cumhail and Ossian and the Fenians and Diarmud and Grainne and Deirdre and Dervorgilla, do you know what all that was?"

"No," said Peter. "You tell us, out of the depths of your old age."

"They wanted to escape," said Tommy judiciously. "They weren't doing anything at all for the country. They were all only a crowd of parasites, thinking they were geniuses because they wint around with their heads in the clouds, so they wanted to escape into the past and try and drag other poor unfortunate people with them. I haven't it all worked out yet," he said, his head on one side, a wisp of grass in his mouth.

"Who are yeh tellin'?" Peter wanted to know.

And the silence then was a better silence than the one that had gone before.

Until the rats came.

Where they came from or where they would go when they left, nobody will ever know, but for some time now they had obviously been swimming from somewhere to that finger of light on the island in the Atlantic, that lit up the tree on the hill, so that it must have seemed like a beacon. But they came, thousands and thousands of rats; legions of rats; big brown rats with their hair sleeked back to their narrow slink-

ing bodies; and they landed in their legions all around this island and then they came on slippery feet, silently towards
the light on the island. If it had been bright what a sight it
must have been to see the clouds of them in the water! What
did the fishes below them think as the unusual cloud passed
over them? What did the seals think? Did they perhaps get
in among the swimming swarms and decimate them, or
would they have been cautious and unused to such a peculiar
dish? Nobody knows. They swam to that island and they
came in on all sides of it and they made their way up the hill
towards the fire. Why did they come? Who called them? Did
they come often before, when no eye was there to see them?

Mico saw them first.

He thought his eyes were playing tricks on him when he
saw many winking diamonds low down near the ground.
He even closed his eyes and opened them again, and still
the diamonds were there, winking, shifting so that now they
were here and now they were there. And then there came a
low squeal and a rat ran across his sight to the other side of
the fire.

"What was that?" Peter asked.

Mico got to his feet.

"I'm not sure," he said in a low voice, "but do you see
what I see?"

The others sensed the urgency in his voice and they got to
their feet looking at him. Mico felt the hair rising on his
neck. The light was shining on more than diamonds now, it
was shining on the wet pelts of those that had closed in on
them.

He bent quickly and pulled a burning brand from the fire
and threw it towards the mass, and it disintegrated with
squealing cries.

"Janey, Mico!" said Twacky, and there was a quaver in his
voice.

"Rats," said Mico. "Look, fellas, hundreds of them, millions of them." He heard a slither behind him and turned.
There was a dim brown wave covering the land behind the

tree. He bent again and caught another brand, smaller, so that it scored his hand and he could have cried with the pain of it. He flung it at them and they retreated.

"Get up into the tree, Josephine!" he called. "Peter, shove her up into the tree for Christ's sake. I don't know what's happening but the island is a sea of rats. Tommy, tear off the tree for God's sake! Pull it down! Feed the fire! Twacky, break up the branches!"

They moved at the command in his voice. Peter had his hands on the girl's body. He felt her trembling. "It's all right," he said. "Stretch for a branch." She stretched and found one and he bent and got his shoulder under her legs and heaved up. She sat there for a moment and then pulled herself up. Tommy didn't move. He sat there with the glint in his eyes and his lower lip hanging. Twacky leaped from the ground and got his hands on a low branch. The thorns went into his flesh, but he pulled down the branch with his small weight and then tried to pull it back. It was too resilient. "I can't, Mico," he called. "I can't break it." Mico took another burning brand from the fire and flung it in front of him and then kicked some red embers from the fire behind him and leaned his bulk against Twacky's branch. It gave and he turned and caught it and exerted the pull of his shoulders until it came away screaming, and then he broke it again across his knee, not heeding the thorns biting into him, and when it broke he threw it at the fire and the fire blazed. He had to go for another low-hanging branch then on the far side away from the fire. He hesitated and then went. He felt a slithery thing under his bare foot so he pressed hard and it gave, squalling. He felt shivers going up his stomach, so he bent down and picked up one of the twelve oddly-shaped stones and used it as a batter, and there was more squealing and squelching, and he reached the branch and pulled it towards him and it cracked off, and he backed and threw it on the fire. Peter and Twacky were like possessed men, pulling at what they could see, and when Peter had a hefty branch he leaned out and hit around him with it, and loathed the scurrying and squealing that it entailed. Tommy was standing up there all this time as if he was moulded from cement.

"Here," said Mico in a free moment, "get up the tree for God's sake!" and he bent and caught him around the legs and raised him up stiff, and Tommy unloosed himself enough to stretch and pull himself high into the tree. The girl was near him and his hand met hers and clasped it, and it was cold to the touch, and his own was burning. The three below got more timber and put it on, and the fire blazed high, and then Mico picked up Twacky and practically flung him into the tree. "Get up, Peter, you now!" he commanded, and Peter did what he was told and then Mico went the round of the remaining stones and caught them up and flung them like a man demented, and there were more squeals and scurryings, and he flung eleven altogether until he thought his heart would break and then he turned and pulled himself into the tree, and the arms reached for him and held him.

He looked down then.

The fire was blazing brightly and it was ringed with rats. Mico couldn't believe his eyes. Or his senses. Any moment now he expected to hear the voice of his mother say, "Come on now, what kind of a sleepy scoundrel are you? Get up for school or Pa will be down for you with the stick."

Where the fire threw light they could see a heaving mass of brown bodies and now and again the glint of the white teeth as they were sunk into the body of a rat that encroached too closely on a neighbour.

Well, to the longest day I live, Mico told himself, I will never believe that this happened.

Peter leaned for the girl where she was perched on a branch above him and pressed her leg. "I'm sorry," he whispered. "You were right. I shouldn't have touched the tree."

"No, no!" She answered him frantically, her hand over her mouth, her eyes big and her face as white as paper. "That had nothing to do with it! That had nothing to do with it, I tell you!"

Mico fed the fire from where he was. So did Peter and Twacky. Tommy came out of his horrified silent trembling sufficiently to break a twig and aim it at the flames below. Mico also gathered the stoutest branches he could get, using Peter's knife, and he stripped them of twigs and branches and used the heavy end of them to lean down and hit at the few rats that braved the fire and tried to crawl up the trunk of the tree.

It went on for hours and then the rain came.

Gently at first like the rustling of a paper bag and after that big drops. A thorn tree is pretty in the springtime when it is in flower and it blazes, but there is little shelter under it from the wind and the weather as everybody knows. So they were soon soaked to the skin. The water drenched their hair and ran into the collars of their clothes.

But it did one thing.

It started to put out the fire.

Now we're for it, Mico thought, grasping the cudgel tightly. When the fire goes we will be in the dark.

And the fire went.

But so did the rats.

As silently as they had come, they went. They were there and then they were gone. Mico didn't believe it. He listened and there was no rustle. He listened and there was no squealing. The others listened too. It took great courage to come down from that tree. But Mico came down, his feet feeling the ground, his inside tensing for the bite of the vicious white teeth in the bones of his foot. His feet rested on the grass and he felt around with them and waited and met nothing, so he walked a step or two. The body-draped tree held its breath as it listened to his movement. He walked farther, feeling the ground with his feet, the tendons of his arms bursting with his tight grip on the stick. He moved farther and listened. No scurry at all. Nothing but the wash of the waves and the dripping of the rain on the grass. He walked to the shore and he walked back again, and then to make sure he walked back up the hill and walked down to the other shore. But he was alone.

They left the tree and they felt their way to the causeway.

They could just make out the wet stones of it glinting a yard or so in front of them.

They crossed the causeway. Peter never let go the hand of the girl. It fitted into his own as if they were Siamese twins. Mico went first and Twacky came behind him grasping a handful of his jersey. And Tommy grasped hold of Twacky, and the girl held on to Tommy and she had Peter by the hand. And they came to the shore and when they came there they sat down on the wet grass and rested their heads on their hands. And somebody cried. It was Tommy. Real tears and a sort of sobbing. "Oh, my God," he would say, "it was horrible, horrible! I'll never forget it." And Mico came and went on a knee beside him and put a large hand on his shoulder and patted it and said, "There now, Tommy, it's all over," he said. "We'll soon be home."

And they faced into the west and behind them they left the island that none of them would ever see or forget again, and just behind the island there was a faint colour of an approaching wet dawn in the sky and it silhouetted the twisted shape of a raped thorn tree that seemed to be shaking a warning fist after them.

Chapter Five

IT WAS FULLY dawn when they stood at the parting of their ways on the big bridge of the town.

The street lamps were still lighted and the rain was slanting in the wind and they looked very wet and woe begone standing there in the early light. The girl's hair was sticking to her head and came down the sides of her face in wet streaks. It made her eyes look vivid, and her cheekbones were high, and the pallor of her tired skin made it look like ivory. With her big eyes, Mico thought, and her head wearily on one side, she looks like the picture of the Madonna hanging up over the fireplace at home. Peter's wet hair was almost dark in colour, but his face was alive and there was a flush on his cheeks. Peter liked it all, Mico was thinking, Peter enjoys nearly everything that happens to him, and maybe that's why people like him so much. Little Iwacky was standing just like a drowned rat or a pup that had been lost by its owner.

"We better go, I suppose?" he said then. "What'll we say at home?"

That gave them all to think.

"We can't say about the rats anyhow," said Peter. "That's too fantastic. I was often beaten at school for better excuses than that."

"I hope you'll be all right," Mico said to the girl.

"Oh yes," she said, tiredly. "My parents won't be worrying. I have an Aunt Julia up near the island. I had been to tea with her before I went there. They'll think I stayed the night with her on account of the rain."

"Well goodnight, so," said Mico, "and God bless ye."

"Goodnight," said the girl, "and thank you. You were very brave."

The girl and Peter watched them until they turned a corner of the long street and then they turned away towards their own place. He had to go a little out of his way to see her there, but he didn't mind. They didn't talk. There wasn't much to talk about now. Wasn't it all too peculiar? But she stopped at the gate of her home and held out her wet hand, and he took it in his and it was soft.

"I ... I ... I'm sorry for bein' a bit rude at the beginnin'," he said.

"It doesn't matter," she said. "I know how you felt seeing the island occupied by a girl. I felt the same about you."

"Well, goodnight," he said, "and I hope they'll believe you."

"Oh, certainly," she said, her head up a bit. "They're very reasonable parents."

"Aye," he said. "Well, so long. Maybe we'd see you again, hah, sometime?"

"Why not?" she said. "I'm often around. Goodnight." And she went in her gate and walked up the concrete path of the front garden to her door – a small garden, you could smell the flowers in it, very neat – and she reached her hand in through the letter-box and pulled the string that was tied to the knob of the door inside, and she pulled and the door opened and she went into a well of dark, and then the door closed and Peter was alone.

He went home whistling, lifting the gun and aiming it at the early birds that sought shelter in the wet trees that were planted along the road.

In many homes that morning there was what might be

called a slight upset of domestic routine. Imagine it! four families and five children not to be found, not a track or a hair of them. Imagine the worrying as ten came and eleven and twelve. Imagine the fluttering about there was, going from house to house, to relatives and friends so that the worry and despair was spread like the ripples made by a pebble in a pond. So it is safe to say that in the town that morning there would have been at least a hundred people whose lives would have been disturbed by the sudden disappearance of five children.

Josephine was the easiest of the lot, on account of the aunt.

"It's all right, I tell you, woman," her father would say to his wife a thousand times if he said it once. "It's not the first time she stayed with her Aunt Julia, is it?"

"No," Mrs Mulcairns would say, "but ..."

"But what?" he would ask as reasonably as he could.

"Well," she would say tentatively, "that road she goes. It's sort of lonely. She likes to be in lonely places, and if ..."

"Sweet God," said the exasperated George, firing down his evening paper which he wasn't getting a chance to read, so that it caught fire from the coal and had to be rescued in the middle of much swearing and smoke and coughing. "Now look what you've med me do! Women! Holy God! How many hours of their whole lives are spent, I wonder, with their minds taken up with themselves being raped or their sisters being raped or their daughters being raped? Half a lifetime if it's a day. It's a bloody Christian country, woman, I tell you. Good honest Galway Catholics don't be goin' about day and night rapin' little girls."

"Maybe no," said Mrs Mulcairns, nettled a little at this typical manly argument, "but there are a lot of queer hawks in it, Catholics or no Catholics."

"Now look," said George, "I want to read my paper. Jo is up with her aunt. I'm convinced of it. It's raining cats and dogs. Her aunt would never have let her home at this hour. All right! Now will you let me read the paper and get on with what you're doing?"

So read his paper he did, but not very well. "Ah, to hell with it," he says then, "we'll go to bed." She undresses slowly and climbs into bed beside her husband and she clutches her beads and she prays. "George," she said then, rising in the bed and switching on the light and shaking the poor man awake. "Suppose she fell and broke her leg up somewhere and she lying out dying in the rain." "Oh, holy hour!" said George. "Will you go to sleep? Will you for the love and honour of God go to sleep?" But of course she doesn't go to sleep. She stays awake there, her eyes tired and red-rimmed, until the pale dawn was whitening the yellow of the window-blind, and then below she heard voices outside the door and she heard the gate opening (George will really have to oil that gate) and she shook her husband awake with a scream, "George, she's come home! She's come home!" and she was up and out of the bed like a rocket and out into the pasage and down the stairs, and her wide cotton nightdress billowing about her, her black hair long on her back and the streaks of pure white at the temples down the long length of it making her look careworn and beautiful at the same time, and she sees her daughter standing in the hall like a little dignified wet duck and she rushes to her and envelopes her in her arms and hugs the wetness of her to her and says, "Oh, my darling, where were you? What happened to you? Oh, thanks be to the Blessed God for sending you home to me!" And behind Father comes out and stands at the top of the stairs, his scanty hair ruffled, blinking his eyes, drawing a dressing gown around him and coming down, saying, "What's this, what's this, what happened?" (Why on earth do they say such awful platitudinous things in emergencies?) And there was much hugging and kissing and swear-words subdued and they half listened to her explanation while they pulled the clothes off her and turned on the electric fire in the living room and her mother wrapped a blanket around her. "Well, that beats all!" George would say. And Mrs Mulcairns would say, "Never, never, never are you to go

- 84 -

away by yourself again. When I was your age I never did that," and much tut-tut-tutting and notes of affection and growls, and the calmest person in the place was Josephine and she explaining it all as if she was describing a peaceful day in the country.

Peter's father, Big Peadar, waiting at the door, looking gloomily out into the rain, nothing on but his striped shirt coming widely over a lean stomach, and his face red and his braces visible and his trousers gathered around his ankles just above the wooly slippers. And he sees his son coming along the street, practically ambling, pausing now and again to aim the gun at a bird and say, "Bang-bang," and coming on as if nothing had happened, and he runs back to the foot of the stairs and roars up it, "He's comin', Mary, here he's comin'!" and just pauses to hear the fervent and tearful, "Thank God! Oh, thank God!" before he rushes out again to meet his son at the gate. "Where were you? Where were you?" he roars. Peadar always roars when he is worried about a lost duck or a fish that got away or a son that's out all night indubitably dead on a lonely hill, shot to death by his father's rifle. Grabs him by the shoulder, "Oh God, where were you, Peter?" he asks imploringly. 'You're not dead, you're alive, and for the love of God give me that rifle." He takes it, looks at it and breathes a sigh of relief when he sees that it is intact. Then he does a strange thing: he slips the gun down the leg of his pants and holds it there through his pocket. "Your mother mustn't know, d'yeh hear, your mother must never know that I gev yeh the gun," and then starts roaring again. Mary, his wife, enfolds her son in her arms and brings him into the kitchen where the stove is red and the aluminium kettle is hopping with the heat, and she sits in a chair and rocks with her son, or rather it ends up with the son practically rocking with her, saying "There, there, Mother, don't be cryin' now. Dry your eyes, can't you? I'm all right. It was nothing," knowing all the time that his father had slipped into the other room to put away the rifle in the case, and thinking how much he loved his father and mother although they were both so different in their own ways, and how lucky he was to have somebody who loved him like this, and still thinking practically at the same time that it wasn't his fault that he had worried them, that after all it was an act of God.

So Peter puts his mother and father to bed and soothes them and kisses his mother and then comes down to the kitchen and makes tea for himself and sits in front of the fire and thinks about it all and sees the girl with the fair hair plastered to her skull, and he says, "You know, I like that girl."

But nobody heard him but himself.

They were practically in the middle of holding a wake for Twacky when he sneaked in like the drowned rat he was. The neighbours were gathered there in front of the open fire, and his mother was in the middle of them her eyes red raw from the crying. And Padneen O Meara's mother was there and two other women, because, although it may seem queer to you, there's nobody in the end like the people who take part in your sorrows. So the Claddagh was a place of mourning this early dawn. There wasn't a soul in the village that didn't know that poor Twacky was dead or drowned or kidnapped, although the kidnapping was questioned by some doubting Thomases who wondered what on earth use Twacky would be to a kidnapper.

Poor little Twacky was avalanched by petticoated women when he came in the door. He was smothered in kisses and talk and screams of delight and rage and oohs and aahs as they felt his wet clothes, and to tell you the truth he wished the lot of them to hell, only dying to get by his father and tell him all that had happened to him with his eyes wide open and his heart panting to bits as he relived it all again for him. But it was not to be, and so he put up with all the slobbering and ejaculations and histrionics as well as he could, and he had to tell his story there in front of them all so that it would go around the whole of the Claddagh like wildfire before an hour was gone, and he was embarrassed and he got a bit sulky and they had to drag it out of him with more oohs and aahs and Nows and What did I tell yehs, and Glory be to Gods and all the rest of it, and it ends up with them going at last and Twacky is there with his own mother and father and she's finished kissing him and fussing over him, and his father is looking at him with shining eyes as if somebody had made him a present of a deep-sea trawler and a thousand pounds, and he tells it better now, and Twacky's mother gets to her feet and storms. "That Mico!" she says, shaking a fist at the window in the direction of the other house.

And Twacky went to bed and the bodies of his sleeping brothers were warm.

And then Mico went home too.

The bounce was gone out of him as he walked beside Tommy, who was sniffling and sneeezing, his whole body going into a bow as he sneezed, and his thin handsome nose was red at the edges so that he looked very woebegone and exceedingly miserable. That makes it all the worse, Mico was thinking, and he had to steel himself again to the fact that he was the villain of the piece. Well, perhaps he was, at that. It was he had suggested the seals on the island and had brought the others there, had urged them on; had kept them going forward when their wavering feet were lagging and they wished to fire a shot or two at the gulls and forget about the island and the seals. I wish to God now, he was thinking, that I had let them have their way.

She was waiting for them as soon as they opened the door.

Her face was tragic. It was drawn and pale and the eyes were starting from her head. She just got up from the stool and riveted her eyes on her son and stood there and then came forward and took him into her arms, her head over his wet head that was on her chest, with her eyes closed.

And the room door above the fireplace opened and Micil came down wearing a shirt and trousers and his big feet bare, and you could see the very white of his skin just below where the neck of his jersey ended. It was like a pillow case left on a mahogany chest.

"So yeer back!" That was Big Micil with a sigh at the end of it.

Delia's hand had gone up to her son's forehead. She started then and pushed him out from her to look into his eyes.

"You're hot," she said. "Your forehead is hot. What happened to ye? Where were ye?"

Tommy didn't answer. It was Mico who answered. Standing exactly where he stood when he came in, the water dripping from his clothes and body, making pools of wet on the concrete floor. He told it short and crisp in a few sentences, leaving out about the rats. She came away from her oldest son then and she approached Mico on her bare feet and her eyes blazing. She raised her right hand and swung it high and she brought the back of it in a stinging crack against the good side of Mico's face. He had been expecting it and his eyes didn't blink, or his body move out of position, and she raised it again and she hit him again and she raised it a third time, but before it could fall Big Micil caught it in his fist and held it and threw it roughly away.

"That's enough now," he said. "That's enough now, I'll have no more."

"From the day you were born, the day you were conceived," she was saying through clenched teeth, "you have been nothing but trouble and sorrow. There's nothin' about you of the bold boy. It's just that there is somethin' evil follows you wherever you go. Somethin' evil."

"Shut up," said Big Micil.

"I'm sorry I ever had you," she said. "I'm sorry I ever ..."

"Shut up!" said Micil suddenly, his face reddening with anger, "or I'll silence you. D'yeh hear me now!"

She went over to Tommy who had sunk on the stool beside the fire and she started to pull the jersey over his head.

"Go on up, Mico," said his father to him then, his eyes kind, "and go to bed. We'll talk about it more tomorrow."

"All right, Father," said Mico and turned and went in the door beside the dresser. There were two bedrooms in the house. The one above the fire where Micil slept with his wife, and the one the other side of the kitchen where Mico slept in the bed with Tommy, and Gran had a bed to himself. It was a tight fit in there. Just room to walk between the two beds. Hooks on the whitewashed wall for their clothes and wooden shelves over their bed that Mico himself had fixed to take Tommy's accumulating store of books.

Mico walked softly for fear of waking his Gran. You wouldn't get Gran to miss his sleep because the two sons of the house were lost and strayed. "Ah, to hell," said Gran, "isn't Mico with them? They'll be all right, I tell ye." The window of the room was small and the ledge was wide and held a pot of geraniums. They were a flash of colour and the patchwork quilts on the bed. Mico stood up and let the clothes fall from him and then got a towel from the end of the bed and rubbed his hair and rubbed himself down. Gran was a sleeping bulk under the quilt. His thinning white hair was visible and his beard jutting out. Mico dried himself as well as he could and was glad to feel the tingling coming into his body. His face was stinging from his mother's hand, and he noticed now that his hands too were very painful where the thorns of the tree had lacerated them in places. He shrugged that off. He had a good healing skin.

"Well, come on," said the voice of Gran behind him then. "Tell's all about it."

Mico turned in surprise. "I thought you were asleep, Gran," he said.

"How the hell am I expected to sleep," said Gran, "with all the noise yeer makin'? I suppose she bet yeh?"

Mico didn't answer. He pulled down the blankets and got in between them and pulled them up around his neck. They were warm and soothing to the touch. He told the tale in a low voice that wouldn't carry. Gran said "Humph" and turned on his side. "Gran," Mico asked, "what brought the rats? Was it the tree or what?"

"Oh, God," said Gran, "why do ye be plaguing me with them questions? Rats often swim about in droves. I saw them meself once. They were goin' across the Bay and they stopped in on the island for a rest, that's all. All rodents swim distances. Look at the lemmings up in Norway that swim out into the sea in their millions and just drown themself to death. You won't get the cute oul rats doin' that. Ye were bloody fools to go on that island. Didn't ye know the times the tides comes and goes? What have I been wastin' me time on ye for if ye won't pay notice to simple things like that? How in the name a God do yeh expect ever to be a fisherman if yeh won't pay notice to things? If you don't even know what time the tides comes and goes."

"Maybe we were witched, Gran," said Mico.

"Ah, witched me ah!" said Gran inelegantly. "You just learn your tides and learn to use your nose and your eyes or some day at sea you'll wake up drowned and find that there was somethin' lackin' in yer education. Yer schooling'll soon be finished anyhow and you can start comin' out with us. That'll keep yeh out of trouble."

"Oh, Gran," said Mico, "can I really go with ye? Can I really go with ye, at last?" He was sitting up in the bed.

"Shush, will ye, and go to sleep for God's sake!" said Gran. "I have to persuade yer father yet. He wants yeh to wait for another year, but I'll be able to get around him."

The door opened then again and his mother was framed there.

"You're goin' away!" she said. "You're goin' away! Do you hear that? Tomorrow morning your father's putting you on the bus and you're going out to live with your Uncle James. He'll find use for your idle hands and he'll take you out of my sight. Do you hear? Out of my sight. You have your brother out there now with a fever high in him. He'll be lucky if he doesn't go down with pneumonia and it's all your fault. Every bit of it is your fault. You'll clear out to hell from the Claddagh and give me and every mother in it freedom from your wanton ways, leadin' their sons into all sorts of blackguardry. I'll have peace for a while with no-body pointing the finger at me."

And she left then, banging the door after her.

"Well, Mico," said Gran, after a pause. "It doesn't seem that you're goin' to sea."

"What's it like, Gran," Mico asked, "out there with Uncle James?"

"I don't know," said Gran. "He must be a poor enough do when he's a brother of your mother's. The Claddagh has always been good enough for me. I was born in it and I'll die in it and no thanks to anyone. Maybe it'll do yeh good, Mico, to go back among the Connemara foreigners. James has a boat anyhow, if you can call their sorts of vessels boats. You can learn their ways and then come back and we'll make a real fisherman out of yeh."

"But, Gran," said Mico, "I don't want to go away. What's she sendin' me away for? Sure, Gran, I never did nothin' to anybody at all. It's just that things happen to me that don't happen to other fellas and then I'm so big that I have to take the blame for everything."

"Look, Mico," said Gran, "you know your mother. If she says a thing, it's done. God forgive your father. It's the pot-stick he should have taken to that woman long ago. But who am I to be sayin' it, a poor oul man with a foot and a half in the grave? Why should I be worryin' about yeer problems. Let ye look after yeerselves. I wish to God it was the mornin' that I was out at sea and nothin' to trouble us except the west wind and the long hard tack across the Bay. Go to sleep, boy, for God's sake and rest yourself. Tomorrow things might be different."

He turned on his side then with great noise and sank his face into the pillow.

Mico lay there and wanted to feel sorry for himself. But he didn't. What's the use, he asked himself, a fella like me?

Amn't I always at the wrong end of everything? God marked me all right, but then He should have left me alone after that. And He shouldn't have given me a good-lookin' brother like Tommy with all the brains and me with a brain like a fog of cotton wool. I never wanted anything but to be a fisherman and to be at peace and have a quiet life and end up like Gran with a slant on things. But even Gran was failing now. He could have ... Ah, what's the use? I'll go back to Uncle James and be a slave for him and maybe I'd be kilt or something and then maybe she'd be sorry after all and see that I'm not as bad as I'm painted; and then he thought, I hope all that island business didn't mean anything. I hope my exile now will take all the harm out of what happened there and that it will never come back again, whatever it is that's troubling me about it. Being young, he was soon asleep, and because he had not many brains, his dreams were untroubled.

And the rain came from the west and attacked the earth and the sea.

Chapter Six

MICO! (PETER WROTE)

The news of your approaching homecoming after your year of incarceration in the western wastelands has taken the whole town by storm. Knowing your modesty I barely prevented having the official reception that the Urban Council wished to arrange for you. Four bands and the Army and the embryonic Navy and the professors and students of the University. Anyhow the Claddagh, mainly, I'm afraid, represented by Twacky, is drunk at the thought of your return. He's going around asking everyone have they heard the latest. You know Twacky with his eyes wide open and he panting and hopping on one leg and you think you're going to hear the best bit of news since they shot the Czar. He'll not sleep a wink the night before you come home. We're all glad you're coming.

Your letter was a mine of information, all seven lines of it. I met Pa once or twice and he was asking for you. "Has he got any ambition yet, Cusack?" he'd ask, hopping his stick on the ground. I said I was sure you had since I'm a good liar in a good cause. "Well, if he hasn't," he said, "tell him to acquire it. What in the name of God is he doing out in the back of beyond? Come home, tell him, and become a captain of a sea liner." Off he goes then. So you're not forgotten.

I'm still storming the Mulcairns' citadel. Now I appreciate how tough it must have been on the old birds long ago who had to take a walled city. I tried holding her hand one night when I manoeuvred her into a walk up Newcastle. Got her into a gateway to look at the moon. "Now," said she, "I suppose we get sentimental and hold hands!" God, can you imagine that! I felt like strangling her, but instead we proceeded to discuss the Pythagoras Theorem in all its subtlety. You'll be glad to hear that she has come out from the clouds of Celtic twilight. (Will you ever forget that night on Rat Island and the Fairies?) That's past now. It's "teenage mush" and so the stately Yeats and A.E. and Campbell and all the rest of them are in the ashcan. T.S. Eliot is the latest. I tentatively mentioned a regard for George Bernard, but she flattened that by saying she had got over him at the age of eleven. Anyhow she keeps me educated reading by the dim candlelight to catch up with her literary whimsies. She's a queer gal and I'm sorry I ever met her, because she has me so that I don't know whether I'm coming or going, but unfortunately she's very nice indeed and I'd prefer to get a hug from her than to own a Galway pub, and that's a big thing because you know the dough there is in one of those. She let me call her "Jo" now. That's as far as I've got after a year's hard labour. Hercules was only a penny-ante boy in comparison to me and Jo.

We will be going back to school again next month after the hols. Everyone is loathing it, except Tommy. Yes, I met him the other day. After Eliot and Jo, it was a bit hard to take Tommy and trigonometry. He's wild about trig. You'd think it was a first cousin to Cleopatra. Algebra is child's play to him. He's dying to get to grips with permutations and combinations and plane geometry. These will really test him, he thinks, and it's about time he was tested. Brother B. loathes the sight of Tommy. Ever since the day in class when he was going great guns on a problem and doing it wrong

and Tommy gets up and says, "That's wrong, sir," and
Brother B. turns and says, "Well, maybe, Mister Tommy,
since you're such a genius you'd come up and do it for us."
And the worst of it is that Tommy does go up and do it, and
what can Brother B. do only hate the sight of him. I know
he'd love to lay hands on him but how can he? Tommy always has his exercises done, and done brilliantly. He always
knows all the answers. In a word he's always right, and you
know how maddening it is to meet somebody like that. But
he has his good points as you know, and it's nice to meet
somebody with the real brains. Your mother still thinks the
sun, moon, and stars shine out of him. I notice the look in
her face anytime I'm down in the house and he's lecturing
me about the failings in Chesterton's style or what's wrong
with H.G. Wells, etc. Gran always gets up and leaves, I notice, and comes back smelling heartily of porter. He's dying
for you to come home.

So are we all, Mico, oul son. Come back home soon and
lead us into temptation. Twacky is dying to fall into sin and
so am I. For a nice quiet fella, Mico, you can make life
around you very interesting. So, until we meet, all the best.
You needn't answer this letter. I know how you *love* letters.
And now I've done me duty, a good long letter with all the
news and I'm off now to meet Jo. I'm still hoping. But I
know. It'll be T.S. Eliot again.

Mico laughed out loud now in the evening air as he thought
about Peter's letter. Fleetingly he wondered why Peter
would be writing to him. All that stuff, some of the names
he had never heard of before even. But you could guess and
it was fun. Peter was warm-hearted. It had been grand hearing from him. It made you want to go home of course, but
now that the time had come for him to really go home he
wasn't as pleased as he thought he would be when he came
first.

He stopped abruptly on the Connemara road and turned
and looked back at his uncle's house just behind him. It was

a brilliant autumn evening. There wasn't a cloud in the sky and the stars were beginning to shine. His uncle's house was built at the very end of Aughris and it was looking straight out on the Atlantic, a most gentle-looking sea now, with barely a ripple on it. It was the very last house on this neck of land pushing into the sea. On his left the sea had eaten its way into the land and ground the stones into the long yellow strands of Omey and cut off the island of Omey from the mainland. And on his right, the sea had cut through the land and raised the island of Inisboffin, so where he stood now was like an index finger to America. When he had come out there first – over a year ago now – through the giant Connemara mountains and beyond them here to the back of beyond, his heart had gone into his new boots every step of the way.

The bleak land! Bogland and stony land with a house here and there, and the casual walk of the people on the roads. Oh, indeed, down to his very boots his heart had gone and he felt like a proper exile. And on directions he walked the long yellow flint road to his uncle's house. Over a hill and into a valley and he could count on the finger of one hand the number of houses he passed in a mile. Strange smells in his nose: of fading heather and sheep on the side of a hill and the breeze laced with strange odours that he couldn't name, and he thought of the noise of the Claddagh; the roaring kids and the geese, city geese, and the screeching of the women in the occasional rows; the creaking of sails rising on the brown masts and the barking of dogs. Now in this great silence he could hear and appreciate them all.

Uncle James was surprised to see him. He had miscalculated the time of his coming. He was very sorry, but he fussed a lot over him and he loosened him up a bit. Boiled the kettle on the hook over the fire and put down two brown eggs on the old tin can he used for a saucepan. And he did cheer up when he lighted the oil lamp and it shone in the kitchen and there was a good fire and he eating and his uncle talking and asking him questions in his slow methodical way. He wasn't a silent man. He lived alone. No, he wasn't married, and why? There's two evils in this bloody world, Mico, and do you know what they are? Women is one and strong drink is the other. You can't have both. If you take one you lave the other. If you take 'm both together, it's dynamite.

He made Mico laugh a bit. And his house was like a new pin, it was that clean. Like his own house at home, a kitchen and two rooms. Mico had his own room and he thought that it was a nice thing to have a room of your own. And when he ct his tay, Uncle James brought him out to the neighbours, where they sat at the fire and talked and Uncle James smoked a pipe and spat large tobacco spits all over the poor woman's floor. That was the house down the road now where he was going to call for Coimín Connolly. That was the first time he met them. The house seemed to be full of them. There was the father and mother and, it seemed to Mico, about fifty children, although there was really only twelve, and he kept worrying about where they all slept. They were interested in him and asked him questions. They remembered his mother well, when she was a little girl going to the school down the road with Mrs Connolly, and they knew Big Micil and they called him Big Micil's Mico, and when other neighbours dropped in they asked them if they knew him, that he was Big Micil's Delia's Mico. It was very pleasant and he slept well when he got to bed.

After that it just grew on him until he was at the end of his year before he even knew it had gone. He had to work hard and learn many new things. Learn how to cut turf up on the bleak bogs with the wind going through him. And how to save the turf, to foot it and stook it and stack it and finally draw it home from the bog on the panniers of the small donkey that Uncle James kept. The same little donkey that, still panniered, drew seaweed from the shore to manure the places among the rocks which they called fields, where they grew their few sparse spuds and bits of oats and mangolds and turnips.

Ach, yes! Life was very hard, and the sea was hard always. His Uncle James had a currach. It nearly frightened the life out of Mico until he got used to the feel of it. Imagine the thought that there was only a tenth of a thickness of tarred canvas between you and maw of the sea. But he got to like the light feel of it, when you got the know-how, but of course you couldn't go very far from land except on the calm days, and the big fish don't come close enough so you had to be content with what you got. And other men then had rowing boats. Heavy double-oared boats that they rowed out past Inisboffin and beyond. But the awful labour of pulling at the heavy oars, all the time! Why hadn't they pucauns like themselves in the Claddagh? Christ love you, boy, do you know what thim things cost? Maybe now the Government'd do something for us.

And now he would be leaving it all.

With a heavy heart too, he thought, as he turned from surveying his uncle's house and the sea, and walked towards the house at the bottom of the next hill.

The day was almost dead, and away behind the corner of the faraway hill you could see the top of the hunter's moon. It will be nice tonight, he thought, and hurried his steps, and then he said, What am I hurrying for when I have to be going away tomorra? That meant ...

He found it hard to admit what it meant to himself, the stir in him as he thought of leaving behind him what he had found. If he could only write like Peter could, he would have written to him and said, Ha-ha, me dear Peter you're not the oney wan that can talk about a Jo. I have a Jo too. At least it's in me head and inside me but it's too embarrasing to be talkin' about or even thinkin' about. Even though I'm over fourteen now and as big as a man. What would Peter make of that? Very little, thought Mico, smiling and jumping on the road so that his hobnails knocked sparks from the stones. He was wearing a pair of homespun trousers too. Right down to his boots they came. His first long ones. His uncle bought them for him. It was gas getting them made. The fisherman that was a tailor too, just known as the Táilliúr. He wore glasses which he didn't need and a long pair of moustaches that always seemed to be full of porter froth ...

Her name was Maeve. There now, he got it out.

It all sprang from his mark.

He might as well admit now to himself that he had been sensitive about his mark. Until he came out here. People in the lonely places were used to things that were marked. They were marked themselves. Many of them wore the scars of their hard living, broken bones badly reset and wounds from a fight that had flared and died and left visible scars. They were used to the mark of God that came on their childer and swept them away to die in fantastic places like hospitals in faraway and incredible towns. God's marks. Mico's favourite in the whole land was Michael Tom's Bridget.

The uncle and himself had gone this spring to help with the turf on Michael Tom's place. After that they went into the kitchen to eat boiled bacon and cabbage and the spuds bursting their jackets. And there on the floor was the loveliest curly-headed girl you ever saw in your life. Red curly hair and blue eyes. Her limbs were soft and well made and she wore a blue dress. She just sat there on the floor, with no word out of her, sort of waving her head, and when Mico got down beside her and looked into her eyes he looked into the vast spaces of nothingness. Ah, she's blind, the poor creature, they said, and Mico felt his heart falling in him.

So they looked at him and saw his terrible disfiguring mark and they said, Ah, the mark, Mico, you have that amac, and how did that happen, and sure you ought to be proud of it, sure people'll look twice at yeh now that'd oney give yeh one look before, and when he saw little Bridget he thought to himself well, indeed, God could have done worse to you than He has. It had been easier to be hurt at home. Boys can be very cruel indeed and he could still hear the jeering cry of "Turkey face" in his ears. But it was different now too, when the stirrings were coming in him and he noticed the silhouette of a boy and girl clasped in an embrace by the side of a gable-end or under a thorn bush or on top of a hill when they were coming home from the crossroads dancing and that.

And one day when he was up on the bog alone he was thinking of these things and of many other things, and he was eating his lunch and there was the placid boghole before him, and he bent over it and looked at his face closely for almost the first time. Looked at is as if he was a girl – say – that was seeing it for the first time, and in cold blood it looked very bad to him. The sun was shining on it, and the water, which can be a terrible flatterer just as much as a pink-shaded mirror, even the water couldn't do much to help it. It threw the whole shape of his face into a sort of fantastic nightmare. And Mico leaned on his elbows and looked at it, and his heart sank slowly but surely, and he thought, Ah yes, it is very bad indeed and if I was a girl and saw it even in a middling dark night I would run home screaming and say to my mother, "Oh, Mama, I've just seen the most horrible thing. I thought I was having a nightmare."

He raised his hand up and felt it and pulled it about.

"The mark doesn't matter really," said a voice above him then.

He didn't raise his head, he looked closely into the pool and he saw another face in there with him. A smiling brown face with the hair falling about it from the bending. He regarded that face just as closely as he had been regarding his own. The hair curled away and fell around it like a frame. Brown hair – or was that the bogwater? – and a slim forehead, brown and shining where the sun reflected from the sunburn of it. Narrow eyebrows and deep eyes that he couldn't see the colour of, only the twinkle in them and the very white whites of them, as clear as the water of a calm sea over silver sand. And her nose divided it and came down sort of flat like the picture of that fella in Tommy's Greek book and then her lips were red, even in the water he could see that, and they were smiling because he could see her teeth gleaming in it and a sort of a dimple in the middle of her chin.

He looked up then.

She was resting her hands on her knees, bent down to him so that he saw her white flesh where the top of her dress came away from the sunburned part of her. And she was still smiling, and funnily enough he wasn't a bit embarrassed like he would be normally. He just rested one hand on the soft bog and sat back and looked up at her and smiled and said,

"Why doesn't it matter?"

She squatted so that she was on a level with his eyes. Her feet were bare, and the dry bog was pressing up between her toes. Behind her a small panniered donkey was cropping the coarse bog grass. She bent down and picked up a bit of grass herself and put it between her teeth and bit it so that it parted with an audible snap. Then she threw away the grass and picked the bitten bit and held it on her finger.

"Well," she said, "sure the skin never matters. It's what's inside the skin that does. Some spuds have very good skins and they're as bad as bad can be in the middle, and some of the spuds with bad skins that you'd think maybe I better throw away that one, well, those are the ones that are very floury and have good hearts."

"Janey!" said Mico, very inadequately, but she laughed and then sat back on a tuft of the coarse grass.

"You're Mico," she said.

"I am," said he, "and who are you?"

"Maeve," she said. "We have the bog over beyond the hill from your Uncle James. Why were yeh looking at your face?"

"I don't know," said Mico; "just a fit that come over me of a sudden." He didn't tell her that he was looking at it as if he was a girl. That would be too pointed.

"Will you be here for long?" she asked.

"I don't know," he said. "For a year maybe or so. Then I'll be goin' back to work in me father's boat."

"You like that?"

"I do," said Mico.

"Do you miss home?" she asked then.

Not now, Mico was about to say, to his own surprise, but then he said, "Ah, yes, you do. 'Tis different, you know."

"What's different?" she persisted.

"Ah, the sea and that," he said.

She laughed then. She pulled her knees up and put her arms about them so that her legs were pressing into her breast. "Ah, that's quare," she said. "Isn't it the same sea that goes into Galway that comes in here?"

"That's right," said Mico, "but they have it fixed up different. Right opposite our house you look out and the sea is a bit away and there's an oul dump where they put refuse and things, filling it all in like?"

"Why?" she asked.

"They're makin' a playin' fields there," he said, "and all that and it's a place to dump all the things from the town."

"It must smell bad," she said.

"It does," said Mico, laughing, "of all sorts of things. Wet clothes and cabbage stalks and tin cans and a sort of red gravel that they cover it with to destroy things and kill weeds. But it's part of the place, you see, and you miss it."

"That's the first time I ever heard of anybody missin' a bad smell," she said, and the two of them laughed again.

"It sounds quare when you put it like that," said Mico. "But they's other things too, like the river and the boats at the quays like, and the smell of the fish and the sight of the old fellas with the whiskers fishing for white trout, and the church spire, and different things."

"And haven't we all of them here?" she said. "We have rivers and boats at quays and fish smelling and old fellas with whiskers, and church spires. Look down below you now," she went on, waving a hand; "I bet ye haven't anything like that."

Mico looked from the side of the hill where they were, into the valley below. At the index finger of Aughris and the sea on the sides of it and the gigantic stretch of Omey beach and the island of Inisboffin rising out of the heat mist on the other side, and the divided fields and the yellow roads cutting up the valley and the sun shining on the white-washed houses with their straw thatches, seeming to have grown out of the hard ground like mushrooms, and the seagulls below them whirling in the air, and the blue lake below glimmering, and the small figure of a boatman in it with the raised rod resting indolently on his knees and trailing into the water. Oh, very good, very good indeed!

"No," he admitted then, leaning back on his arms. "We haven't that, but then you should see the Corrib. Oh, the Corrib lake is somethin' to see."

She laughed again then, clear and long, and he saw the small muscles in her throat working.

"Ah, what's the use?" she said. "We could be goin' on like that for years. Maybe we both like our own places and we should leave it at that?"

"Maybe 'twould be best," said Mico.

They got up then and gathered their asses and walked to their bogs. She was wearing a blue dress, with white dots all over it. It was short and he could see her knees, and they were pointed knees and brown from the sun, and her legs were very nice even though they were bare. The dress was a sort of shapeless one, just made to fit the body, but her shape came through it and he saw that she was as tall as his shoulder walking beside him and she must be about fifteen or sixteen.

"You're very big," she said, looking up at him with her hand resting on the donkey's back and she fitting her walk to his dainty picking stride. "What age are yeh?"

"I'm over fourteen," said Mico, having played about with a lie and then telling the truth.

"You look like nineteen," she said, and that pleased him. He did too. His shoulders were very broad and his chest was pressing tightly against the blue gansie he was wearing. He was glad he was wearing long trousers.

They parted a little above the boghole (Mico would never forget that boghole and this day and what it looked like at the moment, no matter what ever happened afterwards to upset it all). She stood there with her candid eyes on him, her head a little on one side and she smiling. "And don't ever mind the mark again," she said, and she did a very strange thing. She raised her hand and she rested it on his mark. Right in the middle of it. He could feel her hand there and her fingers lightly pressing into his cheek. It was the first time in his life there had ever been any other hand but his own on it. "It's what's inside that counts."

"Like the spud with the bad skin?" he asked.

"That's it," she said, "like the spud with the bad skin," and then she patted his cheek lightly and took her hand away and went on and turned a bit up the road and waved back at him and was gone – but not forgotten. Never forgotten, Mico was thinking now, while the sun and the moon chase one another about the sky and while there is a fish in the water and seagulls over it.

He had seen her a few times since, but never to talk to much. There was always other people, and he was glad in a way. She had got into his mind so much since he had met her that he was afraid she might see it coming out through his eyes and be taken back that a fourteen-year-old boy could be thinking so much about her. She can't be expected to know, Mico was thinking, that I'm much older than fourteen on account of the life I have been livin' and the way I feel. I'm a proper oul man if she only knew, but thank God I'll be seeing her tonight under the hunter's moon as soon as I can collect Coimín and we go down to the beach to be digging up the sand-eels.

He turned from the road in towards the yellow light of the window of the cottage where the purple clematis was reaching from the earth and stretching over the white wall of the house and encroaching on the protruding thatch eaves.

Chapter Seven

IT WAS SOME time before Coimín and himself could escape from the house.

He had to sit by the fire on the little stool when Mrs Connolly cleaned it with a twitch of her canvas apron, and even though he was just after rising from the table of Uncle James, he had to take a cup of tea in his hand and drink it and eat a slice of griddle cake, hot to hold, and melting yellow butter dripping from it. He nearly had to go into a clinch so that he wouldn't have to eat the brown egg, hot from the hen, that they wanted to press on him.

It was a house of bedlam, but a very happy bedlam. Coimín was the eldest of the family. He was eighteen and the other twelve stretched back behind him year after year. Coimín's father, Tadhg, sat in the other corner with two of the youngest children hanging out of his neck and the youngest of all, a small plump childeen with a phoney nipple in its mouth, lying on his knees sucking away and gurgling. Tadhg was a tall rangy man with a moustache that was going grey. He had twinkling eyes and he was reckoned to be the biggest liar in West Connemara, but the point about his lying was that he did it for fun and everybody knew it, since he had a way of telling things with his lips serious and his eyes a riot of laughing at your credulity.

"Stop," he'd say now to the little fair-haired girl hanging from his neck so that her dress would be caught up and her fat bare bottom would swing under his hand. "Stop, will ye, ye devil's spawn ye, and let me be talkin' to Mico. Did ye hear what Coimín did today, Mico?"

"No," shouted Mico above the din of dishes being washed by Mrs C. at the table under the wooden pegs where the horses' harness hung, and the sound outside of Coimín trying to chase a recalcitrant sow into the pigs' house – Hup, yeh cross-grained oul bitch yeh! Will yeh get in, will yeh, or devil a out will I get the night! – and two of the younger boys rolling on the floor and trying to beat each other to death over the possession of an old clay pipe.

"Well," said Tadhg, "he was takin' the oul ass up behind the hill for a load of turf. Stop, will ye! Now listen, Pegeen, I'm warnin' yeh, I'll cut the heart outa yeh, and fair enough you know the soft spot be the river where the Táilliúr has his bog. So here he is and the next thing down the oul ass goes boggin' to his bellyband. Ah, we're humped now anyhow, says Coimín, but devil a hump. Do you know what happened then? Yeh won't believe a word of what I'm goin' t' tell yeh?"

"I'll try hard anyhow," said Mico.

"Well, here's Coimín pullin' at the tail of the oul ass, and lavin' that and takin' a pull on his face, but d'yeh think he can move him? Devil a move! He's as stuck now in that bog as ever he'll be, and be a skeleton there for the sound of the last trumpet. And Coimín is afraid oo his life to come home and tell me what happened, knowing what a fierce man I am and that I'd bate hell out of him."

"Like hell," murmured Mico.

"Well," said Tadhg, thinking with evident relish, but he was never destined to finish, Mico was never to know what happened to Coimín and the oul ass, because Coimín having safely stowed the sow, came to the door, fell over the two scuffling boys, cracked their heads together laughing, and said, "Come on now, Mico, or it'll be time to come home before we get there." And Mico rose and after many protestations and promises to come in to say goodbye to them before he left and to remind his mother of the Connollys and how they were all asking for her and a little to-do and shuffling, they were out on the road and the ascending moon was winking at them gigantically from the middle of its yellow swollen mass.

Coimín was tall. Mico was tall and he was just over his shoulder. He wore a cap and his skin was very clear and his teeth were very white and big and even. Mico liked Coimín. He was something like himself. He didn't talk much (I lave that to the oul fella; he makes up for me); but he thought a lot in his own slow way. Like meself again, Mico thought. He always wore a cap, and the peak of it came down over his nose, giving him a rakish look which wasn't deserved.

They were armed with a bucket and a spade and a peculiar knife Coimín carried with a sort of notch in the end of it. "That's to hook them up," Coimín said. "Wait'll you see."

It was a grand night.

The hard colour of the flint road was softened under the light of the moon, and the bog on either side of the road was mellowed to a uniform dark greyness that hid its bleakness. They walked by the bog and the lake and turned down towards the sea by the church. A different sea. You could distinguish the difference when you got your nose accustomed to it. Smelling now and closing his eyes, he knew that in front of him the sea was washing over miles of the yellow sand. Not because he knew but because he could smell it. Smell fresh sand, newly washed by the departing sea. Leaving all sorts of small things to pervade the air. Not the smell of big weed-covered rocks and things rotting in their lee, but the smell of stranded jellyfish and white cockles before they burrowed, and the mysterious sand-eels.

"What are the sand-eels' yokes like, Coimín?" he asked.

"Ah, like things, you'll see," said Coimín.

"Well, I know what they're like now surely," said Mico laughing.

"But that's what they're like," said Coimín. "'Tis hard to tell. You'll have to see."

"Tell me," Mico asked, "what happened yourself and the ass up on the Táilliúr's bog."

"What do you mane?" asked Coimín. His voice was deep and pleasant.

"Your father was tellin' me how the ass bogged on yeh and he was just about to finish the story when you kem in."

"Ah, another of his yarns," said Coimín. "Don't mind 'm. He has me disgraced so he has. His latest now is that I'm a fearful strong man. Did ye hear what Coimín did today? he asks them. No, they say. What? Well, he says, we wanted to bring home the cock a hay and dammit if the cart didn't lose a wheel, so Coimín says, Ah, 'tis all right, I'll do for it, and then, he says, you won't believe me now, but down Coimín goes with the cart-rope and slings it around the cock and lifts it up on his back and home he comes with it before tea and he not losin' a wisp on the way."

Mico laughed. "Ah, well," he said, "he keeps life interesting anyhow for ye."

"I wish he'd stop on me," said Coimín. "I'm a proper laughin'-stock so I am at him."

"He's a nice man," said Mico. "Sure everybody likes him."

"Ah, he's all right," said Coimín. "Here we are now. She said she'd be up in Mary Cavanagh's place."

Mico's heart started to thump dully. This was the climax now of his evening and one of the reasons he was reluctant to go home. They had met her the other evening coming home from the church, Coimín and himself. Mico admired the great ease Coimín had with her. Talked to her and joked with her in a quiet way as if she was his sister. "And so you're lavin' us, Mico," she said. "I'm goin' home," said Mico. "Now you'll be glad," she says, "because that's the very thing you wanted, isn't it? You and your oul Claddagh."

"Well," said Mico, "if I didn't lave now, maybe I'd never go home to them at all any more." "Have you come to love us so?" she asks. "Oh, begod I have," said Mico fervently, blushing in the darkness when he had said it and hoping they mightn't see how pointed it was. "Ah," she says then, "ah, Coimín," she says, "he can't go home now without waitin' for the full harvest moon and the sand-eels. We must bring him down after the sand-eels." "What's them?" asks Mico. "My God," she says, "you supposed to be a fisherman and you don't know about sand-eels. I bet ye have no sand-eels in Galway," she says. "Well, we might for all I know," said Mico. "I was up the lake once and they fish for eels up there, and they catch them and put them into a big wooden yoke and keep them alive, and I saw thousands and thousands a eels altogether in a big swimming box." "Were they big ones?" she asks. "Ah, big black and brown yokes," said Mico, "that they send over to the English. I don't like them. I do feel them moving in me stomach when I eat them." "The Lord save's," she said, "that's terrible. Ah, but them are only ordinary oul eels. Sand-eels is different. Sand-eels must only be caught on Omey strand under the light of the harvest moon. 'Tis very romantic. Isn't it, Coimín?" Mico felt Coimín stirring beside him, and saying, "Ach, romantic. That's a quare word. You must be after readin' the oul books again." She laughs, nearly petrifying Mico with the tinkling noise of it reaching into the dark night. "Ah," she says, "Coimín is just a simple oul slob. Coimín wouldn't know what to do with a girl if he was catchin' sand-eels with her under the light of the harvest moon." "We'll be goin' home now," said Coimín, setting off, much to Mico's reluctance.

For Coimín was shy and quiet. Some quiet people are shy and some of them are red devils on the sly. But Coimín was really quiet and shy. T'other fellas are quiet and sly and that's the difference.

"Bring Mico," she called after them, "down to Mary's place on the night of the full moon. I'll be waitin' there for ye."

So here they were.

They came out of the mouth of the lane and stood there for a while and looked. It was worth looking at. The tide had just left the strand. A funny tide that was. It came from either side of the island and met in the middle of the strand. It slunk in and it slunk out apologetically, as if to say I'm sorry now for having come sneaking in and covering you up, but just regard me as a sort of sanitary cleanser and it won't make any difference. It never covered the miles of sands much. You could wade across to the island and be covered just over your stomach when the tide was in. The moon was up well now and was shining on the still wet sands so that they were gleaming, and away in the distance you could see the thin line of the island looking like it was suspended in the air. Their feet felt the soft sandgrass under them, just like a thick carpet, and from the great expanse in front of them came a gurgling and an occasional burbling of lonely pools left behind by the exiled sea.

"That's grand," said Mico.

"Aye," said Coimín, slowly. "'Tis nice, I suppose. 'Tis grand and lonely."

"Aye," said Mico with a sigh.

"Come on," said Coimín, "we'll gup to Cavanagh's." He left the spade and bucket lying under the last piece of wall on the road, and then jumped a few tussocks of the green grass with Mico after him, dodging the pools of water, scattering a few frightened birds who had settled down for the night, and then came to the hidden mouth of a narrow lane, and up this they walked and it wound a little and then behind a short hill they suddenly came on the white house with the light in the window. There was a girl standing in the door with the light at her back so that her clothes were nearly transparent. She brought them up short.

"Well, it took ye a long time," said the girl. "I was nearly giving ye up and going home."

"It's her," said Mico.

"Ah, we had things to do," said Coimín, "and who asked

you to wait anyhow? You could have gone home. 'Twasn't us wanted to be going after the oul sand-eels, but yourself."

"Oh, listen to the rude Coimín, now," she says lightly. "'Tis little manners they taught you in school or you wouldn't be talking like that to a lady."

"Who knows," asked Coimín, "how I'd talk to a lady, if I ever met one?"

"Ho-ho," she said laughing. "Come in anyhow and see Mary," and she stepped back a bit and they walked into the lighted kitchen.

"God bless the woman of the house and the man of the house and the little yokeen in the cot," said Coimín, going in and over to the little yokeen that was lying in a wooden cot by the side of the fire. A home-made cot it was with boards and two curved runners under it with protruding ends so that you put your foot on one and pushed and the cot rocked and you sang a song if you liked to croon the child to sleep. So over Coimín goes and bends over the little thing and puts in a large hand and rubs its face, and the young man who was sitting on the settle bed and singing softly sits up straight and says, "Well, the curse a hell on yeh anyhow, Coimín Connolly, and I nearly havin' it asleep!"

"Well, isn't it a nice thing," said Coimín, "for a grown man to be rockin' a baby and he singing to the poor thing with a voice like a *sgaltán*. 'Twasn't asleep it was at all, but goin' unconscious from the batterin'. And how is me little Nuala?" he wanted to know then and the child raises a pudgy finger and takes his own and gurgles awake.

"You're welcome, Mico," says the man of the house. A young man with red hair, reminding Mico of Peter at home. He had bright eyes and he was thin but lithe-looking. "Mary there was baking a cake for when ye come back with the sand-eels. We can have a bit of a feed out of them."

"Ah, that'll be nice," said Mico, looking at Maeve, who was standing in the middle of the kitchen with her legs spread, looking over, peculiarly, Mico thought, at the big form of Coimín bent over the baby. She had different clothes on her now. A pullover, a red one, and a light swinging skirt, and there were light high-heeled shoes on her feet. It made her look different, that and the red ribbon that pulled back the hair from around her face. She was all sparked up as if she was going to meet a king, Mico thought. And she was terrible lovely-lookin'.

"Well, now," said Mary, "wouldn't anyone in their senses think that Coimín 'd have enough a children with all they have at home?"

"He's only an oul soft yoke of a thing," said Maeve. "Look at him, will ye?"

But Coimín remained unperturbed and talked a lot of silly nonsense to the baby.

"And will you be comin' with us after the sand-eels, Peadar?" Mico wanted to know.

"And indeed and I will not," said Peadar, rising from the settle bed and going over to the window and rescuing a large brown pipe from it which he proceeded to scrape with a knife. "My sand-eel days are over. 'Tisn't but a year ago that I went collectin' sand-eels under the moon with a girl and look what happened." He pointed to the baby with his pipe.

"Go on, you scoundrel," said his wife, pelting him with a handful of flour, which he took in the face, and rubbed off slowly, and he looking at her with a smile in his eyes. Mico sat on a chair behind near the dresser and looked at them. They are two happy people now, he thought. Mary Cavanagh was small, and she was well made. Her hair was very fuzzy with many curls in it. Her chin was a bit long and her nose was long, but she looked good all the same. Her eyes were blue and laughed a lot and a blind man with no instincts could see that they were all and all to each other.

"If we're going at all," Maeve asked politely, "wouldn't it be a good idea to be going now, if Mister Connolly'll give over annoying the baby and let her go to sleep?"

"Aye," said Peadar, "if he wants a baby to play with, let him get one of his own."

"Ah, 'tis the mother that's the difficulty," said Coimín rising. "You walked off with the only one I wanted."

"Oh, you flatterer!" said Mary laughing.

"I always knew," said Peadar, "that I was a better man than a Connolly any day of the week, even though he may be a stronger man than Finn McCool ever was."

"Oh, God!" said Coimín, turning, "was me father talkin' to you too?"

"Ah, he was indeed," said Peadar laughing. "Sure when we're all dead, Coimín, you'll be a more famous man than the Fianna. They'll be talking about the famous Coimín that bit a bit out of the land when he was mad, and that was how we got Omey strand."

"We'll be goin' after the sand-eels now," said Coimín, taking Maeve by the arm and ushering her out. "Come on, Mico, and if ye haven't the bite and sup ready when we come back, ye'll hear all about it."

They faced into the lovely night again with Peadar's laugh floating after them.

Mico felt good with Maeve's hand holding his arm. He could feel her warmth all the way down the side of his body that was near her, and the palm of her hand seemed to be burning the flesh from his arm. He walked very carefully along the lane.

"And Mico is leaving us, Coimín," she said.

"He is," said Coimín; "bad luck to it! Just when we were getting him used to us and making him do a bit of work."

"And will you be missing us, Mico?" she wanted to know.

"I'm afraid that I will," said Mico.

"Sure we'll be lonely for you too," said Maeve, squeezing his arm. "But maybe in God you'll come back again sometime?"

"'Twill be hard," said Mico. "I have to work now when I go back. Me father will be needing me in the boat. My Gran is a very good fisherman but he's getting old. I don't think he's able to do as much as he used to do, so I will be welcome with them. So I don't know if I'll ever be back again."

"Ah, you will," said she confidently. "God never makes nice people meet if he doesn't intend them to meet again. Isn't that right, Coimín?"

"That sounds like common sense," said Coimín.

"So we won't be a bit sad or anything because Mico is going away. We'll gather the sand-eels and we'll talk and walk, and it'll be a night that we can remember. So that ever afterwards wherever we are and the three of us meet again we can say, Do you remember the night we gathered sand-eels under the harvest moon on Omey strand? Look at it!" she demanded, stopping at the lip of the beach and gathering Coimín to her with the other hand. They stood there close together and looked.

They heard the sound of voices coming from the strand now. Light laughter and you could see the dark forms of people bent over and doing something with their hands in the strand. And way out in the track of the moon and unconscious of it, there was a boy and a girl and they were as clear as clear could be, standing up facing each other, clasped together. They were silhouetted, like a paper cutting that had been painted black. You could see the cap on his bent head and you could see the wild shape of her hair.

Maeve sighed. Mico felt his heart pounding.

"A nice way to be gettin' sand-eels," said Coimín practically. "Come on!" and he jumped down from his eminence on to the soft sand. "Pick up the bucket and spade, Mico, and we'll be going."

"All right," said Mico and went over to where they had left them against the wall and rescued them.

Maeve lifted her foot and removed her high-heeled shoe and took the other one off as well and left them on a stone on the wall so that they stuck up grotesquely. "I'll be able to get them when we come back," she said, and then jumped on to the sand and ran towards the moon, her loosened hair streaming out behind her and the thin skirt climbing up her thighs.

"That's what the moon does to some people now," said

Coimín, ambling along after her with Mico.

"Ah, she's great," said Mico.

"Do you like her?" Coimín asked casually.

"Oh, I do," said Mico, toning down his fervour a little.

"So do I," said Coimín.

"Well, nobody would ever think it," said Mico, a taste sharply. The way he was talking to her! Sharp answers! As if he was her oul fella!

"Ah, well, that's the way," said Coimín prosaically.

She stopped and turned and leaned her hands on her knees.

"Hurry up, will ye!" she shouted. "Ye'd think ye were going to a wake, yeer so slow!"

They caught up with her. They were close now to the bending people. You could see the piled wet sand that they had dug beside them. They were laughing. Some were serious. Mostly the men were serious if they were together. If there was a girl with them, there was laughter and cries of pretended dismay. "Tommeen Tady, what are you doing with your fingers?" "I will not!" "Now there's a fear of me!" "What would sand-eels be doin' over in the shelter of a big rock?" Tommeen Tady falling back holding his face as she slaps it. On the quiet strand it sounds like the shot from a gun. Laughter from all. Tommeen Tady going into a pantomime of having his jaw broken. Staggering around in circles. Greetings for them too. And is it you now, Coimín? That's a dangerous-lookin' thing ye have with ye! What, the spade is it? No, faith, but Maeve. Is it robbing cradles you are now, Maeve, with little Mico along with you. Little Mico, is it? Sure he's bigger than me own father. It was good natured and light-hearted and beautifully silvery. Even the harshest voice down here on the sand expanse seemed to take on a musical quality, and the peculiar light of the moon on sand seemed to take all the edges off coarse things, so that even the brown clusters of rocks with their seaweed seemed to be bathed in a blue-green glow. And everything so noiseless. No sound of feet or tools hitting rock. Just an odd sucking sound as a boot that was sunk in the wet sand was withdrawn with a clop-plop sound, soft and gurgling.

"This'll do fine now," said Coimín, picking his spot. He bent over it with the slotted knife poised. "Watch this now, Mico!"

Mico bent beside him. He cut at the sand and paused and then finished the cut, and when he drew up the knife there was a sliver of wriggling silver caught in the notch. "There y'are now," he said, "that's a sand-eel."

Mico took it in his fingers and held it up so that the light fell on it. It was a beautifully shaped silver fish about four inches long and as narrow and as thin as the blade of a penknife. It had the shape of a fish too, the long pointed head with the gills on it and the eyes. And it had a tail, and the devil a difference there is between it and any fish I saw except that it is so small and streamlined. He didn't know that all work had stopped and that they were regarding his careful scrutiny of the sand-eel. He looked up at Coimín.

"Sure," said Mico, "this isn't an eel at all. It's a bloody fish."

Well, you'd hear then the laughing that followed this over in Newfoundland. Even Coimín was grinning.

"What's so funny about it," Mico wanted to know, a little indignantly.

"Nothing funny about it," said Maeve. "It's you, calling a poor sand-eel be bad names."

"But," Mico asked logically, "why do ye call it an eel if it's a fish?"

"And what's an eel but a fish?" Maeve wanted to know.

Mico was ready with an answer, but when he thought over it he saw that there was no sense in it, so he raised his head and laughed too.

"All right," he said, "but it's quare so it is."

So he dug for sand-eels.

Why they should come like this, buried deep in sand, is beyond the knowledge of man. They never come either until the time they were supposed to be there. They pick their special places on the strand and they are there when the moon is full. That's all anyone knows. Whether they are there other times, nobody has bothered to ask, but they hardly are. It's a grand time they choose to come. It's a very pleasant thing to be on the strand in the autumn, with the full moon. You dig your hand into the sand and when you feel the queer wriggling thing in your fingers you haul up your hands and hold them full of sand and the little fish. It's a very peculiar feeling the first time you do it, to feel all the wriggling sand-covered bodies in the palm of your hands. It gives you a tingle up the back of your spine. The sand-eels are as fast in the sand as they would be in the water. It's an amazing thing. And when you take them from the sand with your hand or with a spade or with the notched knife, they wriggle a little and then they are still, and they are really like silver shillings that have been battered into shape by the hammer of a gold-beater. But why the sand? When they are so well made for swimming in the sea? And do they ever leave the sand? Or do they come there to spawn in the sand or what? I don't know. Nobody knows and very few care but to be there digging them out, in cans, in buckets, in shovelfuls, and to fill an ass-cart with them if you want to, but when you get tired digging them there is a girl beside you, and maybe sometimes her hip rubs against your own, or a wisp of her hair blows across your cheek, or when your hands are digging they meet your own under the sand, and they grasp each other hotly for all the cold sand, and your heart stops still for a moment and then thumps away dully so that you have to rub your tongue around your dry mouth, and you think, Well, thank God the night is lovely, and in your mind you run over all the places there are on the way home where you can pull in for a minute and let time pass over your head, and indeed is it any wonder that sand-eels make so many marriages?

Mico was tired when the three of them went towards the shore, Mico and Coimín holding a hand each on the handle of the bucket because it was filled and heavy, and he told himself that he must be tired indeed to be thinking that there was a sort of charged silence between Coimín and Maeve. She was silent and that was something. She went along with her head bent down, so that her hair was falling over her face like he remembered her first, and one arm was going around her back and was holding her other arm with the hand and she was kicking stray puddles with her bare feet. And Coimín was walking along with his face to the stars and his chest heaving a little as if he was finding it hard to breathe. And why would that be now, Mico wondered, when he's a fine big man with a stomach as flat as a table and no fat on him, and why should this exertion have taken away his breathing?

I wonder, Mico was thinking then, if fifteen-year-old boys ever got married. Maeve must be two years older than me, but sure that doesn't matter. Suppose I stopped her and said, I know you think I'm very young, but honest to God I'm not that young at all. And every time I see you me heart goes racin' like a *gleoidhteog* in a favourable wind, or a tern on a torrent of stormy air, and that my knees do be shaking a little, and that when I go to bed at night and see you smiling away there at me with the dimple affair in your chin, I do start tremblin' in me bed. If I tell you all that maybe you'll know what it means, and if you feel the same would you ever be content to wait until I'm a man, say in a year, or two years, but stretching at the most until I'm as old as Coimín, and then as true as God is me judge I'll come back one day in my father's boat and we'll gather you into her at the pier of Cleggan and I'll take you home like a man would a queen, all the way down the coast past Omey and Clifden and Costello and Rosmuc and Spiddal and Furbo and Barna until we come into the Bay and I bring you into the Claddagh pier, and there will be all the people waitin' there for us, and we will be married in the church and they will crown you the Queen of the Claddagh and we will be happy for ever after.

He sighed.

They looked up startled.

"What is it, Mico?" Coimín asked.

"What?" asked Mico.

"The sigh," said Maeve. "You let a sigh out of you like a salmon in a seal."

"Ah," said Mico, "I like goin' home, but I'm so used to here now that I don't know whether I'm comin' or goin'."

"That's clear enough anyhow," said Coimín sagely.

So they laughed and Coimín slapped Mico on the back and Maeve took his arm and they went up to the house of the Cavanaghs.

Sand-eels are grand in a mess. You have to clean them, small and all as they are, just the same as you would a right big fish. And you knock their heads off and when you have about a hundred of them done you put them into a pot of boiling water and they are hardly in the pot when they turn over and they are done and you pour them on to a hot plate, and then you pour butter over them, when you have strained them off. And the butter melts into them, and when you have a plate of those with griddle-cake and scalding hot tea you'll go a long way before you taste anything as nice. And they ate them and laughed and Coimín woke the baby up again and Peadar cursed him and there was much laughing and talk in the bright paraffin light before the three of them left and turned for home.

And 'twas then that Maeve broke Mico's heart.

"Will we, Coimín?" she asked. "Will we show him?"

"All right," said Coimín.

"Come on, Mico," said Maeve, taking his hand and hopping the low stone wall. She ran and he ran after her and Coimín brought up the rear as slow as ever. She jumped another wall and then made towards the sea across the swishing after-grass of the meadow, flushing an indignant family of larks and some snipe, and she brought him over another wall and then they came to a small field which had a low hill on one end of it, shutting off the sight of where the sea came pouring in between Omey and the mainland. It was a pleasant level field, and she stopped under this hill that was topped with thorn bushes, bent like old men and growing away wearily from the path of the prevailing wind. It was a sheltered place and the land sloped away gently to the strand which was about three fields away. You could see the pier below in the light and you could see all out by the south side of Omey and away into the misty Atlantic.

"Isn't that nice now?" she wanted to know.

"Is it indeed," said Mico, puzzled.

"Well, that's where Coimín and me is going to build our house," she said. Coimín reached them now and she went over and stood beside him and put her arm through his and she pressed his big arm to her breast and looked up at him. "When we get married," she said with a sigh.

Mico was a long time before the meaning of her words went home and when they did he was thankful for the moon-colour, because it always kills the colour red and he felt his face was flaming. It wouldn't matter anyhow, he thought, with the purple monstrosity on me face. There it was back again, my old friend the face. What a fool I am, he thought, that I didn't see it! All that sparring between them! The way she looked at him bending over Peadar's baby. Talk about Coimín not knowing what to do with a girl under the moon. Lots of other things. Past things when he had been out with Coimín and they had met her. The rudish way Coimín spoke that was a way of hiding love and making it more obvious if you had the eyes to see.

"You and Coimín," croaked Mico. "Indeed and indeed I'm glad."

"Aye," said Coimín, "but it'll be a long time. I have to wait until some of the others are grown bigger so that they can look after things. And it takes a long time to build a house. I will be doin' it in me spare time. Maybe we'll start this winter, or next winter anyhow, and we have to get the walls up and the roof on and the inside of it furnished and we must work and work like hell, because, Mico, it's hard to get married in Connemara."

"Won't it be worth it in the end?" Mico wanted to know.

"We kept it all quiet," said Maeve. "Nobody knows. They'd say we're too young. And nobody gets married here until they are thirty or forty. But not us. And we're not going to be driven out of Connemara because we are young and poor like other people. We're going to build our house and we will be married and Coimín will have his own boat, because he has to make that too, and we'll have a patch of land from his father and my father, and we can grow spuds and Coimín can catch fish and we won't be hungry."

"Aye," said Coimín and rested a hand on hers.

"And we told you, Mico, so that if you ever think of us, you will be able to see us in this spot, with our house going up a stone on a stone, and when we get married we will tell you so that if you have not forgotten us by that time you will be able to close your eyes and see where Coimín and Maeve are looking out at the sea over their three fields and a lot of happiness."

"I will always think about ye," said Mico quietly.

"Isn't that nice?" she wanted to know, her hand feeling his arm.

Mico's face was turned to the sea.

He left them where she went to the right above the church. Coimín went with her to see her home. Mico watched them for a long time. It took them a long time to reach the bend of the road where it wound. A long time. They were very close. Coimín is so nice, Mico was saying to himself. If it had to be anybody I'm glad indeed it was Coimín. Coimín is a shockin' good fella and he will be awful nice to her. Sure amn't I only fifteen after all, he told himself as he turned for home, his hands deep in his pockets. And he talked a lot of sense to himself, but the beauty and light had gone out of the night for him.

Out of Connemara too.

Uncle James was waiting up for him, sitting on the stool in front of the fire, his steel spectacles, so incongruous-looking, on his red nose. He was reading the *Connacht Tribune* with his finger marking the "Connemara Notes".

"You're back, Mico," he said.

"I am, Uncle James," said Mico, sitting on the stood opposite him.

"The kettle is on the boil," said Uncle James, "if yeh want a sup a tay."

"I had tay, thanks," said Mico, "down in Peadar Cavanagh's. We et sand-eels too. They were grand to ate."

"The same sand-eels are the cause a more poor unfortunate devils bein' caught in nets than any other source I know," said Uncle James. "I hope yeh weren't entoiled be a lassie down there, Mico."

"No," said Mico, heavily. "I was not, Uncle James. Sure what would any girl be doin' with the likes a me?"

"H'm," said Uncle James. "We'll be sorry when you lave us, Mico. I'll miss you about the house now."

Mico raised his head then to look over at him. He was very good to me, Uncle James. He was a great laffer. And at sea, it was great to be with him at sea in the light currach. He was sure of himself. And so much he knew, nearly as much as Gran. Oh, a whole lot of things about Uncle James that you'd only remember when you had time to think it over.

"You were very dacent to me, Uncle James," he said. "I was afraid a me life of yeh, comin'. I'll be sorry now to be leavin' you." He emphasized the *you* unknown to himself.

"Did anybody say anything to yeh, down at the strand, Mico?" Uncle James wanted to know.

"Indeed no," protested Mico. "It's just! Ach, I'm tired, that's all."

"I see," said Uncle James. "Well get to bed so, Mico, and sleep it off. Most things can be slept off. Even sand-eels in the autumn. Go to bed, boy."

"I will," said Mico, and went.

'Tis easy to sleep off many things if you can sleep. But Mico didn't sleep. Not much. He tossed a lot in his bed, and Uncle James heard him tossing and worried about him, but being a sage he thought he knew what was wrong with him. The curse a God on them, he muttered to his pillow. Even the childer they do be upsetting.

And the moon grew smaller and travelled far and then it became bigger and died, and Mico wished with all his heart that he was at home; and Maeve moved sleepily in Coimín's arms where they sat and watched the dawn from the comfort of the heather on the hill over the lake.

Chapter Eight

"THE TROUBLE IS," said Peter, beating his fists on the ground, "that we are the lost generation."

"How do you make that out?" Jo asked.

"I'll tell you," said Peter, sitting up a bit so that he could pound a fist on his knee.

The three of them were lying on an island in the Corrib. It was very peaceful. It was a small island. They were lying in a green clearing near the lapping water. Down from them the rowing boat was pulled up on the shore and was rocking gently to the waves coming from the far side of the lake. They were alone in the world except for an occasional diving tern and a cormorant standing on a rock miles away like an ugly black sentinel. Jo was in the middle, her hands back supporting her head, and Peter uncomfortably aware of her thin summer dress clinging to her flat stomach and outlining the push of her twenty-year-old breast. Her hair was cropped just as it had always been, but she had grown. Her nose was a little too big for that and her chin too firm and her eyes too clear. Beyond her Mico was lying on his stomach chewing a blade of grass. He was very big. If you had been trying to see Jo from the other side of him, his bulk would have hidden both herself and Peter. He wore the blue jersey and blue trousers of coarse cloth. But his feet were bare and he raised them now and again and waved them in the air. His shoulders were stretching the jersey and he had grown a column of a neck down which his hair curled at the back. It was all brown now and constant exposure to the sun had bleached it here and there to a sort of golden colour. Peter was ruggedly built except his skin was red from the caress of the sun, pale skin that looked raw. He was sensitive to the sun on account of his red hair, which was untidy and stood up in a bush on his head. His white shirt was open at the neck to disclose a chest with red hair and freckles, and the flannel trousers he wore were held to his waist by a red and white tie.

"Go on," said Jo. "We can't wait to hear."

"We were all born," said Peter, thinking it out, his eyes now closed, now open to the spark that was in them, "at the tag-end and bobtail of freedom. We grew up singing *Kevin Barry* and *Wrap the Green Flag Round Me, Boys*, not knowing what the hell it was all about. Well, heroes were winning freedom for us, unknownst to us. All we knew was that the bobbies disappeared and we got the Garda Siothchana in place of them. That was the outward sign of freedom to us. Then we grew up and we looked around us and what did we see?"

"You're telling us," said Jo.

"We saw bloody nothing," said Peter.

"The heroes of yesterday," said Peter, warming to his theme with a vein sticking out at the side of his neck, "became the politicians of today. They lost their sense of adventure. Here they were, men who had gone and fought and played with death peeping over their shoulders, and the very minute they had their snouts stuck in the flesh-pots they went and forgot the great adventure they had gone through. What an opportunity they had, and how they missed it! They could have really set the people free. They had the people of Ireland in a sack and they could have up-ended that sack and spewed them all into real freedom, and instead of that they closed the mouth of the bag with bunches of green tape and long-term promises. Is it any wonder we'd be the lost generation? The generation of cynics that grew up to see their heroes with fat stomachs. What do you think, Mico?"

"I'm a poor hand at the thinking, Peter," said Mico.

"No you're not," said Peter. "You can think when you want to, only you're damn lazy, that's what."

"He's not," said Jo, indignantly. "He's not lazy. I didn't notice you giving much of a hand to pull us up the lake. Five miles Mico rowed and not a hair astray on him."

"I'm speaking," said Peter primly, "about intellectual laziness."

"Anyhow," said Mico, "they's a lot in what you say, but sure, Peter, boy, the world is made like that, and we have to put up with it."

"Oh God, don't say that," said Peter. "We have not got to put up with it. We should go out and fight and defeat it."

"How?" asked Jo.

"Well," said Peter. "Ah, damn it, there's no how now. It has to be thought about and talked about and the people must be roused to a welter of revolution. That comes after."

"Well, you have a hard job on your hands," said Jo.

"I know," said Peter, falling down on the grass despondently. "Hopeless, because who is there that you can talk to? So that's why I'm going to become a scientist."

"What's that got to do with it?" she asked.

"If I can't help the people the way I want, through revolutions, because I don't think I have the staying power for that, I'm too volatile, then I'll find other ways to help them. I want to find the secrets of life so that things can be got from the air and the sea and the earth and made cheaper for people to live. Oh, I don't know. It's all very confusing."

"Who are you telling!" ejaculated Jo.

"What do you think of your own life now, Mico?" Peter asked. "What does it feel like to you? What do you make of it all?"

"Oh, I like it," said Mico.

"Aye, so you do, but why?" Peter persisted.

"Ah, now," said Mico, "I haven't your tongue at all. How can I say why?"

"Well, dammit," said Peter, "you can try!"

"It's easy for you," said Mico. "You have education behind you. It's so little I know."

"And yet," said Peter, "in a way you know more than I, Mico. Because the things you know are knowledge, while so far I have only an education."

"Ah, now," said Mico, "don't be bottlin' me up before I begin. I have always known that there was only one thing I wanted to do, and that was to be a fisherman like me father. That's clear enough."

"But why?" Peter asked, rising on an elbow. "Why a fisherman? Is it just because your father was one and that was good enough for you?"

"No," said Mico, "I don't think so. I never thought about it. I never wanted to be anything else. If I was to sit back and think now what I'd like to be if I wasn't a fisherman, I couldn't tell you. I thought I'd never get out and at it, and then I did, and it wasn't all that I wanted it to be."

"Ha-ha!" ejaculated Peter.

Jo punched him in the side with a small fist. "Can't you let him go on?" she said.

"Well," said Mico, "it's not easy. It's a very hard life. I found that out quick enough when the first few trips were over. It's not that I mind hard work, mind ye, because a big fella like me needs to be doin' hard work to be able to live at all. It's just that I came to see why so many of the young Claddagh fellas'd be willin' to do anything else at all, sweep the roads even, before they'd become as they say their oul fellas' galley slaves."

He thought for a moment of the way his romantic ideas had gradually faded under the spell of the hard work. It was grand early on. You loved every minute of the important going down to the quay, carrying a net or the bit of food or fishing lines, whistling, looking around to see if everyone was noticing that you were off at last with your father and what a man you were. The creak of the sail, the slither of the water against the rounded bow. All that was terrific, at first. Being on the sea alone, until the rains came and deluged you and the sea rose and tossed you about and you had to learn to hold her in a gale and what to do to meet all sorts of contingencies; what it was to be caught out and to have to run into one of the small little places along the coast for shelter; to hunch up in the small forecastle, crouched over the turf fire burning there, and try and cook and eat and be dry with two very big men like himself and his father squeezed in there, and Gran as well. Maybe for twelve hours; maybe for days. All that. Was it any wonder the lads of the village thought there was no future in it? Give us a fast covered-in motorboat, they said, and let us fish and catch a lot of fish and get home then in the evening in time for the pictures and we're your men. But that other thing! That lying out like a duck! No, thanks. You can shove that up your jersey. You go out and break your heart and suffer worse than if you were in hell, for what? For smart alecks that don't know the front from the back of a boat and care less, for fellas like thim to come down and take the fish off your hands and sell it at three times the price they give you for it. Where's the reward in that? Where's the profit in that?

They are right too, Mico thought, how right they are! But, he went on, there are ways to change all that. And there were people worse off than they.

"The men I saw out in Connemara," said Mico out loud. "Them is the men you might call poor. Not that they aren't cheerful under it. They are indeed, but look, they fish out there from heavy rowing boats. They can't afford to buy a sailing boat and do you know what they pay for their nets?"

"What?" asked Jo.

"Four pounds," said Mico.

"That shouldn't break them," said Jo.

"Ah, God," said Mico, "that's what you don't understand. If they lose a net with a basking shark, or have to cut one away in a storm, they're finished. As true as God, because it would take them nearly a year to find four pounds for a new one. That's true."

"That sounds bad," said Jo.

"Is it any wonder," said Peter, "that what we want is a revolution? There's more poverty than peace in this country. Ah, the whole thing is wrong, I tell ye, and what's the good of lying down here on an island in the Corrib on a Sunday evening and just saying it's wrong. We should be up and doing something about it."

"Aye," said Jo, "what are you going to do? You'll do like all the rest of the intelligentsia do, you'll talk about it until it comes out through your eyes and then you'll go back to Cowper or Shelley or whoever you have on your course for your BA and that's all, because that's all you can do. You can write letters to the paper, or you can make speeches to Mico and myself, but what's the use of pouring your heart out to the converted? It's like that. It'll be always like that."

"Aye," said Peter, "until the poor bloody heroes are dead and buried and the old comrades have fired the salute over them, and the bugle has blown over them, and they have passed from life as weary spun-out old gentlemen and take their place in a history book as the strong upstanding young men with lights in their eyes and guns in their hands and adventure burning in them before they became free and staid and cautious. That's that. *Requiescat in pace.* Well, maybe I'll do something. Maybe when I've got me BA and have gone on and got me BSc, maybe then I'd start to speech out of me on platforms up in the Square. Not the kind of things they're used to, the platitudes that even stick in their own gullets or the clichés that they have been using since they became politicians. I don't care if they lock me up in a home. I'll say things that have never seen the light of day. I"ll stand up and say them. If I only have two boys and a mongrel dog listening to me first, it doesn't matter. I'll say it and I'll say it over and over again, until that square above is jammed black with people, and when it comes to that I'll say, How many of you down there are with me? And there will be a thunderous roar from the throats of the young and we will get a new flag, one that was never in a battle and we'll march with that and we'll clean the country as clean as the flag."

"And that," said Jo prosaically, "is how new political parties are born."

"You never know," said Mico. "Maybe in God, Peter would have it in him."

"Maybe, maybe," said Peter, sinking dispiritedly back on the grass. "What a hope! But I'd do it in a minute, and if I feel like it in three years when I'm finished, maybe I'd do it then. Maybe I would, too."

"And where do I come into all this?" asked Jo, surprising his thoughts out of his head, so that he rose on an elbow and looked at her. Her eyes were wide open and she was looking at him. Looking at him strangely. Peter felt his heart coming up in his throat and sticking there. He thought her breast was rising and falling more rapidly than it had been. There was a silence between them and suddenly the green grass under them vanished away and the rippled water of the clear lake became like the sky and the trees behind them cleared away too, and big Mico went farther and farther away as if he had been on a magic carpet that had suddenly taken off into the blue. Just green eyes and a heaving breast covered with a light frock that did little to hide the sudden strain that was on it.

Here it is again, Mico thought, as he rose to his feet and walked away. He had been with a feeling like this once before. Yeh! Facing a reach of strand under a moon and another girl and a boy that had looked at one another and talked about a house on the side of a hill and how it was to be built a stone upon a stone. Never for me that, he thought, that a number three will be shut out like the night when you pull a blind on it. He walked through the trees, pushed his way through the blackberry bushes, climbed a low wall, frightened two goats and a huge hare that ran and ran as if they were chasing one another and he came out on the far side of the island. The wind was coming from the west so he looked back there, back the length of the long lake where it reached into the mountains. You could see them dimly, lightly blue away at the end, and he saw in between them, saw the sweep of the Maam Valley with the gigantic Maamturc mountains closing it in, and he saw the long winding road on this side of the valley how you went on and on, past the lakes with the solitary boatmen in them, past the bogs and the small towns and the villages and the clinging cottages until you came to the sea, and there she was.

He sat down on the rock, with his eyes fixed on the distant mountains. He thought of her letter. It was nonsensical for a grown man to be feeling that way about a girl he had known when he was fourteen or fifteen. How many years ago? Six say. Six years. It scalded you to read her letter; about the house at last; the description of the toiling and moiling that had gone to its making; the planning and contriving and scratching and making do; the anxious watching of the growing brothers and sisters so that they would be able to take their place and free them for each other. So they were free. Could Mico ever come? No, Mico couldn't come. There were fish to catch and a hard world to survive in. But he didn't need to go. He could see the house looking on to the strand. And he could see them standing up there in the church with the purple light pouring in from the window over the altar. Coimín would have on a blue suit and maybe a collar and tie in honour of the day. And his big face would be clean and shining and fresh-looking and she would be in a blue dress with pink dots (he preferred to think of her that way) and getting married even in her bare feet, because why not since it was his own thinking and he could do what he liked with it. All right. She would be smiling up at Coimín, and probably even there on the altar

- 131 -

Coimín would be pretending to be cross with her or not to be hurrying and to be lazy and all the time the quiet eyes of him would be enveloping her. And all the village would be there. Uncle James commiserating with Coimín dolefully and making them all laugh; and Peadar and Mary Cavanagh, with little Nuala who would be quite big now; and Mrs Coimín would be there crying her eyes out, and Coimín's father, Tadhg, would be there telling outrageous yarns about Coimín's strength or maybe he had new ones now, and the Táilliúr and Tommeen Tady and all the rest of them each passing before his eyes with their smiles or sly jokes or crinkling eyes or moustaches, just the same as if it was yesterday he had been with them. And there would be great dings in Maeve's house. All day and far into the night. The porter that would be drunk! The dances that would be danced! The food that would be consumed! All to be paid for tomorrow and tomorrow and tomorrow, when a good catch was caught or two good catches or even maybe three. And then Maeve and Coimín would walk arm in arm down the lane to the beach and they would turn up a new small lane that Coimín would have made by this and they would look at the cottage they had built with their own hands, and then they would bend and take the key from under the stone and they would enter.

But Mico didn't follow them. He reached his hand and caught up a flat piece of limestone and spun it on the water. It went along skimming and then it sank.

"Honest to God I do, Peter," Jo was saying to his wide-eyed query, and then he put his arm across her, and bent over her face. And she didn't just screw her eyes and let him kiss her as if she was taking a dose of castor oil, or push him away and say, "That's enough now, think of our holy religion," or keep him sitting in her living room with the fire dying, talking about what she thought about the professor's views on *The Playboy of the Western World* and how she didn't agree with this and that and the other, with her mother coming downstairs anxiously, her hair in cloth curlers looking in the door, saying, "It's very late, dear. Isn't it time you were going, Peter? Your mother will be anxious about you." Peter rising and saying, "Honestly, Mrs Mulcairns, I'm not going to seduce her. You'd have to be Shakespeare to do that." Mrs Mulcairns' hand up to her mouth, and Peter going then, tired of dissertation, tired of his love in a literary press. A terrible row of course and Goodbye now, and we don't meet again ever and ever. Never speak to you again. Horrid to my mother. She doesn't even know the meaning of the word. Not half, where did she get you so? A month, six months, a year, a year and a half, two years. Imagine that. But we came back. You and I were born to quarrel, Jo, and born to love too, for ever and ever and ever. There will never be anybody else but you. You're all sour buttermilk to me. What about Norah this and Jane that and Patty the other that you left home from the Engineers' Hop? Nothing to it. Just because I was mad at you or you were mad at me, and what about Paddy this and Tom the other and Declan such a thing? (all this like the dots in the pointed remarks in the College Mag). You weren't holding them at arm's length, I bet, or two arms' length. Oh so! Yes, so! All right. Goodbye, and I hope I never see you again. It was no use of course. There was a long line stretching between them that was unbreak-able. Some need. Two seeds planted in them that had to grow one on the other.

The lovely lassitude of love was in her. His hands were trembling.

Out on the lake a fish rose lazily, plopping, and Mico's stone sank.

Chapter Nine

THEY WERE PLAYING hurling in the Swamp.

Normally it's very difficult to play hurling, or anything else for that matter, in a swamp, but the Swamp was different.

Once upon a time if you lived in the Claddagh with your house facing south you would have a clear view over a rocky marshy piece of land, and the Lighthouse seemed to be outside your front door. You could nearly see the cavorting rats on the rusty wrecked fourmasted schooner that was lying near-in to be stripped and broken up in the course of a decade or two. It was a nice view. But then in the spring tides if there was a south-west wind behind the tide, you would wake up in the middle of the night to find your kitchen floor under two foot of water that had swept across the land between the sea and your house, and you could have found the view alone expendable in the circumstances. There was a lot of cursing and confusion over the same flooding, and many a hot word was spoken and a blow delivered and many a goose was metaphorically cooked in those times. Then the Council decided to do something about it, so they built a low wall across the road to hold up the main flow of the water. But more drastic remedies were required, so they sort of raised the land in a dyke above the shore line and then behind this line they proceeded to dump all the refuse of the city, and in the course of time the whole place was filled in nicely and grass was thrown on it and the grass grew well. It was beautifully manured below by the rotting refuse and the carcasses of old horses and asses and such things that were brought there when they were very old, or when their legs were broken for some reason, and they would pick a suitable spot and put the small gun to their foreheads and it would bark viciously and the eyes of the animal would glaze and it would fall into the hole and be covered up and become a filling at the end of its days. So the grass grew and in course of time enough of the place was covered over to form a nice playing pitch with goal posts at each end. It was called South Park by the Council – the Swamp by the people.

Anyhow here was a playing field. It was a pleasant place to play in because you had a cooling breeze on your hot forehead from the nearby sea, and even if the breeze was tainted with the mixed abounding decay you could forget that in the heat of the endeavour, and if you had time think that in about another hundred years they would be finished dumping all the city dirt in the place and it would be all right.

It was an exciting game they were playing.

The Irish people have always played hurling. It's nearly as old a game to them as the game of chess and that's a long time back. The hurley had always figured in Irish history since God invented the ash tree with its nicely grained curving branches out of which a hurley could be planed to give it a neat substantial *bas*. When the heroes of long long ago had finished fighting giants or stopped raping their friends' wives or stealing their gold and personal belongings or their cattle and bulls, they would rest from the fray and they would have a game of hurling in the nearest park.

It is a brisk game and a very fast game and it can be a dangerous game, and probably that's why the Irish invented it in the first place.

The Munstermen, the scoundrels, are the best players of the game because each Munsterman when he is born only uses one hand to catch his mother's breast, since he's busy even at that tender age swinging a hurley in the other, and it's a thrilling thing to see two teams from Munster playing this game. The small ball, once it is set in motion, hardly ever touches the ground. It is hit from end to end of the long playing field, to be caught by the hand and hit or to be impelled on its way by a beautifully timed stroke. You have to be an adept at sighting the ball and you have to be still more adept at blocking strokes aimed at the ball which might complete an arc and catch you on some part of the body, principally the head, or they might slide down the blocking hurley and slice off a few of your knuckles. But accidents like that are rare by men who know how to play.

In this game now as it is played in a cold March wind on a Sunday after last Mass, there is not as much skill as one would like to see, but there is tremendous endeavour because the opposing teams are the direct opposite of one another in intellect and physique. It is mainly a struggle between brawn and brain. On one side you have the College boys with their red jerseys and white togs (white in the main except for a few who are not fastidious about those things) and their stockings and studded boots: on the other side you have the Claddagh boys and they are togged out in a most un-uniform way. Some of them have their ordinary shirts tucked into short pants with socks and ordinary big boots. And some of them have the jerseys and their long trousers and football boots; and one or two of them even have the whole regalia, but as everybody now knows, clothes do not make men and in the long-ago times the game of hurling was played in the bare pelt, so it doesn't really matter how you play just so long as you do play.

Mico was in the Claddagh goal.

They put him in there, as they said, because he was as big as a house. He was wearing a cap to keep the sun out of his eyes, and a shirt and trousers, with football boots on his feet and his thick woollen socks dragged up over the ends of his trouser legs to keep them from flapping into his way. He had his sleeves rolled over his arms. They were very big arms.

So he custoded there and watched the play that had swung to the other end of the field where they were besieging the College goal. There was a very knacky small squat fellow up there and he was running rings around the nifty College backs. A small powerful frame, and a deep chest swelling well out beyond the width of his upper arms, and his bullet head close shaven. That was Twacky, and Mico grinned now as he watched him twisting and dodging with the ball held as if by magic on the end of his hurley. There were people around the sidelines, not a lot of them. Up near the College goal a lot of characters with heavy scarves even in the heat and their faces red like Indians and they roaring and shouting profanely at the members of their team, telling them what to do to stop their opponents – very sanguinary advice. And there were the Claddagh boys up there too urging on Twacky in no uncertain fashion and pushing and cat-calling, and Mico thought how true it was for the genius long ago who coined the phrase, "The best hurlers are those on the fence", and then there was a roar of rage and a shout of triumph and Twacky jumps into the air with his hurley aloft, and one or two players run to him and clap him on the back, and now, Mico thought, we are in for fireworks because as far as my arithmetic will take me the score must be evens.

He tightened his grip on his stick and bent down as the ball came soaring into the air from the hurley of the other goalie. Came down three-quarters of the field nearly in a strong puck and was sent on its way before it could reach the ground by a flashing stroke from a centre with a red jersey.

This is it now, thought Mico, as he watched the ball heading for the lissom figure of Peter, his hair dimmed by the colour of his jersey, his lithe body straining against the body of the back, big Padneen O Meara, who was wearing shorts and nearly splitting them the way his thickly muscled thighs were pressing against the cloth. They pushed one another from side to side as they watched the ball coming towards them, and Mico idly noted that the shoulders of Padneen were at least twice the width of the shoulders of Peter and yet he was holding his own in the preliminary sideways pushing.

The ball came to them and Padneen swung hugely with his hurley.

Had it hit the ball, it would probably have landed out on the Aran Islands, but before he could connect, Peter's stick was slyly inserted under it and it was swept away from Padneen's hurley and into Peter's hand. He turned quickly and hopped it twice on the *bas* and then he swung it at Mico with all the power of his body. High, high, not for goal but so that it would sneak over the bar for a point, and three points make a goal and it's better to be sure. Oh, the devil, thought Mico, as he stretched his great height for it, but it sailed serenely by just over the top of his hurley like a visible bullet.

"Whoo!" said Peter, jumping and hitting his hurley on the ground. "That bet you, Mico, oul son."

Mico grinned and caught the ball that was flung at him in a large hand.

"Keep a better eye on that fella, Padneen," he shouted to the discomfited back.

"I'll murder 'm," said Padneen, waving the hurley and laughing and then spitting on his hands and rubbing the excess off on his pants and getting a firmer grip on the handle. "Devil a past me will he get agin, Mico."

"Here y'are now, Twacky," roared Mico, firing the ball into the air and hitting it with all the power of his shoulders. It went soaring high, accurate and true, and dropped almost into Twacky's hand in front of the opposing goal. That'll keep them quiet for a while anyhow, Mico thought, as he watched them struggling for it way up above and then let his eyes rove over the watching people.

Jo was there on the side-line. Prim-looking. In a light summer frock that was pressed to her body by the soft wind sweeping in from the sea. Pockets in the frock and her hands sunk into them. Her short hair and her legs spread as she watched. Dependable. Just the kind of a girl for Peter with his sort of boiling temperament. To be with him was something like being at sea. One minute things went gently and calmly and the next minute you were gathered up into a veritable vortex of politics or social science or arguments about the relative merits of writers, poets, or lavatory attendants.

And there was Pa with his stick. Didn't seem to have aged a day. Just a little more bent at the shoulders. His whiskers a little more whitened as if somebody had shaken powder on them. Remembered every one of his ex-pupils by name and knew what they were doing and where they were.

"A goal, Twacky boy," Pa was shouting. "Give us a goal, Twacky."

Twacky did his best to oblige. Mico could nearly see the sweat of endeavour on his earnest countenance from here. Twacky got the ball after much dodging and swinging and conniving, and he drove for goal, but it was blocked and rescued by a back and came sailing out of the field. It was struggled for by the half-backs and the opposing forwards and it rose in the air and Padneen swung at it with Peter trying to hook it from him, but this time Padneen connected with a great stroke and it went sailing back the way it had come.

Mico relaxed.

Gran was there. Standing beside Big Micil and some of the other fishermen who were leaning back against the ugly wall and smoking and spitting and completely unexcited by the view of all the unnecessary sweating that was going on. Gran is getting old, Mico thought, his heart sinking a little.

Tommy was standing up the field.

Well dressed. The sun was glinting from his fair wavy hair. He was sporting a College tie and his shirt was white and well pressed. Mico had a vision of his mother intent on the ironing of it. A grey suit with a nice crease in the pants. And two girls with him, one on each side. He was smoking a cigarette in the nervous way he had, up and down to the mouth and rolling it in the fingers. Not the excitement of the game. Tommy didn't like games. They were for morons. He could prove it to you as well. By quote. Shows you what attraction he held for other people when even the fact that he didn't play games didn't serve to make him unpopular. Maybe if he had pimples and dandruff he would have been. But his skin was very clear and his hair was thick and free of dandruff and Peter's Jo said that he was a very good dancer as well. Out in the Hanger.

The ball came swinging back again.

It was almost a ritual now, the way it always headed for Peter and Padneen. Like a dance it was, the way they pressed their bodies together with the hurleys held on the ready, and pushed one another to get into a strategic position, and the ball came, and Padneen and Peter rose to it, and Padneen sort of turned in the air, and Peter went to sneak it out from him, and no man knows rightly whatever happened then, whether it was Peter below pushing at Padneen and putting him off his stroke or what, but the fact of the matter was that Padneen's hurley with all the force of his great body behind the swing didn't but graze the ball. Instead it swung and all over that great place you could hear the clump of it as it sank into Peter's skull.

There was a shocked silence.

A picture grafted on the eye. Fourteen players on one side and fifteen on the other standing where the blow had found them in awkward positions, legs up or hurleys up or down or sideways, and the people on the side-lines with their breaths held. Just for a few seconds and then Mico threw his hurley from him and ran to the crumpled body on the ground.

As he went on his knees behind him he saw that already the red hair was dark with pouring blood.

"Peter!" he said, turning him over on his back.

His eyes were closed and there was a sort of snore coming from his mouth. His face was paling so that the freckles stood out on it.

"Peter," said Mico, almost shaking him.

"What is it, Mico, what happened?" asked the panting voice of Jo as his back. "What's wrong with him?"

"Nothing wrong with him," said Mico, "he was just knocked out, that's all. He'll be all right in a minute."

"Listen, I didn't mean it," Padneen was saying from the other side of the recumbent form. "I was aimin' at the bloody ball and he come under me and the hurl twisted. Listen, is he all right? Listen, lookit, honest to God, fellas, I didn't mane it. On me oath I didn't mane it!"

"Shush, shush," said Mico. "For God's sake, Padneen, we all know you didn't mane it." He felt for the place in Peter's head from which the blood was oozing, blackening his hair. Red hair, so that the blood didn't look red on his hair at all. It was only when it spread to Mico's exploring fingers that it became scarlet on his flesh. He saw the gaping cut that was dark red and then white sort of flesh inside.

"Oh, Mico," said Jo, her hands up to her mouth.

"Stand back, stand back," said the voice of Pa then, as he waved his way through them with his stick. "What's this, Mico boy? What's wrong with him?"

"He's just knocked out, sir," said Mico. "He got a clout on the skull."

"Let me see," said Pa. He bent over him, mumbled something at the sight of the bloodless face below him, tut-tutted at the slight snore that was coming from the partly opened lips and then felt for the wound. Not the wound itself, but he pressed the skull gently around it with the tips of his small ladylike hands that could deal out such pain in a just cause. He hid the worry as his fingers made the cracked skull creak a little, just the smallest little bit. He looked up at the faces crowding them around. "Here," he said, "one of you College fellows. What the hell are ye doin', boys.

Yeer medical students, aren't ye? Come on and look after the boy!"

Two of them came in and went on their knees beside him and tightened their lips at the sight of his face and the snoring lips and didn't look at each other at all as they explored his head.

"Better send for the ambulance," said one without raising his head.

"Go on, Jo," said Mico. "Chase up the road. The people in the first house beyond the church have a telephone. Go on, can't you? Go on quick!" because she was inclined to delay. The best thing for her anyhow, he thought, and as she went he met Pa's eyes with his own and saw the nod of approval.

"Could we move the boy?" he asked the students then. "We can't leave him lying in a field until they come."

They looked at each other.

"If we're careful," they said, "if we don't be moving his head."

"Right so," said Pa. "What are we waiting for, boy? Speed, neatness, and accuracy." The measure of his flurry that he would use that old cant even at a time like this.

They tied two or three coats together and they made them into a sling. At least Mico did, and his father. Two or three knots and then they got them under him and they wedged his neck and his head with pullovers and shirts and shorts that were thrown at them and they brought him slowly to a low wall and they carefully climbed the stile there, with Big Micil and Mico in front and the two students holding him behind, and they got on to the road and they crossed the green sward of the geese and they brought him into Mico's house.

His mother rose startled from the fire with her hand going to her heart and her face going pale as the red boy's, but then she saw the figure of her eldest son coming in behind and she went forward to them.

They placed him quietly on Mico's bed. There was never

a flutter from his eyes The short red lashes lay like two gashes on his white cheeks. Delia brought a basin of water and she washed the blood from his hair and she dabbed very gently at it where it was still oozing from his skull. "Don't do any more now," said the student who was beside her. "Wait now until they come for him."

"Tell me," Mico asked from the bottom of the bed. "Is it serious?"

"Well," said the other looking at him uncomfortably. "I don't know. I'm not a doctor yet. But anything to do with the head could be serious. It's just as well to be cautious."

Padneen was out in the kitchen, still in his shirt and togs, his gigantic legs throbbing with muscle and the mud of the Swamp still on them. He was waving his hand. The sweat was pouring from him and he'd raise a large hand now and again to wipe at the worry of his forehead, and to use his blunt fingers to swipe the beads of sweat from his eyebrows.

"Lookit," he was saying, "I'd cut off me right hand from the wrist so I would before I'd hurt a hair a Peter Cusack's head. Listen! This was how it was. We both went for the ball and up we go for it and then he must have jostled me from below because the hurl swung in me hand and I heard it hittin' him. Christ, honest to Christ, if I meant to hit him, I tell ye."

"Look, look, now, Padneen," said Micil, coming down from the room. "Will you be aisy, will yeh? Sure nobody in the world thinks that you meant to hit him. It was just an accident. We could all see that it was just an accident."

"But listen, Micil," Padneen persisted, "ye don't understand. I was goin' up for the ball and he was goin' up for the ball, and he must a jostled me or somethin' because ..."

"Silence, O Meara," said Pa then, in a fierce sort of whisper. "It was an accident. Silence now, sir, before I take the stick to you."

"Yes, sir," said Padneen, forgetting to assert his manhood.

"Here, get that boy a drink, someone," said Pa then. "Or it'll be another ambulance we'll have to be getting."

Tommy went to the dresser and took a white mug from it, one with a scarlet rose painted on it and he dipped it into the water-bucket on the table behind the back door.

"Here, Padneen," he said, "drink it up."

Padneen took it with a shaking hand and sank his red face into it.

There was a silence then in the kitchen. So silent was it that you could hear the ticking of the clock hanging on the wall. A clock with a smoke-blackened face and a pendulum, that swing-swung with the whitewashed wall as a background. So quiet that you just heard that, and the slight snore coming like a sleeping man from the other room.

Pa went out through the half-door, with his stick swinging. The numerous little boys gathered out there with their mouths open and their eyes wide – where had they come from so suddenly? Had they been grown from the green grass? Had they burrows, secret ones, in the soil? How on earth could the green be empty of boys half a minute ago and now be full of boys?

"Depart!" said Pa, holding his stick out in the direction he wanted them to go. They went.

Had it been any other time, Big Micil might have laughed.

But not in this silence. A terrible thing to see a young man like that dodging and darting like a red-haired rabbit one minute and the next minute he's snoring on the green grass. A good boy too. One that Big Micil liked. A sharp tongue on him and a fella that was always asking questions. About the sea. About the fish. How are nets made? How do they catch them? What's the international ruling about the size of the mesh? What do you get for a cran of herring? A cran of mackerel? How far out have you to go before you strike the cod? Do you sell the fish to the factories, the codfish with or without the liver? Things like that, and you answered it all, and then he'd be away telling you a story that would be very clever indeed and maybe bawdy so that you laughed at the crinkles that came in his own eyes.

"Lookit," said Padneen, his voice muted instinctively to

the silence of the house. "It was an accident, I tell ye... I was goin' for the ball."

"Ah, shut up, Padneen, for Jaysus' sake," said Tommy.

Padneen looked at him with his mouth open and then sank his hair into his fiercely rubbing hands.

This will put Peter out of the running for the finals, Tommy was thinking, and with Peter out of the running there is no doubt at all that I will get all the firsts. He was really the only opposition, and with the exams coming up in two weeks, he would have hardly recovered before then. Maybe that's a hard thing to be thinking, but after all, he had plenty of time. He's not like me, a scholarship boy that has to scrimp and scrape to find the price of the pictures, the price of taking a girl to a hop in the Aula Maxima; to find the price of the heavy tomes you needed as you came nearer and nearer to the goal of your desires. He didn't have to study like me in a small kitchen with the light of an oil lamp; with the eternal smell of fish in your nose, or tarred ropes, and he didn't have to tumble into a hard board-like bed at two o'clock in the morning with your eyes aching and you tossing and turning on the straw mattress, with the big heavy sweating body of your brother lying inanimately beside you. How he hated that bed and the body of his brother! This would be a first-class honours degree and there had been a few hints that he might be asked to stay on as an assistant lecturer. Sixty pounds a year as well as the prizes he would win for the first places. With that a man might even be able to get a room in town and live there. Except for the mother it would be easy. She would fuss so. But he came first with her. Well, we'd see. It was tough luck on Peter. But there was always next year for him. What did it matter to him? With a home like he had. Carpets on every room in the house. Comfortable furniture. These seemed like petty things but they weren't really. Maybe it wasn't fair to be thinking like that now but after all he was a rationalist. *Nil nisi bonum* boloney, as that chap had said. Well, he's out of the race now, anyhow, he thought. There's a clear field ahead of me now and good hunting.

He raised his head then and saw Pa looking at him coldly.

Tommy was startled for a minute and pulled himself up straight beside the dresser. Then he relaxed again. How could that old fake know what I was thinking about?

Pa turned and went up to the room on his toes.

Mico was leaning on the rail of the bed. Delia was still dabbing at the cut and the young student was standing at the small window with the lace curtain parted, straining his head, listening, hoping it wouldn't be too long until the ambulance came, because he didn't like the look of Peter at all at all, only you didn't say things like that. The first instinct of a doctor to keep your own counsel.

He looks awful bad now, Mico was thinking. He looks shockin' bad now, God, so he does. It seemed like a dream that some short time ago he had been looking at him leaping, and now here they were in the small room with Peter stretched on his quilt and his face as pale as the feather of a goose and he snoring. Mico didn't like that snoring at all. That's bad news, he said. But sure they couldn't kill Peter. Nothing under the face of God's earth could polish off Peter. Not and as lively as he was. The quick darting body and brain of him like a snipe in front of a gun.

And then he heard the whine of the car coming across the green, and out of the corner of his eye saw the student turning from the window.

Gran was outside with the ambulance, the only man with enough sense to wait at the corner so that he could direct them where to go. They'd have been all over the Swamp now, but for Gran.

Jo's face was as white as the wall. She was panting.

The nurse and the driver were very efficient.

No words from them. Just actions.

Before anyone knew they were there, Peter was rolled in a blanket and was in the stretcher and the stretcher was shoved in on its grooves and was away with the nurse inside unrolling bandages from the rack, and Jo beside her, sitting on the other stretcher, holding things for her and her eyes glued to the pallid face of the red-haired man, and nothing at all in her mind only a great fear and a great prayer, all mixed together, and her actions automatically efficient, and her answers to the nurse automatically efficient. And the car rolled softly up by the fishing boats, and across roads and in and out narrow streets, silently and knowledgeably, as if every inch of the roads were known with the pain of the speed that went with them, and they rolled at last in through the gates, and the tyres crunched on the gravel and the doors opened behind and Jo smelled the flood of disinfectants from the gaunt building and shortly afterwards sat on a wooden bench outside a room, sat with her back straight and her eyes on the green distempered walls opposite her, and she was still full of fear and full of prayer.

Mico went over to Peter's parents.

Peter's father, the nice quiet pseudo-fierce man. And Peter's mother, fluffy and nervy and fluttery, but nice withal, treating you with so much kindness that she would kill you, living for a word of commendation or praise or love from the lips of their son.

How would she take this now?

Very well.

As if Peter was there in person to hide her. As if he would be there to josh her back to sensibility if she put one of her small feet a single inch over the borderline. Just a catch in her throat and a fear, a stricken look of fear in her eyes, and then the reaching for her coat with the fur collar that came down nearly to her ankles most unfashionably, and Peter's father going out in nothing but his white hair and his weather-beaten face. He got the car out of the garage, a small car, the inside of it redolent with the smell of dead trout and salmon and the fluttering feathers of shot game, and the upholstery of it covered with the hairs of the Irish setter that had as close a nose for a bird as a froth was on a pint.

They waited a long time in the room with the polished table until after a lifetime the door opened and the tired man with the white coat stood there.

He was thin and his face was thin and the hair on his head was black and going thin too. He closed the door and rested against it. He was tired. They got up from their seats and looked at him. It was like a scene from a silent film.

"He'll be all right," he said then. No lift to it. Just a statement. Peter's mother fell back on the couch then and she started to cry, silent tears that flowed like a waterfall through her fingers. And Jo had to sit beside her again and say, "now, now," and Mr Cusack shifted from foot to foot and his face got redder and redder and Mico was afraid of his life that he was going to cry too, but he just raised a finger like a sausage and rubbed his nose from side to side and "Hump'h"-ed and went over to the doctor and shook his hand and then went back and got Mrs Cusack up from the couch and out the door.

"You can see him in a few days," the doctor said, as he ushered them into the hall and out into the cold dawn. "He had a little concussion. A few weeks here. Then you can take him home. Nothing but rest. No excitement."

"Doctor," said Mr Cusack, "I'll tie him down in the bed." Grimly.

"Good morning now," said the doctor, and watched them get into the car and waited until it had chugged-chugged importantly towards the main gate.

Then he sighed and turned back into the hall.

Thin skull – that was the trouble, he was thinking. So near the brain. Hope it will be all right. It should be all right. But these are dangerous places. We know so little about them really. But anyhow it was a good job even if I say it myself. Touch and go really. Aye, a good job.

Jo said a peculiar thing to Mico as he left her at her own gate.

"Mico," she said, ' do you know a thing I'm after seeing now?"

"What is it?" he asked.

"Maybe because it's the dawn," she said. "It was dawn then too. But long ago do you remember when we were caught on that island? When we got off it was like this except it was raining. And I looked back there. And I thought that thorn tree was shaking a fist at us."

Mico felt a cold shiver up his back.

"For the love of God," he said, "will you not be talkin' like that? Peter is better, isn't he? It'd take more than a clout on the sconce to kill Peter. It might even quieten him down a bit," he said, trying to raise even a glimmer of a smile on her.

A wan smile. "Goodnight, Mico," she said, "and maybe after this now they would leave us alone."

He waited until the door closed on her before he left and turned for home. The slender masts of the fishing boats were silhouetted against the rising sun. It feels, Mico was thinking, like a thousand years.

Chapter Ten

THEY CAME HOME in the early light of the autumn morning.

The wind was over their left shoulder so that the brown sail was well distended and pushed the heavy boat over the sea at a steady deceptive speed.

Mico, half sitting on the hatch, could see the town away on their left, and on either side the other boats were coming home too. They looked small and black and sparse on the breadth of the Bay, like beetles on a sheet, because the sky was grey. There was no colour much in the rising sun. It just threw a pink wisp at the clouds and then rose up behind them. He felt very tired. He felt that his eyes were dropping. His clothes felt stale. He could see his father on the other side of the boat, leaning there with his pipe in his mouth held by a hand as brown and as fish-encrusted as his own. One large arm was across his chest. He looked tired too. His stubble was heavy and was mottled with grey. There were red rims around his eyes, and his heavy shoulders were sagging. Imagine that. Even Big Micil to be feeling the dint of the tiredness!

Mico didn't look back at his Gran with his wrinkled hand on the tiller.

He didn't want to, because Gran wasn't good to look at now on this early morning after three days away. He had looked at him when they set out from home, had seen the purple under his eyes, by main force and terrible will power had refrained from helping him into the boat. Holy God! Helping Gran into a boat! But there it was and somehow it would have to be faced. Not now, his mind said, we won't face it now. Let us put it off until tomorrow. Because the truth was – the blunt truth – that Gran was no use in a boat any more.

Mico sighed.

No, better leave that. Then there was Peter and his strange.... No, get away from that. That is a terrible problem. Even thinking of Gran and his aged uselessness would be better than that.

What are we doing all this for? Mico forced himself to think then.

He looked into the place at his feet. At the boxes of fish. The hold nearly full of fish. All right. Were they worth all this? All that jumble of stiff fish, those rigid mackerel and the gurnet and the few cod and the strange fish with the head of a red gurnet and the body of an eel, plaice and a few black sole. He thought of the hours of labour that had gone into the catching of them. The two nights huddled in the hold or lying cold on the deck in fitful slumber under the stars, at a lonely quayside in the middle of nowhere. Nothing to be heard but the cry of a plover or a nightjar and in the distance, in the middle of the bleak stony land, the bark of a dog, conjuring up a picture of a cottage with a bright fire and men in front of it smoking their pipes and spitting into the ashes with warm beds to go to and wives to sleep with and to ease the grinding poverty of their living and its futility. Was it worth the toil and the tiredness and the rapacity of the men in the middle?

Ach, he thought then, I'm getting morbid. That's the way Peter would be talkin' and we'd be laughin' at him. It was the way the world was made and there seemed to be no cure for it. Since the beginning of it there had been men who would grow rich and fat and fulsome like a black-headed worm on the sweat and toil of others. That was the way it was, and unless Peter hurried up and did something about it in Ireland, that's the way it would always be.

Poor Peter! Poor, poor, Peter!

I won't think of him any more now, Mico thought, and turned and leaned over the side of the boat and directed a dry spit at the hurrying sea.

Too well, Gran thought, I know what he's thinkin'. And I know what Big Micil there is thinkin' too with the smoke of his pipe blue on the air. And sure now it will have to be faced. If I'm waitin' for them two big slobs to face it, I'd be a skeleton here and me hand on the tiller and the water in me eyes. His eyes had begun to water. Only for the last year now. He hated to look into a mirror at himself. He never did now. He clipped his beard by the feel and kept his eyes from the pools and reflections of faces in the green sea.

It was a terrible thing to know you were getting old without having to look at it as well.

He had only to look down at his hand now on the tiller. There was a time when it had been a big hand and broad that could have bent a six-inch nail in the brown grip of it. And he knew the measure of the way his hand had fallen in was the measure of all the rest of him. He didn't have to be told. He wasn't an eejit after all.

All right. He knew all that. But they didn't notice it. There was a lot of things they didn't notice, even if by their silence they told him things they would never get the tongue to say. They kept their heads down. His big slob of a son was a terrible fella. He should have been more of a man. If he was Gran now, he'd have said it straight out. Here you, you silly old bastard, you're no good for the sea any more.

He looked at his son and found the steady eyes on his own. A look and then the big lips opened in a smile and Big Micil winked at him and turned his head away.

The curse a Christ on him, Gran was thinking, the curse a Christ on him, because he's like that. He wouldn't hurt a bitch that was mad with the froth on her mouth. Look at the way he was at home. You'd think he was a lodger. A great big pludder of a man that'd nearly apologize for being in his own house.

"I'm not goin' to come out with ye any more," said Gran in a determined voice, and felt a momentary triumph at the startled way he brought the two heads around to look at him.

"I'm fed up with it all," he went on in a loud voice, waving his free hand violently at the sea. "It's taken enough of me. I don't want it any more. Why should I be goin' out at my age, in the wet and the wind, when I should be at home with me stockinged feet stretched out to the blaze of the turf fire? Answer me that?" he demanded of them belligerently.

They looked at one another.

"Nonsense," said Big Micil then. "You aren't an oul fella yet."

"Is it tryin' to deprive me of me rights you are?" asked Gran.

Micil was hurt at this and shouted a bit, his face red.

"I'm not deprivin' yeh of anythin'," he said. "Did I ever try to deprive yeh of anythin' in your whole life?"

"Well, if I want to go, I go," said Gran, "and there's no need for you to be wantin' to stop me. D'yeh hear that, Big Micil?"

"I do," said Micil.

"Too long I've been fatherin' yeh," said Gran. "Haven't I had yeh around me belt since the day yeh were born? It's time now that you can do without yer father, isn't it?"

"But who said ...?" Micil wanted to know, a bit indignantly, when Gran silenced him with the upraised hand.

"That's enough out of yeh now," he said. "I've heard enough of yer arguments. Isn't it time for me to take a rest? Isn't it time for me to lie abed of a mornin' and hear ye goin' to sea and me snugglin' down in me bed at the creak of yeer sails? And then I'll get up at ten a clock and I'll dress meself slowly and I'll go down to the kitchen and I'll have me salty herrin' and me tay and I'll pull the chair in front of the fire and I'll light up me oul pipe. That's what I'll do, and d'yeh know what I'm goin' to do after that?"

"No," said Micil bemused.

"Well, I'm goin' to walk slowly down be the church to the Claddagh Bar, and I'll climb up on a barrel in front of the counter and I'll have the biggest frothiest pint a porter that ever mortal man had. All that at eleven o'clock in the day. Too long I've been at sea, d'ye hear, and what has it done to me?"

"It never took the edge offa yer tongue anyhow," said Micil.

"Ah-ha, d'ye hear 'm now?" Gran wanted to know. "What has it done to me indeed? Look at thim arms (pulling the sleeve of the jersey up on his skinny arm and holding the tiller with his elbow). Look at it. There's no more meat on that arm now than would be on the leg of a chicken, and time was when it was as thick as your thigh. I was a better man than you, Big Micil, so I was. I could ha' med two of you, d'yeh hear!"

"You could all right," said Micil.

"Yer tonin' down now, are yeh?" he asked, pulling the sleeve viciously down the pathetically thin arm, that was nothing but the big bone and the loosened skin and muscle on it, and it white and yellow where the sun had never touched it. "Aye, it sucked all the juice out of me, the sea did, like a child's mouth suckin' an orange. That's what it did to me. Haven't I done enough now?" he asked. He saw Mico looking closely at him, and dodged his eyes. That fella is too cute altogether. Big Micil, now, is a big slob and he wouldn't know what was going on at all. He didn't want them to be feeling sorry for him. That would drive him into a fury and he'd be saying things then that they'd remember. Because devil a hair of him wanted to leave. Mico, the cute

- 154 -

thing, knew that by the look in his face. But what could you do? People like themselves couldn't sit around the fire and talk about things like that. Things that went into your chest and hurt you every time you thought about them.

"The time has come now," he said in a quieter voice, "for me to leave the sea. The two of ye are big enough now to manage be yeerselves. I can always give ye the word of advice in season, if ye'll listen to me and yeer heads don't get too big because I've let ye out on yeer own at last. I couldn't live another winter in the boat. Not now. I would die, to be feeling it at me. That's all. It's time for me to retire. That's all. You understand that?"

"Yes, Father," said Big Micil, turning his head away.

"We'll miss yeh, Gran," said Mico, and then seeing the old man's face falling he turned and looked over the bow where its big buxom breast was pushing the waves to each side.

Gran saw the sky before his eyes and it seemed to him that there was a mist coming over it. Other people mustn't know. But here now it was come. He thought he might have held out for another year at least so that the cold and the rain might kill him; but it couldn't be, and the way he was hampering them. If it wasn't for him on this trip they would have twice the work done and twice the catch. A man couldn't go on like that, being selfish when so many people's bit and sup depended on your vanished vigour. But all the same never did he think that this that had caught up with him would ever arrive. He had seen the old ones with their white whiskers, holding up the wall of the church and walking slowly between their whitewashed houses and the evening pint, smoking and eating and throwing a line into the river and going home to bed. Waiting to die; that's all it was. Why wouldn't there be some way that old men like himself could be put to death peacefully instead of having to sit on a pier and wait for the old death to catch up with him?

Nothing left now so, but the line by the river and the pint in the evening and the high useless polish on your heavy boots.

"Let ye not forget all I taught ye now," he said, breaking hurriedly into speech. "I taught ye everything ye know; every turn and twist of this Bay and where the fishes lie. I'm handin' it on to ye now, d'yeh hear that, Mico? That's all I have teh give yeh, the heritage of the sea. It's maybe a lot more precious than the things those stupids in there inside their grey walls call money. Money never did any man any good. The day they invented it they took the joy out of life and they put in blood and torture and dishonest sweat and crimes of all kinds. But there's this what you have and you can't go wrong with it. You know where you stand with it. 'Tis a big purse with a long bottom and if you treat it right there'll be no end to it. Remember that now, let ye."

"I'll remember, Gran," said Mico. And the worst of all, he thought, is the way we accept the fact that he is finished, that this is the end of him on his own decision. Hadn't that been the way always? From the time when the first man had built a hut on this reach of the world and when it jutted into the sea it was called *an cladach*, so that they were no different really from all the thousands who had gone before them; and Gran was not the first old man to find he had been sapped by the sea and that he would have to leave it, not because he was so old, but because the sea was younger than himself. Like accepting the fact that a boat was a boat and that a sail was a sail and that it had always been like that, that the sea would take you and use you and you would be finished but the sea would be eternal.

It will be quare all right, Big Micil was thinking, to be without Gran. Think of the boat now without him there at the tail! It didn't seem right. He would miss him out of it. He would miss him very much. Sometimes they had been in tight corners. Big Micil was a very strong man and he knew it, but there were times when his strength would have been useless without the cold brain of his father, or the flick of a knowledgeable wrist on the tiller. Days when he would raise his face to the breeze on the quayside and say, We better not go out today, min, there's rain on the wind. And when he said that it was true, because you were sure to get a gale that would have made matchwood of the sturdiest ships to be caught out in it. Always right, he was, to the fraction. And men listened to him, and God knows it was time for his father to get a rest; to warm his oul feet at the ashes of the fire and to take it aisy. He had deserved it. Micil couldn't see into all the intricacies of the situation at all. He lacked ambition. The one great spurt he had made, he made when he courted and won Delia when she was a grand rosy-cheeked country girl who came to work as a servant in the big house on the hill, way up beyond the town, standing surrounded by trees and quiet grounds. He swept the board then. Ha-ha, many a young twirk's eye he wiped when he won Delia. She was a great woman, even though his father didn't get on with her and never had, but then sure, he told himself, sure no woman's father-in-law ever got on with her and they would get to know one another better when Gran had retired.

Gran ran his eyes over the lines of the boat. The way she curved up a bit at the bow, the steady way the tapered mast rose and the belly of the sail eddying out from it. The fine broad lines of her and she as safe and as solid as a house. Built by men who knew the secret of her.

"'Twill be the oul boat I'll be missin' most," he said, out loud. "Let ye be not abusin' her. She's like a woman, so she is, and you have to ride her gentle. That oul bitch under us now knows more about Galway Bay than the Man that made it almost. That's true. If ye left her out at the Islands on her own, as true as God she'd find her way home again."

He bent over the side with his free hand and slapped the overlapping tarred strips that made her. "As sound as a grown man she is, and getting better with every year. There isn't a whisper of a bad board in the length and breadth of her."

"She's a good boat," said Micil, nodding his head judiciously.

"Aye, she's nice enough," said Mico, rubbing his palm on

the rough boards of the hatch.

The seagulls swung screaming over them, darting and passing, sweeping low, going mad at the sight of the loose fish in her hold. Over the other boats too, all the ten of them you could see, there was hovering a cloud of gulls, flashing white and black and a touch of red, and she rose a little and fell a little, ponderously, and out from her bow they saw the white Lighthouse in the distance and behind it the concealed glow of the risen sun. They saw the low cliffs on their left and then the long road bordering the sea that led to the town. And there the town was, looking nice enough in the early morning, and in the far distance you could see two or three of the white Claddagh houses before the accursed Swamp wall cut them off from your sight. And on their right side the bleak stone-littered hills of Clare with verdant towns at their ends – just like small towns that had been built as toys by a child.

"Here's the oul Aran boat pulling out," said Mico.

She came from behind the Lighthouse, black smoke belching from her stack, puffing as importantly as a great liner, bubbling in her belly, and all she could get out of it was five or six knots.

"Oh, the dirty things!" said Gran. "Look at the dirty oul smoke from her. Like an oul duck with an iron interior."

"If we had that one for the fishin' now," said Mico, "we could go as far as Iceland near for the cod."

"Ye'd get to Iceland quicker in this beauty," said Gran. "Rattle the bowels outa yeh, that stinker would. Look at her. Heavin' up and down like a bad stomach."

"Ah, Gran," said Mico, laughing, "some day maybe you'd have a good word to say for an engine."

"To hell with them," said Gran. "They're agin nature so they are. Ugly black bitches with filth comin' outa them. Look at the way that oul yoke is dirtying up the sky."

The seagulls followed the wake of the steamer and it headed like a plunging mule for the oncoming fishing boats, plodding placidly on with their taut sails a terrible contrast to the rusty steel plates and the belching smoke.

It passed them by. One or two sailors pausing to wave a hand, and the man on the bridge pulling at the whistle. A derisive greeting to the tired men of yesterday.

"And the same to you," said Gran in answer.

There were some passengers up in the bow and they looked curiously at the patient men who sat in their boats. Maybe they even thought for a second that it would be grand to be a fisherman, you did nothing at all, just sat on your behind all day dreaming while a sail pushed you over the water. Couldn't get near enough to see the scum and the scales and the beards and the tired eyes and the relaxed limbs.

At the back a flash of red. On the steamer. What's that now? Mico wondered, idly raising himself, but then it was gone in the moving of the bodies and soon the steamer was behind them and they were heading in past the Lighthouse and swinging left into the channel.

The tide was in.

They went in by the docks and then turned into the river, taking a wide sweep across with the wind on their port side to avoid a tack. Mico stood up and took a pull on the sail-rope, and when they had cleared the main flow of the river he let it go, while Big Micil gathered its folds into his strong arms. The impetus of the last sail carried them close to the quay wall. Mico held it off with his hands, strained with his great shoulders, and took her to the steps. He took the mooring rope in his hand and jumped and scrambled up and hitched it to the bollard.

They were home.

He stood on the grass above and placed his palms on his back to straighten the creaks out of it, stamped his feet, licked his salt-cracked lips and looked about him. People were slowly coming from the cottages. Some of the doors were open and blue smoke was rising from the chimneys. Won't it be grand now to get a cup of strong tea with sugar and fresh bread? They set to then and cleared the boat of the boxes of fish; piled them on the quayside ready for the handcarts or pony carts or trucks of the fish men to come and bring them away, heaved out the net and stretched it on the grass in a great length, tidied their gear and raised it on their shoulders and backs and arms, and turned to go.

"Are you coming, Gran?" Mico asked, bending over to shout down to the old man, who was still sitting in the stern.

"I'll be up after ye," said Gran.

Mico looked at his father, and Micil looked at him, and then Micil nodded his head and they turned to go.

"We'll keep the pot hot for you," said Mico, and then walked beside his father. Tired now that their feet were on land; conscious of a sick hungry feeling in the pit of their stomachs; longing for a pint of porter to clear the salt and the fish out of their throats, and thinking of the small hunched figure in the back of the boat.

Mico tried to whistle but it was a failure.

He dropped his gear outside their door, from which was coming the heat of the fire and the smell of frying bacon that would bring water to the mouth of a Mahommedan.

"I'll just go up the road to give Biddy these," he said.

"All right," said Micil, and went in wearily, saying, "Well, Delia, here we are at last."

Mico went past his own house, the hank of fish swinging in his hand. He turned and looked back once, but there was no sight of Gran to be seen. Mico had a picture of him still hunched there in the bottom of the boat, sucking at an empty pipe. He sometimes did that. He thought of a day many years ago when he was very small and he had stood on the quayside and seen his father and Gran put out to sea. Times had changed, hadn't they? And yet nothing else can change. The sea doesn't change or the river running into it, or the granite on the quay walls. It's terrible that men grow old. Isn't it a great wonder that when God made man at all, he didn't make him to outlive inanimate things like granite?

Biddy was hunched over a small fire, on her knees, blowing it into a small ineffective flame.

"I brought you a few fish, Biddy," he said, going in to her.

"Ah, God bless you, amac," she said, rising awkwardly and sitting back on to a low stool, the tears from the smoke pouring out of her rheumy old eyes. "God bless you. It's few of ye now think of poor Biddy Bee. Let me starve, they would, the creatures."

He got down on his knees and blew at the fire and it flamed. Her kitchen was very dirty. She was very old. She was very dirty. Christ, hope I will never be left like this, he prayed, when I am old. Remember Biddy. Herself and her gander that would frighten the heart out of a saint. And here she was now, growing so old that life was meaning nothing to her but a sort of jumble of childish thoughts and muttered obscenity. A bed in the corner turned back. She slept as she dressed and the years of dirt clung to her. Sometimes the valiant women who came down to the poor descended on her like locusts, and they washed her floor and they washed her clothes and they washed herself. Determined women who did these obnoxious things in the name of God. And they would have to close the door of the house to stop the flow of language getting into the green. All the town gathered outside listened while they stripped her and cleaned her, and you'd hear her out in the Aran Islands calling them for the lot of snobby bitches that they were, comin' down in their furs and upsettin' an old woman like her, and if they think they will get to heaven be that hole-and-corner way, rubbin' red raw the skin oo an honest woman, they had another think comin', buried in hell they'd be with the devil pourin' carbolic on them while she'd be up above in her white nightdress on the right hand a God, pccin' on them from a height, the filthy things. Who asked them to come here? Why couldn't they leave her alone? Let them go home and scrub their lousy childer and their poor bits a men that was out whorin' and drinkin' all over the town while they were down here tryin' t' save their souls be half murderin' a poor oul woman that never did nobody a bad turn in their lives.

"Now, Biddy," he said. "It's goin' fine. Have ye water in? Will I get yeh some from the pump?"

"I have water enough, amac," she said. "Too much water, but little I have that goes with it. I was as tall and straight as a young mast, so I was, and me lips were as red as a petticoat, and there wasn't a young man in the whole a West Connacht that wouldn't ha' hurled me if he got the chance, but they took my love away, love, and left only me" (she was crooning the last bit, a sort of a poem that she had made up, he thought). "We used t' ha' dances at the crossroads then and I was like a goat, so I was, that I could lepp higher than the tip of a ship. Ah, and the twirl I'd do, and all the fine men that were after me because me teeth were like marble, they were that white, like the cloths that does be out on the altar. All gone, love, all gone, even me lovely geese. Nothing left now but them oul bitches that come scaldin' the life outa me with their charity. A hole they should give me, a hole in the ground, and lave me alone, lave me alone, love."

"I'll be off now, Biddy," he said.

"God bless you, God bless you, God bless you," she said, bending over her kettle. "You're a good boy, Mico, Mico, even though you near kilt one a me geese. Ah, well I remember. Sometimes I can remember well and sometimes I can't remember as well as I'd want to remember. Goodbye, goodbye, and close the dure after yeh. Nobody can ate bite or sup in this place with snotty noses stickin' their heads around the door to see what you are havin' for your breakfast."

He closed the door after him and walked away, her mumbling following him. Why should I be getting so many reminders today? he wondered. Biddy would die, and when she did they would pull down the decaying thatch of her cottage and they would level the walls so that the row would look like teeth with one pulled out. They were talking already. We must destroy the Claddagh and give them houses fit to live in. Biddy would be first. They would wait for her to die and then lepp and destroy her house that had been there since the beginning of time near. Maybe 'twas as well. Maybe it would be good to have a new Claddagh.

"Oh, Mico, Mico!" he heard the call and raised his head. To his surprise he saw Jo running across the grass to him. He waited for her.

"Mico," she asked, breathless, "have you seen Peter? Where's Peter?"

Mico's heart went into his boots.

Chapter Eleven

H ER EYES WERE wide and frightened. He put his hand on her shoulder and he could feel her trembling under his palm. Her hair was tossed and he could see the white of her face under the flush of her running. She was wearing a blue coat, the belt of it tied in a knot.

"What's wrong, Jo?" he asked. "How could I see him? I'm only after gettin' in now."

"Oh, my God," she said slumping, "and I thought he might be with you. You were my last chance. Now I don't know where to look."

"What happened, Jo?" he asked her urgently.

"Well, you know the way he has been," she said. Mico nodded, not able to keep the pain out of his eyes.

"He was to meet me last night at eight," she said. "I waited and waited and he never came. Then I went over to his house. He hadn't been home at all. So I waited there a while, just talking, to put them off. And he hadn't come, so I went home. And he never came home. I was down there this morning. They had waited up all night for him. He hadn't come home. So his father took the car and went one way and I came out on my own. I've been everywhere, everywhere that I could ever think of that he might be, and

I can't find him. What are we going to do, Mico, what are we going to do?"

"We'll look again," said Mico. "Come on." He took her arm and turned and walked by Biddy's house and headed out for the road that led by the sea. "We'll just have to think again. Maybe you passed him. Maybe he was one place when you were another and ye just missed."

"I don't know," she said. "I just don't know now, Mico," her head falling down and her hands in her pockets. There was little he could do to comfort her. He was too tired. His heart was heavy enough as it was without having to jump into this. But jump into it he would have to do. Because something was terribly wrong with Peter.

It was like something that grew.

It was fun when he was in hospital. Going up to see him, feeling foolish being so big and a small bag of oranges under your arm. He'd be lying up in the bed, a white bandage around his head, his skin very clear. "That's the bagpipes, Mico, oul son," he'd say, and then explain the repulsive details of how they scoured you like a hose working on the insides of a ship. They were very fond of him. He got many presents of things but he always gave them away. There were two rows of beds in the ward and they were all lying there, men and boys with all sorts of diseases and broken bones. But they liked Peter. You could tell that from the smiles in their eyes. He'd make a cat laugh, they said, and the nurses weren't backwards about liking him either, and the doctor that did the marvellous operation on his head came to beam on him, nearly patting his head. "I'm his favourite operation," Peter would explain to them. Laugh. It was a great laugh.

And they brought him home and it was like a bonfire night. All the neighbours and friends were there. "Hah," said Peter, "if I wasn't here now this would be a magnificent wake," and he looked exactly the same, except that he was a bit thinner and finer drawn, that was all. He was active as ever. Only a few blinding headaches he'd get, and when he got them he'd go up to his room and shut the door and swallow aspirin tablets and come out again pale and drawn with purple under his eyes, but that was all. In a short time he would be as right as rain.

And it was summertime, so he could lie in the sun. And go swimming. He went up the lake often too with Mico pulling the boat, and they swam up there and caught trout and cooked them in wet newspapers in the hot ashes of the wood fire. It was grand. And he loved Jo. They had never been as nice to each other as they were then, and that was something to remember. He became brown and fit-looking and the headaches, he said, weren't as bad at all now when they came. And it was a pity about missing his exams, but it couldn't be helped. Next year. Or maybe in the autumn he'd have a crack at them. It was great to know Tommy had got his. First knobs all the way. Several prizes and things for this and that. First places in everything, so that the professors were going around rubbing their hands and proud of him. "Good job for him I got the knocker," said Peter, "or he'd have had a run for his money"; laughing.

And Jo got through too, very distinguished. So now she was finished with College and she was going to teach. Where? She didn't know. But she would teach. "How could you?" Peter wanted to know. "I love teaching," she said. "I love children." "Don't be giving me bad ideas now." And she would get prim and he would have to soften her up again.

Oh, grand!

It was Jo who noticed his oddities then. She would be talking to him about something. You know the way you are talking away to a person and you don't look at them at all. Most of us are that way. And suddenly she would be conscious of a terrible silence and her words would trail away and she would look at him and his eyes would be fixed on something distant and his teeth would be clenched and the knuckles of his hands would be white and she would shake his arm and say, "Peter, did you hear me? Peter! Did you hear what I was telling you?" And the first time she shook him like that she felt his arm rigid and he didn't hear her. And she got very frightened, because people don't go away like that for no reason, and she got to her knees and shook him again and called in his ear, "Peter! Peter!" and after a little the glazed look left his eyes, and his teeth unclenched themselves, and he looked at her and said, "Yes, yes, Jo, what is it? What's this you were saying?"

If only she could have explained then! Maybe she should have told him then, and about how frightened she was so that she felt the blood drained out of her face. But she didn't, because he looked so pale himself and there were purple shadows under his eyes, and he let his head drop in his hands, and he said, "Oh, Lord, Jo, I have a pain in my head."

Then other times it was more frightening.

Because it would happen to him, the tenseness and the silence, and he would come back to her, maybe after ten minutes, and he would have no headache at all. But he would not remember that he had been away, and that was what sent the cold shivers up her back and the fear buried deep into her heart. She said, "What was wrong with you?" "With me?" he asked. "What's wrong with you to be asking questions like that? What's holding up the conversation?" and it only began to dawn on her then that when he went away like that he didn't know it. So she went to the doctor, and the doctor called around to him and kidded him into going back to the hospital for an X-ray to clear up the headaches, and he went and they took their pictures of his brain and they looked at them and they could see nothing wrong. "It will pass, my dear," they said to her, "it will pass," and patted her hand. After all, if you got a blow on the head like he got you'd be a dead duck long ago. He had a heart like a lion and a head like a six-foot wall.

Mico noticed him worse, the first time.

They were going out Salthill on a summer evening, when Jo was in the middle of her exam and wasn't seeing even Peter.

You know what happens to a town on the sea in the summer. It changes very much. People from other parts of the country who don't have the sea come and see the sea, and people from other lands curious about this one come and see it too. All seaside places are like that. Well, this one was no different. People thronged its walks and paths and roads in the summer so that you could hardly breathe or see the sea, but it was lively and all along by the promenade they strung fairy lights on the poles, and in a big field they brought crazy things, swinging boats and men barking and games, and there was blaring music and the lapping of the sea and crowds and crowds of people, young people and old people, with all sorts of most peculiar dress on them and red faces and brown faces and peeling faces. And Mico and he walked one night out here to view the throng, and they pushed their way into the park where the games and things were, and they went from one to the other with their hands in their pockets just watching, and the music from the loudspeakers was very loud, and Mico saw Peter putting his hand up to his head, so he caught him by the arm and pulled him away through the crowds and out of the field and on to the wide promenade in front of the sea. Out here there was a long seat and people sitting on it, and people leaning on the wall looking into the field, and other people passing, and others just idling, and Peter pulled his hand away from his head and his arm from Mico's hand and he stood out in the middle of the road and he talked. In a loud voice. So that people stopped and looked at him.

Mico felt the sweat in the crooks of his legs and on his face. It poured down his face. The circle of grinning people cut him off from Peter, he was so petrified with the surprise of it. Strangers that were grinning there at the young man in the neat grey suit, the red tie, and the white shirt, with a high polish on his shoes. Was he drunk or what? "You know nothing, you idiots," Peter told them, his fists clenched until the white showed on his knuckles. "You don't know that when the magnet is deflected, having been suspended in the earth's field by another magnetic field, the direction of which is perpendicular to that of the earth, the deflecting force is proportional to the angle of the deflection. I bet you don't know that, you stupid idiots."

Mico had reached him then.

Had taken him into his arms and practically lifted him up, and his body was as rigid as the body of a dead fish, and around the corner from here there was a quiet lane where couples went to court after they had clicked, and he went down this lane with him and he didn't stop until the lights were well behind them and he could no longer see the curious heads of the people pushed over the wall.

There were other things too.

The day of the fair in the Square.

Jo had spent a solid hour in the church praying for Peter. Then she went up the town and was passing through the fair and she saw a circle of people and she was impelled to go over, and there was Peter in the centre with his shoes encrusted with dung and an old ragged street merchant without a shirt standing behind grinning, and there was Peter marching around in that circle of farmers and potboys and tinkers and he playing the man's tin whistle for all he was worth. He wasn't playing it. He was puffing out his cheeks and the noises that were emanating from the piece of tin were half sobs from his drooling mouth and half the plaintive wail of the tin.

She went in and took his arm and took the thing from his mouth and handed back the whistle to the man, and they made an opening for her in the sudden hush that had fallen on the cheers and the jeers and the drunken hurroos, and she walked him out and he was talking, many things mixed up. She brought him down where the river flowed cleanly beside tall trees and she sat down there with him, and the tears pouring down her cheeks and the despair in her heart until she saw the reason coming back into his eyes and he looked at her and said, "Why, Jo, old dear, what are we doing here?"

They thought of all this now as they walked the road.

It was not pleasant thinking.

"And the worst of it is," said Jo, suddenly breaking their silence, and first having to clear her throat before the words would come clear, "the worst of it is that I think he knows."

"What do you mean?" Mico asked.

"When he has come out of them lately I have seen him looking at me in the strangest way, trying to gauge from my eyes; trying to see in them what was wrong."

They went all the way along by the sea out past the houses and the cultivated seashore, with its sands and rocks tastefully laid out for the tourists. All along the miles-long promenade and the diving-place at the end of it, and they left this civilization behind them and they walked the lonely beaches as well, where wild duck rose and fled away and the grazing cattle looked at them inquisitively. And they searched the lonely places under the low cliffs and they came on nobody that they were looking for. Sometimes they stood with their hearts pounding when here and there they caught a glimpse of red hair on a lonely strand or on a beach or high up, reclining on the side of a steep hill, and they approached only to be disappointed.

And they swung wide from the sea and did the great circle of land around the town where Peter had often walked with Jo. Up on the bog road by the Barna village into the bleak land around Lough Inch, past the white monument in a bog to the memory of a murdered priest, and on the hills over the flint roads into the lonely lands of the bogs, thinking that maybe he would have come back here to be alone and to be thinking. But not even the ghost of him walked there, and they went on, tired and dusty and hopeless, and they came back in a swing to the town, past the Rahoon graveyard with its cypress trees, and all the ass carts and horses carts coming back home again with their empty rattling milk churns.

They even went to the island of the thorn tree and stood on the shore and scrutinized it from there. The tide was in so that they couldn't cross into it, and they were glad, and anyhow it was easy to see that there was nobody there, so they turned and crossed the railway line and went into the wood.

Peter often frequented these woods. He would ride out there on his bicycle or pinch his father's car, and study when the mood came on him. It was very lonely. Nothing but the sough of the trees and the scampering of blackbirds through the bushes or the scolding of the birds. Underfoot the decaying vegetation giving off a smell of all sorts of seeds and herbs. Your feet cushioned by the carpets of leaves, year after year of them, layer laid over layer. But it was as bare as the sky on a clear day and nothing disturbed it except those things that belonged to it, with the rabbits abounding.

So they walked back again and there was a confession of failure in the droop of their bodies. Their thoughts were not sharp, because the day's thoughts and searchings had blunted them, so that they had little to talk about. What could you talk about? Eventually they sat on one of the seats that fronted the sea overlooking the Bay on the Grattan road, when they had been back to the Cusacks and had drunk tea in the kitchen and felt their hearts sinking when they looked at the red eyes of the mother and the bewildered hurt look of the father.

The sky was blazing when Mico saw the smoke in the distance pouring from the funnel of the little Aran steamer, chugging its way home as importantly as ever, the black smoke belching from it with the sun going down at the back of it, dying in the sea between the Clare hills and the Islands.

Jo felt her arm being grasped so hard by Mico's hand that she had to pull in her breath with the pain of it.

"That's it!" said Mico, "as sure as God."

"What, Mico?" she asked, holding her bruised arm.

"The boat," said Mico, pointing with his arm, standing up, his legs spread wide. "He was on that boat, I know he was on that boat. I should have remembered. This morning coming home. There were people on it and a flash of something red in the early morning. I'll swear me solemn oath that he was on that boat."

"Come on," she said, not pausing but running towards the Claddagh.

He followed her and caught up with her easily. The boat was bigger now, nosing its way in past the Lighthouse.

If only I hadn't been so tired this morning, he chided himself. If I hadn't been thinking of Gran and all the rest of it I might have looked closer.

"He just went out there for the day. There's where he'd get the places to think it over without a soul near him, only the people in the island of America. That's it now," he said. "We'll get him on the boat."

They went fast, past the Claddagh, and their hearts were much lighter. Jo even felt like a smile. They talked about all the walking they had done and all the searching. How many miles! The poor feet of me, said Mico, that hate walking worse than anything else in the world near. And the people we saw and all the rest of it, and we would have been better employed at home doing nothing at all, just waiting for him to come back.

They raced down the Long Walk when they crossed the bridge, and Mico's thoughts flashed back over the years to a day when they had been fishing for mackerel and they had to fight their way past the boys in the Spanish Arch. He grinned, remembering it, and how Peter with his socks and neat clothes had behaved, and the way they were rescued by Pa.

It was a close run but they beat the boat to the docks, just when it was pulling into its own dock, looking very big there so that you wondered how it could have looked so small and fussy outside. Important calls and throwing of ropes, and water pouring from the side of her, and then she was there and they searched the ship from end to end with their eyes, and the people who were on her, but they didn't see Peter.

They waited until the last heifer and the last squealing pig and the last bale and the last man had swung ashore.

But Peter wasn't there.

Mico talked to the men of the ship.

Let me see now, a tallish fella with red hair. A call to someone else – Here, did you see this fella they want? Was it this morning? Aye. A tallish fella with red hair. Aye. Well, now, let me see. Oh yes indeed, a tall fella with red hair and a grey suit and a red tie. That him? Yes, that's him. Indeed yes, came aboard this mornin' when we were pullin' away. Stood there on the stern all the time. Went up above once and took a return ticket but he didn't come back. He didn't come back? No, nice polite fella, too, not like some of these other unthinkin' scoundrels that'd have yeh waitin' for hours for them while they guzzled porter up in the Aran pubs. I won't be back, he says, I'll be waitin' on the island for a while. Quare it was, Jack and me talked about it. No luggage. Oh, remember him well now. He had no luggage, Jack? No, no luggage. We says what's he goin' to do on the island without no luggage? Not even to sleep in. Ah, well, don't suppose the Aran fellas sleep in anythin' but their shirt so he'll be all right too. Laugh at that. No, he came but he didn't come back, and if you think we're going back again now to fetch him, you have to think again. They laughed at that. It was good fun.

Mico and Jo walked away from the boat, and they had a picture of Peter on the island and they didn't know what to think. They wouldn't know now until the boat went again in a few days and he'd come back on her.

Chapter Twelve

LACED ACROSS THE mouth of Galway Bay there are three islands called the Islands of Aran – the Big, Middle, and South. They stretch in a long ragged line almost from the coast of Connemara to the Cliffs of Moher in Clare. Obviously long ago they were not islands, but were part of the mainland, and they might have been called Galway. But the sea is a vicious enemy of land and it chewed its way in and out and in the middle and it scooped out Galway Bay so the bits that remain after its feast are the islands, and it is obvious that they must be very tough land indeed when even the inexhaustible stomach of the Atlantic Ocean could not digest them. Hard land, deceptively green in places, but nothing but pure solid rock with a thin coat of soil that grows a short grass which makes lovely mutton and grows great men. Naturally they must be strong men and hard men to be able to live at all in this bleak fastness.

You come in on the boat at the pier on the main island and when you clear out of the village of Kilronan and walk the roads up the hill to your right you will come upon good things, like yellow beaches where the sea laps gently when it is not aroused. And you can turn away from the long yellow beach and the sight of the Connemara shore away from you mistily in the distance and the currach out on the calm water with the two men bending their backs to it, or stopping to lift lobster-pots from the sea near the stones, and you climb the sloping hill, rocky and bare with green patches, with the sheep looking at you boldly and the rams very boldly, and the thin cattle, and you climb higher and higher until the breath comes short in your chest if you are not in condition and then you pause and look and you see the stone fort of Dun Aengus above your head. There it is now almost the same as it was a thousand years ago, when mythical men came from the sea and built their fort and held it against all comers. You wind your way through the *chevaux de frise*, slanted pointed rocks buried for your destruction or your delay and you cross over the medley of the outer wall of the fort. And you climb the next wall which is high and very thick, and then you get through the next ring of the circle and when you climb over here you find a lovely grassy sward in the circle of stones. Surrounded all around except for the place near the cliff where you bend over and see the crawling sea hundreds of feet below you beating whitely on the rocks with the seagulls looking very small below, and then if you raise your eyes and look you will see America if anyone wants to see it, it is over there a few thousand miles away.

Peter pulled back from the edge and stretched himself full length on the grass. The sky above him was plastered with white clouds like rough casting.

There was a great silence in the place. He had seen the bobbing tails of the rabbits his coming had disturbed and he could see the fresh dropping of the lark that had soared high indignantly and was now up in the sky fluting away at his song.

Peter's face was very pale, so pale that the freckles stood out strongly on his face. Sometimes as he had come up, thinking his mixed-up thoughts, he had seen one or two people surreptitiously blessing themselves as they passed his red hair and his white face. Maybe, he thought, it wasn't lucky to meet a red-haired man in the evening.

"Oh God, I'm so tired," he said aloud then and he threw his arms wide so that he felt the grass cool against the backs of his hands.

His clothes were crumpled. His last twenty-four hours were like a blur to him.

Where had he been? He could remember if he stopped to work it all out, but raising a thin hand now and pressing his forehead between his fingers, he felt that he didn't want to think.

It was the fact that he had found it hard to think that had first made him afraid. He, finding it hard to think, when the trouble with him was that he had so many thoughts to think that he had trouble sorting them out.

The blow on the head, he thought, must have been harder than I thought.

But he passed that off.

Until he gradually became aware that something was happening to him that he didn't know about. What was happening to him that caused that look of petrified fear and overwhelming pity in the eyes of his mother? All he knew was that he got a buzzing in his ears, a sustained buzzing, almost like an unearthly cornet sounded in a cañon, and that it went on and on and he was listening to it, and then when it stopped he saw his mother with that look in her eyes; or he saw his father with his face red and his eyes bewildered; or he saw Jo with her face stern and a mask over her eyes; or he saw Mico, big nice Mico, with his eyes as soft as the eyes of an animal that was coming to lick your hand when you had broken a leg or shot yourself with a gun.

So something is happening to me, he thought. What is it?

I get a buzzing in my ears and when it goes away people are looking at me in a peculiar way. Even people in the street, people I don't know at all, or else people I know are avoiding my eyes. Therefore that means that when I get the buzzing I must be doing or saying strange things or else people would not notice me at all or would just offer me an aspirin for the pain in my head. That's clear so far. And then he set his mind to what it must be, so that he became half aware even in the middle of the buzzing that his real self was just over his shoulder watching and taking notes on the evidence and annotating them so that they could be all segregated when the buzzing went. So that the day he had suddenly found the buzzing gone and found Jo beside him with tears in her eyes, and a crowd of strange men around him with dung encrusted boots and short whips and sticks in their hands, and the smell of cow dung everywhere with the lowing of cattle, and in his hand was a tin whistle with spittle on it, he had turned away with Jo and he had walked with her to the river and he had pretended that the buzzing was still with him, and then he had raised his head and said, "What are we doing here, Jo?" just so that she wouldn't know that he knew at last.

So he had avoided Jo, and he had watched himself closely and he had found many more things, so that he stayed close to the house and when he felt he buzzing he went up to his own room and shut the door and locked it and let whatever it liked happen to him shut away in there, and he came to himself with his mother and father knocking frantically on the door, shouting, "Let us in, Peter! Oh Peter, please let us in!" And he did and saw their faces and said, Even my room now is no good because it is the same, I always frighten them.

And the buzzing became more frequent.

So he remembered last night. It was last night, wasn't it? And Jo was coming for him and he said, Oh God don't let anything happen to me now, when Jo is coming, but God was inexorable at the breaking of His law of nature and shortly before she came the preliminary silence came on his brain that he knew so well, so he went out the back and climbed the wall and ran along the road outside until he came to the wide field he knew where no one walked. And he threw himself down on the grass there and let the buzzing come, and it must have lasted a long time because it was dawn when he came to himself. He may have been asleep with exhaustion after the other thing, but it was bright and the sheep were around him in a ring looking at him with their heads on one side like intelligent collie dogs. So he arose and staggered a little until the use of his legs and limbs came back to him and he said, No, no, this can't go on, there will have to be a solution, and he walked the sleeping town, looked at curiously by a strolling Guard to whom he spoke and said, "Lovely morning, isn't it?" and went on and why he came to the docks he didn't know, just that he went the Long Walk and recalled the day he had first met Mico, and he went to the docks and there was a sort of half answer to him, the Aran steamer with steam up prepared to put off for the islands. He remembered them well from trips he had made before and he had remembered this place where he was lying now, remembered its loneliness now when the tourist season had ended. You might be here alone for another six months and nobody would disturb you except the animals.

It was hard, on the boat. He knew them, but he had to be curt and stand-offish, thankful that he at least had the fare in his pocket.

He had seen the Claddagh boats coming home. He had seen Mico's boat. You couldn't miss Mico with the early light on his mark and his big father and the hunched old man in the stern. And he had half raised his arm before he remembered and then he had ducked and hoped that the sharp eye of Mico hadn't noticed the sudden flurry of movement.

He had fought the buzz when they were halfway across. He had gone back to the stern of the boat and had leaned over, pressing his chest against the wood and steel, pressed and pressed, saying, You must not leave here, you must stay here all the time when it comes, and he had looked into the green-white churning wake of the propeller and he had let it pass over.

It was gone when the boat was about to draw into the pier, so he shoved his hands in his pockets and muttered to one of the men about not coming back this trip, and had walked on to the stones and past the people thinking his thoughts, the sharp ones, that had been part of his everyday life until the blow had fallen.

So I'm losing my mind, he thought.

Did that matter?

"Why, oh, why, God, did it have to happen to me?" he asked the immutable sky, out loud.

So many things to do; so many things to learn; so many things to work out in my mind. So what are you going to be if you lose your mind? Don't you know? They'll shut you up in a four-storey granite building in the county and for the rest of your life you'll have heavy iron bars in front of your face and a studded door, and in your periods of sanity you will walk so far by so far, and in your lucidity you will dream great dreams that you could have made real, but they will be lost and founder like a ship at sea on the returning waves of your insanity.

There you are now, it's all as clear as a bell. You will not be a lunatic. You will be a lunatic at the behest of God but not at your own will. If my brain is taken away from me I don't want to be that.

I can see my mother, my beautiful helpless fluffy mother that brings an ache in my heart. She was like the child and I the father. Why, I often took her on my knee. And the strangled love he bore for his red-faced father, the sporty man so proud of the brains of his son, boasting about his progress while he shot duck or swung the priest at the head of a gaffed salmon or drank his pint of porter in the little smoky pub by the side of the lake. If I was fundamental now, like my lovable father, maybe I wouldn't mind you taking my mind away from me. Or if I was Mico, maybe I mightn't mind. Because Mico had the strength of ten men from some fount of wisdom that had been planted in him. And dear God, what use would I be to Jo with an impaired mind? Jo was a calm analytical citadel he had stormed with the fury of his mind.

What use is that sky to me, when there is nothing but eyes to look at it like a camera with no film inside? What use is the sea or the sky or my friends or the things I feel when I see scrawny children with the peak of hunger on their faces, or tired, worn men leaning against the Lazy Wall because men have no thought for their welfare. All these things, why should he live to be seeing them when there was nothing inside his head to fix it up? His head now would be like an empty tin can with a pea rolling in it. That for all the use it would be to him any more. They can never knew anyhow. It could have been an accident. There's always that, no matter what they say, they will never rightly know, nobody will be able to prove or disprove.

As the buzzing came back to his ears after the silence he put up his hands to his face and pressed the remaining thoughts into a small space. Not think of Jo, not think of her with her serious eyes or her eyes shut tightly when I kissed her, like making love to a saint in an off-moment; pass over her small figure with her hands held out; shut out the tears in a mother's eyes, the worry in the face of a father, and big Mico with his mark standing up to struggling and poverty and hard living like a great statue; shut out all thought, all thought for ever and ever and ever and ever – and he rolled over the edge of the cliff.

He turned over and over three times with his hands held to his head before his body hit the black stone and bounced slowly from it into the sea, and his light grey suit became black in colour as the greedy water grasped him, and a young boy who had been fishing below from the other end of the cliff face rose and shouted and then ran away shouting, leaving his long line to fall twirling and ravelling slowly to the sea, and from where his body had fallen the seagulls disturbed, rose, outraged, screaming a protest at this vulgar invasion of their domain.

The sky was very red and the sun blazed to death out over the Atlantic.

Chapter Thirteen

THE THREE OF them walked down the long hill from Rahoon.

It was a fine day and they spurned the dust of the road with their heavy boots.

Two big men and Twacky in the middle of them. And they weren't talking. They were too miserable to talk, and each of them was miserable in his own way.

Mico because, well, because. Where would he get the words to be talking about it. He was as full of it inside as a barrel would be full of rainwater. And big Padneen O Meara. Padneen was cracking up. There was no doubt about that. He had not got over the bewilderment of having struck the unintentional blow. He had gone around all the pubs so often saying the same thing about "Listen, fellas, I didn't mane it, the ball comes down ..." and they had got sick if its reiteration. No convincing him that it happened every day, in every game that was every played men had been hurt, rugby and soccer and Gaelic football and American football and hockey and ice hockey and all the rest of them. He wouldn't be consoled and the fact that Peter died the way he did only made it the worse for him. Padneen was drinking now as often as he had the money, and from a fine brute of a man with a stomach as flat as a table he was stooped a bit at the big shoulders and his eyes were bloodshot and he was rapidly acquiring a porter belly. He was dumbly miserable and the only way for him to acquire peace was to drink his thoughts away; to blind his slow mind to its thinking.

Twacky was miserable because Mico was.

Cars passed them by and young people on bicycles.

It had been a young person's funeral. Peter would have liked his funeral. The things he would say about that funeral would be nobody's business.

It meant very little to see the deep grave in Rahoon. All it meant was the sight of Jo's white face and Peter's parents.

"Famous at last," Peter would say when they covered him up. It had been a catchword of his this. "Mico," he'd say, "the only way to make your name famous in Ireland is to have it engraved on a tombstone." He said that often. You are famous now so, Peter, thought Mico, it won't be long now until you have your name on a tombstone: Peter Cusack. Aged 22 years.

He shivered as they left the graveyard behind them. He felt cold even though the sun was shining. There was so much he didn't understand; so much that he would never understand however he sent his slow mind groping for the knowledge of it all. He thought Peter stayed behind them at the gate, waiting to go back. He was afraid to turn, in case he'd see him there standing at the gate with his face pale and a wistful look in his deadened eyes, saying, "Hey, why are ye leaving me, lads, what have I done to ye? Don't go 'way. Come back and talk to me."

"We'll go in and have a drink fellas," he said, his voice hoarse.

Padneen rubbed his hand on his mouth.

"Oh God," he said, "I'd love a drink, so I would, I'd really love a drink now, so I would."

They turned into the pub before they came into their own place. It was a small pub with the big window in front covered in cobwebs and phoney bottles of whiskey. It was dark in the pub. Little light filtered in through the one dusty window. They sat on barrels and took large pints in their hands and drank deep, and there was no talk out of them. They just sat there in the gloomy pub and watched the flies licking at the spilt bits on the counter, and the big man behind the counter raising a cloth to flick them away and retiring again behind the place where he kept his cash. He was a knowledgeable man. He was like a good barber that wouldn't talk unless he felt there was a need for talk.

Mico felt empty and the porter felt good as it went down his throat and into his stomach. We will be going out tonight anyhow, he thought, and out there on the sea with all the hard work it might be easier to forget. Why in the name of God does it take me this way?

"Have another," he said rising.

"This is my twist," said Twacky, putting his half-crown on the counter.

They had another one as well, and then Mico rose to go and Twacky went with him, but Padneen stayed behind. Sometime, Mico thought as they left him, I will have to do something about Padneen. There's no future for him if he goes on this way.

Twacky tried hard as they walked towards the Claddagh. He kicked at the footpath with his big boot, his hands in his pockets.

"Don't be feelin' so bad, Mico," he said. "Sure, janey, he was awful nice, but he's gone and ... ah!"

"Poor oul Twacky," said Mico. "Ah, 'tis only that I've no talk left, Twacky, that's all. When we go out to work it'll pass."

"That's it," said Twacky. "Look, Mico, someday our oul fellas'll get old, won't they?"

"Ther's nothing surer," said Mico.

"And they'll have to be lavin' the boats to us, won't they?"

"'Tis the tradition," Mico answered,

"Well, lookit, Mico, couldn't you and me get together then and be in one big boat? Couldn't we do that, Mico?"

"We could, Twacky," said Mico, "but what about your sons? Won't you be wantin' to take one of them in with you?"

"Is it me to have sons?" said Twacky. "Lookit, I'd sooner drown meself than get married to an oul girl. Oul girls are no good, Mico. I wouldn't marry an oul girl, I tell yeh, if I was to get an ocean-goin' trawler with her."

"Well, ther's very few girls with dowries like that, Twacky," said Mico, "but maybe you'll meet a girl yet, a nice one that'll like yeh for yerself and you'd be wantin' to marry her and if that happens it stands to reason that you will have sons."

"Aw, jay, never," said Twacky. "They're all as cute as oul sharks. Smirkin' and smilin' at yeh until they have yeh trapped and then they treat yeh like you was an oul cuddy they found strayin' on the street."

"Ah, God, Twacky," said Mico, feeling a weight lifting off his heart and clapping a big hand on the other's shoulder. "Yeh have a straight simple view on women and if you stay that way the only sons you'll have'll be in your dreams, and if that's the way you are, ther's no doubt that we'll be able to get together."

"But what about you, Mico?" asked Twacky. "Will you marry a girl maybe?"

"Ther's not much sign of it, Twacky, I'm afraid," said Mico. "Unless I get a rale oul crow of a wan altogether. None a the young wans'd look at a face like mine."

"What's wrong with your face?" asked Twacky, getting excited. "There's nothing wrong with your face. Nobody'd notice your face."

"Ah, Twacky," said Mico, "we're gettin' all mixed up in this argument and 'tis only time will settle it for us. If we're not captured and the sons don't come to 's we'll get together. Will ye be doin' the Sound tonight or will ye be beatin' over the Ballyvaughan?"

"I dunno," said Twacky, "but sure we'll see ye. We'll know before we push off, when oul Gran smells the wind for us."

"I'll see yeh then so," said Mico, parting from him as Twacky turned to go up to his house.

He didn't look back and Twacky stood there for some time looking after him, his eyes quiet and serious. I med him laugh a bit anyhow, he thought then, even though 'twas hard for me to do it. He waited until he had turned the gable-end of the house in his own row and then he put his hands in his pockets and went towards his own house, and even before he got quite near it he could hear the shrill voice of his mother giving out the pay. He could see her thin face and the hair straggling across her forehead as she bent over the fire to get the things on to the table for the dinner. And he could see his father, the quiet man, sitting in the corner with his thoughts far away, letting her shrillness go in one ear and out the other while he thought of pleasant things. "Yap, yap, yap, yap," said Twacky just before he put his hand on the half-door, and then he went in, accurately throwing his cap at the peg over the far table and saying in a loud belligerent voice, "Is the dinner ready? Hey, Ma, is the dinner ready?" She quietened immediately, and gave him her attention. That's the way, Twacky thought, as he pulled in a chair to the table, roar at them, demand things offa them and you have them eating out of your hand. He winked at his father and rubbed his hands together. His mother went to the door and in a shrill voice that would give the dead convulsions she started to call Twacky's brothers and sisters into their meal.

Mico smelled the scallions frying before he got to the door. It would be fried bacon and scallions today. He could see them on the pan before he went in at all. He liked the look of them. Terrible, he thought, how I can eat even after where I have been. It's because I'm so big, I suppose. It doesn't mean any offence to Peter.

He went in.

His mother was bending over the pan. Tommy was at the table in the seat under the window that was once his father's seat always, until Tommy explained how he had to have the light of the window to study his books, even at his meals. He had so much to learn, he had to be at it always or he'd never get through. So Micil had taken a back seat with a laugh. It was all one to Micil. A table was only a place on which you rested plates from which you ate your food. Micil was sitting on the far side of the fire now, with one foot up on his knee and his arms around the back of the chair and his fingers joined. He was looking at Mico, examining his face a little anxiously. Gran was heard up in the room.

The three of them looked up as he came in. He met their eyes and then took off his short coat and hung it behind the door and sat in a chair at the opposite end of the table to Tommy. Tommy's eyes went back to a thick tome that he was holding over his place at the table. There was a silence then except for the sizzling of the bacon and the scallions. He knew they had been talking before he came in, that they had stopped when they heard his feet on the stones outside. He didn't mind.

"You weren't at the funeral," he said to Tommy, just quietly.

Tommy looked up, his eyebrows raised.

"No," he said, "I wasn't."

"Nearly all the students were at the funeral," said Mico.

"Well, they were probably friends of his," said Tommy.

"I see," said Mico, and lapsed into silence. So much he could say, but what was the use? He felt his neck getting red. Here now, he said to his mind, ther's no use venting your hurt on Tommy.

"It's ready now," said Delia, carrying one of the hot plates to the table with her apron protecting her fingers from the heat of it. She placed the plate in front of Tommy. "Come on over to your dinner, Micil," she said then, and to Mico, "Tell your grandfather his dinner is ready." Mico bent back and shouted at the closed door, "Hey, Gran, the dinner!" He turned back to the table again and took up his knife and fork. Micil brought his bulk over beside him and sat down. The table had been pulled out from the window so that there were two seats on the far side. Micil had this near side to himself. He was so big he wanted it. Gran and Delia sat together. They were the smallest.

Gran came down from the room and silently took his place. He rested a hand on Mico's shoulder as he passed him.

"It was a good funeral, Mico?" he asked as he sat down.

"It was a good funeral, Gran," said Mico. "There were a lot of people. He had a lot of friends."

"Humpf!" said Gran.

"He was very young," said Micil. "He was young to die."

"What is it," said Gran, "isn't he only dead?"

They looked at him.

"What's dyin'?" he asked them. "We have a short time. How short a time we have when you look at a stone, even wan that the sea is reducin' for years! How many years does it take the sea to reduce a rock to a pebble? Very long. And yet it's very short when you think of the age of the moon and the sun. Very short. Why, even a boat that's made from timber that can rot from the sea, even a boat has a longer life than a man. That's true, Micil, isn't it? God likes men young."

"That's true enough, Father," said Micil, spearing a steaming potato that Delia turned out from a pot into the centre of the table.

Tommy raised his voice then.

"Well, I hope God likes young Communists," he said, "because that's what he'll get in Cusack."

The three faces rose from their plates and looked at him, so that he moved a little uncomfortably, even got a little red.

Gran went on speaking as if he had not stopped at all.

"Up there," he said, "it must be a quare place if there isn't some young people in it as well as the old ones. It'd be like livin' down in the poor-house in Loughrea to be stuck in any place with oney all oul fellas with long whiskers. So it has to be a careful selection so that ther's a happy mixture."

"Well, in my opinion he was tending towards Communism," said Tommy in a loud voice. "His views were very extra-

ordinary. Nothing at all about this country satisfied him."
Who are these anyhow, he was thinking, that they should try
to silence me? When I think of how little they know.

"I'm telling you," he said, lecturing them with the fork,
"that it was maybe as well for Cusack that he went the way
he did. He was too mixed up. His thoughts were on the
wrong track. He had a weakness of delineation that was
bound to affect him for the worse in the end. I knew from
the first day I met him that there was a kink in him. I knew
there was something wrong. His eyes were strangely restless
and his body could never be still. There wasn't a nerve of
him that wasn't jumping from morning to night. I knew then
that he was unstable, but it shows a great lack of thought
and balance that he should have committed *felo de se* in the
end. There's no greatness about throwing yourself over a
cliff. That's cowardice, and if you are trying to tell me that
God is on the threshold of heaven waiting to welcome
Cusack into the gates with open arms, then you'll just have
to swing away on another tack."

Delia screamed.

"Micil!" she screamed. "Stop him!"

Mico was bending over the table in a crouch. His long arm
had reached for Tommy's coat and had caught it in his fingers and he pulled him to his feet and drew out his other
clenched hand to beat him in the face with it. His face was
pale and his eyes were red. Micil stretched a hand and
wrapped it around the striking arm but he only deflected the
blow. It struck Tommy on the side of the head and he went
back bringing the chair with his legs and he lay down there
looking up petrified with fear, his head against the white
wall. Mico was on his feet straining against the arms of his
father, and Gran was holding him on the other side. Words
came through his clenched teeth. His mind was slow and the
words were fast and almost incoherent.

"You gramophone," he was saying. "You're oney a gramophone. You get things into your head, other men's thoughts,
and you learn them and somebody puts on the record and

you go yah, yah, yah. Peter, Peter, Peter, what was he made his own thoughts. Not other men's thoughts. You yellow bastard, you! You aren't a third the man he was. Not a third the man he was."

"Shut up!" said Delia, suddenly reaching him and hitting him across the face. "Shut up, you ape, you great ape, shut up!"

The wild look went from his eyes. He straightened himself and looked at her.

"All right," he said. "Sorry I hit him. Didn't mean to hit. He shouldn't say things like that. Peter was bigger than that."

"Because you're jealous," she said, "because your brother was born with a brain so that he could be something instead of a stupid fisherman."

"No, that wasn't why," said Mico wearily.

"Oh, yes, I know," she said.

"Delia, Delia," said Micil, shushing her.

"I've felt it in here," she said, hitting her chest with her clenched fist. "I've seen him looking at Tommy. I've seen him fingering his books and flippin' the pages of them. I've seen him measuring Tommy's clothes against himself. Is it Tommy's fault that he was born with brains?"

"I'll go down to the boat, Father," said Mico; "I'll wait for ye there."

He reached for his coat and went out of the door.

"It's all your fault," Delia said then to Gran, who was sitting back at the table eating a potato. "If it wasn't for you it wouldn't have happened."

"Hah," said Gran, "you can blame all now but the right one. Yeh can't see the fault that lies at all with your genius. Blame me away, woman. Devil a hair I care. All I'm sorry for is that he didn't get a proper puck at him. And I better go now before you start in proper and I'll see you down at the boat, Micil. Another mouthful a the food in this house'd stick in me craw like a stone in the gobble of a turkey." And it got him out of the door.

"Are you all right, Tommy?" she asked, turning back to him. He was standing beside the fire rubbing his head. "He didn't hurt you, dear, did he? He didn't hurt you?"

"Ah, for God's sake," said Micil, "he oney gave him a push."

She turned back on him.

"Always, Micil, always you have taken his part. Why? Because no one on earth is useful accordin' to you unless he is able to soil his hands with the fishin'? Is that it? Tell me, is that it?"

"Dammit, woman," said Micil, his face red, "that's not true. I'm proud a both me sons. I am indeed. I like me son to have brains. But Mico is like me. I can't understand Tommy. He's beyond me. I'm only a simple man. Ah, let me out of here, I say. I'm going to sea. God bless it, I say! It's the oney place in the whole world where you can have peace and quiet."

"Right you are," she said. "Run away again, Big Micil. Run away again like you run away from everything else that comes into your life. But you can't be running for ever and you will have to face it when the day comes and Mico's jealousy makes a corpse of your eldest son."

She had to lean out the door and say the last bit after him.

She leant there then for a while and let her head drop. Oh God, she said, what has come over us all at all? What had brought that Cusack boy ever in their path? Since the day Tommy had gone to the secondary school she had been doing nothing but hearing his name. On Tommy's lips or on Mico's lips when he spoke.

She turned in.

"He didn't mean it, Tommy," she found herself saying, surprisingly, because there was a corner in her that struggled to see that Mico was suffering deeply. "'Twas just that he was upset." Maybe I can feel a bit that way now, she thought, because, after all, I have done with my son what I wanted to do with him. I have pinched and scraped and worked my hands to the bone so that he should be what he is now. My job is nearly finished now and nothing can touch him any more. She looked at him. His sullen mouth looked beautiful to her. His long forehead with the fair shiny hair falling over it. His long pointed collar that went with his thin face and the broad blue tie. Why, he has things in his face that you only see in the faces of gentlemen. That's what I have made out of him.

This is the chance now, Tommy was thinking, to break away. Even at his worst Mico can provide me with a lever to do something I want to do.

"That's all right, Mother," he said, waving the incident away and straightening his tie and sitting back at the table. "Poor old Mico was intoxicated with that fellow, that's all. But it points what I was saying. I can't stay here any more. Not if I'm to get my degrees and carry on the lectureship at the same time. I'll have to get a little room on my own somewhere peaceful, somewhere in town."

"Oh, Tommy," she said, sinking down on the chair, looking old and haggard and careworn.

My mother is getting old, Tommy thought, my mother is getting terribly old. I wish she'd take better care of herself. I wonder if it would be possible to persuade her to take to wearing a hat and coat on the street instead of a shawl. Can't have chaps pointing out a shawled Claddagh woman on the street and saying, "Hey, fellas, there's Tommy's mother." But first the room. That was more important for the moment.

Mico was sitting in the boat with his head in his hands and his limbs shaking when Gran got down to him. Gran didn't go into the boat. He let his feet dangle over the wall and looked down at him, taking a pipe from his pocket and sucking at it.

"You shouldn't have lost your temper, Mico," he said.

Mico didn't look up. "I know, Gran," he said.

"It doesn't do," said Gran. "Tempers are dangerous things. Men can't afford them, Mico. They are useless things. Silence is near a worse weapon than a blow from a fist."

"If it wasn't today, I wouldn't ha' minded," said Mico, looking at his hands. "Any day but today. He never liked him. Not because I was jealous, Gran. I'm not jealous of Tommy. On me oath. I'm proud of him in a way, that we should have him in the family. But I liked Peter, I liked Peter very much. And seeing him today going under and then listening to Tommy ..."

"I know, I know," said Gran. "'Twas past bearing. I nearly hot 'm mesel. But he hasn't the brain of a rabbit despite all the brains he has. 'Twasn't worth it, Mico."

"It wasn't a mean way he died, Gran, sure it wasn't?" Mico asked, looking up for the first time.

"I don't think so," said Gran, looking at the sky. "We don't know how he died. They say he slipped. Can't you try and see him slipping, Mico?"

"I'll try, Gran," said Mico.

"That's the boy," said Gran. "It will pass, Mico. Honest to God it will pass. We are not as hurtable as most people, Mico. You hit a landsman with sorrow and he had his feet on the ground all the time. 'Tis like a lightning conductor. But when you are living your life out there on the sea, death and how you died doesn't seem to be as big or as hurtful at all. Because out there everything is so big and man is such a tiny yoke of a thing."

"Ah, well," said Mico, rising and uncoiling the rope from around the mast.

Big Micil came then. There was still some anger in his face. "Is everything aboard, Father?" he asked.

"It is indeed. Who are yeh askin' things like that from for?"

"All right, all right," said Micil. "I was oney askin'. I wasn't thinkin'." He looked down then and regarded the bent back of his young son.

"You know, Father," he said in a loud penetrating voice, "I've been thinkin'."

"Begod, that's a miracle," said Gran, "and no mistake."

"I was thinkin'," said Micil decisively, "that mesel and Mico'd take a long time over this trip. Wouldn't you think now, Father, that the fishing over in Cleggan would be very good for a change? Isn't it about time we followed the herrin' over there for a change now and called in to see Uncle James? What do you think now, Father, of that?" He pretended to ignore the face of his son looking up at him with the mouth open.

Gran looked at him too with his mouth open; even deigned to rise to his feet.

"Well, honest to Christ, Micil," he said, "I never thought you had it in you and here you've done it at last. Whatever dumb thought inspired yeh, I think yeh have the thought of a lifetime."

"Now," said Micil, a big smile on his face, warming under his father's appreciation, "what would you be thinkin' of that plan now, Mico?"

Mico looked up at him. He didn't say anything. Not for a time. "Father," he said then, slowly, "I think it's a great plan."

Micil flushed at the warmth he felt and scratched his head and bustled about. "Well, what the hell are we doin' here now so?" he wanted to know. "Isn't it time we got under sail? Won't we have two days on the job? Let us be off now. We can make Rosmuc tonight and lie up there and then get back west tomorrow."

They bustled, they activated, and it wasn't long before they swung into the flow of the river and the sail caught the wind and they turned to wave back at the small man on the quay. Well, it's no doubt, Gran was thinking, but Micil is a surprising man. He shook his head and grinned a little and then reaching into his pocket he took out the white fishing line that was wound round a stick and he unwound a bit of it and got his jar of worms from behind the bollard and with a sigh he made his way slowly to where an ancient with his hat pulled over his eyes and his finger listlessly holding a line was fishing in the river.

As Gran sat beside him with a grunt, waking him grumbling from his dozing, the black boat rounded the pier and headed bouyantly for the open bay.

Chapter Fourteen

"**H**E WILL," SAID Maeve.

"He will not," said Coimín.

"He certainly will not," said Mico.

"Well, we'll see," said Maeve.

They were walking back to Aughris to Uncle James.

It was a November night and there was a chill on it, even though the day had been remarkably fine. In fact so fine was the weather for this November that old men were racking their minds to dig out one that was as peculiarly fine as it. Cloudless blue with a sort of misted sky over, as if somebody had covered it with muslin, and at night like now there was a moon. It wasn't a big one because the hunter's moon time was gone, but it was a good respectable moon, small and businesslike, as it tried to penetrate the sky mist. You could see the road under your feet and you could see the shimmer of the calm sea on all sides, and you could hear a dog barking over in Inisboffin almost and another lonely cuddy in Omey Island answering him. Maeve was walking between them and she was holding an arm of each.

They had been surprised to see Mico. It had been worth the coming almost to have walked in and surprised them. He had found their house easy enough, because he had never forgotten them showing him where it was to be, and there it was just as they said, as if the fairies had built it in a night for them. There was a wall all around it and a small gate that Coimín had made himself and a walk up to the house with sea-shore gravel on it and the path bordered with white stones from the beach. Nice flowering bushes that were protected from the raping wind by the little hillock, and the white-faced house with red paint on the doors and window-frames and the glass blue from cleaning, with flowering pots behind and they framed by bright chintz curtains. Somehow he knew the house would be like it was exactly, inside and outside.

"My God," said Coimín, "it's Mico, and where did you come from at all, and you're as welcome as good turf weather, and, Maeve love, put down the kettle and get the pot and boil an egg."

"Ah, listen," said Mico.

"In me own house," said Coimín, "and he doesn't want to ate a bit with us."

"Oh, Mico," said Maeve, laughing and going over and hanging the kettle on the crook above the fire.

"I've been atin' in every house from Aughris to here," said Mico. "In Uncle James', and Michael Tom's, and the house of your father Tadhg, and indeed I'd want to have the two stomachs of a cow to be able to eat everywhere."

"Well, you've grown so big, Mico," said Maeve, "that I hardly knew yeh, an' a big man like you sure you'd want the stomach of a bull, not to mind a cow, to be able to support yourself, and come on in and turn and let us have a good look at you."

There was great laughing and snorting and shining in eyes, and they said, Well, now, I never would, and how did you come and what brought you and why didn't you let us know so that we could kill a calf? Ah, it was great! It raised your heart up to heaven to be there talking to them, and he told them about his father and his decision to come over.

That was two nights ago that he had been with them first.

Since then he had moved around.

The fun down at Cleggan Pier when the nights of the fishing came and all the men down regarding their boat. The Lazy Man's Boat they called it as they rallied Big Micil. Their own boats were heavy-oared boats that they pulled with great sweat and labour out four or five miles for their fishing. Look at Big Micil, they'd say, and that son of his. Oh, the lazy bees, they'd shout, sitting down on their ahs and letting an oul bit of a sail do the work for them. Sure ye don't know what fishing is. Isn't it luxury fishing ye are and isn't it a wonder ye aren't ashamed t' call yerselves min and to be goin' out in a yoke like that that does all the work for ye without ye stirring a hand. Big Micil was indignant at this slur on their manhood and pointed out with suitable language the amount of manual labour involved in the sailing boat. He cursed the daylights out of them and they adjourned to the pub and argued long into the night over the merits of the sailing boat and the oared boat, and talked about herring and mackerel and all the rest of it, and it was a great night, and Big Micil blessed the thought that had come to him and started to talk about his holiday in the country, and the next night they went fishing with the others, and they could go quicker and come quicker and go farther so that they returned with a very heavy catch of herring with which the Bay was abounding at this time, and there was more jeering and blasphemy and rejoicing in the pub afterwards.

"And do you think for a minute," Coimín's father, Tadhg wanted to know, "that Big Micil would be able to row one of our boats? Sure isn't he as soft as a woman now, with his sitting in the tail of his pleasure yacht? Sure wouldn't it break his heart now, to come out in my boat and pull at oars for seven hours of a stretch? Wouldn't he be roaring with the pain of it and wouldn't he have to stay in bed for two days afterwards?"

"Feel that!" Big Micil said to him, holding out an arm like an oak tree and bending it so that the muscle bulged against the coat. "Is that fat or isn't it? Isn't that good Claddagh sinew?" he wanted to know, "and if I go out in your boat with ye won't I be oney disgracin' ye with the power of me pullin'? There wouldn't be a man of ye able to hold up yeer heads afterwards for evermore."

"Ho-ho, listen to him, will ye, for God's sake?" the Táilliúr said, his grey moustaches creeping down the sides of his face and the thick hair growing under his eyes where he never managed to shave. "Isn't it oney braggers ever that came out of the Claddagh!"

"I've had enough a ye," Micil swore. "I'll go out with two boats. If ye tie the two of them together I'll man them be meself and row over to China."

"There's no need for that," said Tadhg. "Come out with me tomorra night and you can go with the Táilliúr the night after, and if you're not a dead duck after that at least yeh'll know what hard work means."

It was sealed on pints and curses and loud boastings. All great fun, and Mico was never to forget that evening in the pub and the fun they had with Tadhg and Coimín and the Táilliúr and Michael Tom and Peadar Cavanagh and Tommeen Tady and plenty more.

He had slipped back into the life among them as if he had grown up with them. That was the pleasure of life there, he thought, it moves so little that you can catch up with it, and that's a brave thing to say.

So tonight Big Micil was going fishing with Tadhg, and to make the space for him Coimín was coming to fish Uncle James' currach with Mico, and at the last minute here was Maeve saying that it was about time she could go fishing too, and that she would go over with them and ask Uncle James if he minded her going, and being a gentleman Uncle James would say, Of course, Maeve dear, I will be deeply honoured to have you with us.

"He'll curse like hell," said Coimín. "He doesn't give a damn who's listening and your ears'll be red be the time he's finished with yeh."

"A woman in a boat," said Mico, "is the same as if you

- 197 -

brought the devil into the boat with you. It's bad luck sure. And you know that as well as anybody and you married to a fisherman."

"Ah, ye give me a pain," said Maeve. "That's an oul fable that ye thought up in case the wife would go and see how little work is really done at sea, and so that she wouldn't be with ye when ye come home and ye could be goin' drinkin' unbeknownst to her. Oh, 'tis well I know it all."

"Well, indeed," said Coimín, "you'd be welcome to come fishing. It's only the once you'd be wishing to come, I can tell you."

"What's the use," said Maeve, "when even Mico has turned against me? It wouldn't have been that way with him, the last time he was here. Would it, Mico?"

"I didn't care then," said Mico, "I was young. I'd have let the devil in hell ride with me and not give a damn."

"Ah," she said with a sigh, "'tis a pity we all change."

"We don't change all that much," said Mico. "It doesn't seem any different to me now to be walking along with the two of ye. It doesn't seem so long as all that that we were walking down the lane after the sand-eels. That was a grand night."

"Well, imagine you not forgettin' that now, Mico," said Maeve.

"I'll always remember that," Mico assured her to the pressure of her hand on his arm and he looking down into her face with the bright eyes that was looking up at him. "I can never forget that. It was so grand."

"Aye," said Coimín, "it was a fine night."

"And Coimín didn't change a bit, Mico," said Maeve. "He's still the same oul self-satisfied one-and-tuppence that he was then."

"Haven't I cause to be smirky?" said Coimín.

"Indeed you have," said Mico with a small sigh, that passed unnoticed on the calm breath of the night. He had thought that seeing her again after all this time with children about her (why had they no child?) it would float away on a destroyed dream, the picture he had built up about her. But it didn't. The dream grew up, that's all, and it was a time he was having to stop the dull beating of his heart with the feel of her hand burning his arm, and the shame inside him when he saw the calm Coimín, that he should be nursing a feeling, however innocent, for his wife. But it was buried deep in him and any time he let it drift to the surface of his mind it was so that it might cauterize the pain he felt when he saw a body falling over and over a tall cliff, dying alone, in a bleak place with not a loving soul near.

"Me father," said Coimín, "is on to Uncle James now. Did you know that, Mico?"

"Aye," said Mico, "I heard a few words of it, but it wasn't finished."

"Well," said Coimín, "his story now is that the fame of Uncle James' beauty and wealth have spread far and wide over the Joyce Country and the province of Connacht, and that eligible young women from all parts are making a pilgrimage back to Aughris in the hopes of winning him."

Mico laughed. "Ah, go on. Does Uncle James know?"

"He's heard a few titters," said Coimín, "but he enjoys it more than anyone else although he pretends not to be talkin' to me father when they meet. 'Tis great gas to see the two of them together."

"He was tellin' me the latest saga today," said Maeve. "Last May day, he said, it's reported that there was half a mile of women lined up in Aughris waitin' to have a crack at Uncle James. Isn't it funny, Mico, how ever since you were here he has been called Uncle James?"

"Is it," said Mico, "but aren't you just like a woman! Can't you finish the story and then we can get on to something else?"

"Ah-ha, Mico is the boy for you," said Coimín, laughing.

I wish I was, thought Mico, and said, "I'm sorry for breakin' in on the story. Tell it now."

"So Uncle James pokes his head out the door at half eleven after having his breakfast and washing the dishes and baking the cake, and he says – Let the first come in now. So in comes a grand big black lassie from Clifden and he looks at her and he says, 'Can you talk?' he asks her. 'I can,' says she, showing him her teeth. 'Well, get to hell out of here so,' said Uncle James, 'because you don't suit me, and send in the next one.' She was brown-haired and she came from Costello. 'Can you talk?' asks Uncle James. 'Divil a talk,' says she, having been warned, but forgetting, and Uncle James gives her the door. The next one comes in, a buxom one from Letterfrack. 'Can you talk?' he asks, and she shakes her head from side to side. 'Ha-ha,' says Uncle James, 'that's better. Can you hear?' he asks her and she nods her head. 'Well, get to hell out of here,' says Uncle James, 'you don't suit me, and send in the next wan.' The next lassie comes in. Appears she's from Leenane and she's as fair as flax. 'Can you talk?' he asks her, and she doesn't do anything. 'Can you hear?' he asks her, and devil a stir from her. 'That sounds better,' says Uncle James, and he gets a bit of paper and he writes on it, 'Can you write?' 'I can,' she writes back to him. 'Get to hell out of here,' says Uncle James, 'for you don't suit me,' and he sends her out. In comes then a most lissom lily from Oughterard. She can't talk and she can't hear and she can't write. 'No, but,' says Uncle James, 'you can walk and you can get to hell out of here, for you don't suit me.'"

They were laughing at the way she was imitating Tadhg, the rubbing of the big hand across the moustache and the spit between each incident. And she gruffened her voice and like he did aped the accents of the women and pantomimed their goings-on.

"Had he any more?' asked Mico.

"There were more episodes," said Coimín, "but he hasn't thought them up yet."

"Here we are now," said Maeve, "and although ye won't believe me I am the only woman in the world that can get around Uncle James."

"We'll see," said Coimín, pushing the gate.

Uncle James was inside, wrapping up sandwiches in a brown parcel that would be wrapped then in the oilskin to keep the water out of them. He hadn't aged at all. His body was bent like a bow and he was wearing the same *báinín* coat that Mico knew him in seven years ago. But like all good things it had become yellower and tougher with age, and it smelled like the smoke from a turf fire. He looked up from his packing to greet them. "Ah, there ye are, ye lazy bees," he said. "I thought I'd have to be tackling the ocean on me own. 'Twas aisy known that there was a woman at the back of ye."

"Uncle James," said Maeve, coming in and facing him directly, "would you take me fishing with ye?" Uncle James looked at her wink and then regarded the two young men at the door with their faces split by grins and the look of expectation in their eyes.

"Me dear Maeve," said Uncle James, "it would give me great pleasure and honour if you would come fishing with us."

She turned back to them then. Their grins had gone and their mouths had opened into great Os of surprise.

"There ye are now," said Maeve smugly. "What did I tell ye?"

They gathered their packages and Uncle James reached for the oil lamp and took it from its nail on the wall and left it on the table and curved a big palm around the globe and blew at the palm and the wind put out the wick and they were in darkness.

They walked down the small winding lane to the field where the currach was lying up ended, and Mico and Coimín swung it on their broad shoulders and put their heads under it and walked with it to the shore. A funny sight it was, like a big black beetle with four legs and trousers on them. Maeve told them that, laughing and looking in up under at them as they walked. "Listen," Mico whispered, "how did you get around him? Tell us how did you get around him like that?"

"If you want to be talkin' to women," said Uncle James, "then meself and Coimín'll go fishin' and leave you to it."

"That's how," said Maeve.

They launched the craft beside the narrow pier that Uncle James had built in the cove near the point, and they got out the oars and hit them on the rowlocks and they stowed away the gear, and then Maeve stood back when they were seated, Mico stroking and Coimín behind him and Uncle James sitting in the stern.

"Goodbye now," she said then, "and I'll see you when ye come back."

"You're not coming?" said Mico.

"Indeed I am not," said Maeve. "Is it to bring bad luck on ye, ye want me to? I just wanted to show ye that Uncle James and meself gets on very well together."

"That's right," said Uncle James. "The only woman in the bloody country that's worth a goddam and you have to marry a halfwit like Coimín."

"There y'are now, Coimín," said Maeve. "That'll teach yeh."

Coimín put back his head and laughed. His teeth were white and you could see his throat working.

"Well, the devil is in you," said Coimín. "No man knows what to expect from you next."

Isn't that the beauty of her? Mico wanted to know, but not out loud. How lucky Coimín is! And how lucky she is too, because she has a good man. You didn't have to be long in the place before you knew how well Coimín was regarded. One of the quiet determined ones with the strength of a giant and the fortitude of a bishop. You could see that she knew that too, with the way she looked at him as the light currach went out from the pull of their arms. He felt the flag of the oars as Coimín raised a hand to her and Mico kept looking at her, standing there tall and straight on the shore until she was lost in the moon mist.

"Ah, you're a lucky man, Coimín," he said then.

"Who are yeh tellin'?" Coimín wanted to know, thinking of how grand it was when he would come home now, tired and aching from the sitting and pulling and hauling, to go to his home in the dawn and open the door and find the glow from the still live ashes of the raked fire, and a big jug of milk on the table covered with a muslin cloth. And he would drink that and eat some bread and butter, and take off his big boots and put them away and hang his socks over the crook of the fire, and then he would go up to the room and he would see her in the early light lying on the bed with her hair wild on the pillow and her arms through, out over the clothes, because she was a restless sleeper. And he would see the creamy colour of her neck and breast where her nightdress fell away, and he would put his hard hand on her, underneath her arm, just for a second, to feel the softness of it that was softer than the underside of the wet velvety seaweed. Coimín didn't care if they never had a child, he told himself. She was enough of a child for him, no matter what they said.

Mico could feel Coimín thinking behind him. It made him sad.

They are talking too, the bees, Maeve was thinking, as she went home along the moonlit road. Maybe they didn't mean to be unkind with her, but every time she met a woman she could see the eyes drifting down to her stomach or up to her breasts to see if there was anything doing. But let them talk. In good time it would come. She didn't really care. She had more now than she had ever wanted. Not much materially when you looked at it, but as long as they had their own roof and themselves what more could they want? She knew they were happy.

Oh God, she said, look after us. Don't do anything now to break all this. I even wouldn't want the child if it was to change us. Then she shook herself and whistled and lengthened her stride and turned down to her road home.

I hope to God, Coimín thought, that we will always be like this. I hope to the Lord God that nothing will ever happen to destroy it.

"Isn't that nice now, back there?" Mico asked them, leaning on his oars.

They turned the boat to the slight breeze, and it rose and fell, rose and fell lengthwise to the small innocuous waves. They were about two miles from the point. They could see the sea reaching back into Omey beach and the island bluely beside it, and then there was the stretch of water going back into Cleggan Bay and reaching over to Innisboffin. The moon was still misty, but its light was caught by the waters of the bays and was buried in them, and out from Inisboffin they could see the two rowing boats creeping, and out from Cleggan Bay came four more. They could see the oars gripping the water, in a slow calculated pulling, and the heads of the men rising over the boats. And currachs, lightly bouncing, came out of the narrows between Omey and the mainland, and soon the line of boats and currachs would be stretching for miles and the long trains of nets with bobbing cork lines would be covering miles of ocean.

"Did we come out here to work, I wonder?" Uncle James asked the moon. "Or did we come out to be like eejits lookin' at the moon? Is it any wonder that them Claddagh fellas are feckless fishermen if all they have to do when they go to sea is be lookin' at the moon?"

"Well, 'tis nice anyhow," said Mico, savagely dipping his oars, "and it wasn't the moon I meant at all, but the sight of all the boats and things, and what did you think of it, Coimín?" he asked, turning his head back to him.

"It was very nice, Mico," said Coimín, "and don't be minding that surly bastard of an uncle of yours. He has no more feelin' in him than an oul bull tha'd be spun out."

"Ho-ho," grunted Uncle James.

They laughed, and then Mico brought his head about and saw the boat that rowed silently within three currach lengths of them. Where in the name of God did that boat come from? he wondered. It wasn't there at all a minute ago. It was a rowing boat like the ones that were coming out from the bay. He could see the oars rising and falling, and he could see the backs of the men pulling, but the oars didn't splash when they hit the water, and there was no sound at all from the noise of their dipping, and six oars dipping into the water should make a noise. The bow of the boat seemed to be pushing a mist in front of it.

"Who's that in the boat behind, Coimín?" he asked.

"What boat?" Coimín wanted to know.

"There," said Mico, pointing, "over Uncle James' shoulder."

Coimín stopped rowing and leant out. It took him a little time, as if there was a mist on his eyes which he had to rub away a little, and then he saw the boat pulling a short length behind them and the oars falling soundlessly and the backs of the men.

"Who could them be?" he asked. "I don't know any of them. I can't seem to get a good look at them."

And Mico noticed a strange thing then. Even though neither himself nor Coimín was rowing, and the currach was going very slowly with the headway of the last strokes they had made, the boat behind was still pulling in the same way, the oars were still rising and falling, but it still seemed not to be able to catch up on them.

Mico felt a shiver up his back, and wondered, What's that for? Is it cold?

"Here, Uncle James," he asked, "can you make out who them are in the boat behind us?"

"What boat?" Uncle James asked, throwing a look back after Mico's pointing finger. He was busy at the two nets that he was poising in the back of the boat, ready to shoot them. "I don't see no boat." He turned back again and bent to his nest. "There couldn't be a boat there," he said then, his hands busy at the brown strings. "None of them could have caught up to us that quick."

Mico felt his mouth going dry.

"You see the boat, don't you, Coimín?" he asked in a low voice.

"I do," said Coimín. "Uncle James, have a better look than that, will you?"

Uncle James looked up at them, ready with a curse of his

lips for them, but he saw their eyes and their eyes were staring back over his shoulder, so this time Uncle James turned completely around and he saw the boat three currach-lengths behind them and the oars rising and falling and the backs of the men coming and going, and the boat seemed to be coming and pushing a sea mist in front of it. They were stopped now themselves. The water was lapping against the canvas of their currach and the boat behind was still rowing and still coming, but it didn't seem to be getting any nearer to them and there was no noise at all coming from it.

"Hello," said Uncle James.

His voice boomed out over the water and was lost and faded and died behind them.

The men in the boat behind made no sign.

"Hello," said Uncle James again.

They could hear his voice rolling off the water.

"Row on, let ye," said Uncle James without turning his head.

Mico felt the hair rising on the back of his neck. He felt cold sweat on his hands where they grasped the oar. He dug into the water splashing and the light boat leaped away.

They kept looking.

The other boat followed them.

There was no break in the rhythm of the six falling oars. There was no splash in the water. Mico could see the man in the stern of the boat now. He was wearing a cap and his face was white in the light of the moon. They were near enough only three currach-lengths away, but he couldn't quite make out the face. He felt that he ought to know him but it was just that you couldn't see. Like as if you had a punch in the eye, the way it waters and you see only through a film of water. Like that.

"Pull to the left now," said Uncle James, in a tight urgent voice.

They dug their right oars into the water and the currach swirled away.

A strange thing happened then.

The boat was still behind them. It was still three currach-lengths behind them.

"Pull to the right now," said Uncle James, and his voice was tighter.

They dug their left oars and pulled and swirled to the right and they put terrible power into the pulling because they were afraid.

The boat behind didn't pull left oars or right oars, but when they looked they saw that it was exactly three currach-lengths away and pulling the same.

"Coimín," said Uncle James then, and there was a queer timbre to the tone of his voice, "reach behind you to the bow of the boat where the bottle of holy water is tied with a string. Take it off the nail and hand it down to me. Keep pullin' away, Mico."

"Hello, there!" shouted Uncle James again. "How is the fishing with ye? Is that you, Tadhg? Is that you, Michael Tom? Is that you, Peadar Cavanagh?"

Mico pulled away and felt the boat rocking gently as Coimín leaned past him and handed the small bottle to Uncle James.

Uncle James took it without turning his head from the boat behind. They heard the slight plop as the cork came out of the bottle.

They saw Uncle James take off his cap and they saw the white streak on his head that the sun never touched and they saw him blessing himself with the bottle and then rising to his knees in the stern and spilling the water in his palm and firing it back towards the boat behind and he saying in a sort of loud voice, "In the name of Jesus Christ will ye answer me?"

They waited then, the breath short in their chests, their pulses not fast but slow at their wrists.

There was no answer to his call except the sound of their own oars.

"Turn for the shore," said Uncle James then in a frightened voice, "and row like fair hell and don't stop until ye get there."

Never to their dying day would any one of them forget that row to the point. They felt the sweat on their chests and in their crotch and under their arms, and the sweat of their endeavour was made all the worse by the chills that went up and down them like when you have the flu coming on you and you get the shivers. Maybe that's what's wrong with me, Mico thought, maybe I have the flu. Maybe I'm at home in bed in the Claddagh and this is a fevered dream!

They were about half a mile from home when they looked again and there was no boat with them.

They stopped then after a while.

"Hello," Uncle James called back. "Are ye there, men?"

There was no answer to his call.

All they could hear was the splash of the oars and the voices of the men in the boats who had now cleared the mouth of the bay and were pulling into the open sea.

"Listen to them," said Uncle James. "They're real, aren't they?"

"They are," said Mico, looking closely at the nearest boat and seeing the towering bulk of his father rowing number two.

"Were we dreaming, Uncle James?" Coimín wanted to know.

"We were not," said Uncle James. "We were warned. We're going back in. Pull over to those others. We'll have to tell them."

"Will they believe us?" Mico wanted to know, struggling with his own incredulity.

"More fools they, if they don't," said Uncle James. "Close with them."

They pulled towards the approaching boat and got in ahead of it. Mico's flesh crawled again when he saw how familiar the boat was from the front. Just the same boat. The six oars, the backs rising and falling. But from this boat came voices and the splash of oars and the voices of men, bantering.

"Go home!" said Uncle James as they closed on them.

"For Christ's sake go home, will ye! Tell the others to go home too."

The boats locked, brown hands gripping the sides.

"And what's up with ye now, James?" asks Tadhg, Coimín's father, who was at the nets in the stern.

"We saw something," said Uncle James. "We saw a strange boat. It's a sign, I tell ye. There'll be trouble on the sea tonight. Pull in home for God's sake!"

"Ah, be janey," said Michael Tom, who was there leaning on his oars, "Uncle James is at the poteen again. Come on now, men, open up, give us a suck from the bottle."

"It's serious, I tell ye," said Coimín. "Listen to him, I tell ye! We looked behind and there was a boat and then we looked again and it was vanished."

"Coimín," said Tadhg ponderously, "you wouldn't be holding out on your father, would you? Give us an oul slug."

"Ye fools," said Mico, "we're tellin' ye the truth! We were frightened I tell ye. Me hair was up on end like an oul dog's. Listen, Father. Make them see reason, can't yeh? Go on home!"

"Arrah, Mico," said Micil laughing, "is it gone mad ye are or seein' the fairies? Have a bit a sense, boy. Were ye drinkin' or what?"

"I know what it is," said Tadhg. "This is something that Big Micil worked up with Mico to get him out of the workin'. Look at him. This hard rowing is killing him. He's as puffed up as a stallion with dry straw. He knew well he wouldn't be able for it, so he arranges with Mico to think up a phantom boat so that he can run in home again."

The men in the boat laughed. There were five of them. Micil laughed too.

"Now, Mico," he said, "d'yeh see? You're makin' a hare out of your father. Go on off our that with yeer DTs and let honest fishermen go to work."

And Micil dug in his toes and his oars, and the boat creaked and the others dug their oars too, and Mico got mad and was holding on and for stopping them, but Uncle James caught his arms and said, "Let them go, Mico, 'tis no use. Let them go."

The other boat went away and their laughing floated back to them waiting there in the lightly bouncing curragh. "Fairies," they heard, and "Phantoms," and they heard Tadhg's voice shouting back at them, "Hey, Uncle James, it's me that's the thinker of stories in this place. Don't be tryin' to steal me fame."

They pulled slowly for the point and they got the currach on to dry land and they sat on the stones and they wiped their foreheads with the insides of their caps and they didn't talk. They sat there as if they were tied on springs, so tensed they were, and they watched the line of boats in the sea, the thin line of them, until the pale dawn came in the sky and they saw the boats turn for home, and nothing at all happened, nothing at all, and then they looked at one another and their faces were drawn and their eyes were bloodshot.

"Was it a dream?" Mico wanted to know.

"It was no dream," said Uncle James.

"Won't we feel fools in the morning though," said Coimín, "when they spread this yarn about? Will we ever be able to live it down at all?"

"I don't suppose we will," said Uncle James, rising wearily to his feet. "It happened. Or did it?"

They looked at one another again.

"I think it did," said Mico.

"I don't know what to think," said Coimín, wiping off the seat of his trousers. "All I know is that I was never so afraid in my whole life before and it must have happened or why should I have felt that way? And now I'm going home. Only when I get home and get in beside Maeve will I believe that it didn't happen at all and it was just a dream we had."

Mico stood at the gate while Uncle James opened the front door and he watched the back of Coimín fading into the distance. Have a good time now, Coimín, he said to him, in his own head. Enjoy getting in beside Maeve. He

thought of her that way, wakening up sleepily to see the figure of her husband and the kind capable face of Coimín
bending over her with his white teeth gleaming and the soft
light in his eyes. Enjoy yourself, Coimín, he thought, as if he
were hurling the words after him. He meant them sincerely
too. He felt he ought to run after Coimín and impress them
on him. Coimín turned and waved. Mico waved back and
then the turn of the road took him from his sight.

Later, Uncle James and he were puzzling it out over the
pot of strong tea while they waited for Big Micil to come
home from Cleggan.

"Uncle James," said Mico, "once out there when you were
callin' those names at the people in the boat behind us. You
remember the names you called?"

"I do," said Uncle James.

"Well, why did you call those names?" he asked.

"Because that's who I thought they were," said Uncle
James.

"But they couldn't have been," said Mico, "because they
were in a boat that hadn't come out into the bay at all."

"I know that," said Uncle James with his eyes bleak.

"And did you see the man who was rowing stroke in the
boat?" Mico asked then.

"I did," said Uncle James.

"Was that man Coimín?" asked Mico.

"It was," said Uncle James.

It was a cold dawn.

Chapter Fifteen

IF THERE ARE men in Mars they would have heard the loud roar of derisive laughter that flowed over the land the next day. In the bays and in the islands and in the peninsulas of the province the joke went round of the three men and the phantom boat.

Coimín and Mico went around sheepishly with their heads down and pretending to be enjoying the joke as much as the next one, but their necks were red, and it was the first time in the history of the country that Uncle James had been known to lose his temper. He tried first to reason with their laughter, telling them how it had been known to happen before and that it as a warning of evil things about to befall, but when they kept on laughing he cursed them from a height and back to the fourth generations of ancestors and to the fifth of the fruit of their loins. It was the most beautiful bit of cursing since Moses broke the commandments on the heads of the poor Jews, and everyone was diverted by it, and not a little proud of it, but do you think for a minute that anybody took it seriously? Not a one of them indeed!

They had said a true word the night before when they had thought about how long it would take for them to live it down. It was passing into the folklore already, and Coimín's father, Tadhg, was working on the story that would be handed down as gospel truth and would eventually find its way into the credulous notebook of one of those innocents from the Folklore Commission. Anyhow, as Tadhg said, it would be a change for the poor fellows in place of all the distorted Hans Andersen that was their daily fare delivered through the medium.

From the pub in Cleggan, Micil waited for the Táilliúr to come and bring his crew with him. And the pints were very pleasant in this pub, with tops on them that would water your teeth for you, and just opposite the open door of the pub he could see them sweeping out the small hall where there would be a *céili* tomorrow night.

And the Táilliúr came with his men about seven and they went down to the boats after a few rounds and they felt very good. The air was nippy but the sea was very calm and the moon was out like last night behind the mist in the sky.

And in the boat were the Táilliúr and his son, John, and old Bartley Walsh and Mairteen Delaney from the back of the village and his son, Pakey, and Big Micil.

There were seven nets to be loaded aboard as well as themselves.

Micil thought it was very awkward to have seven nets in the boat. He had thought so last night, but he was too polite to say it. And why shouldn't they anyhow? They were too poor to get a bigger boat, and although the nets cramped them a lot and you had to be an acrobat to be able to fish at all, if they had to labour at oars for hours and hours they had to have some return from their sweat and striving, so why wouldn't they have as many nets as they could fit in? He thought it was a clumsy way nevertheless. The nets were shot, and as one was shot it was attached to the next so that a train of nets was spread in the sea, and then after a time you went back to the beginning of the first net and you started to haul, slowly and laboriously, stripping the fish and hauling the net, so that by the time all the fish were in the boat and all the wet and weedy folds of the seven nets, there wasn't room to spit even. They were the leading boat and the other three boats came slowly after them, their bows heavily heaving at the small waves that were forming from a gentle north-west wind. They saw the dark shapes of the two Inisboffin boats pushing out from the land when they had reached the mouth of the Bay, and turning his head Big Micil could see the slight currach out ahead of them with the two figures in it.

Mico and Uncle James were indeed way out ahead of them.

He was afraid to ask Uncle James if he felt as nervous as he did himself; if there was sweat on his body that wasn't just the sweat of work but the sweat of incipient fear. Uncle James felt just as badly as he did if he only knew it. Uncle James thought they shouldn't have come out tonight at all, even though the fishing was good and they needed the fish and the money they brought to keep body and soul together. So he was afraid, but he'd admit it to no one.

Mico believed now, here on the water, that they had seen what they had seen, even though he had managed to persuade himself during the day that their imaginations had been working overtime last night. But that was when you were on land and there was no moon and things were bright. But here now repeating their movements of last night, with only Coimín absent, it was all very clear to him. So they rowed from the point and he judged they were about the same distance from land as they were last night when the mysterious boat had closed with them. And he waited and waited with his eyes wide and the tenseness in every muscle of his body, but nothing happened. And soon they were far, far from land and behind them the rowing boats had cleared well out of the Bay and into the sea, and nothing happened, so he relaxed and his grip on the smooth handle of the oar became easier.

He wiped the sweat off each palm on to the seat of his trousers.

"Well, Uncle James," he said then, honking like a seal to

get the words out, "it doesn't seem that the yoke is coming back to us."

"No, thank God," said Uncle James with a sigh. "I've been waitin' for it every minute, and now I declare to God I'm ready to believe that we oney imagined it, that's all."

"Maybe 'twas the mist and the moon," said Mico.

"You know, Mico," said Uncle James, his voice brightening, "it could have been something like that. There's many strange tricks that nature, God bless her, is able to work that all them smart alecks that knows everything accordin' to themselves, bad luck to them, that they know nothing about at all. We'll pull another half-mile now and we'll shoot the bloody net, God bless it."

"Aye," said Mico, and he felt so cheerful that he could have sung a song if he could remember one and if he hadn't a voice like a crow.

So he pulled strongly and wondered at the power that was in a thin man like Uncle James, the power that with a tug of the shoulder and a twitch of a narrow wrist could send the boat bounding on, and it was all Mico could do to match his stroke, big and all, and strong and all as he was. And they pulled for another half hour and then they rested. The land seemed like a dream for them and all of a piece, it was so far away and mistily and calmly blue in the moonlight. The water was smooth. They could see the other boats closing on them and spreading out, taking their own allotment of ocean like a garden and preparing to dig it. All the rowing had stopped and the men were unravelling the nets and ready to let them slide over the gun'les.

Uncle James shifted his weight agilely to the stern and prepared to pay out the net. Mico took a firm grip on his oars and rowed gently away from them. It was easy at first, but as the cloying water found the net and soaked it, it became a little harder. Just a little. It was a nice thing then to see the bobbing corkline of the net; the awkwardly cut piece of cork that held the net suspended seemed to be bouncing like fairy things on the smooth waves.

They had paid out the whole net when suddenly as if a gigantic hand had been held over the moon its light went out and it was pitch black.

"What's that?" Mico asked.

They looked instinctively at the last position of the moon and indeed, it seemed to be covered by a black hand that had crept in from the ocean. Then the fingers of the hand opened for a moment and the moon shone. It shone clearly. The mist had gone as if it had been heated by a gigantic magician and blown away in wisps of steam.

Everything was as clear as the broad noonday. No outlines were dimmed. It was the same as if they were all suspended under the reflected light of a powerful search-light, as bright as day. Mico looked around him. He could see the land as clear as clear, with the white cottages standing out in them. And he could now see the bays cutting into the land. And he could see the faces of the men in the boats behind them, looking up at the moon, their busy bodies and hands momentarily ceased from their tasks. All that he saw in a second, and then the whole body of the ocean became what men out there call *"blátha bána ar gharraidhe an iasgaire"*, white flowers in the fisherman's garden.

One minute the sea was as smooth and as soft and as unruffled as a basin of water on a table, and the next minute it was just as if somebody from below had pushed millions of small white buds up so that they blossomed miraculously and rested on the top of the water.

They felt a cold wind on the sides of their faces. A remarkably cold wind. One minute they had been sweating in their heavy jerseys and rough clothes, and the next minute this sudden short sharp wind had pierced their clothes right into the skin as if every curve of the wind was a small hand holding a sharp knife.

And then the moon departed under the black hand.

And next it seemed as if the same black hand had reached down and stirred up the water with its terrible fingers. The light boat rocked to the swell of a great wave that came from nowhere, raised them up and smashed them down so that Mico had to reach for the sides of the boat with his hands and grasp them tightly to save himself from going over the side. He felt the rock of the boat as Uncle James was thrown off balance.

"Are you all right, Uncle James?" he shouted, wondering, Why am I shouting? and then realizing that he was shouting because there was a howl to the gentle wind. What gentle wind? The one that was with us a moment ago. What has happened to it? Nobody knew. It had been frightened away by a howling wind that suddenly hit them with terrible force. He could feel the rise of it. He could feel the boat under him being raised six feet in the air.

"Uncle James!" he shouted, instinctively feeling for the oars to steady her and in his bewilderment even pulling her bow to meet the strange things that were coming from the open sea.

"All right, Mico," he heard his uncle shouting. "'Tis all right. We'll have to haul the nets. I ought to've known! I ought to've known. Turn her into the wind, Mico, and tack back the way we came if you can. Or keep her nose to the wind and I'll haul it."

Mico only heard words of what he said, here and there. The other words were snatched contemptuously from his lips and hurled away. Mico thought that his arms were being pulled from their sockets when he had her bow into the wind. Into the wind? Into the gale! How was it possible for a wind to become a gale while you could say it?

The dying moon must have hit a weak spot in the clouds. Mico suddenly saw again. He saw Uncle James with speed in his hands and the wet net coming over the side with wriggling greeny silver things in the mesh. And away to his left he saw men leaning over the sides of their boats and hauling in their nets with what even appeared from here to be panic. He had a quick look over his shoulder then and he nearly swallowed his tongue with what he saw. Behind them the sea had reared itself up into white-topped mountains that were coming towards them and their boats with the speed of a train. The water wasn't blue now. It was white and black. There was just the two colours in it. And away behind the oncoming waves he could see the black sky as black as a black cat and it seemed to be pushing in front of it a solid wall of white threads. And then the moon was gone and the wind howled and Mico felt as if it had reached into his heart and squeezed it and stopped up his breathing.

This couldn't be, he thought furiously. This couldn't be at all. To no people in the world has it happened for a thing like this to descend without warning. Without warning? Then what about last night? Didn't Uncle James say then that that was what it was, a warning? The bow of the boat shook then as if it had been beaten with a heavy sledgehammer. Oh God, Mico thought suddenly, we are going to die. He felt the passing wave wetting him up to his waist and he felt its cold touch that went into the front of his boots and wrapped itself around his woollen socks. He felt it on his feet and it was as cold as the skin of the dead. He thought of the boat under them. He had seen them made. You get light laths and you shape them on a frame and when they are all together you put a spread of canvas over them and then you paint this canvas several times with tar. Thick sticky tar.

What is it then? It's nothing else but a canoe.

A wave caught the boat and spun it around as if it was a spinning top caught under a giant whip. Mico was flung from his seat, his hand reaching out, when the oar was snatched from it. His jaw hit with a crack against the side of the boat. A crack then sent the blood to his head and the water to his eyes.

"Mico! Mico!" he heard his Uncle James say. He was near him. Mico reached up his hand and felt the warm cloth of the *báinín*. It's real anyhow, he thought, Uncle James is real. "Are you all right?" he heard the shout that came to him as a whisper and yet Uncle James was only inches away from him.

"Yes," Mico roared, getting on to the seat again, putting up his hand, feeling the sticky thing on his jaw-bone and knowing it was blood.

"We'll have to cut the nets, Mico," he heard Uncle James say.

Mico felt for his oar with his sticky hand. It was jammed back tightly against the side of the swirling boat. He could hear even above the wind the water in the bottom of the boat. It would be up to his ankles at least. He thought of the nets. Four pounds a net cost. Where would Uncle James pick up four pounds to buy another net? When would he?

"Don't," he shouted, putting his back into the oars and gradually with a heartbreaking effort getting the light boat about to face into the wind. "Use them to anchor. Wind'll blow us along to the end of them. Maybe 'twould hold us. Hold us until the storm blows out."

The boat was lifted in the air and then there didn't seem to be anything but air under it. Mico felt it falling but he held on to his oars and reached them and held them level to break their fall. They fell. The jar went up through his bones and rattled his teeth. And then despite the pull of his arms on the oars, they were spun again.

"They're gone," he heard Uncle James shout. "Get her around, Mico, get her around. Have to chance it. Get her around and let the sea take us. Only chance we got."

The currach sprang loose as if it had been freed from a retaining spring.

"Mico, Mico," he heard his uncle's voice then, "the oars are gone."

Lord! Mico thought, holding tightly on to his own.

"Try and get her around, Mico, for the love of God," he heard him say, "or we're lost."

Mico dug in his oars, when he felt they were on the top of a wave. He dug in his two oars and held them there. It was as if four men were hanging on the blade of each oar trying to pull them out of his hands. He held them there with his face to the sky and his teeth biting into his lip. He could feel every muscle in his shoulders groaning and it seemed to him that somebody was running a sharp knife along both his upper arms. But he held them there and the pull gradually lessened. I'll have to time it, he was thinking. I'll have to time it on top of a wave. He held her level in the trough and then he got ready again for the awful pull. It came. As if someone had a rope tied around his heart and was pulling it. I'll never be able to do this again, he thought. I will have to try and get her on the next wave. He rested in the trough and when the next rise came almost immediately, he loosened his left hand, shifted it over and took a grip on his right hand and the oar-handle and pulled with every bit of strength that was left in him. It stuck for a minute and then the currach took a sharp turn around and was off cresting on the waves.

With his hands still holding the oars then he let his head fall down between his knees and tried to breathe. He felt as if he was draining. Behind him, Uncle James wedged himself into the stern of the currach and took the beat of the running waves on his back. Thump, thump, thump, like the pounding of the potato skillet on the boiled potatoes. But he stretched his arms along the gunwales and held them tightly and took the beating on his back. He could feel the blows and then he could feel the water rising on his back and flying over his head and pouring along each side of him. And what went over his head poured on top of Mico so that he was soon as drenched to the skin as if he had slipped into the sea. In fact they seemed like part of the running sea, a slimy black slithery part of the sea that was running with the waves.

Mico looked up then and the white following threads that had been running behind them hit him full in the face. White thread, and as cutting as white thread pulled into the flesh. White gleaming icicles of solid sleet, cutting and as cold as the heart of charity. Mico cried out, although he didn't know it, and sucked in his breath when he felt the cut of them on his face and the pricking of them at the skin of his hands that were gripping the oars. He closed his eyes to the pain of them, but opened his eyes again to the feel of cold rain, and then he wished that he had not opened his eyes to see what he saw. Because when the white threads came they brought a sort of artificial light with them that lighted up the blackness, and just to his right Mico saw the boat.

There were seven men in the boat, and two of them were leaning over the side hauling at the net. He wanted to shout at them, No, for Christ's sake run, run, but no man could have heard him. He saw the faces in the boat of the men that pulled the oars, the wet on their clothes so that they shone, and he saw the wet of the shining part of the tossing boat. He saw the wet on the keel of it as it was raised into the air end on, just as if a hand was put underneath the bow and the whole thing was toppled over. He saw its full length high in the air and he saw the oars falling away from it, and he saw it shining and he saw the black bodies of the men falling from it, and over the wind, over the waves, over the unbelievable and incredible hell of it all, he heard the voices of men screaming. He heard strong men screaming. And then there was nothing behind them, nothing at all. The whole lot had been swallowed as if they had been taken into the belly of a whale.

"Oh, Jesus, Jesus!" said Mico, and he dropped his oars and he let his face fall into his hands.

"Mico! Mico!" he heard his uncle pleading. "The oars, Mico! Mico, for the love of God, the oars!"

He put his hands out then and he caught one, and the other was on it way off the rowlock and about to be hurled into the night when he caught it and held it and battered it into place with his fist so that he felt the flesh of his fist cleaving under the blows, and then he had it right and he dipped them at a wave and raised them over another and he could hear an odd groan from the stern of the boat as Uncle James took the beating of the waves on his bowed back. He could see Uncle James. He was beginning to assume vague outlines now because the sleet was piling up on him and he was becoming visible like a snowman in a land of ink.

He put the screams away from him. Oh, God, if you think of those and you are dying, what's the use of thinking of them and who are they, are they my own father; oh, God, don't let it be my own father or any of those men I have come to know. What devil was it that got into them that wouldn't listen to the voice of men who had died before they had died at all and had come back to tell them not to go to sea, that there was death piling up for them out in the Atlantic, and coming in the shape that no mortal man here had ever known or heard of before?

Why in the name of God had they not looked at the sea and the sky and smelled the rain on the wind? They were too busy thinking and laughing at the tale of the phantoms to pay attention to the sky, and they, Mico and Uncle James, were about to die and they had brought their deaths on their own heads because they had been ashamed of their visions and had not looked at the sky. If only Gran had been with us, this would never have been. Gran would have put his face into the wind and he would have said, "No, no, for the love of God not tonight, there's rain on the wind." If only Gran wasn't a poor man who had become too old for the sea, who had to stretch his feet into the ashes of the turf fire and fish for eels off the river bank; he would have been with them and then no man would have gone to sea.

Mico should have known himself; he had been long enough under the thumb of Gran to have learned a little of his lore. So he just sat in the currach, that was racing towards destruction like a greyhound closing on a hare, with his face being cut to pieces by the howling sleet driven by a bitter wind. Felt it gathering on his closed eyes and on his eyebrows and felt it soaking into every bit of him and his flesh went dead. His fingers still holding the oars didn't seem to belong to him any more and he thought, God, when we die and are sucked into the water it will be even down there; before we are suffocated with the water pouring into our lungs, at least we will know that the sleet can't cut into us any more.

There could be no hope for them. He had seen the heavy-oared boat upended as if it had been a toy boat on a duck pond. What would the wind do now to this thin toy? He heard the screams of men about to perish ringing in his frozen ears and he saw them falling awkwardly and undignified to their deaths. Oh, Christ, he prayed, when it comes for us now don't let us go like that, let the sea just go over our heads and let us go down, down, swallowed by a wave, not falling into its arms with waving hands and legs and screams in our ears.

Where is my father?

Was my father one of the screaming men who fell?

Not my father, God. If only we had the luck to bring the big black boat with us. He thought of her rounding swelling breast, of her stout timbers, of the heavy limestone ballast. The sail would be torn from the mast like you would tear a used sheet between your hands, but at least she would be left her body and her steering and she would weather this filth. She had weathered no worse maybe, but she would have weathered this. If only ...!

"Mico," he heard his Uncle James then. It wasn't a cry. It wasn't a scream. It was a hoarse unnatural noise.

He opened his eyes. He thought they would have to be torn open. He saw his uncle's hand pointing over his shoulder.

He turned his head painfully. He could see nothing at all, only something faintly phosphorescent behind them.

"Rocks, rocks, rocks," his Uncle James was saying.

Mico dug his oars. His hands were sliding from them.

They had been about at the middle of the back of his head, that speck he had seen. Uncle James knew his Bay even by the light of pitch-black night in the middle of this desolation. I can only try as hard as I can, he thought, and if I fail, I fail. And why should I be trying anyhow? There is no hope for us under the sun. And then he thought of a body falling over a cliff. Into water like this, the same water that washed and roared at the Aran cliffs.

He dug in his oars and he took a pull with his left hand. Edging. Edging. Edging. That was all he could do, there was nothing else any man could do because he was so tired. So terribly, terribly tired, and what was the use anyhow?

"Faster, faster, faster, Mico!" he heard his uncle say. If there is a chance for him, he thought then, why shouldn't I give it to him? He thought of the currach hitting the sharp rocks. He could hear the tear of the canvas, the split of the thin laths, and the pounding of his body against the points of the rocks. That would be no way to die. No way at all. He let go his right hand and he grasped his left hand and he pulled and pulled and pulled. Out of the corner of his eye he saw the oar he had freed being taken up and pulled away and soaring off ahead of them. Well, we're done now anyhow, he thought, but he pulled at his left oar until there wasn't a pull left in all the frozen blood in his veins, and then he saw the boiling whiteness on their left side. A fearful boiling maelstrom that was sucking and sucking loudly enough to be heard over the scream of the wind, and the sight of it showed him the speed they were travelling and soon they were cut off into inky blackness again with one oar in his paralysed hand and no feel to it. He tried to hold on to it; tried with all the will he had remaining, but it was no use, his numbed hands refused to clench themselves any longer and he saw the oar being whipped away as if it was a wisp of straw. He slid off the seat then and felt himself sitting in the water that was in the boat, felt it seeping into his already seeped clothes, and then he let his head fall on his hands. His face was as cold as ice and he could only feel it with part of his palms.

How long have we now? was all he could wonder then, wondering if it was possible to feel so cold; it it was possible to live for much longer in this awful tearing white-hot cold.

How long later was it he didn't know, but he felt the

heave of the boat. He felt it rising into the air, and then it went down again, but this time he knew that the bow of the currach was never coming up. It went down, down, and he saw that Uncle James, with his hands still grasping the boat, was higher than he, and then the water closed over him and he felt the boat being sucked from under them.

It was an instinctive gesture that made him reach then for the *báinín* of Uncle James. He felt it bunched in his hand and he held on to it. He even reached his other hand and grabbed it with that too – the dying grip of the drowning man – and then he felt something under his feet. Rocks? The bottom of the sea? The boat? But it was firm and he stood on it and he stood straight, and to his cold surprise he felt air around his head and he hauled on the *báinín* and Uncle James was in his hands, a tired heavy weight, and then the feet were swept from under him again and he felt the water pouring into his lungs, and then it seemed that he was caught by hands and raised into the air and his body thumped down on black slimy things that must be rocks. He freed an arm and grasped with it. It closed around seaweed. He pulled with the other. The soused white *báinín* with Uncle James came up beside him. He felt the water pouring over him again, and he dug in his hand and he rode the rock with his knees as if he was on a horse, and he was ready when the sea went back sucking, and he pulled himself up more, and then with an effort which he would never again in his life be able to emulate he stood up on that rock, and he pulled the limp body of his uncle up with him, and he took a step and he took two steps, and then he fell, holding tight to the coat, and he felt rough sand on his face like the cloth of a tweed coat, and he pushed with his knees and got to them and he was hunched like that when the water broke over him again thundering, and he took it on his bowed back and when it retreated, still sucking, he got to his feet again, but he couldn't pull any more at his uncle. He walked forward and he dragged him behind him, and he walked four paces and he fell again, and it was still sand and the sea washed over him, but it seemed to have lost its power, so he rested there a while and then he rose again and he went on again and he kept going on. He couldn't open his eyes at all. They seemed to be ribbed with pain. They seemed to be suffering the pain of having red-hot needles stuck into them; but he went forward and then he fell and didn't feel the sea, just felt it reaching for him behind, so he crawled this time on his knees, still hauling at the limp body behind him, and then he paused and reached with his other hand and he pulled the body far, far up so that it was level with himself, and he felt for the face with his hands and found it, and then he laid his chest against the chest below him and he placed his frozen face against the frozen face under him, and that was the last he remembered.

Chapter Sixteen

H E CAME TO himself with a hand shaking his shoulder.

"Mico! Mico!" the soft worried voice was calling.

He heard it in his ears and he moved his body. He was hugging sand. He felt it under his face and under his hands. The salt smell of sea-shells was in his nose. He tried to turn on his back, and ragged pains shot through him, so many of them that he couldn't know where the seat of them was. But he got over on his back and he opened his eyes, and then he shut them quicker than he had opened them and brought his arms over to cover them. Opening them was like the pain you get when they pull heavy sticking plaster from the hairs of your arms or your legs. Short and agonizing.

"Are you all right?" the voice asked.

"Yes," he said, "I'm all right." It was an effort to talk. His mouth was dry and sticky and his jaws were sore and he felt a dull pain from his cheek. He made another effort then and opened his eyes. They were very painful and they watered, but he could see a sort of grey sky with wildly scudding clouds. He closed them again and winked them and opened them again, and this time it wasn't as bad, so he kept them open and sat up, his big hands resting on the sand and propelling his body upwards. He turned his head then and looked into the anxious eyes of his Uncle James. His face seemed to be coated with salt. His eyes were puffed and red-rimmed. "Are you all right, Uncle James?" he asked then.

"I am," said Uncle James, "but I was afraid. I woke up and you were half lying on me. So I got out from under. There was no stir from you. I thought you were a goner."

"'Tis hard to kill a bad thing," said Mico, not meaning to be funny, because even if his body was sore his head was clear. It was too clear. It took up immediately where it had left off last night. His eyes fell then to Uncle James' hands.

"Holy God," he said, "look at your hands!"

Uncle James held them up. They were red and raw and blue in places and they were swollen up to three times their normal size. You couldn't see any muscles at all on them or any knuckles. They were just two lumps of red-blue flesh. He lifted his own and looked at them. They were not swollen but the left one was split and there was dried blood around where it had been cut open from hammering home the oar on the rowlock. He flexed it. It sent searing stabs of pain up through his arm. "You'll have to get something done to your hands, Uncle James," he said then.

"I'm lucky to have hands," said Uncle James.

"Yes," said Mico. "What about the others? Where are we?"

He got to his feet. His whole body groaned protestingly so that he had to bite his lip, and then he found that his bottom lip was already cut from the way he had bitten it in the boat, and it hurt very badly so that he almost groaned, and then when he pulled his face with the groan the split on his cheek opened up and sent another searing of pain through his face.

"You have a bad cut up there, Mico," said Uncle James. "It will have to be stitched or something."

"Yes," said Mico.

He looked around him. They seemed to have landed on a desolate part of the coast. It was a miracle that they had hit on that one patch of sand. All the rest of the coast as it wound around the bay was nothing but great jagged brown-coloured rocks, with heather behind them running away into bog, and small mountains rising from those so that it was a terrible sight of bleak brown land, and over it the sky was ringed with black-bellied clouds all around the horizon, and the scudding clouds over their heads were grey and pregnant with rain and storm. The wind was high, but the rocks on the left of the little bay were sheltering them from it. He could see that the sea was raddled. There was no order about it. The waves were being blown all ways and were lashing themselves against the coast. There was nothing now on the sea but a churning mass of white foam. A mile or two across the bay he saw the land rising mightily to the peak where the Lighthouse was, and over beyond that he could just see the tip of Boffin pushing out and taking a terrible beating from the sea.

"Where are we?" he asked then.

"We're several miles down from Cleggan," said Uncle James.

"Did you see any sign of any of the others at all?" Mico asked.

"No," said Uncle James, looking at him, and his eyes were very bleak, "I saw nobody at all."

"Maybe," said Mico, "they were blown into Boffin or into Omey?"

"One boat at least wasn't," said Uncle James.

"Did you see that too?" asked Mico. He had been hoping that he had only imagined that.

"I heard it," said Uncle James with a terrible emphasis.

"But our boat was so light," said Mico. "Their boats were heavy. If we came free from it, they must have too."

"If they didn't wait for the nets," said Uncle James, "they had a chance to run for it. Waiting for the nets, that killed the boat we saw. Their nets are so precious. We are all so poor. But life is sweeter than poverty. It's not worth a net."

"Will we walk along by the coast a piece?" Mico asked.

"We will have to do something," said Uncle James.

They walked. Slowly and creakingly and haltingly at first, with the aching of their limbs and the feeling of the cold wet woolly clothes that were embracing them, but as they walked their blood warmed and the dampness of their clothes became warm too, and more bearable. They came to the extent of their sandy beach and then they clambered over the rocks. This was very painful. Uncle James had to use his arms instead of his hands to lever him over the bigger ones.

They found their currach. It was wedged between two rocks, and the body of it had been ripped as if it had been done deliberately with knives. They didn't stop. Mico just hauled it clear and up above the highwater mark on the rough grass where the edge of fresh seaweed was piled in a long line. Uncle James threw it a casual look. "It might be fixed," he said, and then went on.

When they rounded the next headland they had to climb a monstrous rock with a flat top on it. Mico stood there and looked back. He could see a lot of the coast. Right back to Cleggan and beyond. He could see figures moving on the roads and on the beaches, small figures, colourful too. A lot of red, which meant that the women were out.

And then Mico looked down at where the water was hitting the base of the big rock and he saw a body in the water. It was the body of a man with his face down and his arms spread out as if he had fallen. He was being washed in and he was being sucked out, washed in and sucked out helplessly. Mico's heart stopped beating. It was the body of a very big man and it was dressed in a blue gansie and rough blue trousers. The hair on its head was stretching out from its skull. It was dark in colour.

"Uncle James," he called in a low voice, and he felt him moving to him. He pointed down with his finger. No word out of him.

He felt Uncle James sucking in his breath and then he jumped down into the water. It wasn't deep. It came to his waist. He didn't feel the wet of it. He got beside the body and put a big arm around it and he walked with it pushing it along the water and to the far side where the sea curved around the huge smooth base of the rock.

Uncle James was there when he arrived and he could do nothing. "My hands, Mico," he said. "Ther's no feeling in them at all."

"All right," said Mico, and he came from the water and bent over the man lying helplessly there on the edge. He caught the body under the arms and pulled it, still face down, over the round rolling stones, as gently as he could, so that it came slowly with the legs trailing and the heavy boots disturbing the stones, and then he placed it there with his mind blank and he turned the body over. It was an effort. It was a big body. He sucked in his breath then.

"Do you know him?" he asked.

"I do," said Uncle James. "I know him. God rest him now."

"Was he in my father's boat?" Mico asked.

"No," said Uncle James, "he wouldn't be."

Mico didn't press it any further. If he wasn't in my father's boat, whose boat was he in? What kind of an answer did you want to that?

They carried him out of the *bruth-fá-thír* and they left him to rest on the grass above on the headland. Placed him there with his face to the sky. A face that had been as brown as mahogany and was now blue like the colour of the flesh of Uncle James' hands. The beard on the dead man was two days of age and it was strong and virile. He had probably been a young man. You couldn't see very well now, but the thick lips were open and swollen and the white teeth were there, a little yellow near the gums from the tobacco. Mico had no coat, only his jersey, but they managed to take his uncle's coat off. It was painful. They had to tear it near the sleeves because the hands were too big for them, but they got it off at last and put it over the dead man's face and saved his wide open eyes from regarding the leering, exulting sky.

"There's something there now," said Uncle James, pointing farther down the coast. "That's on the shore, isn't it?"

Mico looked. A scattered splume of smoke coming from something burning on the shore.

"That's like something," he said.

"You go and see," said Uncle James. "I'll wait here with him until you come back, and then one of us will have to go and let them know in the village."

Mico went methodically, jumping a rock or avoiding a rock, his hob-nailed boots slippy on the stones. He kept his mind blind. He didn't want to think at all. Thinking wasn't necessary now. The eyes were seeing too much, too much altogether to be sending it to the brain.

He approached the smoke. It was on the far side of a tall cluster of rocks so that he could see nothing of it but the smoke rearing high and being scattered then by the shifting wind. He got on top of the rocks and looked down. For a few beats his heart didn't go at all and then it went on steadily and faster than was its wont.

"Hullo," he said, looking down at the men under him who were around a fire.

The big man looked up at him. Something stuck in his mouth. It was open and then it was closed and he swallowed.

"Hello, Mico," said Big Micil.

Mico jumped down on to the small sandy beach that was like their own.

"We lit a fire," said Micil. "The Táilliúr is gone blind on us. The sleet got at his eyes."

"Is that Mico?" said the Táilliúr, who was squatting there with a once white handkershief tied around his eyes. He had lost his hat. His hair was very grey and thin and there was a white band around his forehead which the sun never saw for the cap. But his moustaches were dry and were standing out from his pale cheeks. "We're glad to see you, Mico," said the Táilliúr.

"How are ye, men?" Mico asked the others.

"We're alive, thank God," said the Táilliúr's son, John. He was a tall young man with a great width of shoulder. "Bartley Walsh has got his hands bad. Look at them. As big as sods of turf they are."

Mico looked at the hands of the old man. Big and swollen.

"Uncle James' hands are the same," he said.

"We got the boat back too," said Micil. "Look at it!" pointing to where it was drawn up on the beach.

"Yeh, but we lost the oars or most of them," said Mairteen Delaney, a big man with a wet *báinín* and huge red hands and long teeth in low-hanging gums.

"And the nets," said his son, Pakey.

"To hell with them," said the Táilliúr. "We better go now."

His son helped him to his feet. Micil kicked the burning embers of the wood fire into the sea.

"I feel the better for the heat," said the Táilliúr. "I couldn't ha' moved a step without heat. Are we right now, men?"

"We are," said the men, moving up the beach after them.

"We found a man above," said Mico then, a bit louder than he meant. "He's up above."

"Oh," said the Táilliúr. They all paused for a moment with their gaze fixed on the ground and then they went on.

Micil walked with Mico behind them.

"You're all right, Mico?" he asked, almost casually, without looking at him.

"I am," said Mico. "Just a few cuts and things and a bit stiff, but I'm all right."

"I never thought ye'd live in that currach," said Big Micil. "I never thought you would for sure."

"How are you?" asked Mico then. "Was it bad?"

"Ah," said Micil, "'twas just a bit risky for a while, but then it was all right."

Saga of the sea. He reached a big hand and pressed Mico's arm.

Mico felt like weeping now. It was just a feeling.

"Aye," said Micil, "just a bit risky."

They went slowly to where the men were bent over the body.

Five pitch-pine coffins on the floor of a hall.

A hall that should have been resounding to the spirited music of melodeon and violin and the stamping of heavy boots, broken by wild hurroo cries and flushed faces and the sweating of bodies, with the music of the dance heating the blood and making it fit for anything violent, love or bloody battle. Instead, five pitch-pine coffins on the floor with the dead men in them: five out of so many was all that the sea gave back to them. Six boats put out from shore and one boat comes back alive and five dead men after them. All day at the seashore the figures of weeping women and old bent men searching, searching, lifting the heavy roots of seaweed that had been torn from the farther bottom of the sea. Looking for something more precious in the wreck than the gutted things of sea-destroyed ships. Looking for the bodies of men who were all in all to you a few brief hours ago.

Three guttering candles held aloft as the evening fell, and the lids of the coffins are raised and the people pass them by to look at their dead. Is this my son or my father or my husband or my lover? The smell of candle-smoke guttering in the air. The shuffle-shuffle of feet on the boarded floor. And then a cry that rises above the wind, and there is a woman bowed and bowed with grief, and the black shawl pulled over her head. Every home is bereft. Old men are left without their sons and old women without their husbands. And children crying on the night air.

And the lids go back on the coffins and they are screwed down and they are raised on the shoulders of the few men who have remained from the holocaust, and a long train of sorrow stretches for three miles to where they are placed row upon row in the little church over the hill.

They might have been cardinals or kings, lying in the aisle under the light of the candles and the faint aroma of incense. They had company for the night as if they had been the greatest in the land. And the people placed their foreheads on the smooth wood of the lids and they placed their hard hands on it and they prayed if they were able. It was hard to pray and say it is the will of God, with Peadar Cavanagh somewhere out there waving to and fro with the lift of the tide. He was too young to die. And in the house of the aged dead you had Tadhg. He was old right enough, but what were you going to do without him and his outrageous yarns, and the laugh-wrinkles round his eyes dug in deeper than a furrow under a plough? And what's little Bridget going to do without her father, Michael Tom?

The long line stretching across the yellow sands of Omey. The coffins on the backs of men, canted to their size, and the sea at either side of you there to applaud jeeringly. All my own work. Clapping its hands greenly at the behest of the dying storm.

The grave is big and they lie together, side by side, the men who died. And the priest prays for them, with tears in his bewildered eyes, feeling for the moment his inadequacy. The Latin words intoned on the clear air and the soft fall of the yellow sand on the glistening coffins. So the graves are filled and the green grass is laid over them, and some time, some day there will be a modest headstone raised with their names on it, but there can be no monument at all to the men who are waving out with the weed at the bottom of the sea.

And the people straggle back across the great strand away from the green grass of the island, and then the small houses swallow them, and over the fresh mound in the island the great gulls wheel and swing and cock their heads sideways, wondering at the rectangular disturbance in the green grass, and come down from their great height and peck at the descending worms, before they burrow below to humble mankind.

Mico closed the door and leant with his back against it.

She was sitting at the fire. It was burning slowly and it lighted the side of her face nearest to it. She was sitting on the stool, and her hands were falling listlessly between her knees. She didn't look up at all. Not even when he lifted the latch; not even when he closed the door. Maybe I shouldn't have come at all, he thought.

He went over to her then, his feet barely kissing the floor, and he got to his knees in front of her and he reached for one of her hands. It was cold to the touch.

"Maeve," he said.

She raised her eyes slowly and looked at him. She barely saw him, he knew. Her eyes were not red from weeping. They were nearly as cold as her hand. What could he say now? Wasn't he just a great big lout that was as useless as if he didn't even have a tongue at all? She waited for him.

"I'm sorry, Maeve," he said. Oh God, was this all he could say now?

"What happened your face, Mico?" she asked, her eyes on the sticking-plaster holding the split in his cheek, right in the middle of the mark on his face.

"Nothing," said Mico.

"It's all right, Mico," she said. "It hasn't touched me yet. Don't be sorry for me now. Save it up until I need it. 'Tisn't as if he was one of those that was buried in Omey. 'Tisn't like that at all. Maybe he isn't gone, Mico. Maybe he's on some desolate part of the coast and that he can't get home to me for a day or two. It might be that, you know. Couldn't it maybe be that way, Mico?"

He saw one of the bodies lying in a coffin. It had been found off the Cleggan pier with a length of net wound tightly around it. He had been a man who had been in Coimín's boat.

Her voice rang hollow in the house. Over her head hanging on a nail was a coat and a cap. Mico looked at them, and he knew that Coimín would never fill them again.

"You don't think so," she said, her voice disappointed, as if he had failed her. Wouldn't it be worse for her to be getting a notion like that and waiting every day in this lonely little house by the shore, waiting for the sound of a foot on the gravelled path and the lifting of a latch? Wouldn't that be far worse for her? Mightn't she stay here an old woman for ever and ever waiting for the sound of a latch to lift?

"Maeve," he said, "if he was anywhere in the world he would be home now."

"Nobody can help another person, Mico," she said then, her hand up to her forehead. "Nobody at all. You'd want to be given a new mind when things happen to you, so that it would be clean and new and more misfortune could be written on it. I used to think that we were too happy, that we hadn't a child because we were too happy and that God didn't want to give us any more happinesss, that we had enough as it was. Now I have no child and I have no happiness and I have nothing but an empty house, that was once a lovely dream, and if I can't have the sound of the lifting of the latch, then I have nothing, nothing at all. So I will wait for that. It might come. It might come tonight or tomorrow morning or in the middle of the noon or tomorrow night or next summer. That's all I have to hold on to is the lifting of the latch, and if I haven't that I haven't anything at all."

Her head was in her hands.

He raised one of his big hands then and rested it on her hair, lightly. Her hair was as smooth as the web of a spider, but it had lost its glisten, it was dull.

"Maeve," he said, "I'm a useless class of a fella when it comes to the feelings of people and their minds. I can't know enough about these things at all to be able even to speak about them. But I am big and strong and I can do things materially, like. If ever you want Mico to move a mountain for you, or to kill a man for you or to work for you or to do anything else for you, let you remember me.

Maybe some day Coimín will come back. Maybe some day the latch will lift for you. I don't know. If that's the way you want it, maybe it will happen that way."

He got to his feet then, and looked down from his great height at her bowed head.

"Goodbye now, Maeve," he said then, softly. "I'm no use to you now. Maybe I never will be. But like you waiting for the liftin' of the latch, I'll wait for some day that maybe you will find some way for me to help you. I don't write much, 'tis only but the few lines I can put together and that same is hard on me, because I was of rare use in school, but maybe you wouldn't be insulted if I was to write to you. Sometimes when we're at sea there does be a chance of a night when we are in a little place and we do be hunched in the small place in out of the rain. Maybe sometimes I will write to you and you won't mind."

"I won't mind, Mico," she said, but she didn't look up at all.

He left her then. He walked backwards to the door and reached for the latch and raised it softly so that it made no sound at all, and then he opened the door so that the fresh wind, with its dying whistle around the headland, could be heard there, and he went out, and he saw her there with her head in her hands and her hair falling about her face and the flickering fire lighting up one side of her, and then he closed the door so that the latch would not click and he walked so that his feet made no sound on the gravel and then he went away.

On the morning tide they left the pier.

There were some of the people there to see them off. Even at this time. Uncle James was there with the bandages around his hands, and the Táilliúr was there with his eyes red and raw, but a little of the seeing coming back into them, and his son and a few of the others. They even joked a little with them. About the yacht and the two Claddagh gents that had finished their cruise in the Connemara waters and were now returning to their mansions in the capital. They even laughed. But Big Micil couldn't whip up a laugh at all. He just stood big and dumb winding a rope.

And they waved their hands and they pushed away.

They saw the people on the pier with their hands raised and then they traversed the Bay. It was playful now. The waves were dancing. The sun was shining on them benevolently. The waves slapped the black boat, gently and chidingly, and the boat soughed softly as it glided over the great graveyard.

They should change the name of it now, Mico thought, and call it the Bay of Tears. There were enough of those to fill it.

And they sailed into the Atlantic and the sun was warm and the air was fresh, and over the bodies of the dead men the sea was as peaceful as the heart of a nun.

Chapter Seventeen

IT WAS A Saturday morning and it was nearing Christmas.
That was why Mico was finding it so hard to push his
way through the crowded streets. They were packed
from side to side with cars coming and buses going and all
of them honking impatiently at the slow men with the
horses and carts and asses and carts who were tangling up
the traffic in an incredible confusion of hee-hawing asses
and honking cars and the horses with their heads pulling at
the reins, and the boggle of the tied-down turkeys in the
carts and the squealing of confined bonhams and the cackling of indignant chickens.

There was a great smell of fresh porter pervading the air
from the pubs, mingled with that of the fresh droppings of
the various animals on the streets, and the blue smoke that
rose in the air from noisome but sweetly pulling pipes. Big
women with the baskets and soldiers on leave and under-
the-breath-cursing Civic Guards trying to reduce order from
chaos. It was very colourful and necessary, but modern civilization hadn't caught up with it yet, and would be standing
back scratching its head, wondering how on earth it would
ever be possible for it to blend with the primitive invasions
of unaccountable things like asses and horses, and iron-shod

wheels. Had these people never heard of the pneumatic tyre? Didn't they know that the horse was on the way out ten years ago?

Mico enjoyed it all and exchanged loud shouts with the people he knew.

He felt like shouting. He was dressed in his Sunday suit although it was only Saturday. It was a double-breasted sort of reefer jacket suit, and the tailor's creases were still on it, and he swelled it out well as he pushed his way through the throngs. His neck rose from a blue-striped shirt with no collar that was as clean as a sheet in the sun. He wore no cap and his thick hair was unruly on his head. He was freshly shaved, the side that could be shaved, and the other side looked a little peculiar with the white scar-tissue dividing it. He was a very big man, but it would hardly be noticed here when the countrymen were in practically undisputed possession of the town, and there were big men there from all parts, from Spiddal and Barna and Furbo and out from the Moycullen and Oughterard direction, and from the Claregalway side too, and they were dressed in *báiníns* and ceanneasna trousers and in rough homespuns, and the Aran men were about with their shuffling pampooties and their ashplants, and their blue rough clothes, and there were men in frock coats and frieze coats, and coats that had been made in modern multiple stores, and there were tinkers with any sort of clothes they could get on them, with their great hairy chests open to the December winds. All big men, that was about the only thing they had in common; their clothes were different and their accents were different and their voices were different.

A great sight it was.

The shops were bursting with people and many citizens were to be seen trotting home with a turkey grappled by the neck or the heels and its head trailing in the dust of the channels; and there were geese too going home under an arm with their legs tied with bits of rag and their heads proudly erect as if they were facing the thought of the chopper like Christian martyrs. The whole place was bulging with people and it was an effort to get through them. Mico cast an anxious look at the town clock as he passed, but its face assured him that he had plenty of time yet to meet the bus.

He had never met a bus in his life before, but he had had no reason to. But this was worth having waited for. The bus would stop and he would be there and with his eyes glued to the door and then Maeve would step down and look around her. How would it feel to see her again? How would she look? Would it take them long to get used to the feeling of meeting again? He didn't want to take up where they had last left off. No fear! But that was just over two years ago now, and no mind can hold a tragedy fresh for ever no matter how long you hold on to it. It must dim surely. The mechanism of memory would have to dull or how would you be able to live at all? He just knew her from the odd letters she wrote to him in answer to his own.

He had seen the change coming in her. Had sensed it although he didn't know much about sensing people from scratches on paper. He thought that well over a year ago she had stopped waiting for the latch to lift. And then he had read the emptiness. In a word here or a word there. Maybe he could understand that. How empty the house of theirs would seem, how empty the whole place would seem; how terrible a thing it was to be looking at the sea that still held the body of your husband.

Ah, well, that was over now, and God rest it. So at last she could not stand another Christmas there. She would have to go. Where would she go? Mico thought the sky had fallen the day he read that. Where would she go indeed? She had a little money, a few pounds from the Disaster fund and a little here and there she had collected from the sale of the house and the bits and pieces that were in it. Now what?

Pa was the answer. Mico saw Pa.

He treated it just the same as if it was an equation and the solving of it therefore to him was inevitable. Hum! And Ha! And then the blessed chance that had driven him to the house of Peter, and drinking his cup of tea in the kitchen he had told Mrs Cusack the story of Maeve. It had brightened her up considerably. Her thin frame had reared a little. Mico hadn't meant it that way at all, but she said, "We have a spare room, you know." That was Peter's room, that was as untouched now as the night he had left it never to come back to it. Was that a queer working of God now, that would give Maeve that room? Would it be possible now for two great tragedies to cancel each other out? It maybe might. Gran thought so, and if he thought so then it meant something.

And Pa came back after solving his equation.

"She will serve her apprenticeship to the drapery business," he said decidedly. "Normally a fee is required for such a thing, but one of my past pupils is in need of assistance, and he doesn't anyhow believe in this prehistoric and monstrous throwback to the Middle Ages where you are required to pay so that you can work like a slave. Therefore it is all fixed. She will get just enough to keep her alive, and as time goes by and if suitable she will be rewarded by higher wages. I will keep my eye on the girl and also on my past pupil. In time, if she remains a widow, it may be possible to arrange a little advance from another past pupil so that she can set up in a little shop of her own, if such is her wish. Does all that please you, Mico?"

If it was possible, Mico felt like kissing him.

"I will make it my business," said Pa, "to pay her a visit tomorrow, in Cusacks', you say, and I will arrange all. There's no need to be thankful, my boy. If I can't make a liner captain out of you, the least I can do is to raise a finger for you." And off he went with himself, Mico standing with his hands on his hips looking after the tiny figure. He seemed to get old by growing smaller, nothing else showed on his face.

"Greetings, Mico," said a voice to him then in the middle of Shop Street, and he came from his thoughts to look at the sardonic face of his brother.

"Oh, hello, Tommy," he said quite warmly. They didn't

see much of Tommy since he had moved himself into a room in the town. That was over two years ago now. First he had come back quite a lot for his meals. But since he had got another big science degree or something (Mico always got mixed up in the letters) he had gone into the chemical departments of one of the factories. Now he only appeared when he had bought a new suit, which was quite frequent, and he came sometimes when they were all there and handed over pound notes to his mother. It was very dramatic and good in a way, to see the way his mother's face lighted up, and she looking at them with pride in her eyes. Now what did I tell ye! Didn't I tell ye that some day he would be doing this?

He had a blue pin-stripe suit on him now, with a white collar and a red tie, and there was a shine on his shoes that you could see your face in. There was a girl beside him. She was tall and had long hair that was arranged to fall over her face, and her face was fashionably white and she had grand red lips that were opened to show you her teeth. They were good teeth. Her eyelashes were as long as the fins of a fish. Tommy was looking very well. Very well shaved and his fair hair was gleaming and wavy. He was as tall as Mico.

"Where are you off to, all dressed up like a Sunday?" he wanted to know.

"I'm going to meet a bus," said Mico.

"I hope the bus appreciates the effort you are making for it," said Tommy. The girl laughed, opening her white teeth. Mico could nearly see her tonsils.

"Still as funny as ever, brother," said Mico, going red.

"Ah, I didn't mean that, Mico," said Tommy. "Will you come in and have a drink with us, Christmas and all that?"

"Thanks," said Mico, "I can't. I still have to meet the special bus."

"Very well," said Tommy. "We'll meet again perhaps. I'll be down with you all for the Christmas dinner."

"That'll be nice," said Mico. "Goodbye now," and off he went.

Tommy stood looking after his broad shoulders pushing their way through the crowds. "Now what," he wondered aloud, "could have made the modest Mico dress up like that on a Saturday afternoon, and what bus could bring a light like that to his eye?"

The face of the clock with DUBLIN TIME written over it hurried his feet up the remaining street and out into the Square and down the side of it where the bus would come. It was free of buses for the moment, so he stood there, idling, watching the men opposite in the pub, with the glasses in their hands, and the sticks in the other ones, and they pressing on top of one another. A voice from the inside of the pub singing *My Shawl of Galway Grey*, in a real pub manner with dramatic pauses and scoops like a coalheaver in the docks, and the slowed applause of the near drunk, and the exhortations, and the singer started in and gave them *The Old Bog Road* and drew tears from them all about the bit where my mother died last springtime when Ireland's fields were green, and the neighbours said her waking was the finest ever seen; snowdrops and primroses piled up beside her bed, and the little church was crowded when her funeral mass was said. It'd draw tears from a turnip and even the arguers near the door turned to listen and shook their heads, and one old man drew a red handkerchief from his pocket, put it to his nose and blew it like a bugle up in the barracks playing lights out.

And then he saw the bus pushing its way up the street and he stood there with his heart pounding and his feet in their new brown shoes moving uneasily on the pavement.

It stopped then beside him with a squealing of brakes, its great red dust-coated body panting from its long exertions, and then the conductor descended and the passengers began to alight, their faces tired, their clothes crumpled from their long sitting. He stood back near the railings, his hands in his pockets to try and stem their trembling, and she was nearly the last one to come out from the bus.

She stood there blinking her eyes in the glare of the unheating sun. She seemed to Mico to have become small since he had last seen her. She was wearing a brown coat over a red dress, and her head was bare and she was holding in her hand a battered cardboard suitcase that was held together by a piece of strong yellow cord that seemed to have been plaited from straw.

Then her eyes moved and she looked around her.

Before her eyes met his own as he moved towards her, Mico noticed how thin her face had become. Her cheeks had fallen in a little so that her teeth seemed to be pushing her mouth out more than he remembered, and her nose was thinner and straighter, and the cleft in her chin seemed to have become deeper. Her eyes were black-looking and were sunk in her head, and they were circled with a purple tinge. And then her eyes met his and he wiped out the misgivings the sight of her had put in his heart and he went forward to meet her. Her eyes came alive as she saw him and she smiled a little, and he saw her then as she had always been. Nothing wrong with her; just lacking a bit of flesh, that's all, and flesh could be put back. Her eyes seemed to be calm too.

He took her hand in his. Was it always as thin and as brittle as this?

"Hello, Mico," she said, the first to speak.

"I'm awful glad to see you," said Mico.

They looked at each other then for a short time. Behind her eyes Mico saw the sorrow that had been baked out of them. The lonely places where you can only go alone and bring nobody at all with you, but out of which you have to come some day.

Maeve saw big Mico like you would see a big port if you were a ship and had struggled in from the boundlessness of a great and lonely sea. There was a great depth of kindness in the eyes that were fixed on her, and a warmth in the huge palm that was holding her own hand as if it was an eggshell. She noted the deep eternal brown that his face had acquired, slightly yellowed by the winter seas, and she saw the lines that had grown on his forehead, permanently grooved, and the many lines around his eyes from peering into the sun and the sky. And the gap in the middle of his mark showing shiny and white. She turned her eyes from that. It brought up memories of high seas.

"Have I changed such a lot then, Mico?" she asked.

"What are ye ravin' about," he wanted to know. "I'd know you among a million, so I would. You're lookin' great. A bit skinny you are, but after a while here you'll be like a Christmas turkey."

She laughed.

He bent for her bag.

"Will we be going?" he asked.

"All right," she said, "where do we go?"

"Over here," said Mico, putting a hand on her arm and feeling it thin under his fingers so that his heart sank again. They waited for a cart to pass and a bus to pass and two motorcars and a sidecar with men up on it singing and swaying

"There's a lot of people, isn't there?" said Maeve. "What's up?"

"Ah, nothin'," said Mico, "it's just the Christmas market and a lot of them do come in for it."

He ushered her across the street.

"Is the place far away, Mico," she wanted to know, "where I am going?"

"It isn't too far," said Mico. "Are you tired?"

"Oh no," she said, "it's just that long way in the bus. You do get tired in it."

"We won't be long," said Mico.

"Will the woman like me, Mico?" she asked then. "Maybe she won't like a strange girl from Connemara to be put in on her."

She laughed at the look in Mico's face.

"Me dear girl, what are you saying?" he asked. "You'll be a sort of lifeline to her, I tell you. It's very hard to explain, but with a bit of luck you'll do her more good than you have any idea." He didn't say that he was hoping that it would work the other way too. But the idea of not wanting Maeve! As if a surly person would bang the door in the face of the Blessed Virgin on Christmas Eve.

They crossed the street again through the traffic and went down a long wide street where the buildings curved at the corners.

Outside the Post Office they were stopped again. By a tall young man standing in the middle of the path and saying, "Well, there you are, Mico?" and looking inquisitively at the girl walking along beside Mico.

Mico stopped.

"Oh, this is me brother, Maeve," he said in a synopsis of an introduction.

Tommy held out his hand.

"How are you?" he said, his eyes examining her closely.

"Well, thank you," said Maeve, giving him her hand, surprised at the difference in the softness of his hand and Mico's big one as solid as seasoned timber. She looked at him, her eyebrows raised.

"I know," said Tommy, "nobody would take us for brothers, but actually we are from the one clutch. Somebody laid a foreign egg in the clutch and we don't know whether it was Mico or myself, but anyhow we are brothers."

She smiled at him.

"It must be nice to be a brother of Mico's," she said.

Tommy threw back his head and laughed. His teeth were strong and white.

"Well, that's rich now," he said. Mico waited with his lips tight for the expected bout of repartee, but Tommy stopped laughing as he looked at Maeve's surprised eyebrows and decided that she was serious. "We'll pass that one," he said. "Actually I was very curious as to why brother Mico should be dressed up in his best and his face shining and he off to meet a bus. Now I know. Mico never tells me anything. We have grown past the stage where we used to exchange confidences in the depths of our feather bed. Isn't that so, Mico?"

- 248 -

"You got away from us, brother," said Mico. "If we wanted to tell you anything now, we'd have to look for you first."

"Ah, well," said Tommy, "I won't detain you, but we will meet again perhaps."

"It's likely," said Maeve.

He stood aside.

"Till we meet so," he said, and stood there looking after them. Now where, he was wondering, did Mico get her. A very interesting face with those steady eyes and the life behind them. A bit thin. And those rather country clothes as if they had been made by herself in the candlelight. But a very interesting face.

"He's not a bit like you," Maeve was saying.

"You mean I'm not a bit like him," said Mico.

"I didn't think he was like that," said Maeve, "from the way you talked about him. I thought he was a sort of fellow with a weak chin and glasses, the way you talked. He's as big as yourself."

"That's right," said Mico. "Maybe it's because we're so different. He makes me feel small. It's a shocking thing to be thinking how stupid you are every time you meet your own brother. It comes from all the times he was standin' over me when we were young, and he tryin' to bate sums into my thick head. Maybe that's why."

He showed her the town as they walked. He was hoping she would like it. He was hoping she would like it enough to stay in it. The fear Mico had in that groping thinking of his was that now she had pulled her roots maybe she wouldn't want to stay in the one place. It must be a terrible thing to pull your roots. Would any place then seem worth planting them in again? So he showed her the cinema and the church, and he brought her around and showed her the sweep of the river and the flowers on the banks of it where it rushed brown and tumbling under the Salmon Weir bridge. Up that way he walked her and by the calm road where the University was, and around then and out by the hospital that always made him think of Peter from the smell of the disinfectants. Shortly they were knocking at Mrs Cusack's door.

He saw that Maeve was tired. Her face was drawn and her breath was short even after that walk. She looked as frail as a wilting flower. Holy God, he thought in despair, how is one ever going to make her forget it?

The door opened and Mrs Cusack stood there.

An awful lot depends on this now, Mico was thinking. Let it be all right. Mrs Cusack was as frail herself as a sparrow. Her hair was white and it was pulled back tightly over her head into a bun at the back. Her face was small and there was no spare flesh on it. The skin was tight across her nose. Her eyes were pale blue, and lines had eaten into the pale yellow of her skin. The cardigan she was wearing made her look like a tiny man, so little bosom had she. It was pale brown and she wore a cameo brooch in the front of a blue blouse. A black skirt and black shoes and stockings.

She looked at the girl in front of her. She smiled shyly. So did Maeve.

"Come in, my dear," she said then, after pressing her hand.

Maeve felt the carpet under her feet, and saw the hall bathed in the blue yellow light from the coloured glass of the door and the fanlight. Then the door closed and they were in the warm kitchen. Red tiles on the floor and the small range polished like a pair of shoes, so bright it was, and the table was laid. On a white cloth there were cups and saucers with blue Japanese designs on them. And a bowl of flowers in the middle of the table and gleaming cutlery and an almond cake, richly brown against the white of the cloth, and another cake with white icing on it and *A Merry Xmas* was picked out in pink icing.

"I thought," said Mrs Cusack, "that we might as well cut the old Christmas cake, since it's so near Christmas anyhow. Father had to go out for a few minutes, but he'll be back shortly and we can have tea. Give me your things, dear. Take off your coat. Come on upstairs and I'll show you your room." All in a spate it came.

When Mico bent for the suitcase, she said, "No, no, Mico,

you wait here and warm yourself, I'll bring it up for her," and she bent down and took up the case and was off up the stairs like a bird, and Mico stood huge and very near the ceiling and his face red with worry, and Maeve smiled at him before she followed the old lady up the stairs.

She wasn't used to stairs. She felt the polished wood smooth under her palm, the thick carpet cushioning her feet. And then she was on the landing and Mrs Cusack stood there with the door open and a shy smile on her face, like as if she was saying, "I hope you'll like this." A very brave act because it was Peter's room. Maeve went in and looked around her. A single bed under the window with a blue eiderdown on it. A fireplace in the centre of the wall and making a cubby-place on either side that was packed from floor to ceiling with books of all kinds. And there was a fire in the grate and it lighted the room, and there were starched lace curtains on the window that seemed to be blinding, the way they caught the light.

Maeve thought, This room is smiling. She went over and sat on the edge of the bed and dropped her head.

She was tired. The engine of the bus was still throbbing in her brain. You pull your roots and you are like the fluff holding the seeds of the dandelion being blown in the wind. This room and the bright kitchen below and the feel of the little anxious woman in the door; another woman who had travelled to the lonely places and come back. Maeve felt her, and felt her anxiety and felt the way she was groping like herself, like being in a dark room and holding out your hand in front of your face in case you hit your head against the wall. And then your hand meets a hand and you are safe, or you are on the right road. She felt all this, and the woman behind her in a strange way too felt all this.

So she at least wasn't surprised when the girl with the tragic eyes threw herself forward on the bed and rested there with her face hidden and her shoulders suddenly started to heave.

Mrs Cusack went over to her slowly. She didn't speak. She

just reached out a frail hand and placed it on the girl's back. A bony back, with her shoulders sharp peaks. How much thought had gone into making those sharp peaks maybe Mrs Cusack knew. So she laid her hand on her back and then she went away and she closed the door loudly enough so that it would penetrate to the girl on the bed, and then she went down the stairs and her eyes were shining.

"She will be all right, Mico," she said to the big man in the kitchen. "She will be all right now."

Mico looked closely at her. The ways of women. How could you read them? There was something now in the eyes of Mrs Cusack. Was it a purpose? It was something anyhow. Something that hadn't been there before.

"She's very tired, Mico," she said, "but she'll be all right now."

"She's very thin, Ma-am," said Mico. "Do you think is she too thin?"

"That can be cured, Mico," she said. "I might even get fat myself now."

"I better go, I suppose," said Mico wisely enough.

"Maybe if you did, it might be best," she said, agreeing with his thoughts.

He stood on the step and looked into her eyes. With questions. Suppose Mrs Cusack didn't get on with her? Suppose there was more unhappiness in store for her? Suppose a million things that put a crease between his eyes. Mrs Cusack put her hand out and rested it on his shoulder.

"She'll be all right, Mico," she said. "Don't worry."

And she will too, he thought, looking at her. She will indeed. It lifted from him and he smiled. She's in good hands, he thought. There has to be that. Who could doubt that? She would be all right.

"I'll come back tomorrow," he said, and turned and went out of the gate and latched it and waved to her as she closed the door, and looked up at the window where Peter used to sleep, and then he turned off home and went towards it, whistling.

Chapter Eighteen

ALTHOUGH HE KNEW that Maeve was in a house behind him and that in all probability she was weeping in a strange room, somehow Mico didn't feel too sad as he went home. He halted his steps at the Claddagh Basin and looked into the water for a while.

All the boats were at the quays. The old men were sitting on the bollards, their black flopping Connemara hats shading their eyes from the sun reflected blindingly but coldly from the smooth waters of the engulfing tide. At the far side of the church, the younger men were standing, smoking and talking idly, watching the passers-by, greeting them if they knew them, letting them go with a stare if they didn't, and the cries of children were rising from the Swamp where the kids, free of school for the Christmas, were watching a football match, and an old lady with a long coat and a flower-pot hat was throwing bread to the swans, dipping her hand into a brown-paper bag.

Mico suddenly decided to go into the church. It was no easy thing to do. It was not the accepted thing to do for a young man to walk into the church in the middle of the day for no apparent reason, and that under the eyes of the young men of his own age. But now suddenly he thought that it would be a good thing to kneel for a while in the silent church under the placid light of the sun shining through the stained glass windows. Maybe he would be able to work something out. To hell with you, my hearties, he thought, as he hitched his belt and walked to the gate of the church.

Comments floated after him, but he closed his ears to them, grinning, and feeling a bit hot under the collar.

Why is that, he wondered?

He climbed the stone steps and dipped his hand in the water-font and blessed himself carefully. He opened the door then and made his way into the church.

That's what I mean now, he thought, as he made his way up the centre aisle, and listened to the sighs and sibilant prayers of the two old shawled women in the back seat. It was very silent except for the sincere prayers of the old people. He got into a seat behind an old man with white hair and knelt down.

The old people. It was a refuge for them, the church. They seemed to have nothing left in life except it, that and waiting to die. The altar seemed to be miles away from him, and the sanctuary lamp, gleaming redly, was like a star in front of the moon in the evening. He could see the pink scalp of the man in front of him, ringed with frail, snow-white hair. He knew him. There were rosary beads twined round his fingers, just like they would be when he was in his coffin. His prayers came in faint whispers. So it was all right to kneel here with your head in your hands, disturbed only by these sounds that belonged to the place, and if you listened closely enough you would hear the muted roar of the turbulent town outside in the middle of its market and its noise. So you pressed a finger at the drum of your ear, and that was shut out too and you were really alone.

His thoughts?

What do I want? Sure God above must know what I want, not to have me bringin' misfortune on everybody I meet, that's the principal thing. I want to be left alone, so that I

- 254 -

can go me own quiet unobtrusive way without bringing misfortune on everybody's head. He had come to believe that
now. Let things rest for a while, and if they go on fair and
square for a good time, mebbe I can say then, Ah well, the
jinx has gone now to scrape somebody else, and it will be all
right for me to take a cautious step or two in the direction I
want to go. That was easy. He wanted very little. His bread
he could earn himself, and if it was slack he could tighten
his belt. He just wanted her, if that was possible. It seemed
terribly impossible at the moment, but surely stranger things
had happened than that. She was used to his face anyhow,
that was something, and since the sight of it must have
grown on her, then she wouldn't even see it. So that was
one hurdle over, but there were as many more left as up on
the racecourse at Ballybrit. There was Coimín. Could anybody after living with Coimín want to come and live with a
fella like Mico? That was a nut. And even if so, what about
the difference in the place you would have to live? Where
would a house be got and what class of a house? And even
if so, what about the kind of life with Mico at sea and the
girl at home? What about that? Wasn't that the toughest nut
of all? Hadn't it happened once before and wouldn't you be
afraid of your life of it happening again?

Mico heaved a great sigh.

Ah, no, he thought, 'tis impossible, and if ever a miracle
was worked, as true as God it will have to be worked now.
And that's that. Amen.

"Hello, Mico," said the voice of the girl who came softly
and knelt beside him.

He turned his head, his eyes wide, as if he was afraid he
might have said some of the things out loud.

"Hello, Jo," he said then, surprised.

"I came down to see you," she whispered. "I just saw the
tail of your coat coming into the church. Come on out now,
I want to talk to you."

"All right," said Mico, rising and wondering. He genu-
flected to the altar and followed her trim figure out.

He hadn't seen much of her since Peter died. He didn't want to. Somehow he had guessed that she didn't want to see him either. What was the use of starting, Do you remember with each other? Not when a man was dead. That did no good; that was only robbing a grave. He knew she had become a teacher. He had seen her once or twice at the annual processions, and she shepherding a whole troop of little demons looking like angels in white dresses with white veils on their heads.

They had met and they had spoken a little, about How are you? and What are you doing now? and they had looked at each other's eyes and had looked away again and she would say, "Well, I have to be going now, I have so many exercises to correct," showing him the pile of ink-stained copy books under her arm with the huge unformed writing of names on them.

She turned as she came down the steps and looked up at him. She looked at him and didn't turn her eyes away, and she smiled. And it revealed a lot of her, of a good, thoughtful, intelligent girl who was very capable.

"You're looking very well, Mico," she said when he reached her, and she put her hand on his arm. "Let's go over to the river," she went on. "We can talk there."

"All right," said Mico. "You're looking very well yourself too. It's a long time since I saw you."

"It is," she said. "Too long. I meant to come and see you many a time but I kept putting it off. Now I don't mind. It's all clear."

They came out of the gate, her hand still on his arm, and the men at the church wall released low whistles, and one of them said in a loud voice, "Now we know what he was goin' into the chapel for!" and another said, "Is there any more like that left in there, Mico?"

And Mico turned his head to them and laughed at them, and Jo, unperturbed, turned too and smiled at them and waved a hand, and they raised their caps to her quite respectfully, and then the two forgot them as they crossed the road and walked on the grass towards the wooden bridge over the lock gate, and they crossed this and walked over the grass until they came to the quay wall and they could look down at the river boiling below them, and Jo let herself down and tucked her legs under her, and Mico heaved himself beside her and let his legs hang over the water.

"I'm going away, Mico," she said, "so I wanted to say goodbye."

"Where are you going?" he asked her.

"I'm going away to be a nun," she said, and then turned her face fully to his to watch his eyes. She knew so well by now the look that could come into the eyes of people when she made the simple statement.

When Peter had died she had stayed in her own room for three days and three nights and she had not come out of it at all. Not to the entreaties of her mother or the threats of her father or the coaxing of the twins. And when she came out, she came out not much different to what she had been when she went in. From that day she had spoken to none of them about Peter. It was just the same as if she had never met him or as if she had never gone and shut herself into her room for three days. The only concession she made to them was to kiss the ravaged and worried face of her mother and say, "I'm sorry, Mother. I didn't mean to worry you." That was all. She had finished her studies and she had gone to teach children. She loved teaching children. She was a very good teacher. She had a way with her. She was neither too cross nor too kind, and deep inside her there was a great well of patience. She found that in her room and it was never to leave her, ever.

She had taken her time. She had allowed two years to pass over her head. Then she had told her mother and she had watched the look in her eyes. Disturbed. Incredulous. Her mother was a good woman. She was a good wife. She regarded all woman's duties as being those two things. And the way to do them was to cohabit with a man and enjoy it and have children and suffer them, and bear with a husband. That was life. That was woman.

Mr Mulcairns didn't take it lying down. No, sir. He knew a thing or two. Of course he respected nuns. They were good women. They did a lot of sterling work. But dammit all to hell, that was for other men's daughters and not for his. What kind of a wasted life is that, shutting a woman up in a convent? What the hell good were you doing? Wasn't it the most selfish life in the world? Shutting yourself off from the struggles of humanity; to shelter your fear of the future behind high walls; an egotistical seeking after salvation for yourself; what kind of a life was that for a girl? Damned if she would and double damned. And he called for his slippers and he called for his supper and he called for his paper and he sat into the chair and pulled the paper over his head and Jo knew the look that was in his eyes. It was hurt.

He was an ordinary man. All his friends were ordinary men. How could he meet them over a pint in the club, and say, "Look, men, that daughter of mine is going to be a nun"? Nuns were out of their kens. If a nun came within eight miles of them they would shuffle their feet and feel as awkward as a pup in a doll's house. Nuns to them were the robed figures of saints in the church with their chiselled eyes raised to heaven and carved crosses in their ethereal hands. It put a fellow a bit out of the ordinary to have a daughter a nun. It was nearly worse than if she was going to have a bastard. That was natural. It was near home. Men could understand that since it could happen to their own just as easily. But a nun! In time of course he would mellow. It made a fellow a little different. Men drinking pints would look at you a little differently. Mulcairns' daughter is a nun. Did you know that? It might even moderate their language a little as they thought about it.

But there were her father's eyes. Hurt in them.

Friends' eyes? Astonishment. Mockery. Incomprehension.

And here were the simple eyes of Mico. What?

"I hope you'll be happy," said Mico.

"You are the first that said that, Mico," she said.

- 258 -

They both looked at the water.

It was a rushing river, normally shallow, that piled over a ragged bottom so that its torrent was broken into white foam and big curving sprays. Now the sea was swelling it, but the rushing over the stones was not lost. The wide sweep of the river was broken by heavy undulating waves. And out in the centre there was a black cormorant riding the tide. He dived and they waited for him to come up and when he came he had the wriggling body of a small eel in his beak. They saw an evil eye flashing over them and then he dived again as if he was afraid that they would steal the eel from him.

"I was always queer," said Jo "With fellas, I mean. I hated to be touched. It wasn't being prim or anything. It was just that I didn't want to be touched. It used always make me feel a little ill to have the hands of a man come near me. That was always the way. Even with Peter. Peter joked a lot about it. He was puzzled. He couldn't understand how everyone couldn't feel like himself. I think I was the only one who ever succeeded in giving Peter a complex, apart from himself. Maybe it was because I was like that. It was grand talking to him. It made you feel alive talking to him. Sometimes you would be exhausted. Sometimes you would be so stimulated that when you went home to bed you couldn't sleep for hours. You'd see him in front of you waving his hands and his red hair flapping and his eyes alive. Now that things are as they are, I am very glad that Peter could touch me and that in the end it pleased me. But we fought a lot. Not he, really, but me. I didn't deep down want to be pleased because he could soften me. I didn't want to be like that, for some reason I couldn't analyse. I didn't want to be under the spell of this red-haired man. I didn't want to be under the spell of any man. And it came to me too, that suppose some day I married Peter with all the unrest and glorious movement and uncertainty that marriage with him would have meant, and suppose I did and that one day it came to me, maybe eating breakfast with him in the morning, that I had been led away from the substance by the shadow, and suppose after all that time that one day he touched me and I shrank from him, what would have happened to him? What would have happened to his eyes? That thought.

"All this I finally hammered out in my room when Peter died. I cleared it up a little. Don't think I didn't love Peter. I did. I loved him very much. I loved him more than my mother or father or my own brothers or anybody else I had ever met, but it isn't because of Peter that I'm doing this. There was always someone else – really. I waited. I have learned patience. But now I know, Mico. And now you know. That's my story. That's why I came to say goodbye to you."

There was silence between them.

The main feeling Mico had was the lack of surprise that was in him.

He wasn't surprised. It had always been difficult to get close to Jo, as if she had gone away and come back; every time you met her you had that feeling. Was there a purpose in Peter's dying after all? Such a terrible death. Was the purpose big enough? Mico didn't know. It was too complicated for him.

"We'll think about you," was all he could say to her.

"I'll think of you too," she said. "Peter was very fond of you, Mico. I wouldn't give Mico's big toe, he'd say, for the whole of humanity. Not even for me? I'd say, and he'd say, Well, maybe I'd sacrifice a second of Mico's toes for you."

Mico laughed.

"Poor oul Peter," he said.

"Poor oul Peter indeed," said she, and then she got to her feet, standing straight and tall and sure against the sky as he looked up at her. Then he got to his feet and towered over her. She held out her hand.

"I'll think of you, Mico," she said, "out in the sea and you coming home with the tired look in your face."

She smiled, and she walked away then and left him, walking towards the main road beside the bridge. He stood there and watched her. She ducked under the link of chain swinging between the wooden posts that divided the entry from the road, and then she turned back and waved her hand at him.

He waved back at her and then she walked firmly across the bridge under which the swollen river tumbled to the sea.

There's one has come now, Mico thought, and there's one has gone away.

I hope the one that's come has come to stay.

He went home.

Chapter Nineteen

MAEVE SAT ON a seat on the promenade and watched the fishing fleet coming home.

It was a summer evening.

The water of the Bay before her was barely rippled and the black boats, apparently unmoving, were like paper cut-outs stuck on a photograph of what she was looking at.

Around her there was movement. There was colour. The colour of the dying sun in the sky, dying in a technicolor dream, and on the promenade young girls were passing and laughing or chatting, with or without young men in tow, and a few older people were sitting on the seats, their hands resting on the crooks of their walking-sticks. Pipe smoke was blue in the air and cigarette smoke.

She was thinking.

Of the way she felt. Of the changes that had come over both herself and her thoughts in a short few months. It was only last Christmas that she had left home, and yet now she felt as if she had been out of it for generations. Was it possible for the human mind to be so callous in its forgetfulness?

Well, it was no wonder in a way that she had begun to forget. You couldn't, after all, keep thinking for ever. And then when she had chosen to change her place of living, she had unconsciously chosen what would be the best way to forget. Among people. So many people that it was confusing, and that was the start. You endeavour to sort the people out, and give them names and occupations and listen to them talking. It became extremely difficult to fit in Coimín in the middle of all this, so the shape and memory of him had to be shut up in a private room in her mind, and she could open the door then sometimes, but the opening of it became infrequent as she struggled to understand and fit herself into this new and confusing life about her.

It showed in her now.

The tall fair young man who was coming up the prom on her left saw the difference in her.

He saw a girl on a seat and her hair was brown and worn long so that it reached her shoulders in a silken tide, rippling like the waves of the sea. He could see the clear-cut face near him where the hair was pulled back behind her ear, the clean line of the jaw and the straight forehead and nose with the lips slightly opened. She was sitting straight and her hands were listless in her lap hiding the line of her breast, emphasizing the outline of her lower body. Very nice, he said to himself, before he came closer and saw who it was. It couldn't be? That girl of Mico's. But she was such a dowdy little thing. Clear eyes all right, but her clothes were like as if they had been cut out in the dark by the local tinsmith. There was little about her now that betrayed the hand of the amateur. She had no stuff on her face except colour on her lips. There was a slight flush over the tan that the sun had given her face, and as he closed and stopped beside her, and his shadow fell on her, she looked up, and he thought, this girl is not the same. Her face was striking. There was something in the clear eyes and the cleft in her chin; a clarity of vision and suffering behind her that had put slight purple shadows beside her sunken eyes. She parted her lips and he saw her teeth behind the slight smile she gave him.

"Hello," she said.

"So it is you," said Tommy.

"Who did you think it was?" she wanted to know.

"You've changed a lot," he said, one hand on the back of the concrete seat, the other pulling the crease of his trousers up so that he wouldn't bulge it with his knees when he sat down. It was a good suit. It was brown gaberdine and it went well with the bleached fairness of his hair.

"We all change," she said.

"Yes, but not so much," said Tommy. "The last time I saw you you were just off the bus. Mico was with you. Outside the Post Office."

"Yes, I remember," she said. "I have been down to your house a lot since. I never met you there."

"Is that a rebuke?" he asked.

"Why, no," she said. "Why should I be rebuking you?"

"Why indeed?" he said. "What are you doing here?"

"Sitting," she said. "Watching Mico's boat coming home. Thinking."

"Oh," he said, shifting his eyes from her face to the sea. "Yes. There they are. The poor devils."

"Why do you say that?" she asked in a genuine surprise.

"It's a literal remark," he said. "They are poor. Even the devils must have a softer time than they have. That's all. What a life! That's what I mean."

"They don't think so," she said. "It's a useful life."

"What's useful about it?" he asked.

"Well," she said, "they work. They do something for their living."

"Excuse me," he said, "they don't work. They slave. Slavery is always expendable. Do you think that I don't work?"

She turned her eyes on him. They were a little cold.

"Why, I don't know," she said. "I have never thought about you at all."

"I see," he said. "Was there never any dialogue at all about Mico's brother?"

"Your mother talks about you," she said.

- 264 -

"Yes," he said, "she does. The others don't. They dislike me. Mico doesn't like me. Of course there's no need to tell you that, is there?"

"I don't know what you mean at all," she said. "Mico talks about you as if he was very proud of you. You've grown away from them, that's all. They like having a man in the family who is successful. Are you successful?"

"Why do you ask that?" he demanded.

"Well," she said, "if you are successful, I'm wonderin' why you are goin' around wondering what people think about you."

He half rose from his seat to go then. His lips tightened. She thought he was about to take off. She was glad. She thought he was a smug young man. Then he sat back again and turned to her. His eyebrows were pulled down over his eyes.

"I want you to understand," he said tightly.

"But why me?" she asked.

He looked fully at her.

"I don't know," he said. "I'd just like you to. You have come from people like them. It's hard for you to see anything beyond brown sails and the smell of fish."

He thought that would hurt her. She smiled. And he flushed. He felt like a small boy.

"Dammit," he said then in a burst, "you'll have to listen to me!"

A passing couple paused to turn raised eyebrows to them. He glared back at them until they averted their heads.

"Please," said Maeve. "What's happened? Two minutes ago, I was quite happy here on this seat, thinking. Why should you come down and upset me now? When I've only met you once in my life? I'll be going now."

He put out his hand and rested it on her bare brown arm.

"No, don't go, please don't go!" he said, his eyes very soft, like Mico would be sometimes. She noticed that his hand was long and thin and strong looking, the nails very clean, the cuticles very regularly attended to. She sat back again. "It's as peculiar to me too," he went on when she was sitting. "I just came along and saw a girl sitting on a seat on the promenade and I admired the look of her and approved of the cut of her until I came up and saw it was you."

"The admiration ended there and then," she said, and laughed.

"No, no, I don't mean that," he said, wondering what in the name of God was coming over him that she, a little girl from the country, could be tying him into knots like this. "Tell me, what do you know about me?"

"But what does it matter?" she wanted to know. "Why are you going into this?"

"Just to know," he said. "Sometimes I get a bit mixed up. It's a lonely thing sometimes to be up on a hill. I am on a hill, you know. I meet nobody I can acknowledge as my intellectual equal. That's true. It's not boasting. I can suffer them for a while, but then they make statements that are so moronic and so stupid that I have to leave them. Besides, I'm going away soon."

"Going away?" she asked. "From Galway is it? From home?"

"Yes," he said.

"Does your mother know?" she asked.

His eyes were wide.

"What does that matter?" he asked her. Maeve felt then like getting up and going, but she held herself down.

"No," she said, "I suppose that doesn't matter to you."

"You don't understand," he said.

"I find it hard," she said. "From what I know if it hadn't been for your mother you'd be out there today on the Bay hauling fish with Mico."

"That's not true," he said. "It's where people go astray about me. If I had never had a mother, if I was born in a mud hut in the middle of the Connemara mountains I would have done just what I have done. Some people are born to be just what they are. I'm one of them. It was appropriate that I should have had a mother who would see what I was and not put obstacles in my way. But I would have done it anyhow. I got where I am by what I had myself, and now this town is too small for me. The country is too small for me. So I am leaving it."

"I see," she said.

"I know what you're thinking," he went on. "You're thinking that you have never met anybody in your life or conceived of anybody you could meet who would be as egotistical as I am, but you're wrong. This country is only starting to become industrial. It's back now starting where the English were a hundred years ago. My work, small and all as it is, has attracted notice, so I am leaving. I'm going to a big combine in England. For how long I don't know. And I'll go on from there. You see, the world has changed. Once upon a time a scientist was an old buzzard with a beard and a test tube in a cobwebbed room, but now life has become so complicated that they can't perform even a function of nature without having a scientist at hand to approve it for them. The whole world is moving into the hands of science. But not here. Outside. You have to go outside to find the immensity of it, and do you know the whole trouble with me?"

"No," she said, interested in spite of the spate.

"I don't think I ever wanted to be a scientist. That's the tragedy of me."

"How?" she asked.

"Have you heard of a chap named Peter Cusack?" he asked her.

"I have," she said. "I sleep in his room." She saw the enlarged picture of him hanging on the papered wall over from her bed. The face of a red-haired young man with a grin, the sides of his mouth turning up. She saw his mother looking at the picture. She heard the mother talking, quietly, philosophically; she saw his father, who had lost interest in his guns and his fishing rods, who came home most nights now apologetically drunk, his pale blue eyes abashed. "Yes, I have heard of him," she said.

"He had a fairly good brain," he said. "But he let it wander into side issues instead of applied knowledge. We were together at school and at college. He wanted to be a scientist. I didn't, until he wanted to be. And then I thought, suppose he does and makes use of it and becomes very famous? And I said, what he can do, I can do. So I did. I don't think I wanted that. I wanted to know things. I wanted to be able to read Sanscrit and to read the old Bible in the original. Lots of other things. And to write too. I can write now, but I haven't the time for it. So I turned away from all that to this. This is not easy. But once you have learned the fundamentals, and if you have a good brain, it's quite simple. I like mathematics. But sometimes I'm worried. He's dead now. But how do I know he's not laughing at me?"

"I don't know," said Maeve, looking at him, barely understanding what he was trying to tell her, but thinking that he was truly a complex character, and feeling sorry for him in a way. He looked childish now, looking out unseeingly at the sea with a deep cleft between his eyebrows. "Maybe you think too much about it," she added lamely.

"My God!" he said, turning on her. "Isn't that the whole trouble with this bloody country that we do so little thinking? Isn't the whole brains of Ireland as rusty as a six-inch nail in the sea from lack of thinking? Look at the people walking around you. Look at them bathing. Look at them soaking themselves in the mediocrity of mediocrities churned out twice a week from the great moron factory called Hollywood that is choking the whole world, strangling it with the glorification of the mundane."

"I like the pictures," said Maeve. "If you had been all your life and never seen them, you'd like them too."

"I thought you were different," he said bitterly.

"Why should I be different?" she asked.

"I don't know," he said; "just that Mico never likes anybody unless they're different."

"Is it possible," she asked, "that you have some respect for Mico?"

"Of course I have," he said. "Mico is something I wish I was in my saner moments. He's placid, like a big good-humoured bull. I wish I was that way. I wish sometimes I had never been driven to becoming what I am, so that I wouldn't be driven now to go on, and go on, and go on, and when I do go on, what's the end of it all?"

"You will know more," she said.

He looked at her closely.

"That's true," he said. "I will know more. Few people like me you know."

"I don't wonder," said Maeve.

That startled him.

"Why do you say that?" he asked.

"Well, you despise people so openly," she said.

"Do I?" he asked, his elbow resting on the concrete supporting his head so that he was turned sideways looking into her eyes.

"Yes," she said. "Maybe you're very clever. I don't know. But some people are clever and other people aren't clever. But I think you should try to be a little bit more kind to people. They never did anything to you personally. If you think they are slow, that's no reason for you to feel that you're God Almighty and look at them as if you were sorry for making them at all. If the Lord God thought that way, he'd say what's the use of making millions of morons when they are all inferior to Me? But sure He didn't. He took the broad view, and said, Ah, God help the poor creatures. Sure we may as well let them have a bit of fun."

He laughed.

"Will you come and dance with me?" he asked her.

"Where?" she asked.

He waved a hand back behind them. She listened. From a big tin shed that was hot in the sun she heard the faint strains of music.

"In there," he said. "Afternoon dance."

"I don't dance very well," she said.

"Where does Mico bring you so?" he asked her.

"Oh, Mico doesn't bring me many places," she said. "He's not often at home. I've been a lot of places. All around the town and out by the sea and the woods and up the lake."

He stood up, pulling down his coat to get the creases out of it.

"Come on," he said.

She thought about it and then she consented.

"All right," she said rising. Her head came to his chin when she stood, he noticed. Her body was slim and her limbs long and rounded. All the hollows he had noticed before had gone. He thought she was very atractive. He liked the directness of her. She would stimulate you to anger or argument and you couldn't say that about a lot of the girls he knew now. He wondered if she knew Mico was in love with her.

"You like Mico?" he asked while they stood on the edge of the prom waiting for a stream of cars to pass before they crossed the road.

"Oh yes," she said. "I like Mico. Why do you ask?" looking up at him.

"What harm is there in asking?" he asked.

"I don't know. With anybody else it would be just a question," she said. "But when you ask questions, I don't know what is behind them."

"There is nothing behind this," he said, taking her arm and shepherding her across. The feel of her cool bare flesh was nice in his palm. Maeve thought she liked the soft feel of his hand on her arm. It was smooth. No callouses on it. Her own hand were nearly bare of callouses now, too, after her soft life in the town.

Nothing behind his question. But she had answered him more than she knew. Yes, she liked Mico. She should be afraid of Mico, he thought. Mico would wait around without opening his mouth for seventy years, if he thought that it would be right then. But she was too good for Mico. Look at her now, so neatly dressed and sure of herself. What could Mico do with her apart from making love to her? Nothing. Throw her into an old canvas apron like his mother. Put big boots on her and crack her hands with the soda of the Monday washing. That's where the lack of thought came in.

Maeve felt a vague stirring in herself as she walked beside him down the leafy lane that led off the main road. A sort of excitement that she hadn't felt for a long time. He was a change from all the travellers coming into the shop and telling her it was lonely to be a commercial traveller and could they interest her into coming to the pictures or out for a little drive in the car?

"Did Mico ever bring you down here?" he asked then, indicating the lane they walked in with the grass edges and the low-lying thorn bushes that bordered the lane until farther down it wound and was entirely roofed in by tall chestnut and birch trees.

"No," she said. "Why?"

"This is Lovers Lane," he said. "It's traditional. I believe that's why they erected the dance hall one side of it."

"Is that so?" she said. "No, Mico and me are respectable people. Whatever you think about us, we find there are others things in life for us. I wish you'd stop talkin' about Mico. You think you know him, but you don't. You've been too busy trying to make yourself out."

For a moment he felt like becoming huffy, but he didn't. He laughed.

He held her hand to assist her over the stone stile into the field of the dance hall. It was a short cut with a gravel path leading in. There was no need to hold her hand. He liked the feel of it. It made the muscles twitch on his forearms, and when shortly their feet were sliding over the polished floor he felt a trembling in his limbs at the closeness of her; the soft bulk of her breasts against his chest; the wisps of her hair that touched his cheek; the feel of her warm flesh moving under the thin stuff of her dress.

Maeve liked it too. But more the concentration of keeping her feet moving; listening to the blaring of the band; getting a glimpse of the two of them, like strangers, in the big mirrors of the hall, and looking up into his face which was surprisingly young-looking as well as good-looking and smiling at him as if to say, I am enjoying this.

The black boats were swinging wearily in towards the mouth of the river.

Chapter Twenty

THEY HAD LONG left the harbour and had covered the Sound, and the pale October day was half dead, before Mico drew himself from his thoughts to regard the sea around him. It was like waking out of a dream and finding yourself at sea, and saying how did I get here, and have I done this, that, and the other without noticing it at all. Seeing his father back at the stern with his legs spread and his boots sideways on the boards, he puffing at a pipe, still-dying fish wriggling between his feet, and a quizzical look on his face and his eyes crinkled with a smile as he met the eyes of his son.

"It's a nice day," said Mico.

"It was," said Micil.

It was no wonder really. He had so much to think of. His dreams were coming so near the point where they might be capable of fulfilment that he was holding his breath with fear. He was slightly shocked at the advances he had made himself towards the fulfilment of them. And the trouble in a way was that it had all been comparatively easy.

It had started when he had walked around the back of the village to Fair Hill and watched them destroying the white cottages. Cheerful men in dungarees and lime-encrusted boots, with bared arms rippling with muscles and browned by the sun. Caps on their heads. They tore into the cottages and before you knew where you were you were seeing the inside of a gutted house; the whitewash seeming very white when they exposed the blackened walls near the roof; the smell of the centuries of straw and scraw that had gone to the making of them; the seeing that it was a very small space for a whole family to have lived in and wondering how on earth they had.

And shortly they had raped a row of them, and torn them up by the roots and scattered the whitewashed stones to the four corners of the world, and tall scaffolding poles went up, reaching stripped arms to the sky, their butts sunk in barrels that were filled with stones, and you heard the chug of the donkey engine on the small concrete mixer and the loud talk of the labourers and their bawdy cheerfulness, and you could see them sitting on the nearest handy thing with their legs spread and their thick thighs pressing against the stuff of their clothes and their teeth closing on thick slices of bread and butter, and they drinking tea that was as strong and brown as bogwater, drinking it out of tall cans, blackened and battered from their casual fires; and from the decayed ruins of the rows began to emerge the thin shape of new houses. They would be two-storey ones, strickly utilitarian, fearfully ugly, but they would have a garden in front and a garden in the back, and there would be a real lavatory, and a range in the small kitchen.

"I wonder, Gran," said Mico to him one day, as they stood there looking on, with the lovely pleasure one gets from looking at other men working, "I wonder, suppose a fella, a young fella, wanted to get married and he had no house at all, and he wanted to get married, would there be any hope now of gettin' one of those."

"Hum," said Gran. "'Tis hardly likely. They take the people outa the houses they are going to destroy and they put them somewhere else, but when the houses are built they'll have to have them back again, because they are fishermen and they like to be near their work and not living up in the wilds of Bohermore."

"I see," said Mico, with a sigh.

"Of course," said Gran, "this whole world was built on a wangle, there's no doubt at all about that. It's possible that things like that could be fixed if we went about it the right way."

"Ah, no," said Mico.

"Me dear man," said Gran, "everybody knows that towns-men are as crooked as rams' horns. If they weren't, what would we be doin' slavin' for them while they live in their fat mansions up on hills? There's only one way they can be hurtit. That's to threaten their profits. There's a few men in this town that makes a lot of money out of the sweat of the Claddagh, and suppose they were approached and told that somebody else might be given the chance of swindlin' us in-stead of them, maybe they'd see the daylight."

"But," said Mico, "if be any chance in the world, and it is a very slender one indeed, and almost incapable of happen-ing, that I ... I mean that a young fella that wanted to get married got one of them houses, well, supposin' such, wouldn't he only be depriving people of a house that is in line for them?"

"A devil a one," said Gran, spitting at a heap of gravel. "The houses is for the fishermen. Some of the fellas that'll get those houses knows no more about fishin' than cats know about weddin' bells. The closest they will ever come to a fish is a salted herrin' on Friday. In all probability the very labourers on the houses will get them. It wouldn't sur-prise me at all. And some of the men that have gone up to live in the town will abandon the fishing. I know that. So it is only just that if a legitimate fisherman wants a house, that all manner of things should be done so that it can happen like that. We will gup and see Pa about it."

So they went to see Pa.

A retired Pa. A changed man. Very white now instead of being very grey, his tweed clothes hanging loosely on him.

Wearing glasses, a thing he had never done. But he was an old man and they took his school away from him with words of praise and a presentation of a silver tray. What in the name of the Almighty God good is a silver tray to me? What will I be doing with a silver tray at the end of my days? They took away his school and his boys and they might as well have cut his throat at the same time. He stayed at home now always, reading. So many things I want to read before I die that I never got around to before. Every day at twelve o'clock, he put on his hat and took his thick stick and he walked out on the promenade. He spoke to boys and admonished them for such things as firing stones at cats or tying tin cans to the tails of dogs, or firing pellets from airguns at the bulbs in the light stardards of the Electricity Supply Board, or lectured them in the buses about not rising politely and giving up their seats to the aged and infirm. He sometimes went back to the school and had a look in there. He wasn't very welcome now. There were newer teachers and younger ones, and naturally they thought their own ways were better than his had been.

He visited his past pupils. None of them ever forgot him. He hadn't aged for them at all. There was respect for him still in their eyes and that made him sit straighter and brought the words flowing more strongly from his whiskered lips.

A problem presented to him.

Let me see. Who is on the Council now? Such a one and such a one. Oh yes. I know him. I know him very well indeed. And the other fellow, what's his name? Yes, I think he would like to do me a favour. And the other one daren't refuse to do me a favour. So that's three I can get after, and how many can you handle, Gran? Oh, I can fix two and in a pinch I could manage another fella. Well, there you are. We must arrange it all. Marvellous in a way, the power of the common people. True democracy that is. That an old schoolmaster and an old fisherman, both retired, both, in a manner of speaking, on the rocks, can stretch out a hand

and take a share in the democracy of humanity.

So there, almost before he had expressed the wish, he was promised a house. He even knew the number of it, and that it would be ready at Christmas. So he'd have to hurry on. He went down and watched it often. It seemed to be rising too fast for his peace of mind. He saw the walls and he saw the wooden planks laid on, that would be the ceiling of the rooms below and the floors of the rooms above. He felt sometimes that he'd like to go up to the building chaps and say, "Listen, fellas, don't go so fast, will ye, I want more time to think this out."

So he had spent today thinking it out. Facing it out. Could a girl spend her life with him? Would her heart sink at the thought? Not if she was Maeve and if she wanted to. But this was a different Maeve. This new girl that went around so well dressed with her hands white and clean and soft to the touch. Think of her side of it. Her life was easy now. In the shop and only that work. Would she be ready now to throw all that up and become the wife of a common fisherman? Holy God! Then think of Coimín. He had been a fisherman too and look what happened to him. Would she want to go through all that again?

So you face it. Now. As soon as possible. If the auguries are right. He was still afraid of bringing bad luck on people. If there was only a sign that he wasn't bad luck for people any more! But that would have to be chanced.

They rounded the headland then and saw the trawler.

"The bastards!" said Big Micil, rising to his feet, the pipe in his hand.

On their left were towering cliffs with the waves a white foam at the feet of them. Here and there the tall cliffs were broken by small coves, comparatively peaceful. On their right was the south island of the Aran group, looking green and brown and slightly bedraggled with the approach of winter. The sky over their heads was closed from sight by fairly low-lying clouds which sent a not very stiff breeze to swell their sail and ruffle the sea they sailed into a sort of grey mass like wholemeal porridge boiling in a pot. For the time of the year it wasn't cold. It was sticky. They had the sea to themselves except for the other Claddagh boat that was rounding the headland behind them, and the working trawler in front of them.

"What is it?" Mico asked.

"It's English," said Micil, "may the devil scald them!"

"They have a seine net too," said Mico.

"They have, the filthy things!" said Micil.

"Can we get their number from here?" Mico asked.

"No," said Micil, grimly hauling the sail tighter, "but we'll bloody well go and get it. I'm sick of them. If it isn't English it's French, and if it isn't French it's Spanish. Why in the name of God can't they stay in their own grounds?"

Close-hauled the big black boat started to hiss its way towards the distant trawler. It was about half a mile from them and fishing about a mile from the line. Foreign fishing boats were permitted to fish in other people's waters, but they were supposed to stay three miles off shore in order to leave a few fish for inshore fishermen. Sometimes they do and sometimes they don't. They do if they are afraid of the navy of the country where they are poaching: they don't if they think they can get away with it and not be caught and fined and their gear confiscated. You ask the Claddagh men about the foreign trawler and you'll see a crease coming between their brows and you'll see a disdainful spit coming from their mouths followed by language. Who cares? Isn't Ireland an open sesame for them all? We had a navy at this time. It was a great navy. One boat it was, older than two grandfathers, and they called it the *Hound of the Sea*. Hound me ah, said the men. Trawlermen in the three poaching countries regarded the Irish fishing grounds as a man'd think of heaven. They couldn't believe their eyes. You knew they were Spanish if the bow of them rose like an old galleon, and you knew they were French from the poop, and you knew they were English the way you recognize everything else English. Cut down and spare, and no dash

- 278 -

like the Continentals. This was English all right.

"Get up on the bow," said Micil. "I'll swing her about so you can get a good look at the number. It's the only thing we can do. If only we could get aboard her and get our hands on them! But that's not possible. So get their number and write it down and we'll send it in and maybe in ten years' time they'll do something about it."

Mico swung himself up on to the bow and stood there, tall, with his hand holding on to the rope of the foresail. He saw a slighty flurry on the trawler as they approached. He heard a shout over the closing space of water. A black silhouette of a man pointing and shouting and running back to the small wheelhouse of the boat. Then he saw a bigger man coming out and coming up forward and holding a hand over his eyes and regarding them, and then three more men made their appearance.

They closed on the trawler. The burnt-in number of the bow was faint and misty at this distance, and he peered forward to try and get a closer look at it. The big man on the boat shouted then and waved a hand and two of the crew went back and then came up to the bow carrying something. There was a flapping of the thing in the breeze and then a tarry tarpaulin was thrown over the side of the boat and covered the number.

"They've covered it up, Father," said Mico. "Swing her over quick to the other side."

Micil's powerful arms worked on the sail and tiller and the rope, but the boat's speed slackened as she stalled, and stood, and then slowly picked up speed again from the pull of the sail, but it was too late as Mico saw. They had gone back again and returned and another tarpaulin was soon flapping over the other number. He could see the men standing up there then, and he could see their teeth white as they laughed. He felt himself going red and the primitive anger of helplessness was rising in him. Big Micil didn't swing away from the trawler. He kept the nose of his own small boat pointing straight at her. What they meant to do they didn't know. What they could do, was anybody's business, but it didn't amount to much. If only he had the *Dun Aengus* under his hands he could have done something, but for the moment just anger kept the boat going towards the trawler so that she could clear her bow and swing around.

He saw the big man looking at them, and the others stopped laughing and the big man shouted at them and they went back and disappeared, and then the big man went into the wheelhouse again and the slow trawling speed of the boat changed from a smug chug-chug to a louder and stronger note, and Mico saw that the bow of the trawler was pushing aside the waves at a fast speed and making towards them.

They were very close. He could see the black dirt of the white paint that was clinging to the wheelhouse of the trawler and the dirty lacework at the neb of the bowsprit.

"Swing her, Father!" he shouted then. "The dirty divil's going to run us down."

There was little Micil could do. All he could do was to haul tighter on the rope so that the sail took more of the wind in less space and crowded on a little extra speed. He felt the muscles of his stomach tightening as the trawler came straight for them. One of two things saved them from being rammed. Either the fact that the trawler was still trawling the heavy seine net and this was retarding her, or the sudden appearance on the other side of her of another black Claddagh boat, with a stocky figure up on the bow waving a fist in the air and shouting. Indecision came to the trawlerman then and he turned aside to have a look at the new enemy buzzing on his other side.

Mico's boat just scraped the trawler. He could have reached out and scratched his fngernails along the side of it. There was nobody to be seen on the boat, just a head glimpsed darkly through the dirt of the wheelhouse window. Mico raised his hand and shouted. "What's the idea, ye dirty divils? Do ye want to kill us, or what?"

That was all he got in before they swung away from one

another, and had rounded into the white wake of the trawlers propellers. They kept straight ahead and looked.

"It's Twacky's boat," said Mico, recognizing the stocky figure in the bow with the rubber thigh-boots falling about his legs. The trawler had changed direction and was now heading for Twacky's boat with the determination that it had shown for their own a moment ago. Mico saw Twacky standing up watching it, and then he saw him shouting back to his father who was at the tiller and he saw the flutter that came on the black boat, its stalling as the sail was swung over and its change of direction and slow gathering of speed.

"Bring her about, Father," he shouted then. "Bring her about. They're after Twacky now."

Micil moved very fast. The boat came about in a slow sweep, the sail flapped and then caught the breeze and they headed for the trawler with Mico leaning out on the bow and waving a fist and shouting. It gave the trawler more pause as he saw the other boat closing on his port side, and Mico saw the black tip of Twacky's mast passing by the trawler on the other side.

"They must be mad," he said. "We'll have to turn about and get out of here, Father. If only we had a gun or an engine or something! Hey, Twacky, Twacky, Twacky," he roared then, his hands cupped to his mouth, as the other's boat cleared the low bulk of the trawler. He saw Twacky leaping up on the bow and he waved his hand towards the tall cliffs behind him, waved and pointed and saw Twacky nodding his head. "I lead in for the Priest's Rock, Father," he said to Micil, jumping down. "It's very shallow in there. If he follows us in he won't have enough draught and we might be able to lead them up on to a nice sharp rock."

Micil was swinging the boat around even while he was talking. Mico saw the trawler taking a wide sweep to come after them, but before it had completed its turn, their own boat was headed in towards the cliffs and getting up a nice speed from the following wind. Twacky's boat was about fifty yards ahead of them, and if he didn't feel so mad Mico might have been able to laugh at the look of him. He was standing in the stern looking behind him, his hands on his hips, his grey cap pushed to the back of his head, and a mixed-up look of rage and surprise and blasphemy on his face.

They weren't far from the land. They headed for one of the breaks in the cliffs where the waters of the thundering sea were calm-looking and glassy – a very deceptive look as Mico knew. They seemed to become smaller and smaller as they approached the cliffs. They were like two rough black swans being chased by an outsize in cormorants. The trawler was closing behind them fast. It was a sound Mico would remember for a long time: the sound of the trawler closing behind them and the sound in front of them of the sea thundering at the bottom of the cliffs.

He saw Twacky's boat breathe its way into the clear water and wind a bit as if it was going up a river, towards the cover that was hidden from the sea. A small narrow place it was, between the cliffs with black rocks on either side and a sort of sandy beach. They had often fled here before when the sea was very bad. It always reminded Mico of some of the places you'd read about in *Treasure Island*, even though it was far from being tropical. He turned his head over his shoulder and he saw the trawler was only ten yards away.

He felt the change under his feet as their own boat got into the smooth water.

"He's caught now," said Mico, "if he doesn't stop and fast."

He heard the sail on Twacky's boat come screeching down, but he kept his eyes on the trawler. It was a good job that the trawler had the net or it would have caught up with them long ago. Another twenty yards now, Mico thought, and he'll find himself on top of something he had no wish at all for. He held his breath.

He nearly laughed then.

If the trawler had had brakes they would have screamed

with anguish as it turned away. Only in time. He saw the scurrying about. The sudden emergence of the crew, the shouting and orders that came across the water. He could almost see them holding their breaths as the trawler swung away, slowly it seemed and painfully, the side of the boat almost kissing the edge where the sea was deceptively calm.

Mico relaxed then. "We missed," he said.

"Too bad," said Micil, "I wisht they had come on. If they had come on and struck we could ha' got aboard them and told them what Claddagh men think of them. That would have been very nice."

They closed up to Twacky's boat where it was riding idly on the water, Mico jumping down and releasing the sail so that it fell from its high eminence. He gathered the fold of it into his arms and piled them there. They caught on to Twacky's boat and looked at one another.

"Look at them! Oh, look at them now!" said Twacky, shaking his fist at the ugly backside of the trawler as it scurried away. "Did ye see them, Mico, did ye see what the dirty bastards were tryin' to do to's! Oh, if oney I could lay me hands on them! Oney for five minutes if oney I could lay me hands on the fella that was at that wheel!"

The trawler went around a headland and was lost from their sight.

"What's the world comin' to at all?" Twacky's father wanted to know.

He was a grey man with a moustache. Not a bit like Twacky at all. Wearing a blue gansie and a reefer jacket and heavy boots, to Twacky's shirt without a collar and dungarees and soiled fish-stained coat of what had once been a tweed suit. A cap on his head and the white insides of the rubber boots flopping angrily about his legs. Twacky was raging. He was clenching his fist and hitting it on the palm of the other hand. Twacky was powerfully squat. He was like a man who had been caught between two great hands and concertinaed a little so that the whole of a seven-foot giant was squeezed into a five-foot-five man.

"I'm damned if I know what the world is comin' to," said Big Micil indignantly. "Isn't it enough for them to be comin' into the Bay and takin' the fish out of our mouths, without tryin' to kill us into the bargain? What's the Government doin' about it?"

"The Government!" said Twacky with great scorn. "You know what the Government can do, do you?"

"Don't tell us, Twacky," said Mico. "We have enough troubles."

Twacky told them anyhow. At great length, with very colourful language. What he didn't say about the Government and the *Hound of the Sea* had been said before many times, but he resurrected it.

Twacky reduced them to the semblance of good humour. He aired their vapours for them. They sat there and smoked until the memory of the trawler was gone from them and then they turned to go back to their fishing.

Mico stopped them, after looking at the sky. It was coloured now with a light bronze and the breeze was no longer warm and sticky. There was a cold nip in it, and way out over the Atlantic there was a bank of white raddled mist closing on the Aran Islands.

"We better go home," said Mico.

"Go home?" said Twacky. "But we're oney after comin' out."

Big Micil followed Mico's finger.

"Aye, bejing," he said, "we better go home. Will we have time for even that, I wonder?"

"I think so," said Mico. "I think that we should about make it."

"Oh-ho," said Twacky's father, looking back at it and putting away his pipe, "there's a lot of dirt there. There's a few days' dirt in that."

Mico agreed with him. He started to haul the sail.

Twacky grumbled. About fresh-water sailors. What was the use of going home again with no fish at all? What were they to live on? Why hadn't they known before they came out this morning that the weather was going to be bad so that they needn't have come at all? Why didn't they have decent boats so that if they did have to come out in a bit of bad weather they wouldn't have to be running home again like dogs with their tails between their legs?

But they hauled their sails and stole out of the cove, and the sea was building up and the breeze was much stronger and was blowing directly at them, with all the power that its journeying over a great stretch of sea had given to it. They had difficulty in rounding the headland even, but once they did they ran down the Bay very fast, and spread out before them they could see the other boats, too, scurrying for home.

They cleared the Bay before the mounting storm caught them.

They were about to swing into the calm mouth of the river when Mico looked over at the docks and looked away and looked again. He shouted at Twacky who was close hauled behind him, and pointed with his hand. Then to Big Micil, "Do you see what I see, Father? Is that an English trawler lined up at the docks?"

Micil looked.

"Be the heart of God it is," he shouted, rising to his feet.

"Is it the one?" Mico asked him, still looking.

"It's no other," said Micil, and swung the tiller so that the boat slewed over protestingly to the yawning dock gates.

They tied up the boat at the concrete steps outside the gates, and Twacky's boat came alongside them, and they mounted the steps and they stood on the quay. Two very big men with day-old beards on them and grim faces, and a tall man who was a little thin and a stocky squat man with his legs spread and great power in a big chest and a small tight red face far from serene.

There was an idler leaning against a bollard.

"Here, Jack," said Mico to him, "is me man long in?" thumbing at the trawler.

Jack spat scientifically, watching the brown stain hitting the green littered water of the dock.

"An hour or two since," he said.

"He must be our man," said Micil.

"It has the very cut of the fella," said Twacky's father.

"'Tis no one else, at all," said Twacky.

"Then," said Mico, hitching his coat, "let us go and talk to them in the name of God."

They walked along the quay by the customs shed and they stood where the trawler was tied up and they looked down into it. There was nobody about. Just the sound from below in the engine room of a voice singing. An unintelligible song of sorts.

Mico shouted. "Hey, you; hey, you!"

A red face appeared after a time. Red and black with dirt and sweat. A man wearing a singlet that was as black as the face. A sweat-rag around the neck. Long, thin, thickly tendoned arms.

"What ho, what yer about?" it said or something like that.

"Is the skipper aboard?" Mico asks.

"What, him?" the man asked. "No fear he ain't. Up in the boozer he is with a lovely pint I bet."

"In the pub, is it?" Mico asked.

"Here," said he, "where were you brought up? That's right. One up the road."

"Thanks," said Mico, moving off.

"Here," shouted the other after him. "You keep one or two up there for me, chum."

"We'll keep something for you all right, chum," said Twacky back to him.

The man stayed there rubbing his hands on a cloth for a time, looking after the figures of the four determined men going up the dockside, and then he shrugged his shoulders and went below again and he took up his song where he had left it off.

Chapter Twenty-One

MR McGINTY POLISHED his spotless counter with a clean duster.

The most remarkable thing about Mr McGinty was his cleanliness. He was a fairly big man. He carried a lot of flesh, but not an excessive amount. His head was bald and pink, and what hair he had left was silvery like the flash of a turning trout in water.

Mr McGinty was used to all classes of people frequenting his pub. He had heard the voices and languages of many lands, since he plied his trade so near the docks. He had heard Frenchmen and Spaniards, and Germans, and Lascars, one or two Chinese, and also the English. So he polished his counter now unnecessarily and listened to the five Englishmen talking. There was very little talking going on among them. They were too busy lowering Guinness to be bothered with the dialogue. The man nearest him, who was the skipper, since they addressed him like that, was a very big rangy man wearing seaboots and heavy trousers with a camelhair duffel coat over a thick jersey. His hat was on the counter. He had been fair of colour, but the bunch of hair that was left when his head had been clipped close to the skull was turning grey. His head came down in a straight line from his poll into a powerful neck that was red. He had a big nose that seemed to stand out from his face. His eyes were wrinkled sadly from the sea, and he had a jutting chin that didn't come out as far as the tip of the big nose. A hard man, Mr McGinty would have called him. Hard and tough and reasonably honest.

The skipper was a hard man, and he was thinking now that it was unfortunate that he had been caught poaching in Irish waters. Not that it mattered, but it would stir things up. And he was thinking also that it was a pity that they had to come in here for supplies, and that there was such very dirty weather coming in from the Atlantic. But his mind was easy. No man could prove that he had been fishing inside the limit. Also he thought that the fishermen who had attacked them would be out in the storm, and that they would have to run for shelter, and that it was unlikely that they would be back, and even if they were, what matter? No proof.

"Here's how, mate," he said to the man drinking near him.

"How," said the mate, raising his glass. A small powerful little man, mate was, wearing a tweed cap. He had very little neck and his face was big and round and his hands small and powerful, his arms and legs short, so that all of him seemed to have been concentrated between his neck and his fork. Dressed in heavy woollen jerseys and navy-blue suit that was shiny from wear and weather. His eyes were small and peered out almost leeringly from his fat face.

The counter was circular, built of solid mahogany with a brass footrail for the foot, and bevelled edges that were decorated underneath with a fretwork design. There was a double door with frosted glass and the name picked out where they had rubbed off the frost. There was a big window on either side of the door with the dummy bottles of coloured water, looking pretty from behind so that you could read the label through the glass of the bottles. There was a table with six wooden chairs under each of the windows. At the moment there were only the skipper and mate and three of their crew in the pub. The three men were at the table drinking. Three men with days-old beards, two fair and one dark, tall, small, and indifferent.

"We better go and get in the supplies now," said the skipper when he had drunk his pint and wiped his mouth and clapped his hat on his head.

"What's the rush?" mate wanted to know. "We ain't going out in that dirty weather, are we?"

The skipper didn't know. He thought they might. They had been a long time out now. It was a filthy trip. They were dogged with bad luck. A poor do to have to come over to Ireland looking for fish. What was wrong with the bleeding fish anyhow?

"One for the road," said mate and placed a two-shilling piece on the counter.

The skipper hesitated and was lost. They had another, and after that they had another. It did little to them. They might as well have been drinking water for all the effect it had on them.

They had been about an hour in the pub when the door swung open and a very big man stood there looking at them, a young man with a strangely marked face. He came in and an older edition of himself followed him, and after that a tall man and then a squat fellow with a huge chest. Their faces were grim and they looked at the skipper. Mico knew it was he from the side view of his face. It was the same profile he had glimpsed for a moment at the dirty window of a wheelhouse. And the sight of the small man with white teeth in a black-bearded face. He had seen that face laughing. Still it was all very nebulous. Apart from impressions they had very little to go on.

McGinty stopped polishing his counter and looked at them. At their tight faces, at the pulled-down eyebrows. They didn't look like men who had come in for a pint.

"Hello, Micil," he said.

"Hello, Mr McGinty," said Micil, not taking his eyes off the skipper.

"It's blowing up," said McGinty.

"It is indeed," said Micil.

"Hello, gents," said the skipper.

Mico had seen the flash on his face when they had come first. It was just a raising of the eyebrows, and a quick dart from the eyes. Now it was composed. One foot resting idly on the rail, the nearly empty pint held negligently in a big brown hand.

"What's the idea of trying to run us down out there?" Mico asked.

An expression of elaborate surprise came over the face of the skipper.

"What you sayin', mate?" he wanted to know. "You say that again."

"You were fishing inside the limit," said Mico. "You tried to run us down with your boat."

"Here that, mate?" said the skipper to his own mate. "Hear what he says. D'jou ever?"

"I never," said mate, raising his glass, a half-full bottle in his other hand.

Mico knew they were right. Knew it from the tension that had crept into the place; from the stiffened attitudes of the other three men behind them at the table. What could we do, he wondered? He felt a wave of anger coming over him as he thought of the bow of the trawler heading for them.

"To be a thief is bad enough," he said. "It's no skin off your nose with your boat to go wherever the hell you like for fish. Why you should come over here to steal the fish from men that can't afford an engine to get farther away. I can't see that. But to make a deliberate effort to ram us down. That's different. That could have been very bad."

"Listen," said the skipper, "you must be ravin', chum. Don't know what you're talkin' about. If there was a boat doin' a thing like that, it must have been some other boat. We don't do things like that. Do we, mate?"

"No," said mate. "You should have got this boat's number, cock, and then you'd know."

That was a mistake.

They all knew it was a mistake. The skipper and the three men behind who came to their feet when he said it. He even knew it was a mistake himself just as soon as the words were out of his mouth. Even at that nothing might have happened apart from the further grimness of the faces of the fishermen. What could they do? They could do nothing to prove what they knew was true. But the slight sneer in the sentence of mate brought Twacky from behind the group with his face white and a glare in his eyes, and before a hand could be raised to stop him he came forward with his boots flopping and he said, "You swine," and he swung a fist and hit mate on the side of the face. Mate, who had been filling a bottle into his pint, went down on the sawdust with the bottle clutched in his hand. He was not badly hurt, just surprised.

McGinty was very worried. He said "Gentlemen!" in a loud voice, but it was ineffective. The skipper came away from the counter and the three men at the table closed in and Mico loosened his shoulders and Big Micil came up a step or two with flame in his eyes and it is undoubted that there would have been a riot in McGinty's pub on this evening if the man on the ground hadn't moved like lightning and done what he did. He did two things. He swung his heavy-shod feet at Twacky's legs, a surprise scissors kick, and Twacky went down with his arms wide and as he kicked mate broke the head of the bottle on the brass rail and very quickly he straddled the falling Twacky and raised the pointed edges of the broken bottle and proceeded to bring them down on the face under him.

Mico would probably for ever remember that moment. He saw Twacky's surprised face on the ground and he saw the broken bottle coming down with the light glinting on the green gashes of it. In a moment he would see the sharp points piercing Twacky's eyes and he would see the bright scarlet mixing with the green of the glass. Oh God, was what he thought, it has come up with me again. He saw a

Twacky rolling on the ground with blood pouring out of his fingers held over his mutilated face, and after that he saw a Twacky with a stick and empty eye-sockets, a forlorn figure sitting on a bollard on a Claddagh pier waiting for the boats to come home.

He was helpless. There was nothing at all he could do. It would be over too quickly; even Micil and Twacky's father were too far away; anything they could do now would be too late.

The skipper from where he was flung the contents of the glass at mate's face. They saw it going into his eyes. They saw it brown on his face and they heard him cry, but he still brought down the bottle on the petrified face of Twacky. It was a wild swipe, however. It went the far side of his face. The skipper had followed up his attack by reaching a foot and kicking at the other's arm. He fell over and lay on the ground and wiped his face with the sleeve of his coat.

Twacky rose up from the ground like a cat, a look of outrage on his face, his fists clenched and blood flowing freely from a small cut on his left jaw.

"Bejay!" said Twacky. "I'll kill'm. I'll kill'm."

"Hold it, Twacky," said Mico, reaching for him. It took him all his time to hold him. Twacky was straining at his hold like a stallion. Micil came over and put another huge hand on his shoulder. "Ease it off, now, Twacky," he said. "Ease it off."

"Let me go! Let me go!" Twacky roared, struggling. "Oh God, let me go at him!"

"Twacky, now, Twacky," said his father soothingly.

"Get up, you bastard," said the skipper, bending over mate and hoisting him to his feet. "What did you want to do that for? Did you want to get us all killed, did you?"

"Aw, lay off," said mate, pulling his arm free and trying to get the stinging porter out of his eyes.

"He's that way because he has drink taken," said the skipper, turning to the others. "He's bad with the drink."

"All right," said Twacky. "I'm all right now."

They released him.

The fight was gone out of the lot of them. It had been cold anyhow. If they could have met those men in the heat of the dodging on the sea, there might have been enough hot blood to make for action. But it was cold. And even if it wasn't, the sight of Twacky's face under a descending broken bottle had cooled them anyhow. It had even cooled Twacky.

"If I see you again in this town," said Twacky to the mate, "I'll kill you as true as God. And if we ever see any of ye in this town again ye'll not get out of it safe."

"Come on," said Mico. "We'll go." He was glad to go. In a way it was he had led them into it. He had spotted the boat at the docks. If he hadn't they wouldn't have bothered. It would have been just a tale without an ending. It was that now. There was little ending, but he knew that if that broken bottle had gone where it was going his own chance of happiness would have been at an end. He knew it clearly now. Here, he thought, is a sign if ever I wanted it. If that had been a year ago that bottle would have gouged out the eyes of Twacky. But it didn't. It wasn't his fault that it hadn't. But it had been his fault that they were there at all.

They paused outside the door and looked at one another.

"Here," said Twacky, "what the hell are we doing?" dabbing at the blood on his face with a piece of rag, and turning back again to the pub.

"No, Twacky," said Mico, holding on to him. "Leave it rest."

Twacky was furious.

"What kind of men are we at all?" he asked them. "To let them do things like that to us and then just walk away as if it was nothin'! Won't they be laughin' at us for the rest of their lives, won't they? Won't they be tellin' tales of the Claddagh simpletons in every port in the world, won't they?"

"Ah, Twacky," said his father. "What good would it do to fight? What good would that do anybody? You started the fight and it's oney the grace of God and that man that you're not up in hospital now with the eyes hanging out on your cheeks. Let it rest now for God's sake. We can report it to the police and let them deal with it."

"To hell with the police!" said Big Micil. "If we haven't a photograph for them it's no use to us. Come on for the love of God and let us go home and forget the whole thing."

He set off with long strides towards the docks, Twacky's father following him up.

Mico stood up there and watched them go, and terrible and all as it seemed he felt very happy. He watched the wind sweeping the litter on the dockside as if it was a giant invisible broom, sweeping before it wisps of straw and hay from the channels and brown pieces of paper. The smooth water of the docks was troubled even by the rising wind, just as if the same broom had swept lightly across its surface. Farther out beyond the dock gates the sea was wild. He could see the waves dashing over the island of the Lighthouse. The clouds were very low and dark. The light was going out of the sky and the black storm flag was up on the standard on the far side. I'm going to do it now, he thought, I'm going to do it tonight. I'm not going to let tonight pass before I do it.

"What are yeh standing there grinnin' like an eejit for?" Twacky wanted to know in an aggrieved tone.

Mico threw an arm around his shoulder.

"Twacky," he said, "at this moment I'm the happiest man in Ireland and do you know why?"

"Why?" asked Twacky.

"Because me man missed yeh with the bottle," said Mico. "Listen, Twacky, if that fella had got you with that bottle I don't know what I'd ha' done. I'd ha' killed'm."

"You would not," said Twacky, "because I would ha' killed'm first!"

"It didn't happen," said Mico. "That's the best thing that happened. Come on, we'll go. I want to go home. I have a few jobs to do."

He set off with long strides across the road and walked quickly down by the Customs Shed near which the English trawler was tied up.

"Here, take it easy, will yeh?" said Twacky following him up. "What's got into yeh, Mico?"

"The divil," said Mico without turning his head.

"Take that," said Twacky, spitting into the English boat as they passed, "and may ye meet destruction in the coming time."

The two older men were waiting impatiently for them.

"Here, here, what's keeping ye? What's keeping ye?"

Gran was waiting for them on the quayside.

"Aha," he jeered, "the fair-weather sailors comin' runnin' home from a little breeze."

"That's a hairy oul breeze, Father," said Big Micil. "There's as much dirt in that breeze as ever I saw."

"It's a great wonder," said Gran, "that ye had the sense to come in out of it."

They emptied the boat of what they had to and tied up the sails and fixed the rope fenders in position and then Mico left them.

"I'm in a bit of a hurry," he said. "I have something to do. Leave some of the things there and I'll drag them up when I'm finished."

He ran from them, across the green grass, startling the grazing geese.

He laughed as they hissed him, and paused to remember a scene from long ago when he had hit Biddy Bee's gander on the head with a tin mug. The fear and the fright he had got from that oul gander. And Biddy Bee. Where was Biddy Bee now, with the tongue on her that would chastise the Pope? Not a sign of her to be seen. Her cottage was at the end of the row and she was dead. And her cottage was dead. They had pulled the dirty thatch from the top of it and they had levelled the walls, in case people would have sneaked in to live there. The white row of houses was ugly now with the two or three gaps, like black yawnings in a mouth when teeth are pulled. Soon, soon, the row would not remain at all. They would be tearing at them and destroying them, and building the ugly two-storey houses in place of them. It wouldn't be the same ever again. Idly, as he ran, Mico wondered why they couldn't have built houses that might be somewhat the same as the cottages they were destroying. Why couldn't they have got some fella, a building fella, what do you call them, architects, that's it? Got one of those fellows to design a new village with modern cottages. People all knew the Claddagh. It was a famous place. Because it was like it was, different to other places, but when they had the other awful houses put up, it would lose its identity, and it would be the same as any other slum clearance area with cabbages in the front gardens and railings of iron rusting in the sea winds.

Ah, well, he thought, if they have no imagination, what about them? A house is a house and a roof is a roof, and to hell with them. And our children will never know what the Claddagh looked like before they destroyed it, and for the rest the people who want can look at pictures of it. That's all that will remain. A picture of rows of white houses with geese grazing on the green grass.

His mother was in the kitchen.

"Is there any hot water, Mother?" he asked. "I want to shave."

"Yeer back," she said, rising from the chair. "Your grandfather was worrying about ye. He was afraid that ye wouldn't be able to read the signs."

"Were you not worrying about us at all?" he asked as he pulled off his coat and threw his cap on the side table.

She looked up at him very surprised, pausing to wipe back a wisp of her white hair with a thin hand.

White hair. She was very white. She was getting old. His mother was getting old. The skin was stretched tightly across her nose, Tommy's nose. The gleam had gone out of her eyes. What does my mother feel now? he wondered as he pulled the thick blue jersey over his head. What is she made of? He liked her. She had mellowed a lot with the years. She had really begun to mellow, once her son had become all that she had wanted him to become. After that she rested, like God was supposed to have rested on the seventh day.

"Why, no," she said, "I don't think I was worried. I might have been worried about your father, but then you were with him so ye'd be all right."

Pulling off his shirt and standing there looking at her with the muscles leaping on his big naked chest and arms, his hair tossed from pulling off his clothes.

"Is it you mean that when he's with me he's all right?" he asked.

"I suppose so," said Delia.

Mico laughed.

"You remember the time, Mother, that you wouldn't trust anything at all with me, in case I'd bring them to destruction?" he asked her.

She smiled a little.

"Aye, Mico," she said, "I do. You were a great worry to me, so you were."

"To meself too," said Mico, "but I'll tell you something now, Mother. The jinx is gone. As true as God it is. I'll be the safest man in the world from this out, so I will."

"That's good, Mico," she said. "I'm glad to hear that." She poured hot water from the iron kettle into a basin and put it on the wooden chair. "You were never a jinx. It's just that trouble follows some people like a can tied to the tail of a dog. God has been good to us in His own way." She left the kettle back and brought him a clean towel and red carbolic soap.

Mico got a shaving-brush from the window and wetted his face and then lathered it as well as he could with the red soap. He didn't look at his face much, just the way you look at it when you are shaving, like you'd look at a piece of wood if you were a carpenter or a stone wall if you were a mason. But his mother paused to look at him. Why, what's up with Mico, was her thought? What are his eyes gleaming like that for?

I want somebody to love me, Mico told his face as he shaved the bristles from the good side of it. I seem to have spent all my days being disturbed by people I like myself, and suffering for them and being moved for them and about them. Has there ever been anybody at all who could look at me, and say, Ah, I must look after Mico? It was hard to believe. Because he was so big and seemed so well able to look after himself, and his face was big enough and kind enough to be able to take care of somebody else's sufferings.

Maybe, he thought, the razor poised, maybe Maeve thinks that too. Suppose she never thought of me like that at all. He had never said anything to her. He was sort of pinning his faith on the fact that she would know when the time came; instinctively; inside of her. He hoped, he hoped, he hoped.

He moved fast in case his resolution would dissolve.

He washed himself, splashing the floor of the kitchen in the process, and then he went up to his room and threw off his old trousers and boots and dressed himself carefully in his shirt and his new blue suit and his brown shoes, and he came back to the kitchen and dipped the comb in the water to slick back his tough hair.

"Where are you going?" his mother wanted to know. "What's all the dressing up about?"

He wanted to tell her, but he knew it wasn't on the cards. He had never been close to his mother.

"Oh, just out," he said, "to meet a fella. I'm just going out, that's all."

He went.

The rain was beginning to fall in scattered showers. Light and almost pleasant, but with a sharper promise behind it all.

"Where the hell are you off t'?" Gran wanted to know with his eyes wide when he met him in the middle of the green. "Where are yeh all off teh on a dirty evenin' like this and you all got up like a duke?"

"Gran," said Mico. "I'm goin' on the most fateful journey of me life, so I am."

"Go on," said Gran.

"I am," said Mico. "To hell with it. I'm sick of waiting. I'm sick of the shadows of the dead. I'm a live man, amn't I? I've a good body, haven't I? I'm not too repulsive, am I, if you look at me in the right way? I'm sick of waiting and saying I will, I won't, I will, I won't. I'm off now, Gran, and it's going to be faced one way or another within the hour."

"The blessin's a God on you," said Gran, "and I wouldn't be in your boots for all the fish in the ocean."

"Isn't that nice encouragement?" asked Mico.

"To hell," said Gran, "what encouragement do you want? Aren't you the best man in the County Galway and what are you afraid of?"

"I don't know," said Mico.

"Go on," said Gran. "It's gettin' dark. Things like that are best done in the twilight. That's the quare time. I'll see you later on and you can tell me about it."

"I hope," said Mico, "that I will have something to tell you."

"One way or the other," said Gran, "you will."

"That's right," said Mico, and he pulled his cap low on his forehead and buttoned his coat and left his grandfather. Gran stood and looked after him, the big figure striding across the grass. I don't know, he was thinking, I don't know. Mico seems to be cut out for the wrong things. And aisy to hurt too under all the bigness of him. I hope to God he's not goin' to be hurt now, I hope to God he's not goin' to be hurt.

"Where are yeh off to, Mico?" Twacky asked with his eyes wide.

"I'm off on a bit of business," said Mico.

"Bejay," said Twacky, "you're like a Christmas tree. Will you wait till I dump all this stuff and I'll be up the road with yeh?"

"I will not, Twacky," said Mico. "Where I'm goin' can't wait and I have to go there alone."

"Is it turnin' into a secret drinker you are, Mico?" asked Twacky.

"I wish it was," said Mico, and then he lost his caution for a moment and hoped at the same time that he'd not have cause to regret it.

"Listen, Twacky," he said, his hand on the other's arm. "How would you like to be best man at me weddin'?"

"Ah jay, no!" ejaculated Twacky.

"Ah jay, yes," said Mico and laughed and left him, striding through the shower of leaves that were being stripped from the trees in the church and scattered like confetti over the road and the Basin and the river.

"Mico! Mico!" he heard Twacky calling after him pleadingly, but he didn't turn, just waved his hand and hurried on.

I have a date with fate, he was thinking.

Chapter Twenty-Two

MR CUSACK OPENS the door, glasses on his nose, a paper in his hand, slippers on his feet. His sparse hair was untidy and he needed a shave. He blinked his eyes.

"Ah, it's you, is it, Mico?" he asked unnecessarily. "Come on away in. Hey, Mother, it's Mico."

Mico steps into the hall, taking off his cap, and the figure of Mrs Cusack appears at the kitchen door, wiping her hands on her apron.

"Ah, come in, come in, Mico. You are welcome."

He steps into the cosy kitchen and sits on a chair, feeling his face burning; cold from the wind outside and being lighted up from the glowing in the range.

"And how are you?"

"Oh, I'm well, I'm well indeed, and how are you all?"

"Oh, we can't complain, thanks be to God. Himself there has a bad cold. But sure it's no harm, it'll keep him at home for a few nights with us instead of being up in that place drinking."

"Now, now, Mother, it's not as bad as that. Mico will be thinking that it's a regular boozer I am."

"Indeed no," says Mico, "nobody would think that";

looking away carefully from the pale face with the nose that was beginning to turn violently purple. A face that had once been clear and tanned, always. And he had a stomach that was as flat as an ironing-board for all his age just a few years ago. Now he had a stomach hanging on him, dropping away from the round of his cardigan.

"Is Maeve upstairs?" Being sure she was. It was the way. He would come like that and he would sit in the kitchen and he would put the question and Mrs Cusack would go to the foot of the stairs and shout up, "It's Mico," and her voice would call back and then she would come down the stairs.

"She's not in at all."

The statement shocked him so that he blinked his eyes.

"Oh," he said, "I thought she would be in."

"No, your brother called for her. He was to take her out for tea in the café and then they were going up to his place. She was to listen to records he has. He keeps a lot of musical records, you know."

"No, I didn't know," said Mico. What do I know about my brother? Nothing at all. He had been once to the place where he lived. In his rooms. Very elegant. Like places you knew, but hadn't yourself or never had any hope of having. Strange, Maeve going up there with his brother. But what was strange about it? Nothing at all. She had mentioned once that she had met his brother a few times and he didn't seem to be as bad as he was painted. Mico wanted to know who had painted him badly. And she thought and then said, "Why, nobody really, I suppose. It was just an impression I had."

"Yes," said Mrs Cusack. "He's a very nice boy, your brother. He makes good money too, I believe. He seems to be very clever."

"Oh yes," said Mico.

"Grand clothes he wears," she said. "He gives Maeve a lot of books. It's nice for her to have somebody intellectual like that to talk to."

"Yes, it is," said Mico, wondering if she was trying to hurt

- 302 -

him. She wasn't. Her eyes were kind. She wasn't meaning anything particularly. "I'll hop along up there and contact them," he said, rising.

"Won't you have a sup of tea, Mico?"

"Oh no, thanks, I just rose from me meal before I kem."

"Come in with Maeve and have a bit of supper so?"

"I will, thank you very much."

Into the night again. A little worried. About what? About nothing. Just that he hadn't known that Maeve and his brother were reading books together and having tea together and listening to records together. Maeve hadn't said anything about that. Why should she? No reason at all.

It was instinct with Maeve. Not deliberate. To say to Mico, You know, Tommy is not at all bad. He excites me. I have been dancing with him and I have been to the pictures with him and I have listened to him and he stimulates me. I feel different with him. He doesn't remind me of Coimín's Connemara at all. When I'm with him I feel great temptation. It's like committing suicide to be with him. Suicide in the sense that all your past life begins to die from your memory, and the pain of it isn't at all as sharp. With Mico a whiff of fish or a slow turn of speech drives you back to the small kitchen of a cottage and you looking dry-eyed into the fire, or lying on your back in a cold bed and thinking of how warm it used to be. Here then with Tommy is sweet forgetfulness. Never a dull moment. Wasn't I a fool all my life, the simple things that gave me pleasure, when I should have left it all behind me and gone out into the great world and seen the wheels turning. She saw Galway, which had been big to her such a short time ago, and looked at through the right eyes it was only a little country village in the West of Ireland that was hardly bigger in its way than Clifden, or less dull. Mico belonged to the part of the world that was simple and unassuming and put up with its lot with a smile. No ambition. Mico would fish for the rest of his days. He didn't want anything else. He was quite happy to be that way. So that in his way he was a temptation too. To sink back into the indolence of unambitious living. And it was a relief sometimes to get to him, to walk beside him, rest a hand on the giant strength of his arm. It restored a sense of balance. But there was little choice. Was there? You had to go back to the pain in your heart. Or you could forget it?

Well, I'm glad Tommy took her up a bit, Mico was thinking. It must have been lonely for her here. And she would meet a lot of young people and have a bit of fun. It was good to have a bit of fun. As long as she wouldn't see him, Mico, now, through the eyes of his brother. He always felt shabby beside Tommy. He always felt inferior. Even though he believed firmly himself that he, Mico, had the best part of it all. You didn't have to suffer so much internally, it seemed to him, when you had chosen the simple way of living.

"Ah, well," said Mico to the howling night.

He came to the end of the quiet road, having passed the lighted windows of Jo's house. Where was she? In a quiet place with long, long corridors in it and doors opening off. Statues in alcoves and the red lights burning in front of them. Polished floors, shining linoleum, and the black-clothed sister gliding along as if she was on skates. Her robes whispering in the corridors. And the white coif on her head, hiding her face, so that she couldn't see to the left or the right but had to look ahead. He tried to see her face surrounded by the black and white that cut off her features, but he found it hard. He remembered her only in a coat and skirt and silk stockings, ducking under the iron chains at the Claddagh bridge.

He passed by the hospital and he saw Peter's face on a white pillow with the circles under his eyes and the feverish light in them. He could get the smell of disinfectants and he saw the black bulging smoke from the chimney-stack behind, being scooped up and scattered disdainfully by the rising wind. Away in the far places behind the Clare hills he could hear the rumble of distant thunder.

It was really raining now, so he quickened his steps. The

drops that had soaked his cap were falling from the peak. His collar was tight around his neck and he felt the ends of his trousers flapping stiffly against his socks.

Past the hospital and straight ahead and then he came to the gate of the house where Tommy lived. A modern house aping the English style with gables and tall chimneys. Green sward in front of it and an overhanging porch shading the door with the coloured glass. There was light coming from it. He went in the gate and he rang the bell.

He rang it again, shaking his arms to free them from the heavy rain.

Actually he rang the wrong bell. There was a bell on top with a sliver of white pasteboard that said Tommy's name, and the other was for the owner of the house. The owner appeared – a small man with an aggrieved face.

"Oh, dammit, I don't know how many times I have to answer. Why don't ye press the right bell? Yes, I think he's in. Upstairs and the second door on the landing. There's the bloody bell and the next time you call would you mind pressing it! Think I have nothing else to do but actin' the skiv for that young gent. Can't think what the wife sees in him. I'd have him out of here like a shot if it wasn't for her. And I don't give a damn if you tell him so. You can tell him anyway. I don't give a damn. He knows the way I feel about him. How do I know what he does be doin' up there? Go on!"

He closed the door and went down the hall and into an opened door which he banged loudly after him. Mico shook himself again and started to mount the stairs. Carpeted stairs, that caressed your feet. Thick carpet.

He stood outside the closed door and he tried to order his clothes. He'd feel bad enough under Tommy's eyes with his best, but dishevelled and soaked like this! Maybe, he thought, I oughtn't to have come at all. Won't it only make me feel discontented? But he had come and he would have come anyhow. He'd have gone to China tonight for her if he had to.

He put his hand on the knob, turned it and stepped into the room.

There was no music, he thought. No music, as he stood there and looked at them, standing in front of the fire.

There was a terrible pause before they sensed his presence.

He saw the look in his brother's eyes then. The sort of haze leaving it and the recognition coming into it. He saw his hand falling away from her breast.

He didn't look at her at all. He just saw the deep couches and the carpet on the floor and the gramophone open with the needle still going around the groove of the record, a ploppety-plop, ploppety-plop, and the small table with the used glasses and the bottle standing beside them.

Then he saw the fear in his brother's eyes and he saw him reaching his dropped hands behind him, and he knew that he was going to kill his brother. He knew he was going to go forward slowly and reach his powerful hands for his neck and wind them around it and keep them there until the last breath had gone from his body.

He didn't feel himself moving into the room. He just saw the face of his brother with the look of terror in his eyes that brought him back to a night when they had sat in a tree and swiped at rats with branches. It was a cringing look. He didn't hear the shout that she let out of her, a sort of a shout a person would let if they were awakened in the night to call a name. "Mico!" she shouted. A lot of pictures flashed through his mind, boys fighting by a river and mackerel in the dust. Open jaws shouting "Turkey-face"; a hurley crunching its way through a skull, and his hands drawing a drowned body through sea water. Pictures, pictures, pictures. So many pictures that he stopped there when his hands were reaching for him and he let them fall by his side, and then he turned and made his way out of the room fumbling, like a child in the dark.

They heard no sound of him. Just a dull shaking as his heavy body ran down the stairs and then the banging of the door.

Maeve looked at Tommy. He was not a nice sight to see.

He was crouching back against the farther wall, as the terror slowly died from his face. She twitched her head so that the hair that was falling about her face was swept back. She knew her face was white. She could feel the skin stretched across it. The fumes that were in her head were fading. So were the colours. She looked at the room as Mico must have seen it. She thought back and brought up the picture that Mico must have seen.

She said, "Why didn't you tell me? Why didn't you tell me that Mico felt like that?"

He couldn't answer her.

She went over to him and shook him, crumpling his lapel. "Answer me, will you?" she said.

"You knew," he said. "Everybody knew."

"No," she said, "I didn't know. I didn't know." She stamped her foot on the ground.

She was wearing a white silk blouse. There was a Peter Pan collar on it and the sleeves were fluffed out. She was wearing a black skirt that fitted her closely and her stockings were sheer and made their way into high-heeled court shoes. She looked down at them. What are they doing on me? was her wonder. What am I doing here at all? What must Mico have thought seeing me like that?

It couldn't be explained now. It would have to be suffered. That it was all a sort of climax that was anti-climaxed. The music and the food and the chatter in the restaurant and the love music of Strauss. A sort of striving, striving, striving. For what? So that she could see a breath of the world come in and stand there big in a door and not look at her after the first frantic look? Stand there, and then the whole of him to be exposed like that, horribly naked, in his eyes, and then to see the murder come into them. Red-hot murder. She saw the great chest rising and the brown work-worn hands clenching until the white showed at the knuckles, and she saw the measured advance of murder in the few steps he had taken. And that it should have been only then she had known that Mico wanted her! Only then!

For this too! Looking over at Tommy. He was straightening up. His eyes were shifting from her. He was smoothing the lapel of his coat, setting his tie straight, his shapely head bent down.

"You know," he said hoarsely, to his tie almost, "that brute was on the point of killing me."

She bent her head and sank where she was on the carpet in front of the fire, and she cried. Silently, her hands in front of her eyes, and the tears forcing their way through her fingers.

Chapter Twenty-Three

MICO CAME OUT from the house as if he had lost his sight. The wind tore at him and flapped his coat about his back. The sheets of rain violently driven by the triumphant wind pierced to his body through the thin stuff of his shirt.

The tarred road was a smooth black river with the rain sweeping over it like waves. The trees of the College grounds, tall trees, strong trees that had been planted for generations, were being waved about as if they were immature bushes on a hill overlooking the Atlantic. They were swishing and moaning in their torment. The wind screamed through their denuded branches, their leaf-raped twigs, and tore past them screeching. The wires on the electric standards and the telephone wires whistled and sang as if they had suddenly come alive.

He didn't know where he was going, only that his feet automatically took him in the direction of the Claddagh.

Down past the College and turning down by the canal, a placid clean canal, rarely used, that was as tossed and tormented as if it had been a river in the middle of the ocean and wide open to the winds and weather. Now and again the night was lighted by the flashing lightning that was still playing away beyond the hills of Clare, causing the men who braved the night to look over in that direction and say, "Ha, they are getting hell over in Clare tonight."

It was a fitting night for Mico. Fishermen are not supposed to mind. They are only simple men, the nearest things to morons that you could find, great big clods of unfeeling flesh. He felt like crying aloud to the black sky like a dog that had been kicked in the belly.

All the hidden feelings that had made him shrink when he was young were back again with him. The wide-open gobs of the cruel playmates with their faces red and their physical feelings hurt, screaming, "Gobble, gobble! Gobble, gobble!" The awful way youth could put a finger on a nerve and make it scream aloud with variations.

He raised a sleeve and brushed the rain from his face.

They took away everything from me now, everything. 'Twas so little he had wanted after all. He had taken very little out of life. He had wanted only a small part of it, and here it was kicked out from under him so that he could see nothing but a great big face in the night and the left side of it a great red and purple nightmare. He raised his hand and rubbed at the mark as he started to run, rubbed at it and rubbed at it until it hurt, so that it seemed that his calloused palm would tear the skin from it.

No good, no good that at all, and he stopped his run and walked on, his great chest rising and falling, his head bent down.

A smiling girl on a bog with an ass, and a hand raised, a brown hand, and placed against his nerve centre. It was so cool. It doesn't matter. A moon over sand and the feel of a wriggling sand-eel in your palm. The sight of a smile at the corner of a mouth, a cleft in a chin that you wanted to put your finger on. Hair falling over a face, and a bare shapely leg with the toes spread on the grass. Oh, God. He stood with his back to the door of a cottage, and he saw the hair falling over her face, and outside he saw, somewhere on the sea, a dead drowned body, swaying to the lilt of the tide.

He wanted to take her in his arms and let his tears fall on her bowed head. He could have reached in the sky and torn the heavens apart from the sorrow he felt and the wish he had to show what he felt for her. He had never felt different. He saw her coming off the bus, with her dowdy clothes and her face thin and the flesh gone from her bones and her eyes deep purple pools of suffering, and he saw her as he had seen her a moment ago with the flesh back on her bones and her face filled out and her good clothes fitting her as if they had always been like that; and of the two he blotted out the last and saw her only with the tired drawn face and the suitcase in her hand.

Oh, what have you done to me at all? Or was it me? You should never have come. Where has your coming left you? Where has your coming left me?

Goodbye to a two-storey concrete house rising uglily on the side of a hill. Goodbye to the smell of fresh distemper and the sight of a coal range gleaming in the winter night. Goodbye to me and you hand in hand walking up a stair with the smell of fresh paint. Saying, "This is where we will sleep, in this room," and you look out the window and you can see Renmore Barracks across the Bay shining on a green hill under the sun of the early morning. "And this room for a cot maybe sometime." She would say, "But no, I won't maybe. Because God never gave any at all to Coimín and me. Maybe God knew what he was doing." "You will now, wait till you see." The fun of that. And of going out to the boat and knowing behind you you were leaving something of your own. That she would be worried about you maybe until your dauntless black boat like a black substantial swan came home from sea in the late evening of the flushed sky.

There had been no world but that. Everything else in life had seemed to be worth the living of it for the sake of that. Because there could never be anybody else, and now she was taken away, as a man who painted a picture could wipe a figure away with the rub of an oiled rag.

He groaned and ran free of the canal on to the main road and ran across.

The Claddagh Basin wore a tortured look as the storm raged over it. He saw her standing beside him on the Long Circular walk around the town, and they looking down at the City of the Tribes spread at his feet, and there's where we are. And farther up you see where they are knocking down the old Claddagh houses and building the new ones. Look, even from here you can see the tall poles rising, and won't it be queer some day to look down and see no sight at all of the yellow thatches shining in the sun? How could anybody be so cruel? How could they be so different from what you had them all fixed out to be? Of all people how could she have been like that? With a level head on her like no other head in the whole world. That she should have surrendered without a fight to the unsubstantial things that Tommy and his way of living had to offer her, she who had seen and suffered the real things in life and had tasted them and had seen what they meant. How could she if she wasn't what he had made her out to be? Was all her talk to him and the kindness in her eyes when she had looked at him, was that nothing at all? Was it just the way that you would look at a dog you had in the house, a great big collie dog that you were fond of and that you would throw into the quarry-hole one day when you looked at him and saw that after all he had the mange; that after all he had a most repulsive mark on his face? That you would be ashamed to be seen with him; ashamed of the looks of people who were walking or eating or talking about you? Look, Jane, at the big fella over there. My, what a face! Look at it. It'd frighten the children. And what on earth is that handsome girl doing with him? Doesn't she know? Sweet Mother of God, imagine waking up in the early morning and seeing that monstrosity sleeping on the pillow beside your face!

Mico groaned and he raised his hands up and he covered his face with them, his soaked shoes, once brown in colour, now dark and wet and slobbing with the wet, slithering and splashing in the pools of water that were gathered by the sides of the Basin where only the iron railings stopped him from falling into the water.

He paused at the quay where his boat was tied. Paused there for a single second to look at the sky and then turned and ran towards the boat. His movements were feverish. He freed the stern rope and tossed it into the black maw of the boat, and then he ran and tried to untie the rope at the bow bollard. It was difficult. The rain had soaked and tightened it, but he fought it free, tugging and pulling at it with all his strength, and then the rope was in his hands and he was holding the big boat that was dancing and bucking to the toss of the waves coming in from the river.

He didn't hear the voice of Twacky shouting behind him as he ran towards him. Twacky, who from the shelter of his own house had seen the stumbling figure of Mico come down and turn to the quay. Who had paused unbelieving until he was sure that his eyes were not playing tricks on him, and had run into the rain then, calling his name. "Mico! Mico! What are yeh doing?"

Mico felt him pulling at his arm and turned his eyes on him. He saw the rain streaming down his face. That was all.

"Let me alone!" he shouted. "Let me alone, do you hear!"

Twacky was frightened, because although Mico's eyes were looking at him they didn't seem to be seeing him.

"Hold on, Mico!" he shouted. "Hold on! You can't take the boat out on a night like this. You'll be killed, Mico!"

"Let me go," shouted Mico, twitching his arm. Twacky's grip was too tight.

"Mico! Mico!" said Twacky pleadingly, and then Mico raised his free hand, raised it high and brought it down, and Twacky fell.

He didn't wait. He leaped into the tossing boat with the rope in his hand. It was miraculous how he managed after that, that the boat wasn't blown to pieces against the granite walls of the quay. He reached for the rope tying down the sail and put his hands under it and exerted his strength, and the thick rope broke in his hands. He reached for the sail-rope then, freed it with a tug and hauled and hauled. The boat behaved as if it was mad when the skirling wind caught it, but he tied it off and reached back to the stern and took the tiller in his hand, brought it about, and the boat headed like a hound into the raging river. A most outraged boat. A big kindly bitch of a boat that was used to more skilled and more deft handling. But it headed out hissing, and when it came to the middle of the river it was hit by all the might of the wind, and stalled and groaned as if it was in pain, and then slowly and turbulently, diving and ducking and emerging, it headed for the sea.

Twacky, rising to his feet, watched it out there. His hands were sticky with the mud of the puddles into which he had fallen. He felt frightened. He felt like he had felt at school when he was frightened of Pa; he felt like he always felt when he was in the company of women. He could see the boat. It was so black and the water was so white, like whipped cream. "Oh God, he's dead," he said; "he's dead," and then he turned and ran to the houses.

Ran shouting. "Oh, the bees! The bees!" Twacky was shouting suddenly thinking of Mico and "Will you be my best man?" That's it now, he was thinking savagely, and how he'd like to hit her in the face, and how justified he was, and what a terrible thing they were, and how right any man was to stay away from them all!

He burst up the placid peace of Mico's home, standing in the door dripping, with the bit of sticking-plaster on his face where the bottle had cut him, and the look of pain in his eyes and the rain falling from him in streams. Big Micil with his feet and only socks on them held out to the blaze and the *Galway Observer* in his hand, looking up at him in amazement; Gran holding his pipe out from his mouth, the mouthpiece of it wet; Mico's mother looking up from darning a sock, looking at him with her dark eyes from the thin face.

"Mico is gone mad!" says Twacky in a sort of a shout.

"He's gone out. He's taken out the boat. He'll be kilt. What'll we do?"

"God!" Big Micil reaching for his boots. Gran running back to the pegs behind the door and stretching for the oilskins. Automatic. Delia rising to her feet, fear in her eyes, and something else inside her too. Mico in a boat on a night like this.

"What happened to him, Twacky?" she asks. "What's wrong with me son?"

"I don't know," says Twacky. "He comes raving down and then he lepps into the boat. I tried to stop him but he got away." Not even to himself could he say that Mico had hit him. He'd forget that. He'd put that out of his mind now as if it had never happened at all.

"Women are bees," said Gran. "I knew it. I knew it. I knew it." Struggling into his oilskins.

"Where's me shawl?" she asks, going over to the door.

"Don't come out, you, I say," says Big Micil, rising to his feet. "What's the use of you comin' out?"

"Where's me shawl?" she asks, reaching for it and throwing it over her white hair and brushing past Twacky.

"Here!" says Big Micil, struggling into an oilskin. "Come back! Come back!"

They left the house. The door was wide open. The sheets of rain were shown up brightly from the rectangle of night that was illuminated by the yellow light of the oil lamp.

They ran, a thin line of figures, down to the quay. They scanned the river. In the reflected flash of lightning from Clare they saw the tossing sail of the boat just clearing the river.

They ran down by the Nimmo's Pier, and halfway they went over the stile into the Swamp and they stumbled on the grass and ran towards the seashore. A line of people, oilskins gleaming, breaths panting, only Gran staying behind to help up the woman as she stumbled and fell, moaning. "Mico! Mico!" she was saying as she reached a hand to help herself from the ground, her hand red as if it was stained with blood from the red chemical gravel they poured on the top of the banked refuse.

Mico felt the sea and its power when he cleared the Nimmo's Pier. It took the cap from his head and snatched it away and sent it on the scream of wind. Jeeringly, as if to say, "Take off your cap, you unmannerly fellow, when you come into the wind." He had to lean hard on the tiller as the boat took its beating from the right. But she weathered it and stormed ahead, jolting like a young horse. An undignified jolting for a boat of her years. What did the creaking timbers think of it? Timbers that had been lovingly planed and shaped and joined by the rough horned hands of delicate craftsmen years and years before Mico was born.

She weathered the estuary and headed for the Clare Hills, across the mountains that the wind was tossing in her path. Mico had been wet before, but now the waves lashed over the side of the boat and drenched him to the skin. He felt it all over him and he rejoiced in it. It was heaven. It hit him across the face, and lashed at his body and pricked at his hands, but it couldn't get inside him at all to quench the fire that was in him.

I wanted nothing at all out of life but the little simple things that other men don't want at all. I can see that Peter would not live in the world as he saw it and see the things that were wrong, and sometimes not sleep at night because they were so wrong and there was nothing you could do except wear yourself out talking about them. Mico was content enough with things as they were. He could have cheered from the sidelines if Peter or someone like him had won a victory for the common people. But just cheer. He was one of the people they could despise because he was content to let things go on as they are. Because he was content with the things that his father and grandfather had before him. He liked the leaping fish and he liked the labour and torment of their catching. He liked the sea and hated it as all men did, but he was content enough to carry on the eternal struggle against it. He didn't want meat every day for his dinner. All he wanted was what he had with a roof over his head and children and the woman. That was all. It was simple enough, what he wanted. Why couldn't he have got it?

Because he was too simple? Because he wasn't willing to fight for it? Was that it?

Because he who had learned to brave tempests was driven to die by the sight of his brother's hand falling from the breast of the woman he loved, was that it?

Where was he going now?

He rubbed his hands across his eyes, to wipe the streaming rain and sea from them, and he saw the waves on all sides of him, gigantic and green and white, and they glittering sometimes in the light of the reflected lightening, and he knew well where he was going, when his eyes cleared. He was going to his death because no man or no boat could live in a sea like this. He looked up at the brown sail. It was being strained to within an inch of its taut life. The boat was heeling over like a pleasure yacht in a middling gale. It was bucking so that sometimes he could nearly see the black keel of her as he bent over to gain his equilibrium. Very well. I'm going to die. He didn't turn his head to the right, where along the bleak shore the small figures of waving people were spread despairingly. He might have looked. It would have maybe meant something to him. He might have imagined the face of his father, with the imminent tears on it as he saw the sea swallowing the only son that was left to him, a helpless, gigantic figure, that would have jumped into the sea and swum to his son if he could. As it was, he was standing in the lashing waves up to his thighs, futilely shouting and waving and calling to the hard to see, vanishing dot on the bosom of the incredibly turbulent ocean. He might have seen his mother, with her white hair unloosened and pitifully thin and waving in the wind, and her thin hands starting out. And Gran, standing bent and small, his hands by his side, his lips moving, whether cursing or praying no man could know, and he waiting with all the patience that the long years and his calmly awaited death had brought to him. He might have seen Twacky, standing there shifting from foot to foot, like he was a little boy and somebody was asking him a question he couldn't answer. He might have seen all those and the other figures hurrying to join them across the wet grass and the discarded refuse of a town, stumbling and falling and rising and hurrying to where the figures were silhouetted against the lightning in the sky.

If he had turned and seen those, he might have been surprised, because he might have thought, Well, yes, people do mind if I die after all. They don't think I'm just a simple ignorant fisherman with a terrible mark that no eyes can bear to look on calmly. They just think I'm Mico, and that I'm a nice fellow and they like me just because I'm Mico and they wouldn't give a damn if I had a tail like an ape and ten fingers on each hand.

His head was clearing as he fought the tossing boat. Power to control her was almost being taken from his hands, but he fought her with all the great strength in his body. And he held her nose to the wind and felt that he was pitting his strength against something that was stronger than himself and holding his own. As he felt his head clearing and the power flowing into his body, he thought, What am I doing?

And the storm answered jeeringly, You are running away. You ran away, it said, and it's too late now. You ran into your own death, like all cowards.

And then he thought.

What am I doing to my poor black boat?

And the poor black boat, groaning and tumbling and suffering, answered him, You are killing me, Mico. What have I done that you should do this to me? Haven't I been a good boat all your life and all your father's life and all your grandfather's life and all his father's life too, and is this how you are going to reward me, to have my old body smashed and beaten and thrown up on a strange Clare shore across the Bay? Am I after all my toil to end up driftwood on a strange rocky shore?

What am I doing at all? What will happen to my father and my mother and my grandfather if I take away their livelihood with my own poor body? How long will it be until they can have a new boat to sail under them? Where will they buy it? How will they build it? What will happen to them while they are doing that? Will my father have to go and get a pickaxe and a shovel and dig ditches for a few shillings under the eye of a County Council ganger. My father!

What should I have done?

I know! I know now when it is too late!

I should have hit my brother a puck in the kisser and I should have taken her by the arm out of that place, and said, "What kind of going-on is this? What do you think you are doing at all? Aren't you bloody ashamed of yourself to be doing things like that?"

That's what I should have done. And that's what I'm going to do!

And he leaned on the tiller and turned her about.

Now, you old black boat, he said to her as he strained, if ever you served let you serve now. It's all on in this. We either go or we come. He even reached a free hand and patted her, as she paused, was left static to become the plaything of the incredulous waves. He thought his heart would burst; that his arms would be pulled from their sockets; that the old boat would be taken apart like a biscuit in the hands of a child.

She groaned and she groaned and she creaked and her sail flapped and he ducked low as the boom swung over his head. He caught the strain of the sail-rope wound tight around his arm, and he nearly screamed as it bit deeply into his tendons. But he held the tiller and he held the rope and slowly, painstakingly, pantingly, the old boat turned, and the waves poured into her and tried to grasp her and drag her under, but she turned slowly and slowly and then she bounded away like a greyhound released from a leash.

The people on the shore couldn't believe it. They only saw the struggle in flashes, taking place about half a mile away from their petrified and rain-soaked eyes.

They'll never do it, Micil thought, linking the man and the boat.

They'll never do it, Gran thought, shaking his head, thinking of the timbers older than himself.

And then they saw her rising out of the waves and coming back the way she had gone, and they stood there for a moment and then they turned and ran back the way they had come, waving and shouting, the shouts whipped from their mouths by the wind.

It was Gran who reached the girl.

She was on her knees looking at the sea, the hair plastered to her face by the rain. She wore nothing but a blouse and a skirt. A white blouse that was sticking to her body as if she was naked. Her skirt was wet and ruined and torn. Silk stockings hung from her legs in shreds and her high-heeled shoes had been sucked from her feet in the grip of the green mud.

"Get up, get up," said Gran, "he's coming back."

Big Micil paused by them and looked and whipped off his oilskin coat and flung it around her, and then ran on.

Gran helped her to her feet.

"Go on," he said. "Run like hell. He's all right now."

She looked at him, and then she turned and followed the others along the shore.

When Mico neared the mouth of the river he turned his head and saw them. He saw them waving. He saw them shouting. He saw the slim figure in the rain and wind and the lightning flashing. He saw them all. The coat had fallen from her shoulders and she stood there. White and black, white and black, the hair plastered to her face.

He saw Twacky.

Oh God, I hit Twacky!

I love Twacky! I'll marry Twacky!

And he leaned over and patted the leaping boat on her rough side.

"You're a great oul bitch!" he said aloud. "You're a great oul beautiful black bitch!"